> "This book is a work of fiction, but some works of fiction contain perhaps more truth than first intended, and therein lies the magic."

Copyright © Ben Galley 2013
The right of Ben Galley to be identified
as the author of this work has been asserted in accordance
the Copyright, Designs and
Patents Act 1988.
All rights reserved.

No part of this book may be used, edited, transmitted in any form or by any means (electronic, mechanical, photocopying, recording or otherwise), or reproduced in any manner without permission except in the case of brief quotations embodied in reviews or articles. It may not be lent, resold, hired out or otherwise circulated without the Publisher's permission. Permission can be obtained through www.bengalley.com.

All characters in this book are fictitious and
any resemblance to real persons, living or dead, is purely coincidental.

DS2PB1:
ISBN: 978-0-9567700-8-0
1st Edition
Published by BenGalley.com
Cover Design by Mikael Westman
Original Illustration by Ben Galley
Professional Dreaming by Ben Galley
Printing by Lightning Source

Want an eBook instead? Dead Stars Part Two is available on Kindle, Kobo, and Nook. Scan the QR code below to find out more:

about the author

Ben Galley is a young indie author and purveyor of lies. Harbouring a near-fanatical love of writing and fantasy, Ben has been scribbling tall tales ever since he was first trusted with a pencil. When he's not busy day-dreaming on park benches or hunting down dragons, he runs the self-publishing advice site Shelf Help, zealously aiding other authors achieve their dream of publishing.

For more about Ben, Shelf Help, or for more about Emaneska, visit:
www.bengalley.com

Simply say hello at:
hello@bengalley.com

Or follow on Twitter:
@bengalley

The names below are those of the downright glorious group of people who helped edit my book. These are the esteemed Beta Readers of Dead Stars Parts One and Two, and each and every one of them is a star in their own right.

Thank you very much for all your help. Great work. Neato gang.

(in no particular order)

Nancy Clark
Kevin Richard
Jason Bennett
Sarah Clark
Paul Nelson
Sam Leeves
Marj Crockett
Genevieve Taylor
Luke James Wardle
Cathy Villars
Sheila Billings
and Helen McKenna

Dead Stars
Part Two

By Ben Galley

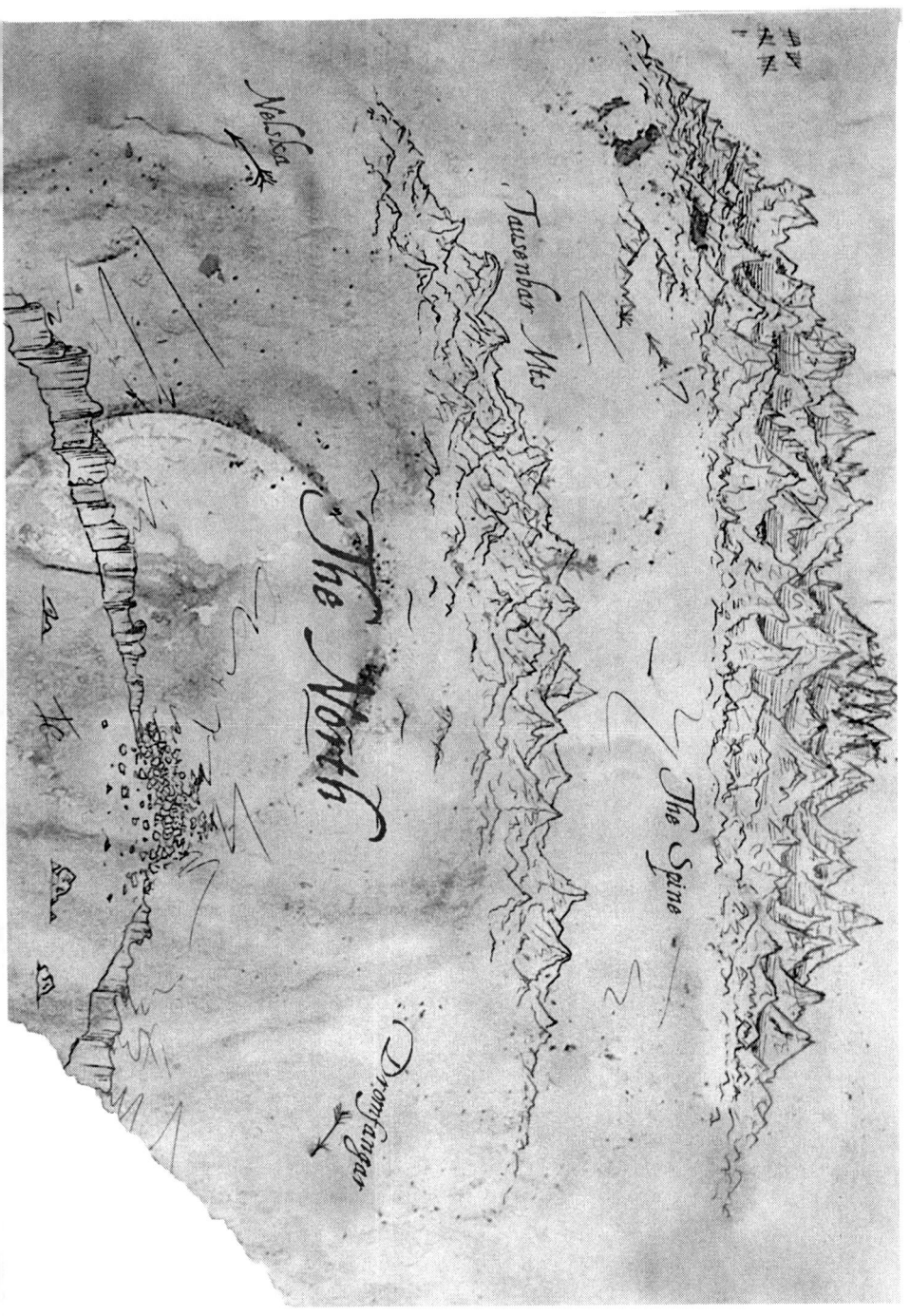

A whaler's sketch of the far North, showing both The Spine and the Tausenbar Mountains.

Prime Map of Emaneska, created by Arka scholars of Arfell in the year 819.

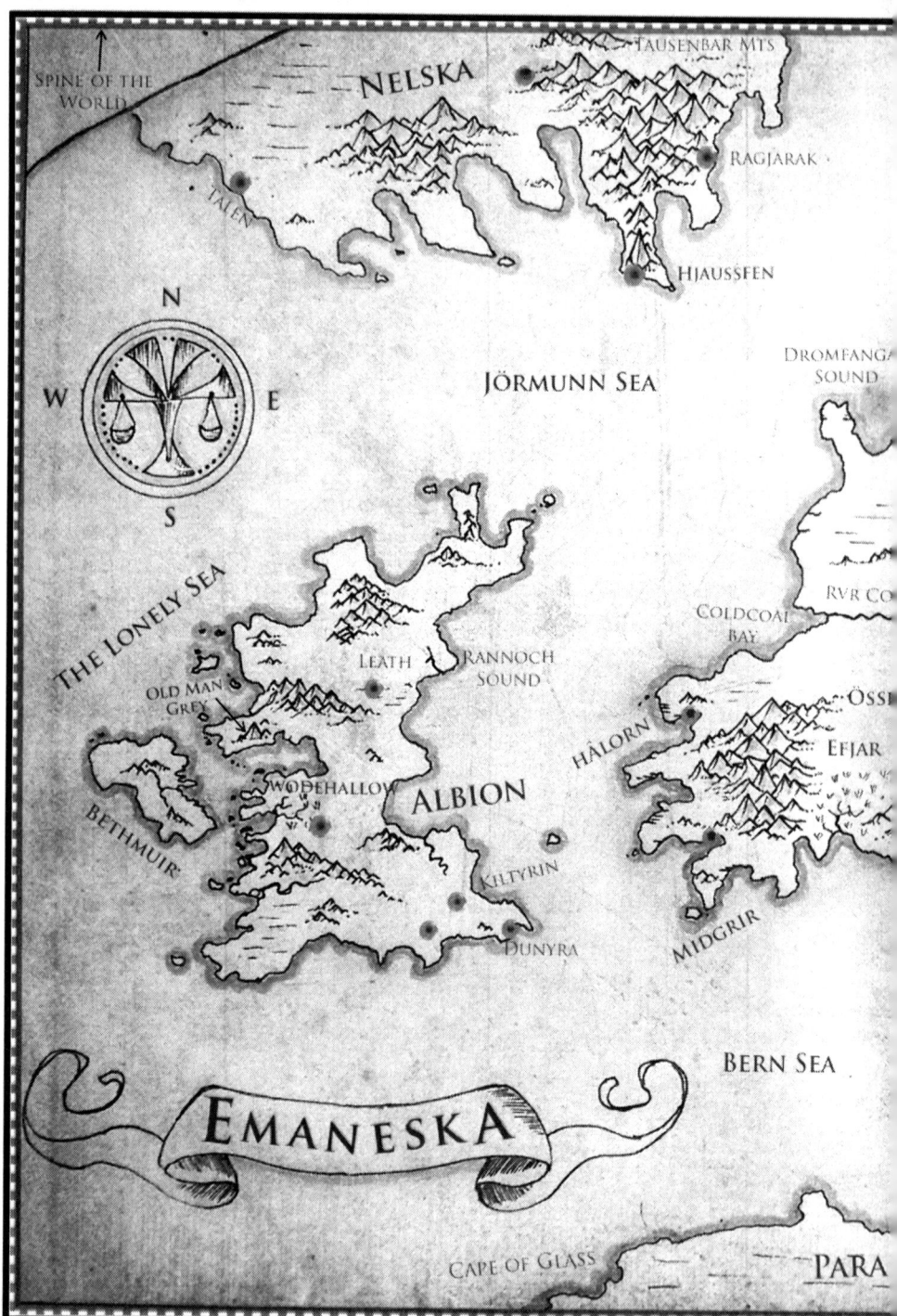

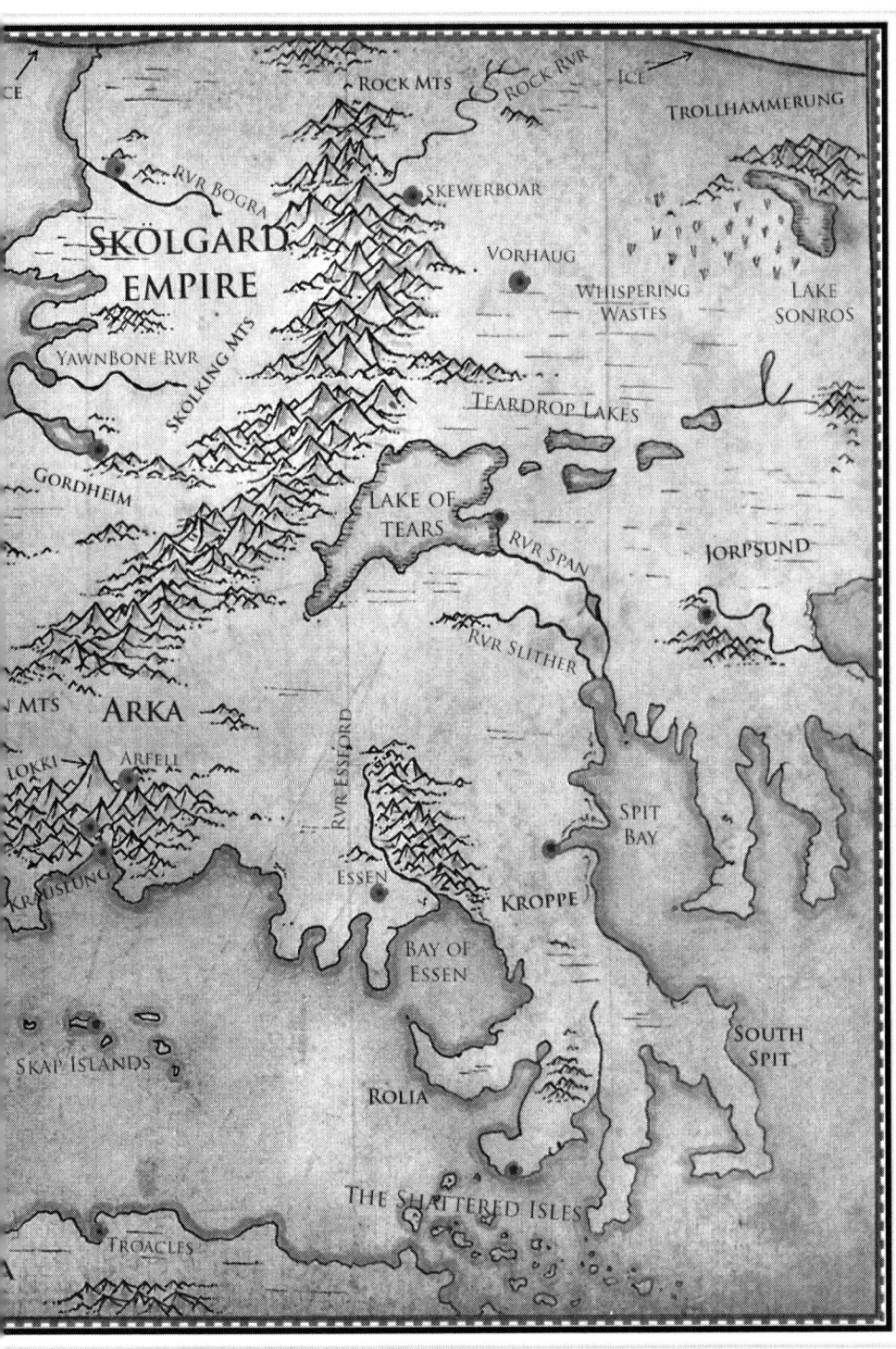

part one
of grimsayers

"It is foolhardy to believe that we humans are the only wielders of good and evil in this world."
Words from the scholar Lasti, scribe to the Arkmage Los.

'War.' The word was a fleck of spit on sun-warmed stone. A hot lump in the throat of its utterer. A dark scowl in the eyes of the nearby. Durnus let its hallway echoes die like a thief sent to the city noose. Alone and unwanted. Unloved.

'Is it?' asked Tyrfing, between the squeaking of his boots.

'Of course it is!' Durnus snapped back at him.

'Then what a strange war it is,' muttered Farden. The three fell silent. Silent as graves once again, silent save for the pacing of Tyrfing. He strode in impatient circles and tight, angry figures-of-eight. His armoured hands were clasped firmly behind his back while his face tried its hardest to imitate thunder. He would occasionally go to the window, press his nose up against it, and scowl at the city and its beyond. Smoke rose in three pillars from the distant hillside. Black, oily smoke, tinged with the sulphurous yellow of a dead daemon and the broken Spire. Word had it that a crowd had gathered to marvel at the creature. Vultures of curiosity, the lot of them. If this was war, then they were the only three men who knew it.

Durnus, still dirt-clad from the field and the fight, slouched on the wooden bench, sagging with more than just the simple tiredness of battle. His patience was stretched like cheap silk over a brothel bed, and getting thinner by the minute. Keeping his eyes screwed shut, he listened to the frantic sounds from behind the door across the hallway. Sounds of vials clinking, hurried whispering, and an Undermage fretting, yelling, snarling.

For once, Farden was the only smidgeon of calm the three could lay claim to. He lay a short distance away, sprawled on the floor with his hands firmly clamped to each side of his throbbing head. His feet would occasionally kick out, suddenly eager to stand up and get moving, only to remember the reason why they lingered.

For the mage, the world was suddenly very simple. Upside-down and shaken to shit, but simple nonetheless. Maybe that was why. He was used to that view.

It was the first time in decades he had experienced such decisive clarity. The mist of his nevermar withdrawal momentarily lifted, his was an unflinching clarity realised in beautiful simplicity. Farden saw his tasks like stepping stones, cast out before him. He spoke them aloud, whispered in little breaths. *Save Elessi. Beat the truth about his vambraces out of Loki. Hunt his daughter down. End her.* Simple. Sort of. No doubt there would be other little tasks here and there. No doubt it wouldn't be easy as four little breaths, but they would come at their leisure. Farden had never been so set on anything in his life. It was almost like a medicine to him. He lay on the floor and let the clarity heal him.

Tyrfing went to the window again and stared down at the streets. Crowds were gathering outside the Arkathedral doors. Crowds bearing banners and painted signs. Crowds headed by people in robes and home-made uniforms. 'The vultures are circling again,' he muttered.

'Speaking of vultures...' Durnus growled.

The sounds of vehement, striding shoes were quickly approaching. Ten, maybe a dozen of them. Farden begrudgingly got to his feet and stood with the others. They were met with the sight of Malvus and ten of his finest council sycophants rounding the corner, marching towards them as if they were playing soldiers. Malvus had his fists clenched and firmly clamped to his side. His clothes were even grander and smarter than usual, regal, with a dab of something military about them. Shrewdly chosen. His face was the perfect picture of political indignity, a lovely shade of russet purple. 'There you are! What in the name of the golden scales is going on?!'

Durnus took slow steps to meet him. His patience was now wearing dangerously thin, frayed and parting ways. His gentle pace couldn't have been more at odds with the storm that burned inside him. Malvus, of course, hurtled on, skidding to a stop in front of Durnus, indignant spittle flying from his lips.

'We demand an explanation for this chaos! There are riots springing up all over Krauslung, riots of fear and panic. People are petrified that those *things* will return at any time! Every eye is on the sky. It is pandemonium out there, and all you're doing is sitting here? What sort of game are you playing here, Durnus? Tyrfing?! You have my word, *mages*, that you will not spend another day on those thrones of...'

'Shut up, Malvus!' Durnus bellowed, inches from Barkhart's face. Malvus shuffled backwards, plainly taken aback. Durnus wished he could see the man's face. 'You dare to call this a *game*? Thanks to our efforts, and those of our brave army, this city has been spared a foul fate. Spared from enemies so dire they make you look like an irritating wasp. And where were you, Malvus? Busy counting your coinpurses no doubt, or busy scheming with the rest of your Copse? Yes, we know of your Marble brethren. How dare you accuse us of toying with this city's fate, when not two hours ago we were fighting hard with our bare hands and spells to preserve it.'

Malvus had recovered some of his confidence. He looked to his supporters. They nodded eagerly, heads bobbing, urging him on.

'My fellow Councils,' he began, turning back, 'tell me that most of the army was deployed this very morning, *before* those things arrived. One can only assume that you must have known about them, hmm? Yet again you try to keep us in the dark, and we have to pay the price for your secrets! Krauslung and I demand an explanation!'

'Krauslung will get its explanation, Malvus, but not before we have seen to our fallen, our Elessi. You can wait, like the rest,' Durnus hissed.

Malvus looked confused, and even more indignant, if that were possible. 'Elessi? The woman married off to your lap dog? Ah, so that's what you're doing here. You would choose to fret over a fat chambermaid instead of tending to the angry voices of your city. Typical!'

Further down the hallway, a door quietly clicked shut. There was a sharp intake of breath from the gang of councillors. Durnus shook his head, and backed away, a smile twisting his grey lips. 'Poor choice of words, for once,' he sighed.

Modren was a shade of red so dark it bordered on brown, as if every pint of blood he held in him had suddenly rushed to his cheeks. His knuckles, now shed of their polished steel, popped and clicked as he clenched them. The Undermage could have turned pebbles to sand in those fists. There was a cold sweat on his brow. His eyes were as red as his face, and were busy boring a hole into Malvus. He began to walk towards him, slowly at first, burning with murderous intent. He probably would have satisfied that intent, too, had it not been for Farden.

Just as Malvus was turning ashen with well-deserved fear, Farden took a step forward and swung a fist. It caught him on the chin, a lucky shot for a tired mage, and the Council's eyes rolled up into his head. He sagged like a melting candle, right into the arms of his cronies. They began to shout and yell for the guards, cawing like skewered gulls.

'Outrage!' they yelled.

'Council Malvus has been attacked!'

'Guards! A Written has gone mad!'

'Assault!'

It may not have been Farden's wisest decision, but it had done its job. Modren stopped dead in his tracks, fists poised in mid-air, crackling with flame, now utterly purposeless. He could only bare his teeth at the unconscious Malvus and the yelling councillors, shaking with rage.

Farden bent down. Malvus was already coming around. It hadn't been a hard punch after all. He blinked like a startled owl, a little blood gathering at the corner of his mouth. He recoiled when he found Farden's face so close to his own. 'Think I just saved your life, Barkhart. So, if I were you, I would leave before my good friend here decides to try again.'

For the first time in a very long time, Malvus was speechless. As were his men. They may have been a bold bunch when it came to politics, but when faced with three angry Written, a furious Durnus, and a slim hallway bereft of witnesses, they quailed.

With a nod from Malvus, he was hauled upright. He made a show of brushing imaginary dust from his clothes and cleared his throat again, trying to recover some dignity. He would have had better luck trying to squeeze it from the marble.

'If I see any of you again before the sun sets, I'll show you what a mad Written looks like. In fine bloody detail too!' Modren shouted after them as they swiftly retreated.

'They're gone,' said Tyrfing.

'Probably for the best,' grunted Modren. He nodded to Farden.

Farden returned the gesture. Behind him, Tyrfing scuffed his boot along the floor. 'It does take an age to get blood out of this marble.'

'How is she?' Farden asked the burning question.

Modren swallowed something hard. 'They... they don't know,' he said quietly. 'She's barely breathing. She's ice cold to the touch, as if she were already two days dead, but somehow she's still alive. They tell me that much, at least.'

The others bowed their heads.

'Can they do something about the poison?' Farden asked. 'Is there an antidote, or something?'

'The healers have never even seen a daemon, never mind its poison. They're stumped. Utterly clueless.' Fists clenched like punctuation to his words. The blood had fallen from his face. Underneath the dirt and sweat that clung to him, Modren was now white-pale, almost grey.

'Can we see her?' Durnus asked, and Modren nodded, waving a hand towards the door.

In silent single file, the others went to the door, gently turned the knob, and went in. The smell of the room, a square and simple affair with a single bed, was one of bitter chemicals and vinegar, of the clinging, dusty odour of cotton and blankets. That iron tang of blood, the salt of sweat. The scent of frustration. Elessi lay on the narrow, iron-barred bed, surrounded by healers and their servants. She was wrapped in blankets, almost as if she were already being prepared for the pyre.

Durnus and Farden parted the crowd of healers and knelt down by her bedside. Modren was right; she was as cold as winter, and grey as it too. There was not a pinch of blood in her cheeks, not a single flutter in her eyelids. To the casual eye, she looked dead, but somehow she was alive. Squinting, leaning close, they could see that her chest, still wrapped in the golden bodice of her wedding dress, rose and fell in tiny amounts, powering whatever shallow breaths she clung to. The ugly purple wound on her neck and collarbone bled slightly, another sign that her heart still pumped. Durnus laid a hand on her ribs and tried to feel it beating. It took all his concentration to sense its feeble fluttering.

Modren had entered the room. He stood behind them all. Eyes wide and fixed on his wife.

'She lives,' said Durnus.

'Though we don't know how,' sighed one of the healers, a middle-aged man as tall and as thin as a willow. There was a spot of blood on his cheek, half-dried and cracking.

'Can't you give her something? It's what you do isn't it? Heal people?' Farden eyed him.

The healer stared right back. 'Not a single potion or spell that we know of has worked on her, mage. This poor woman is at death's door and we have no idea how to bring her round.' He sighed. 'It's hopeless, sirs.'

Farden made a move for the man, hands ready to throttle a solution out of him. 'I'll give you hopeless,' he hissed, but Tyrfing grabbed his nephew by the collar and dragged him back to sense.

'I tried that,' muttered Modren, gesturing to the healer's colleague, a shorter, younger man standing nearby. He nervously twiddled with a vinegar-soaked bandage. The beginnings of a glorious black eye blossomed above his cheek. 'They've done their best, Farden.' The pain in Modren's voice was palpable.

In silence, he and the others left the healers to watch over Elessi. When the door was closed, Modren went to the window, while Farden and the others stood in a circle. It was a while before anyone else spoke.

'So what's the plan?' This from Farden.

Tyrfing shrugged. 'Your guess is as good as ours, nephew.'

Farden crossed his arms. 'But there's always a plan.'

'And perhaps that is why we are in a dire situation, yet again. What is the old saying? The best laid plans…?' Durnus trailed off.

Tyrfing finished for him. 'We've never faced foes like this

before, nor on so many fronts. Daemons, daughters, politics, they're all clamouring at the door.'

'I can't believe what I'm hearing. The very best of the Arka, lost and clueless?' Farden sounded as though he were about to laugh.

'What would you have us do, Farden?' Modren spoke into the smudged glass of the window, as if he were speaking to the city, not the mage. He eyed the black smoke in the north. 'Krauslung's rising up against us. Malvus has called for the Arkmages to step down. The daemons have vanished to gods know where. Your daughter is still free, ready to attack again at any moment, and Elessi, my new wife, is inches from death.' It was hard for Modren to hide the hopelessness in his voice, but it was a hopeless moment, and the others let him have it. It was painful to hear a man of his strength admit such truths, and all the more painful that they were truths, not lies. He turned around to face Farden. It looked as though a tear was hovering on his cheek. Perhaps it was the light catching a fleck of broken glass. Nobody dared look too closely. Modren shook his head. 'What possible solution have you got for all of that, hmm? Because fuck me, I'd like to hear it.'

Farden crossed his arms and stared right past Modren, at the mountains. 'Me,' he replied. There was a sliver of defiant confidence in that response that jolted the others like a spark. This scrawny Farden suddenly looked like another Farden altogether, one they'd lost a long time ago.

'You?' Modren couldn't help but snort.

Farden frowned. 'Would you have said that fifteen ?'

'Fifteen years is a long time.'

'What's that supposed to mean?'

'You know exactly what I mean, Farden.'

'Well, pardon me for being the only one here with a solution.'

'*You* aren't a solution, Farden. You're the bloody opposite.'

'Am I now?'

'Modren...' Tyrfing warned.

'No, no, let him carry on, Uncle. I know what he's going to say.'

Modren let his angry words loose like snarling dogs. Every accusation was a sharp prod of a finger in Farden's chest. Farden took it all without flinching. '*You* are the reason that bitch of an abomination exists. *You* are the reason she attacked today. *You* are the reason those daemons fell from the sky, and *you* are the reason that Elessi, my *wife*, is lying in that bed right now! You're the poisonous root of all that's happened here today! You're a fuck-up, not a knight in shining armour. You're... you're nothing but a *curse*, Farden! You hear me?!'

For a long moment, nobody spoke. Modren's finger remained firmly entrenched in Farden's chest. The two mages simply stared at each other, almost nose to nose, while Tyrfing and Durnus waited, holding their breath. They all expected Farden to explode like a raging volcano, or at the very least storm off down the hallway.

He was full of surprises today.

'Are you finished?' he asked, after a time. There was an annoyingly confident shine to his face. Only Farden knew where it stemmed from; that unwavering, unflinching clarity... Modren wanted to slap it off.

'Yes,' spat the Undermage.

'Good,' began Farden. 'You're right. This is all my fault.' He spared a moment to look at Tyrfing and Durnus, whose expressions were nothing short of bewildered. That alone made him surge on. He turned back to face Modren, and pushed his jabbing finger off of his chest. 'But you're also wrong, and for one astoundingly simple reason. I can fix this, and even better, I will.'

'How?' asked Durnus.

Farden crossed his arms. Proving them wrong was almost as gratifying as proving them right. *Unflinching clarity.* 'First off, Elessi needs saving. If those useless healers in there are out of options, then I vote we go somewhere better, somewhere with healers that managed to fix me when I was banging on death's door, half-dead from a shipwreck. Healers who have access to a lot more ancient lore than we could ever dream of.'

'The Sirens?'

'The Sirens.'

'We haven't heard from them in months.'

'Then we'll go to them.' The others looked unconvinced. Farden ploughed on. 'Unless of course you want to consult the Arfell scholars, and have them spend the next three months trawling through their libraries?'

Durnus nodded. It made sense. 'Fine. What about the daemons?'

Farden clanged his wrists together, grinning. 'They wouldn't come near me once they saw I was wearing this armour. You all saw it happen. I challenged him and he slunk off. It must be the Nine. We find the rest of this armour, and we've got ourselves a deterrent. Or a weapon. Or both.'

Modren couldn't help but laugh. 'That simple, is it?'

'Godblood,' Farden retorted.

'Godwhat?'

'Godblood,' repeated Farden. 'It's what that daemon whispered before he disappeared.'

'And what is it supposed to mean?' asked Tyrfing. 'Besides the obvious?'

Farden shrugged. 'How am I to know? But what I do know is that we happen to have two gods in this very Arkathedral who just might. I say we ask them.'

Tyrfing held up his hands. 'Say you do all this. Say the Sirens can save Elessi and you can fight the daemons. What about your daughter? And the rest of the daemons? I would bet my Book that

Ragnarök was never just three daemons. There will be more soon. And lots of them too. More importantly, Farden, what about you? How are you, in your current state, going to fight them all off?'

Farden turned to face his uncle. He smiled wryly. 'I guess we'll have to see, won't we? After, all, I didn't say I'd fix this alone, did I?'

The others shook their heads.

'So?'

Durnus shrugged. 'Well, it's rough. And simple. And I have no idea how you're going to pull it off, but there we have it.'

'Sounds a shite plan to me.' This from Modren.

Farden stared at each of them in turn. 'Anybody got any better ideas?'

Tyrfing sighed. 'No.' He found it odd that it was so difficult to admit that. He should have been practically prancing with joy at Farden attempting to take the reins, but instead, he couldn't help but doubt him and his perforated plan. He felt a trickle of guilt run through him. He looked at the floor.

'Be sure to let me know when they pop into your head,' Farden replied, almost sensing his uncle's doubt. He looked to Modren. 'And you? She's your wife. Nelska could save her.'

Modren looked back at the door, and thought of his wife on the narrow bed, as grey as stone and as cold as a winter morning. He thought of the healers bumbling around her, mopping up sweat and blood. Useless.

When he finally spoke, his voice was small and cracking at the edges. He prodded Farden once more in the chest, but this time there was no anger behind it. 'You bring her back to me, Farden. I don't care how, just bring her back,' he said, small, and cracked.

Farden met Modren's eyes, and the look they shared was as hard and as binding as steel. He didn't reply, he simply nodded.

'Well,' said Durnus. 'If you are intent on going to Nelska, I suppose you will need a ship.'

Farden turned so fast his neck almost snapped. 'A *what*?'

'A ship, Farden,' replied Durnus, breathing in the sharps sea air of the port. 'A sea-going vessel. Usually propelled by sails or by oars, and normally fashioned of stout wood. Or, in this case, wood and iron.'

'I know what a bloody ship is, Durn... Wait. Iron?' Farden sputtered. He could feel sweat under the collar of his fresh tunic. 'Last time I checked, old friend, iron sank in water.'

Durnus winked with a misty eye. 'Not on this ship, it doesn't. She is rather special indeed.'

Farden eyed the ship as a farmer might eye a sabre-cat he'd just that moment found snoozing on his doormat. Fondness wasn't a word that sprang to mind when ships were mentioned, especially in the dubious context of stepping aboard one.

'Examine her all you want, Farden,' Durnus said, a hint of pride in his voice. He didn't need his eyes to know the ship was a masterpiece, he'd run his hands over it enough, had every line and rivet described to him countless times. 'She is the first in a long line of warships that we will build. The Arka need to rule the sea again. She is no *Sarunn*. Tyrfing and the shipsmiths have seen to that.'

That she was not.

The ship was a monster. In every angle the eye could take. Tall, long, and wide, it towered into the cloud-painted sky with deep red masts the colour of bleeding mahogany. It stretched along the wharf-side like a sleeping giant, barging the choppy, oily waters of the port aside with its swollen sides, bristling with circular shields of iron and arrow-slits. Yet despite its size, it looked as nimble as a pike, as though it had been forged, no, *born*, in the stormiest of seas. Stout, sharp, and deadly. It lounged in the waters like a smug king on his throne. Farden's misgivings started to fade.

The ship was stern-on to the city, nuzzling up against the fender-lined arc of the busy, rime-encrusted wharf. It had been invaded by big crates and yelling workmen. Farden slowly traversed its well-trodden planks, feeling drowned by the bustling bodies. Seagulls and rimelings filled the air above, whining and harassing each other in the meanwhile.

The mage examined the tall flanks of the ship. They were made of stout oak beams, Hâlorn timber by the pale shade of it. Obsidian pitch seeped from where the joins overlapped. And there, as Durnus had said, the higher planks were clad in riveted iron, dull in colour but polished to an inch of its life. It glittered with sea spray.

Farden waded through the crowds to the bow. There, splayed across an iron flank in white paint and steel letters, was the monster's name: *Waveblade*. What a blade it was. The bow looked like it would slice rock in two, never mind the rolling waves. It arched out of the water like the curve of a Paraian scimitar. Every inch of that bow was clad in the same dull metal. Thick, riveted plates of iron. Barnacles dared to cling to a few of them, but they were swiftly being evicted by a gang of sailors dangling from ropes, brandishing chisels.

At the very front of the *Waveblade*, just beneath the sharp bowsprit, a figurehead sprouted from the metal. She was a twisted mermaid, tail slapped against the iron. She held a huge broadsword aloft. Farden stared at her, half-expecting her gemstone eyes to stare right back. His eyes wandered down her naked body. Her tail and Siren-like scales had been painted a dark orange and sulphurous yellow, so perfect and bright that they too looked as if they would shiver into life at any moment. Her silver sword ran along the underside of the long bowsprit, like a spear aimed at the distant blue-green sea. Mermaids were vicious creatures. A fitting figurehead, for a warship like this.

Farden reached out to touch the armoured bow. The iron was cold, even in the morning sun. It felt rough to the touch, despite its polish. Salt-bitten, but without the faintest hint of rust. Tyrfing had put something special into it, he could tell. Farden ran his thumbs over the rivets that pinned the metal to the oak beams. Runes and spells hid here and there between the overlaps, whispering of shipsmith's spells; sealing charms, strength runes, and whatever else his uncle had seen fit to include. Had Farden looked down into the dark waters trapped between the ship and the salty fenders, he might have seen more runes, glowing dimly in the half-light. Script battered onto the iron keel, like the ink of a Written's book. The ship was a monster, indeed.

Farden slowly made his way back to Durnus through the crowds of servants, sailors, and general gawpers. The Arkmage hadn't moved. He stood alone, yet surrounded. Narrow-eyed guards stood in a circle around him, wary of the shouts and calls coming from the boardwalks not too far behind, where the crowds were.

'Remind me again why we can't use the quickdoors,' asked Farden, hands thrust firmly into his pockets once again. He threw the ship one last dubious scowl.

Durnus shook his head. 'Aside from the quite obvious fact that you in your current state would fail to handle the journey, the magick has made them unpredictable, dangerous. The last mage we sent through came out bent double,' he said.

'That doesn't sound too bad.'

'Bent double. Backwards. Spine snapped like a twig. I am still trying to forget the screams.'

Farden winced. 'Point taken.'

'I hope so,' Durnus replied.

'And Ilios?'

'After his encounter with Samara, he is lucky to have any wings left. The fall nearly broke both. He has only managed a few short flights since, if hopping and fluttering can be called flights,'

Durnus replied. Farden frowned. A shout rang out from the boardwalk then, from somewhere in the depths of a cowardly crowd. The guards murmured. Durnus closed his eyes and let his ears drown in the noise of the dissenters. 'It is getting worse.'

Farden glared at the busy boardwalks. Peaceful for the most part, but, like the morning embers of a campfire, they were an inch away from igniting. 'Ungrateful bastards. The lot of them,' he said.

'No, Farden, they are the misled masses. Coerced by coin and religious talk. Blindfolded and conquered by cheap notions. It is people like Malvus, and the rest of the Marble Copse dissenters in the council, that are the ungrateful bastards, the greedy whores, and the power-drunk liars.'

'What are we going to do about them while we're gone?'

'We? No, Farden. I am staying to hold the fort.'

Farden was genuinely disappointed. 'Alone?'

'Better alone than abandon this city altogether. Though I suspect that Modren will stay also, given the circumstances. The people have been given enough to complain about without absent Arkmages and Undermages. He and I will remain, to fight Malvus in the great hall, and to show the people that we are not as inept as they have been told. Truth is a blunter dagger than lies, but it is of a stronger steel.'

Farden found himself smiling. He watched his old friend's face as it creased into a frown, like bleached paper crumpling. It was a face that had seen several thousand years waltz by, and yet now there was a a depth of life underneath it that could never be understood. 'Gods, I've missed your pearls of wisdom,' Farden mused.

The Arkmage shrugged. 'Hmm, they have been rather scarce of late. Scarce and dun.'

'So have a lot of things.'

'Speaking of scarce, your crew has finally arrived,' Durnus changed the subject.

Farden looked around. 'Where?'

'In the streets. Behind us.'

Farden looked over the Arkmage's shoulder, bewildered. 'How did you…?'

Durnus tapped the corner of his eye with a finger. 'You'll get used to it.'

As predicted, a long file of people emerged from the crowded boardwalk, flanked by a phalanx of spear-waggling soldiers and mages bedecked in light, sea-blue armour. They were silent, stoically ignoring the insults and shouts, the spit and the glares. One bystander had the audacity to fling what looked to be a rotten orange. Luckily for him, the timid little missile missed.

The group descended a wide set of stairs and strode across the lower boardwalk, weaving through mountains of crates and barrels like a lazy eel. Farden counted their faces. Tyrfing and Modren, both grim-faced and stern; Jeasin was there too, led, by a mage he didn't recognise. Loki and Heimdall walked behind them. They were as blank as virgin parchments. Behind them, bringing up the middle and the rear, were the Written. They were in full armour, straight from the battlefield, visors down, hoods up. Every single one of them had a bow and quiver strapped to their back, a sword dangling from their hip, and a weapon of choice balanced in their steel palms. Nobody dared fling anything, never mind an innocuous orange, at these men and women. Not a thing.

As the line drew alongside Durnus and Farden, the Written, the soldiers, and the sailors peeled off and headed straight to the gangplanks of the *Waveblade*. The others lingered behind, silent, pensive. Modren most of all.

'What a fine day for a sail,' remarked Farden, as they all stood in a rough circle. He looked up at the towering stern of the ship, built like the swollen turret of a castle. 'And what a fine vessel,' he muttered.

'Something wrong, Farden?' asked Tyrfing.

'Ships and Farden don't get on, if you'll remember.'

'Mmm.'

Farden turned to Modren. 'I hear you're staying?'

'I am,' grunted the Undermage, absent-eyed and distant.

Farden nodded. 'That makes sense, considering Malvus.'

Jeasin piped up. 'And it looks like I'm staying too,' she said. Farden had guessed as much. It was probably for the best. He had dragged her around enough. She crossed her arms. 'I don't suppose I'll be of much use to you on a ship.' Then she put a finger to her chin. 'Then again…'

There was a pregnant pause. A few eyes swivelled to Farden. They knew the manner of woman Farden had brought back. 'Er…' he attempted.

But Jeasin didn't wait for his answer. 'Don't like ships anyway. Don't even like boats. Make me sick. Besides, I've 'ad enough of followin' you 'round, mage. What's one more whore in Krauslung, anyway?' sighed Jeasin. She couldn't help but sound very alone. 'And there ain't point in goin' for the sightseeing, either.'

'That there is not, madam,' interjected Durnus. 'Perhaps the two of us should pool our resources. Two blind people are better than one, after all.'

Jeasin looked a little shocked by that. She hadn't realised she wasn't the only blind person in the group. She found herself curtseying in Durnus' direction, and said no more.

'We are wasting time,' said Heimdall, his voice like rolling boulders.

Modren nodded and waved his hands toward the *Waveblade*. 'That you are.'

'All aboard then,' said Tyrfing, pointing the way. Farden stood by his side, and waited to catch Loki's arm.

'You and I have unfinished business, god,' he hissed in his ear.

'Which side of this face would you like to hit this time? The right, for a change, or the left again?' Loki tapped each of his cheeks with his finger.

'I'm not going to hit you, despite how much I would like to see the colour of a god's blood.'

Loki chuckled quietly. 'I invite you to try, mage. You'll be sorely disappointed.'

'I bet it's gold, perhaps with a dash of red.' Farden squinted at the god, trying to glean some smidgeon of truth from his reaction. But Loki's face was utterly blank. In fact, his expression actually bordered on confused.

'Are you attempting to bludgeon me with riddles now, mage? Or is there something you wanted to ask me?'

Farden sniffed. Perhaps he had the wrong god. His eyes flicked to the stern of the ship, where a taller, darker god now stood against the railing. He met the mage's eyes and then turned away. Farden slowly released Loki's arm. 'Lie to me again, and I'll bury you in those neverending pockets of yours,' he whispered darkly in his ear, but, annoyingly, Loki departed chuckling. Farden turned back to those who had stayed behind.

Durnus was wide-eyed, fuming like a forge. 'I trust that Loki was joking about you hitting him?' he hissed.

'Oh,' Jeasin smirked. 'He weren't.'

Farden thought about glaring at her but shrugged instead. 'Gods don't know how to joke, old friend,' he replied. Durnus barely fought off the urge to give the mage a piece of his mind. Lectures could wait. 'Anyway, has Ilios or Heimdall had any luck in hunting *her* down?'

'Ilios is clouded by her. He always has been. Heimdall has better luck. A faint trail,' he said, 'leading north into the mountains. It was all he could see. She's shielded herself again.'

'Why north?'

Durnus raised his hands. 'Who can tell? I can only hope she keeps heading that way.'

'If she does, then we'll catch up with her.'

'Elessi first,' Modren growled. 'That bitch can wait.' And that was the entirety of his goodbye. The Undermage pulled his hood over his head and strode towards the boardwalk. He ploughed into the crowds, daring somebody to get in his way. Farden watched him leave and sighed. He knew his pain, a little of it at least.

'Tyrfing has your supplies, and a few trinkets from the markets,' Durnus said.

Farden nodded. 'Be safe. Both of you. I don't suppose all our enemies are heading north.'

'And you,' Durnus said. He clasped Farden's hand and then followed in Modren's wake. Jeasin felt for Farden's face and gave him a stiff kiss on the cheek.

'Durnus will look after you,' Farden quietly said. 'He'll do a better job than I've been doing.'

Jeasin stared at him, her blind gaze missing his only by a fraction of an inch. 'I don't know this mage. You're not the Farden I knew from the cathouse,' she said. As Farden took a breath to reply, to tell her he was sorry, tell her that she would be fine, to tell her anything, she caught it with her hand, touching his lips softly, like she had done in the dark of their nights together, when she had been bought and paid for. It felt strange, now that it was free. 'Keep it up,' she said. 'Maybe I'll be here when you get back. Maybe not.' And with that she walked away, guards following, tramping out a rhythm with their steel-plated boots.

'Farden!' came a cry from behind him. 'Stop wasting time!' It was Tyrfing, hollering from the upper-decks. Farden did as he was told.

As the mage negotiated the final ridges of the gangplank, he was faced with the swarming platter that was *Waveblade*'s deck.

Tyrfing stood to his right, high on the aftcastle. There was a snap-crackle above him as the first of the sails were unleashed from their furling bags. Shouts chased each other through the rigging as a horde of sailors plied their ropes and pulleys. They worked like ants, strong and nimble.

Farden was barged aside as politely as a sailor can manage, and behind him, the gangplank was hoisted aboard. Farden heard the scrape of others too, and all of a sudden, the rime-slick wharf below seemed very far away indeed. Farden stared at Krauslung. A little quiver of panic flitted through his stomach then as he felt the ship sag. The mooring ropes were being let loose. He could hear the squeak of the fenders as they were finally allowed to exhale and relax. The *Waveblade* had been unsheathed, let loose.

The iron monster floated after all.

'Farden!' came another shout, above the clatter of commands and the cacophony of boots on wood. Farden began to make his way through the strangely ordered chaos towards the aftcastle stairs. Applause rippled through the crew as the mooring anchor was cranked aboard.

The stairs to the aftcastle curved up towards the ship's wheel like two horns, left and right. The mage took the steps two at a time, passing deck after deck until he stood atop the towering stern. It was no less bustling there. Officers ran back and forth, yelling at their respective deckhands. Getting a ship out of port seemed to be all one big shouting match.

Farden finally made it to his uncle's side. 'So here we go again.'

'That we do!' Tyrfing was trying to remain blank-faced and hide his excitement. It is hard for any man, never mind an Arka, to stand at the stern of a fine ship and feel her buck and race towards open sea without cracking a smile. Tyrfing was managing, but only just. Farden looked back at the rapidly receding wharf. The city and its ivory Arkathedral shrank behind it. No cheers to waft the morning air, no applause to rustle across the boardwalk, no flags to flap and wave, not a scrap of a send-off, nothing, as they set off to save the world once again. The world, and one maid. Farden shook his head. *What a thankless task it was, this saviour malarkey.*

'Wheel! Two points to starboard, quick as you like!' yelled a deep voice from behind them.

The wheel ratchets clacked and snapped and the *Waveblade* swung to the right to line herself up with the mouth of the port. The sea beckoned like a forgotten mistress. Farden could already feel the waves building beneath the slick hull far below. The ship shuddered with anticipation. Or was it the crew? The shouting had not died, but the men had slowed, keeping their heads up and their eyes on the sea, biting their lips.

There was a glorious moment of silence as the *Waveblade* put her nose through the gap in the mighty sea walls. A moment of silence where nothing but the slap and slip of the waves echoed back at them from the flat-faced stone. Then there was a hiss and a roar as they sprang free, and suddenly the world seemed to erupt with noise and a cold, salty wind. The *Waveblade* sliced through its first wild wave and sprayed the deck with its foaming entrails. The crew applauded again, and the ships of the harbour rang their bells in salute. A piercing whistle rang out on the wind, making every man and woman aboard flinch. It was Ilios, perched on the bow. Despite his nervousness, Farden had to smile too. Perhaps there was just a scrap of a farewell after all.

'You alright?' Tyrfing asked as Farden took a wider stance. Sail after sail was dropping now. The faster the *'Blade* went, the less she moved with the waves, but it would take a while to reach her finest speed. For the meantime, she was at the mercy of every trough and crest. Farden felt like his stomach was plotting an escape.

'I'm fine.'

'You look as white as the sails.'

'No. Fine.' Farden kept his replies short, lest his mouth stay open for too long.

'Come meet the captain, Farden,' Tyrfing gestured, and the mage moved eagerly away from the railing. Farden caught the eyes of one of the Written, a tall man with red hair. His face was also pale and his mouth firmly clamped shut. *At least he wasn't the only one.*

The man Tyrfing brought him to had all the dimensions and vital statistics of a barrel. From his bare, calloused feet, to his huge, calloused hands, to the mop of black hair tied back into a tail behind his head, the man was simply round. He wasn't fat, not in the slightest, and he looked as though he would twist the neck clean off of anyone who dared call him such a thing. This captain was pure rope-hauling, anchor-lifting, wheel-turning muscle, and he looked proud of it too.

'Farden, this is Captain Nuka, one of the finest sailors ever to drop anchor in the Port of Rós.'

Nuka took his sharp, gravel eyes from the horizon and affixed them to Farden instead. His concentrative face broke into a beaming smile that looked as if it couldn't hold any more teeth if it tried, and he reached forward with two hands to grasp Farden's one. He shook the mage's hand vigourously, laughing a laugh only a barrel-shaped chest could manage. 'Well if it isn't the nephew,' chuckled Nuka. 'Truly a pleasure to have you aboard, sir.'

'And you, Captain,' Farden smiled back, immediately liking the man. Still holding onto Farden's hand, Nuka spared a moment to bellow at one of his officers.

'Get a barrelman up the mainmast sharpish! I want storm reports hourly!' he yelled. The officer saluted and turned to yell at his inferior. Man by man, the order was passed on down the ranks, losing none of its volume or intensity, until it found the sailor in question. He dropped whatever he was doing and jumped into the rigging like a cat after a bird. This truly was a ship of war. It made the *Sarunn* look like a grimy fishing boat.

Nuka turned back to Farden and finally released his hand. 'I've heard plenty about you, you see. And, might I say, it's a fine thing what you're doing for this maid of Modren's. How lucky it was that we hit port this morning, eh, Tyrfing?'

'Divine coincidence,' Tyrfing smiled.

Nuka nodded. 'Speaking of divine, where have the, er, other guests gone?' he asked, looking suddenly wide-eyed and wary. 'Don't get me wrong. It's an honour, and I've got a fine, loyal crew. Don't spend long enough on dry land to pick up any ideas besides ale and naked women, if you get my meaning, but they're still sailors mind, and superstitious as the next. Just a bit disconcerting, to tell the truth. Having the likes of them on board. Want to make sure they're looked after. Kept quiet.'

Tyrfing looked over his shoulder. The gods were nowhere to be seen. 'I'm sure they're fine. They want to remain inconspicuous. Special treatment might raise eyebrows.'

Nuka winked. 'Right you are. And these wizened old brows don't need any more raising,' he said, pinching his wiry salt-and-pepper eyebrows between finger and thumb. He grinned and turned to Farden. 'I almost forgot,' he announced, clicking a calloused finger.

'What?' Farden held his breath. The ship was moving around far too much for his liking.

'Might I introduce my second mate,' Nuka moved aside, and pointed to a woman standing a few paces away. A very familiar woman indeed. Farden couldn't help but squint to make sure his eyes weren't lying to him.

Lerel strode forward, as sturdy on her feet as any practised sailor. She wore the smart and simple *Waveblade* uniform, and a little smile on her face. Farden had all but forgotten what she had looked like, but the memory suddenly punched him hard.

Perhaps it punched him too hard.

Farden's stomach chose that moment to strike. As the bile rose up his throat, Farden mumbled something strangled and barged his way to the railing. As he spewed his guts into the rushing water below, he heard the sighs and chuckles from behind him. *And so it begins*, he groaned to himself.

How right he was.

1566 years ago

the sand *was hot on his knees. Even through the metal of his armour. He could hear the pebbles grating against the greaves, trying in vain to scratch them. Fools.*

'Come here,' Korrin whispered. The wolf licked its lips at him. A skinny thing, a bag of bone wrapped in flea-bitten grey fur. Sand covered one side of its face like a leper's mask. One of its ears was notched.

Korrin waggled the scrap of meat again, leaning forward another inch. The red meat glistened in the baking sun. It wasn't the freshest, but it was likely better than anything the wolf had eaten in weeks, months even.

'Come on,' he muttered. 'I won't bite.'

The wolf inched forward, broken claws pressing into the whispering sands. Even in the blistering heat it was shivering. Poor thing, thought Korrin. He squinted at the wolf's eyes, little shrunken orbs of deep dark brown. He moved the meat back and forth. The eyes didn't move. They were fixed on his breastplate, on the wolf engraved into his own armour. A little growl escaped from its throat, more of a strangled little howl. Korrin went to toss the meat, but the wolf quickly backed away, disappearing behind the lip of the dune.

'Not a fan?' rumbled a voice. Big Balimuel. There was a scraping thud as a huge broadsword dug into the sand beside him, its blade crusted with sand and blood and bone. It was almost as tall as Korrin.

'Apparently not.' Korrin stood and hurled the little scrap of meat over the dune, hoping the wolf would find it on his own.

Balimuel cast a nod behind him. 'Trust me, lad. There's plenty of meat on this field for him and his kind. He'll be so fat tomorrow, he'll be rolling up and down these bastard dunes. Give me snow any day,' mumbled Balimuel. The giant was right. There was no shortage of meat behind them, if it could be so callously described. Korrin glanced over his shoulder, letting his tired eyes rove over the bloody mess that was the battlefield.

The undulating dunes were covered with the detritus of battle. The black of charred bodies. The ugly red of spilt blood and innards. The dull, smoky glint of abandoned weapons. The wind caught the moaning of the dying and the muffled flap and caw of the gathering vultures, and carried it to their ears.

Such was the aftermath of battle. Korrin's eyes were dulled to it now. He had already seen so many scenes like this one, in the two years since they had first donned the armour. So many battles. Hard-fought. Hard-won. Not a single piece of armour nor a single Knight had been lost, or barely even wounded for that matter.

He shrugged. He could see the rest of the Nine, standing a little way off, gathered around a hooded figure, kneeling bent and broken in the sand.

'Come,' Balimuel shrugged. 'Let us see the fallen King.'

King Halophen was a battered axe-head of a man, all bones and scars. He growled as they yanked the rough sack from his head, making him blink in the hot light. Korrin knelt down by Lop and stared at the king. Smeared with blood, the king's face was a tapestry of war and violence, its threads the knotted purple of old battles, the fresh crimson pink of new ones. His hair was tied back in a braided tail, while his beard, black and wiry like all the men of Zeuter, spread down his chest like a rash.

The glint in his eye was nothing short of murderous, and also something curious. Amusement, Korrin judged it. Usually it was fear, or repentance, anger maybe. Never amusement.

'The Nine of the North,' rasped the old king, looking at each of the Knights in turn. Gäel, Demsin, Chast, Estina, Rosiff, Lop, Gaspid, Balimuel, Korrin... they all stared straight back, confident as their armour made them feel.

'Halophen Ad-Gara,' began Gaspid, speaking in a tired, flat tone, 'for crimes against your people and their allies, you will be...'

But Halophen had begun to laugh then, a dry, sand-choked chuckle, prickly in its contempt. The Knights tensed and scowled. Estina even reached for a knife.

Gaspid tried to continue but Halophen spat something red in the sand. 'They put a crown on me in my youth, a terrible heavy thing, all jewels and white gold. They put it on hot, see, to give you the first scar of your rule. First of many. I wondered, for a time, why it was the crowd didn't cheer, when I came to the balcony, why they mumbled and chatted amongst themselves as they read my name, instead of falling to their feet before me. You know why, Knights? Because a crown don't make a king, no more than a scar makes a boy a man.' Halophen showed them his yellow teeth. 'No more than a suit of armour makes you lord and master, judge and jury.'

'They cheering now, old King?' hissed Estina, lips pursed.

'What?' Halophen spat again.

'Are they cheering for you now? Your people?' Estina looked around at the bodies, splayed around them in a ring. They had begun to stink. 'Don't think they'll be cheering anything, let alone you.'

'And whose swords cut them down?'

Gaspid shook his head. 'And whose tongue and whips drove them here, against their will? For your greed no less.'

Halophen chuckled again. 'The others won't put up with you for long. You think you have a say, in these lands, so far from your tower? Pah! You think they will listen? No. They will hunt you down, and rip that armour from your hides.'

Lop leant closer, bringing his nose close to the bloodied mask that was the king's face. 'Let them try.'

'Balimuel?' Gaspid looked to the giant.

Balimuel shook his head. 'It's Korrin's turn. I took the last one's head.'

'Korrin?'

Korrin had been staring up at one of the circling vultures. 'Me?'

'By my count,' rumbled the giant.

Korrin paused, counting in his head. There had been so many this year. So many kings of the south and east already fallen. Quite a dent, they had made, in their violent machinations. Dictators and maniacs all. Korrin shrugged, and wrenched his sword from its scabbard. It came free with a sandy rasp. 'If you say so,' he replied. He raised his blade to the crystal sky and gripped it hard. So many this year, and look how numb he was to it now. What was it his father had once said? Ain't no pride in killing a man, no matter how you flourish your sword.

Korrin looked down at Halophen's exposed neck, a mottled mosaic of bruises and blood. His father had been wrong. There was pride in ridding the world of filth like this. There was honour in the spilt blood of warlords and murderers. And what had he once said to his father? He was good at this.

'Last words, King?' sighed Lop.

Halophen grinned at the sand. 'Your time will come, Knights. Soon. Very soon.'

'So be it.' Gaspid cleared some dust from his throat. 'Korrin? As you please.'

Halophen chuckled to the very last swing of the blade. Not a single Knight would have admitted it, but it was unnerving, to say the least.

Chapter 2

"I'm of the opinion that the phrase 'hopelessly lost' was invented, and remains privately reserved, for those who dare to wander the lofty crags of the Össfen Mountains..."
Words from 'Mountain-Climbing - A Fool's Hobby' by the explorer Aspold the One-Legged

Mist clung to the scree-slope like gnats to a bog. It held the mountain close, seeping into every crack and crevice. It was cold high in the crags, cold as graveyards in winter. The wind cut like a blade through the gaps in their cloaks. The footing, slivers of shale from the grinding of mountains, was tricky and treacherous. It covered the steep incline like a frozen avalanche of rock. Only the tired jabbing of a boot seemed to stir it to action, and when it did, it slipped like a sudden river, building as it flowed. It paid to dig feet in deep.

Samara was exhausted, more exhausted than she had ever been. The ground tugged at her weak muscles, but she fought it, as stubborn as she ever was. At least she was conscious now. Lilith could stop moaning about carrying her. Only her shoulders, ripped and torn from her spell, slowed her down.

Samara negotiated a steep section, hopping weakly from a protuberant boulder to a flatter section of shale. For a moment it sagged beneath her, its edges crumbling away, and then remained steady. She smirked and took a moment to look around her. She even dared to look down. It was a long fall and a lonely death that spread out below her, faint in the mists. Samara threw the fall a contemptuous look. This mountain should be so lucky as to play host to her grave.

Lilith was not feeling so confident. As her younger companion dragged herself over yet another lip of rock and disappeared from view, Lilith braced herself against the shale with her good hand and gave her poor lungs a moment to rest. The cold was getting to her. It burned in her chest. Her withered hand shivered uncontrollably. Curse this mountain, and curse the brat for choosing this direction, she hissed to herself. They should have listened to her stones. East, Lilith had said, not north. East to the forests, to wait and to train. Lilith mumbled her tirade under her breath; her lungs hadn't the breath to spare for words.

Samara must have felt her anger. 'Come on!' she hollered down the slope, still lost to view. Lilith grudgingly pushed herself upright and began to climb again. Not because she had been told to, but because it was either that or sleep in the scree, waking up to who knows where, who knows what, if she woke up at all. *Broken skull and twisted limbs*, most likely. Night was gathering once again.

Lilith used her weak arm to hold her steady while she dragged her skirts up to her knees. She managed to get a foot onto a solid rock, and pushed herself awkwardly up to follow in Samara's rattling wake to flatter, sturdier ground. Curse this ageing body of hers. What a decrepit husk.

It took her half an hour to reach the jagged crest of the slope. It too was draped in monochrome curtains of mist. There was nothing but grey around them. Nothing dared to grow in such a place. The air was too thin for animals. Even birds stayed below, where the food was.

Lilith wilted onto a boulder and caught her breath. The summit was like a grey blanket hung between two sharp poles. They sat in the dip of it, a ridge with barely a yard of flat land on either side of it before the world dropped away into a misty, slate abyss. Samara was bent double at one edge, wiping the sweat from her hair. A smear of brown blood ran across her cheek, between her nose and her ear. Despite the strain on her body, she looked pleased with herself, as though she had just conquered the whole of the Össfens, not one simple crag.

'What are you smiling about, girl?' spat Lilith, digging a pebble from her stolen shoe. They had escaped in their borrowed clothes. There had been no time to change. No time except to run. They had barely made it to the mountain crags east of Manesmark without an arrow in their backs, It was a miracle they hadn't been hunted down already. Nothing made a distraction like a trio of daemons falling from the sky.

The aforementioned smile quickly faded. 'I'm not smiling,' replied Samara.

Lilith scowled. 'Good, because you've got no reason to. You failed. An' miserably too.'

'What are you blabbering on about, old woman?'

Lilith's rock-bitten fingernail jabbed the misty air. 'You! You failed, like I said you would. You weren't ready.'

'Shut up! I didn't fail, I...' Samara faltered, along with her confidence. 'It was too hard. I didn't have enough of a grip... Oh, you wouldn't understand!' snapped the young girl. It was in moments like this that she looked her true age; a petulant child still yet to teeter on the cusp of adulthood. Moments like this made Lilith more confident.

The old seer got to her tired feet. 'You weren't ready and we should have waited. Now you've ruined your perfect chance to hit 'em all at once. We're lucky to have escaped with our lives!'

Samara thumbed the crusted streak of blood on her cheek. A fresh trickle had started to worm its way out of her nose. 'I had orders...' she mumbled.

'I'm the one who gives you orders around here, you little runt!

I'm the one who tells you what to do, as I always 'ave! Who 'ave you been talking to? Hmm? Who put ideas in your head before you were ready?'

'We did,' boomed a voice that rattled the shale. Lilith fell to the scree in fright.

'They did,' smirked Samara, slowly bowing to one knee.

As the mists coalesced into charcoal muscle and flinty bone, the night seemed to fall like a landslide. Veins of shadow knitted together like the plaited wicker of a basket, wrapping around them and their little ridge of shale. Teeth emerged from the mists, in two glowing mouths. Eyes ignited. Claws and toenails found the earth, thudding and scraping as the daemons took their steps forward out of the dark haze. They shrank as they moved, going from twenty feet tall to ten in less than a step. Suddenly there they stood: two daemons, arms crossed, fiery faces blank, waiting for a response.

Lilith was reticent to give one. Samara bowed her head. 'Cousins,' she said.

'Stand, daughter of nefalim,' said one of the daemons, the one with many eyes.

Samara stood, but kept her head bowed.

'I'm sorry,' she blurted, sounding like a child again. Even she realised it this time. Something that might have been called fear trickled down her spine. Fear of failure. Of consequences unknown. It was all well and good talking to dead rats and gibbet-cages, but now two daemons stood before her, as real as the stench and the claws they brandished. 'I couldn't do what you asked. It was too hard. I tried, but I couldn't do it.'

'No, but you shall, in time,' said the other, one with bitten wings and curled horns. In the murky darkness behind him, something resembling a lion's tail swished back and forth. He had large, wild eyes; grey, tinged with red. They were disconcertingly human in proportion. He was grinning with all his teeth, looking possessed, if that were even possible for a daemon. 'You will!' he laughed.

Samara glanced at Lilith. 'But I've already failed you,' she said.

The other daemon, the sterner one, flicked a many-eyed gaze at the old woman, who was still wallowing in the pebbles. He was taller and darker than his comrade. His skin was a mottled black, scaled like the hide of a snake. His claws were curved and curved again, wickedly sharp. He had no tail, but wings of smoke and shadow. A cluster of orange eyes squatted above a scant nose and a mouth that resembled a blast-furnace. Thin wisps of greasy white hair trailed from the back of his ridged scalp, falling across a muscled set of shoulders. 'And who said that?' he asked, slowly.

Samara didn't even hesitate to point at Lilith. The seer glowered. 'She did.'

'Ah yes! The pebble-caster. Future-spinner. Fate-seller. You have been quite busy keeping our cousin from her task.'

Lilith scrabbled to her feet in protest. 'I've done no such thing. I did everything Vice asked! And more besides.'

The grinning daemon sniggered. 'I don't remember our dead cousin or his father asking for the skins of mages, do you, brother Hokus?'

'I do not, Valefor.'

Valefor snickered at that.

'It matters not. I've seen this one's future,' Hokus smiled a smile at Lilith that would chill an ice bear. It certainly chilled her. It sent a rattle down her spine.

'A fire, methinks,' announced Valefor.

Hokus shook a claw. 'A small one, for the Watcher might see.'

Valefor bent to it. He cupped his mottled hand and dragged some of the shale into a pile. 'Not here, behind the mountains,' he said. 'I don't sense his gaze.'

Hokus let his forked tongue taste the air. 'It is good to sense anything again.'

'That it is, brother.'

Lilith looked across at the pile of shale. 'Where's your firewood? Wet rock won't light no fire,' she told the daemon, her brashness nettling both Samara and their fiery visitors.

'For a seer,' sneered Hokus, 'you know very little.'

Valefor had finished piling up his rocks. Once he was satisfied, he stood up and spat a gelatinous globule of grey saliva onto his hand, and then let it drip onto the rocks. He then gestured to Samara. 'If you please, cousin,' he said, bowing.

Samara clicked her fingers, making Valefor and Hokus swap glances for a moment, and let a ribbon of fire swirl around her wrist. She touched it to the rocks. The spit caught like whale oil, and in mere seconds the shale was alight, bubbling like lava. It hissed with an orange flame, belching a thick oily smoke and throwing out a blistering, dry heat. It was like no fire Samara and Lilith had ever felt.

'Sit,' ordered Hokus, and the strange quartet sat down on the stones.

Samara spoke first. She sat like a half-empty sack, bent over and withered. The exertion of the day and its summoning sat on her bruised shoulders like a heap of granite. She felt sick with fatigue. Only her acute stubbornness kept her eyes from drooping. 'So,' she began, tentatively. 'I haven't failed you? He's not angry?'

'Not yet,' chuckled Valefor, gazing upwards. The daemon's smile was like oil.

Samara breathed a loud sigh of relief, letting her head droop in her hands. 'What do you want me to do?'

'You will try again, of course,' said Hokus.

'Now?'

Valefor shook his head. He swung an arm to one side and held it above the shale. As he wriggled his claws, the slivers of rock began to twirl and rise into the air, gently and slowly, as if they were dancing, twirling on their tips. 'The magick here is strong now. Almost as strong as we remember, perhaps, in the first days. But it is not quite strong enough for you and your task. You did not fail us, the magick failed you. For the most part.'

Samara let her chin dig into her palm, balancing her head. Her eyelids drooped, tiredness, relief, both tugging them down. Lilith leant forward. 'So that's it then?' asked the seer. 'The magick isn't strong enough?'

Hokus spoke then. 'Centuries of planning and prophecy, and you imagine us to be foiled by something as elementary as this, seer? Your lack of faith in your masters is deplorable. I have half a mind to see you punished.'

'I *am* rather hungry, brother...' ventured Valefor. He let his floating slivers of shale fall one by one, to the rhythm of Lilith's chattering teeth.

'I do not imagine she would taste very good,' mumbled Samara, flicking the old woman a look that ordered silence. Lilith shrugged, callously, almost fearlessly. She knew her fate. They weren't it. 'She's all dust and daemon-blood as it is. Tough as boots,' Samara was saying.

'Mmm,' mused the daemons, licking their lips. Lilith didn't reply.

'So what then? Do we wait?' asked Samara.

'You go to where the magick is strongest.'

'And where is that?'

'I think you already know the answer to that,' Hokus replied.

Samara rubbed her eyes. Did she? Her mind was a tangled, tired mess. The magick in her veins burned insolently as she quizzed it. Then she realised she already knew. It felt as though she had been living beside a strong river for all her life and only just realised in which direction it flowed.

'North,' she said.

Hokus nodded. 'All the way north,' he said. Lilith's face turned ashen at that.

'To the Roots,' Valefor chipped in.

'The roots of what?'

'Of everything.'

'And then?'

'And then you will try once more. Unhindered this time,' said Valefor, smiling again. His smile bled duplicity, for in the next breath he added. 'And mark my words, cousin, failure will not be tolerated a second time.'

Samara simply nodded.

Lilith spoke up again. 'What of Farden, and Ruin, and the others?' she asked.

Hokus flashed teeth. 'The years of fretting over his precious Arka have made Ruin weak. He may have killed Alpheron on the hill, but mind is weak, human, and petty. His father has something special planned for him.'

'And Farden? What about him?'

'Last we saw, they have gone west in a ship.'

A tired sneer. 'He's fleeing?'

Hokus stared into the mists. 'No, but he does not pursue you either. Not yet. The god-shadows are with him.'

Valefor spat on the rock-fire and sent a burst of flame into the sky. 'None of them will matter once you reach the Roots.'

Samara instantly got to her feet, albeit a little shakily. The daemons followed suit. Lilith preferred to stay where she was. 'Then let's go,' Samara said, her voice as tremulous as her legs. She was met by Valefor's chuckling.

'You cannot travel with us. That sort of magick is god-trickery. Your journey is by foot, cousin.'

'You rest tonight. You will need it.'

Samara fidgeted, as if eager to prove herself that very second, right there on that mountaintop. But the daemons were having none of it. As they began to fade back in the mists, as their bodies began to deliquesce and trickle into the darkness, their voices rattled the shale. 'We will be watching,' said Hokus.

Valefor's grin was the last to fade. 'Sleep tight.'

And so it was that Lilith and Samara were left staring at the gathering darkness, a fire of stones and a sticky silence between them. The girl pondered her frustration, her unsteady future, her looming task, and the fate of failure, while Lilith contemplated her own doom, knowing she had just leapt a little closer to it. *The far north*, she quivered. *Anywhere but there.*

She remembered an old phrase she had once heard from a drunken sailor. He had crossed her palm with coin, and she had cast his stones in the pipe-smoke air of a bilge-ridden tavern. He had been sacked from his merchant ship, given a bottle of wine for his troubles, and cast into the city. Lilith had asked him the reason behind his sacking. His gruff, addled answer had been two simple words that at the time, she hadn't understood.

Surplus to requirements.

All of a sudden, Lilith understood him perfectly.

For a while, neither of them spoke. Samara kicked at the rocks and fought off unconsciousness while Lilith stared at the fire. Night descended on them and their mountain, and soon they were stranded in a black void, with only the odd flames and their twisted shadows for company.

'You've got no respect,' muttered Samara, finally.

'Now you know how it feels.'

'They'll see you dead, if you keep acting like that around them.'

'I'm touched by how much you care.'

'Don't care one inch for your skin,' Samara coughed. 'I may need you, is all,' she added quietly.

'You forget, girl, that I am a seer. I know my journey, even if I can't see yours. Don't you worry. I'll make it jus' fine to the north. Those daemons won't touch me,' she whispered, stretching out on the shale, feeling her old back click and moan. She found her pack and the thick, square object hiding in it. A book crammed with bloody pages. *Her insurance*, she inwardly sighed. That's what it had been designed to be, when all this was over. A little bargaining power, a little something to stave off her fate. Keep her in blood for a little longer. Fat chance of that now. Not if they were heading north. She'd brought up the child, done her work. Now she was baggage, being dragged to the place she'd avoided for years, to an ice field, to black rocks, to a dripping knife... she shuddered as the old vision flashed through her mind once again. *So soon...*

Samara shrugged. That was all the sentiment she had to offer, it seemed. 'You just watch your tongue around them. And don't be dragging me back, either. This is a race now.'

Samara ended her sentence by booting a flat pebble into the black void. She didn't hear it land and Lilith didn't reply. She had nothing to say to the little girl and her callous words. After all these years, she'd grown quite accustomed to them.

With a frown and a curse, Samara lay down on the shale, and finally gave in to her exhaustion. The darkness of sleep quickly took her. Only one thought wandered through her mind before she slipped away.

It was a thankless task, bringing the world to its knees.

Chapter 3

"You can put a sailor on dry land, but you'll never turn his gaze from the sea."
Old Arka proverb

'I'm not used to men throwing up at the mere sight of me, but as I know how you tend to react to ships, I'll let you off.'

The words floated to Farden on a murky sea of darkness, muffled and adrift. There is a fine line between dreaming and waking, and Farden found himself straddling it. Sleep sucked him downwards, while the orange light sneaking through the slits of his half-cracked eyes bore him up. He felt like a man halfway into a warm, and not entirely unpleasant, bog.

A hand gently pressed on his chest, and he was slowly brought back to the world of the living. Wood was the first thing he saw, staring down at him. Still wreathed in the remnants of his dreams, the sleepy-eyed mage could imagine faces in the knots and whorls of the oak beams, like the faces in the candles he used to carve. They wrinkled their faces at him.

'Farden,' said a voice, and another face came into view. This time it was a real one. Lerel stared down at him, a faint hint of concern on her features. There was also a hint of impish humour there too. 'Did you hear what I said?' she asked.

'You look different.' Farden squinted at her. This was not the

Lerel he knew from his crumbled memories. Not her at all. Her dark hair was shorter now, cropped and cut close to her jaw-line and neck. The tips of her ears peeked through it. Rings of silver and gold hid there. He looked down at the hand resting on his scarred and sweaty chest. He looked so pale against her nut-brown skin. The Paraian tattoos on the back of her hand led a swirling path up her arm, slipping under her shirt, and blossomed across her neck, like fingers of ivy. Another reached down from behind her ear. Desert script. Newer than the rest.

Her mahogany-brown eyes roved over his grizzled and gaunt face. He imagined the same expression being worn by a merchant assessing a rusty antique. She sniffed, her nose wrinkling for a moment. Still as feline as ever. 'Fifteen years will do that,' she said.

'Lazy,' he mumbled.

Lerel smiled. 'What did you say?'

'It's what I used to call you,' he said. 'In a room just like this one. On a similar voyage. When you were a cat.' It felt as though he had lived three lives since then. A foreign time, misty, rusted.

'I remember,' Lerel reached below the bed with her other hand and produced a wooden bucket. It was empty, for now. 'See?' she asked, with a wry smile.

Farden groaned. He took a deep breath, rubbed his eyes, and ran a hand through the matted mess that was his beard. 'How long this time?'

'Barely a day,' she answered. She leant closer to wipe a patch of sweat away with a cold towel. Farden couldn't help but flinch. His skin was hot. 'Tyrfing told me. It's the nevermar again. Not just seasickness.'

'Mmhm,' hummed Farden, avoiding the answer.

'Well, looks like you sweated most of it out for now,' she said, wiping her hand on a nearby towel.

'I just need to rest.'

'No, you need a bath. And a shave. And some food. And some good sea air.'

'I'm allergic.'

'To which one?'

'To all but the food.'

'You're a liar. Get up.' Lerel slapped his chest lightly with her hand. Farden tried not to show that it hurt. His skin was so thin and sensitive. It felt as though she was made of thorns.

'Fine,' he winced. He made a little circular motion with his finger, and she nodded.

'I know, I know.' She went to stare at the opposite wall, impatient hands resting on her hips. Farden took his time getting up. He had no choice. Dizziness pounced as soon as he raised his head. He squinted at the bucket and told himself no.

With a throaty groan and a lot of effort, Farden arranged himself into a sitting position and put his bare feet on the soft floor. It took a moment to realise that it wasn't wood that his toes were kneading, but thick carpet. 'Gods,' he muttered. 'Carpet. This ship must be special.'

'Done yet?' Lerel moved to turn around but Farden grunted for her to stay still. A shirt had been left on the end of the bed. Red, like Lerel's. Like the ship's uniform. He stiffly put it on.

'Finally,' she said, as she heard the mage get to his feet. His head nearly brushed the ceiling. 'This way, come on.'

Farden had no choice but to follow. She opened the door and pushed him out into the corridor. 'My boots?' he asked, tossing his little cabin and bed a forlorn look, as they were dragged away from him.

'You don't need boots in a bath.'

'Oh for f…'

'No arguments, mage. You smell like we just caught you with a hook and line.'

'He smells worse than that,' called Nuka, from the end of the long corridor. The barrel-shaped man filled its whole width. He wore a wide grin. 'I've had to batten down the hatches. Keep the men from mutiny.' He leant casually against the wall, with one foot tucked behind the other. 'When you've shown that stench to his bathing, I need you at the charts, m'dear. You know these waters better than the rest of us.'

'Aye, Cap'n,' replied Lerel as she shoved Farden down another corridor.

'Aye, Cap'n?' echoed Farden with a smile, as he was nudged and prodded towards his soapy doom. 'Charts? You've really taken to this sailing thing, haven't you?'

'As I said, fifteen years is a long time. There's a lot you've missed,' she replied. Farden might have been mistaken, but there could have been a tinge of regret, or perhaps the tiniest hint of resentment in that reply. He stayed quiet until they reached the bathroom.

It was a square affair, no bigger than his cabin, and no different either, save for a wide copper tub sitting right in its centre. Steam choked the air. The smell of soap and cleanliness made his nose itch.

'The door locks from the inside, so nobody will disturb you. Take as long or as little time as you want, but if you come out smelling the same as you went in, I'll have your uncle come below-decks to show you how it's done,' she said, hands on hips yet again, stern, yet subtly playful. Farden shook his head.

'Yes ma'am,' he said, and began to close the door.

Lerel leant forward. 'And Farden?'

'Yes?' he poked his head out of the door. Lerel gave him a quick kiss on his cheek and then grimaced as she was stung by his matted beard. She rolled her eyes and began to walk away.

'I'm glad you're back,' she called over her shoulder.

Farden watched her until she disappeared around the corner, a bemused smile on his grizzled face. He locked the door as she'd instructed and turned to confront the dreaded bath. He shrugged off his shirt and dipped a finger in the steaming, soap-slick water. Vials of perfumed oils and scrubbing brushes had been left on the side. The mage shook his head.

'Fine,' he sighed, and hoisted himself into the near-scalding water. As he melted into it, he could almost feel the dead skin and dirt flaking away. He let his eyes droop and his body sink. It had taken a decade to get him into a bath. Oh, how he had missed it.

❦

In the end, it was a probably a miracle he didn't drown. When Farden awoke nearly two hours later, the water was almost ice cold and his skin had shrivelled to a prune-like texture. He quickly hoisted himself out of the tub, muscles shaky and unsure of themselves.

Farden wobbled his way to the door, threw on a robe, and shuffled down the corridor. The ship was alive with noise. All around him the creaking of a ship at full speed sang in harmony with the roaring and hissing of waves sliding over wood and iron, the orders of the officers, and the occasional *whump* of something going on above decks. Farden pulled his robe about him and found his way to his door. It was unlocked, and the room empty.

Somebody had put a pile of fresh clothes on his pillow. Not his usual sort of wear, but all he had. His old clothes were nowhere to be found. In all likelihood, they had been tossed overboard. The folded pile shivered and twitched as Farden reach for it. Farden caught sight of a tail and seized it, hauling a large rat out from a trouser leg. The mage peered at its furry features. 'Whiskers,' he muttered, once he was satisfied it was indeed his rat. He was on a ship after all. Nothing goes together like a rats and ships. How glad he was that he had remembered to bring him, hidden in his cloak pocket.

Farden placed Whiskers back on the bed and got changed into the crisp, scratchy clothes. Ship's trousers, the thick cotton sort, dyed a dark red. A cold white shirt with too many buttons. Thick socks that hugged his damp feet. A pair of black leather boots with waxy laces. A cloak, the sort he liked, with a low black hood and pockets upon pockets. Farden put it all on.

He discovered a razor underneath the pile of clothes. It was the cut-throat kind, with an ivory handle. It had a curly *T* carved into its handle. Tyrfing's. Farden twiddled it around in his fingers while his other hand ran around his face and neck, pulling at the wiry strands and long locks. Farden pulled a face. A clean start needed a clean shave. It was a small decision, but, like ants, they often carried the most weight.

Farden cast about for a mirror, grimacing at the thought of facing his reflection again, but thankfully he found himself without. He used his towel to dry his face and then began to carve away the thick black hair that had infested his jaw and cheeks. Whiskers teetered on his back-legs, watching the wisps of black hair fall to the wood. Farden winced with every tug of the blade. He'd imagined a blacksmith, of all people, would have kept his razor sharp.

It took half an hour of scraping and grunting, but in the end he got every last hair his calloused fingers could find. He ran his hands around his sore, reddened face and pulled a strange smile. He didn't need a mirror to know it looked better.

After strapping his Scalussen greaves over his trousers, leaving the gauntlets for Whiskers to curl up in, Farden left his room and headed for the top deck.

※

Farden poked his head out of the hatch and was rewarded with a faceful of wind, sharp as glass, fresh as ice, and salt on the lips. He felt it swirl around his shaven skin and freed ears, rolling across his bare hands and between his fingers. It was glorious, as though it was the first wind he had ever tasted on his skin. Farden stepped higher on the step and felt it tug at his clothes.

It was then that he heard the clapping of a crowd somewhere behind him, no doubt on the aftcastle. A few cheers went up. Farden slowly picked a path through the ropes and hatches and bustling sailors, intent on seeing what all the fuss was about.

Nuka was there, leaning gently on the wheel. He was staring up into the pure blue sky, watching the flaming mess of a bottle tumble out of it and land with a hiss in the frothing wake of his ship. A group of mages stood at the balcony. A gaggle of officers clustered behind them, surreptitiously swapping bets of tack biscuits and dribbles of coin. At the back a row of soldiers, dressed in their sea-blue armour, looked on.

Farden wove his way through their lines and found Tyrfing standing at the railing with the mages. He was brandishing a brown glass bottle swathed in sailcloth.

'Ready?' he asked the Written to his left, a skinny woman with a shock of white hair and pink eyes. Farden couldn't help but recognise her from somewhere. The Written nodded, and held her hands out flat, as if spreading them across an invisible tabletop.

'Go,' she muttered, deep in concentration.

Tyrfing let the bottle lie loosely in his palm. The wind twirled between his fingers, growing stronger and stronger until it was snatched up and away, flying high and far above them.

'Njord, it's too high,' one of the officers tutted, flicking a coin to his mate.

'Stay those greedy fingers, lads and ladies. I've seen this trick before,' muttered Nuka, but still loud enough for them all to hear. There was something in his tone that reverberated certainty. The coin and biscuits froze in mid-air.

Nuka was right of course. He had seen this mage in action before. The snow-haired woman jabbed her hand at the sea, like a spear, and twisted it. Fifty yards from the wake of the ship, a wave broke in two, right down its centre. One half foamed and spat and bubbled as it curled upwards. The Written clenched her fingers and the column of water swiped the bottle from the sky. It fell to the sea in pieces, puckering the rolling waves with glass and spray. A lonely scrap of sailcloth drifted away on the wind.

'Water beats fire, six to five!' called a sailor, and the biscuits and coins were swapped with an equal measure of grins and grimaces.

'Another round!' somebody cried, but Tyrfing held up his hands.

'We're all out of bottles, I'm afraid.'

'What a shame,' mumbled a familiar voice, as the crowd began to dribble away, back to their chores.

Tyrfing turned to face his nephew. 'You're alive. What happened to your face?'

Farden rubbed his cheeks, wincing. 'Somebody left me a dull razor.'

'Nonsense,' Tyrfing grunted. 'You'll sully a good blacksmith's name.' While Farden picked at a spot of dry skin, Tyrfing cast a glance over his shoulder. He drew a little bottle from the inside of his coat and raised an eyebrow at his nephew. 'Fancy raising the score to six apiece, Farden?' he quietly offered. A few of the nearby officers heard his words, and slowly the crowd began to knit itself back together.

Farden looked at the bottle as if it had fangs, sharp gnashing fangs. 'Er...' was all he could say, as his uncle stared down at him, wind tossing his hair to and fro. Farden looked around and caught the stares of some of the Written. He sucked his teeth. His skin itched uncomfortably.

Tyrfing smiled and tapped the bottle, waggling it in front of

Farden's face. 'Dust off that Book of yours. Cast a spell or two. The reputation of fire is at stake here.'

Farden shook his head. 'I don't think so, uncle.'

'Come on. Modren told me about the lock spell you broke.'

Farden cleared his throat sharply. He dusted off his cloak, even though not a single mote of dust could be seen on it. 'A fluke. I gave my magick up a long time ago,' he quietly confessed, but the wind carried his voice further than he would have liked. There was a muttering between the nearby mages, part disbelief, part told-you-so whispers. Farden bowed his head. He had half-expected this. Alienation from the other Written. The lone wolf, once again.

Tyrfing looked down at the deck. His hands fell to his side. His brow was furrowed like the cracks of dried mud. The ship rocked under them for a wave or two, and then the Arkmage shook his head. He asked the question on everybody's bitten lips. 'Why would you give something like that up?' he asked, simple as a river stone dropped in a millpond.

Farden knew it was a question without an answer. At least, without an answer that had the sting of a long and guilty explanation. An answer for the privacy of a cabin, not for the ears of the onlookers, the eavesdroppers, the ones looking down their noses at him now. Farden turned to the sea, hunching his shoulders.

Tyrfing clapped his hands. 'Back to your training!' he ordered, 'or back to your bunks. Some of you are on watch later. Get to it, or…!' A cough cut him short, and Tyrfing put his hands to his mouth. He turned away, leaving Farden to stare at the sea.

It was an age before anyone bothered to speak to him. It was probably for the best. The mage had his thoughts. The two kept each other company. Three would have been a crowd.

It was Nuka that finally ventured over. Farden felt a heavy hand on his hunched shoulder. He found the captain brandishing a mug of hot beer at him, like a club. 'Drink?' he grunted.

Farden sniffed the proffered mug. It smelled of spices and barley, of the tang of alcohol. It was early afternoon but the wind and his stillness had made him cold. He took the steaming drink in both hands and thanked the captain.

'Don't mention it,' Nuka said, and moved back to his wheel. He tested the wind with a wet finger and hummed to himself before jerking the wheel starboard. The mage, boots now somewhat attuned to the movements of the deck, felt the ship respond beneath him. The distant, rocky headland came in line with the needle-like bowsprit. Sea-Water, rainbows in its spinning droplets, sprayed over the bow as the ship clove a wave in two. The clouds frothed overhead, slow and steady, greys and blues.

Farden frowned as the order was given to take in a little sail. It felt as if they were slowing. In fact, now that he thought about it, they hadn't been going very fast for the last hour. 'Heading inland?' he asked.

Nuka nodded. 'Avoiding the squall.'

'What squall?'

'That squall,' Nuka flicked a finger at a patch of ugly cloud loitering in the southwest, a bruise of granite and indigo against the rest of the sky. It was nowhere near them, and Farden said as much.

Nuka smiled at him. 'How many ships you sailed on, Farden?'

Farden thought about that. 'Three, I think, and the last one sank.'

'Then I'm guessing you wouldn't want to make a repeat of the last time, eh?'

'Not particularly.'

'Then west nor' west it is.' Nuka slapped the wheel with a hand that resembled a side of ham. He turned to one of his officers, the first mate by the looks of him, a narrow fellow with a chin like a spade, and smiled. 'As if a squall could sink this lady, though eh? Just slow us down a mite.'

The first mate shook his head and returned the smile.

Farden sipped his beer and found it sweet with a bitter, malty tang of an aftertaste. He washed his tongue around his mouth. 'Won't heading into the coast slow us down anyway?'

'I'm aware of the shortness of time, good sir. The Arkmages have explained the situation to me at great length. This ship is faster than any that the Arka, or anyone else for that matter, have ever built. No doubt it took you three days' sailing, last time you saw the Midgrir beaches, am I right?'

Farden nodded. That it had.

'Well, it's taken us barely two.'

'But aren't there rocks that we'll have to avoid? Islands to go around?'

Captain Nuka threw him a warning look. 'Farden, friend, don't be mistaking my kindness and calmness for an invitation to keep rambling on and telling me how to sail my ship. I know you're anxious. We all are. Elessi is a good friend of mine and Lerel's too, so hold your tongue and be patient.' Here Nuka left his wheel and came close to Farden. 'Or, you can go belowdecks and sleep yourself into a better mood. It'll be three days yet 'til we make anchor in Hjaussfen,' he said, one bushy eyebrow raised, awaiting a response. Farden said nothing. Instead he went back to the railing, taking his mug of beer with him. He sipped at it, shivering as the warmness slid down into his belly and reminded his skin how cold it was. 'Patience,' he whispered to the wind, as a gust of it slapped him in the face. Seaspray followed in its wake. Farden winced. *Patience*, he repeated the word in his head, clutching at it, pushing it deep into his mind and hoping it would stick.

'Steady as she goes!' Nuka bellowed over the sound of

rattling pulleys and the thundering of a hundred shoes pounding up and down the long deck. The sails were being hauled down and rolled away. Sailors swung through the rigging, caring little for the fall or the choppy sea. The ship squirmed with activity.

And rightly so, for in their path an orange cliff stood boldly against the crashing waves, still a mile or two away yet, but tall enough to seem very, very close indeed. So close in fact, that for every two glances that the sailors gave their work, they gave a third to the cliff-face and its pounding, thundering roots.

The waters at the southern tip of Midgrir were a strange and vibrant green, a mixture of the sandstone seabed and the deep blue of the water that had drowned it. It made the danger a very colourful one, as if they were already stuck fast in the oily paints of some artistic rendering of a disaster to come.

Farden had put himself at the very back of the ship, where an enormous lantern hung out over the iron stern and its foaming wake. He looked back at the open sea behind them, and saw the squall was hot on their tail. He could already see the lightning flashing at its heart.

Lerel was beside him, bent over a table with a compass and a dagger. She stared at the maps closely, prodding their script and symbols, fingers twitching with her lips. Occasionally she would call out directions and warnings to Nuka, who was glued to the wheel. He had plied this channel many a time before, in many other ships, but this time was the first the *Waveblade* had tasted its emerald fury.

Wave by wave, they drew closer to the cliffs. All the sails but a skinny few had been left to catch the wind. The closer they got to the cliffs, the faster the water around them seemed to flow, as if they were stuck in a river, rather than a sea.

Less than half a mile from the rocks, the *Waveblade* turned her starboard flank to the sheer face of the cliff and the sailors held their breaths as a narrow dagger of rock sidled by, casual as a statue, too close for comfort.

'Port two notches. The island is close!' Lerel hollered.

'I see it,' Nuka barked, as the keen edge of the cliff drew back to reveal a tall column of stone, built like a tall, ochre turret in the sea. Farden felt his jaw drop at the sight of it. Then the noise hit him, the noise of a million cliff-birds greeting them. It was deafening, a cackling, piercing roar like no other, only made worse by the hiss and rumble of the waves. He could see Lerel's mouth moving as she yelled another direction, but her voice was lost in the cacophony.

Guillemots, swippets, cormorants, puffins, foamsnatchers, rosklints, terns, and seagulls, they came in whirlwinds and waves, smothering the ship and her tall masts. They swarmed the deck, squawking and screeching and cawing and as they swooped and dove. A few snagged in the rigging, and had to be clubbed into silence before they frayed the taut ropes. The *Waveblade* surged on, unabated. She was poised for something, Farden could feel it.

'Mages!' yelled Tyrfing, from the port side. The mages emerged from their hiding places in the crew and began to throw random fireballs into the thick flocks. It worked like a charm. The birds, terrified by the fire, beat a hasty retreat, fleeing back to the sheer walls of their strange island, hissing and screeching from afar.

'Five notches to starboard, Captain! Watch for the Bodkins!'

'Aye!' acknowledged Nuka.

'The what?' blurted Farden, as he remembered his tongue. He darted past Lerel and looked over the port side. His stomach clenched with what he saw: sharp rocks jutting out of the water at all angles, barely a few feet from the hull.

'The Bodkins,' Lerel was shouting. 'Needle-like rocks that lead a path to the Bitch!'

'The *what*?!' Farden turned back to her.

Lerel jabbed her dagger at the towering column of rock that stood directly in their path. 'The Bitch! That great thing! Now shut up!

I'm concentrating on not getting us killed.'

Farden strangled the railing with his hands. Memories of the *Sarunn* made his teeth chatter. He winced as he spied a tooth of rock, unsheathed by a falling wave. It curved upwards like a fang. An old anchor was wrapped around it, just below its dagger-edge. A gravestone to some lost vessel. Farden was close to crying out when he heard the rattle of the wheel. The ship kicked, and they slid past it with only inches to spare. 'Why'd we even come this way?' he hissed, swearing under his breath.

The bosun, a man Farden had heard being referred to as Roiks, stood at Nuka's side. Hearing the mage's cursing, he turned to grin at him. 'Pickles the mind, don't it!? But by Njord's festering bollocks, you'll see. Ain't a current like it in the seas!'

'Steady!' Nuka shouted over the roaring of the waves, the wind, and the seabirds. It was then, leaning far out over the railing in the clutch of the most morbid curiosities, that Farden saw the method in Nuka's madness. By some peculiar quirk of rock and sea, the channel between the Bitch and the cliffs caused a tidal race, one that flowed at a breakneck speed. Farden could see the water streaming between the rocks; frothy, pale, a blur ripped from the depths. It made him feel nauseous to watch it.

Farden tried to stand as steadfast as the sailors around him. He clutched the railing with one hand, holding the other over his eyes so he could stare up at the lofty, dizzying heights of the cliffs and the Bitch. He couldn't help but notice they were still heading straight for the face of the Bitch herself. It could have been the shit-painted rocks, it could have been a trick of the light, but it almost seemed to be smiling at them.

'Now, Captain!' yelled Lerel, jabbing her dagger into the crease of the map. Nuka and Roiks went to the wheel with a frantic will. *Waveblade* lurched like a stung sabre-cat, twisting almost around her centre to show the Bitch her port flank. Suddenly the surge of the channel snatched at them, and the ship sprang forward like a bolt from a bow, wind howling. Nuka and the rest of the crew let loose a mighty cheer. Roiks even spared a moment to flick two fingers at the Bitch as she flew past, her squawking parapets inches from the tip of the main boom.

'Release!' yelled Nuka, and the sailors sprang their trap. Clockwork and cogs clattered across the ship as levers were yanked by calloused hands. The sails burst into life, wrenched downwards and outwards by clever ropes and weights. They puffed like the chests of heroes, and the ship lurched again as the wind added its strength to the tidal race.

Before Farden could even blink, they were skipping across the waves of a tranquil bay, the squall, the cliffs, the Bitch, and her Bodkins already shrinking behind them. 'So that's why,' he muttered to the sudden quiet.

Lerel teased her dagger from the wood. She winked. 'That's why. Now we can all can relax for an hour or two.'

Roiks sauntered up, wiping a hand across his tanned brow. The bosun was a thickset man with cauliflower ears, younger than his weathered hide might have suggested. He had a mouth that would make a thug's mother faint and that could goad a dead man from the grave, so it was said by the others. His hair had jumped ship long ago, and his knuckles bore the scars of many a fight. Despite all that, Farden supposed he seemed friendly enough. He had met worse characters in his time.

'Feck me and that was close,' he chortled, nodding to Lerel. He grinned a grin that was surprisingly full of teeth. 'And we've got eats too, by the looks of it. The gods are just pissing luck down on us!' The bosun gestured to the deck, where the sailors and soldiers were picking up the fallen birds, some already part-roasted, thanks to the mages.

'Get the pots out lads!' Roiks clapped his hands as he went

down onto the deck. Heimdall was standing by a hatch, looking around at the feathered carnage. Completely unaware what sort of passenger Heimdall truly was, the bosun swaggered up to him, dead bird dangling in one hand. Roiks clapped the god hard on the back, thrust the bird into his hands, and winked. 'That was bloody close, weren't it?' he chuckled, before jauntily strutting to the forecastle.

Farden couldn't help but wince.

Loki was toying with a frayed bit of rope, slowly unwinding its braids. He looked up at Heimdall, who seemed frozen, staring down at the limp and bloody bird draped over his hands. It was a swippet, a bright blue and yellow cliff-bird with a long, curving beak and a crest of soft spines about its little head. Heimdall wrinkled his nose.

'And you wanted to remain anonymous,' muttered the young god.

Heimdall let the bird fall to the deck. 'It would be different, if they knew the truth.'

Loki looked up at the aftcastle, where Farden stood between Lerel and Nuka. 'I am not so sure,' he replied. Heimdall didn't answer. Loki tossed his rope overboard and put his hands in his pockets. He moved to stand beside the older god. 'Any sign of them?'

Heimdall flicked his eyes to the cliffs now retreating behind them, up to where their crumbling tops were fringed by spiky grass and teetering pebbles, where two creatures sat like clouds of smoke, grinning right back at him. Nobody had seen them but him. 'Still they watch us.'

'Why do they not strike?'

'They are biding their time. This ship and its crew are strong. They will not risk it, until...' Heimdall's words faded away.

'Until she tries again.'

Heimdall nodded.

'And is there any sign of her?'

'A faint echo, to the east. Heading north still. I will climb the mast at sunset to make sure.'

Loki turned his head to look towards the bow, where the forecastle offered a small platform to the sky. Ilios lay on it, curled up in a big, feathery ball. The gryphon had slept through all the excitement.

'Do you think Farden's plan is a sound one?' Heimdall asked him.

Loki looked back as if surprised that he was being asked that question, or any question at all for that matter. It was the first time Heimdall had asked his advice since they had fallen. He sucked at his teeth, making Heimdall narrow his eyes. A most human expression. 'Save the maid, chase the girl. I think the priorities are backward, but if she is heading where you think she's heading, then I suppose we might just have time.'

'Precious little.'

Loki shrugged. 'For immortal souls, we have such trouble with time-keeping.'

Heimdall nodded and turned away, squinting into the distance. He couldn't help but think of it, but that was the fourth time Loki had mentioned souls in the last two days. A strange occurrence, nothing more, he told himself, but it nibbled at his mind nonetheless.

ॐ

The sun died and with it the winds.

As the bruised sky darkened to black and purple, the *Waveblade* found itself floating on a millpond sea, like a knife sliding gently through the glass of a mirror. It was a stillness that would have been peaceful, had it come at a different time. Not for Farden. Not on this journey.

The mage stood at the stern of the '*Blade*, busy glaring at the star-speckled sky as if he were eyeing a crowd of thieves, hunting for the one that had stolen the wind away. They were as silent as the sea, and after a few minutes more of accusatory squinting, Farden relented, and decided to blame the sun instead. He sighed. The culprit was already long gone. He would have to take it up with him in the morning.

A silver sickle-moon hovered in the east, looking for all the world as if some great creature had taken a bite of it. The stars clustered around her, concerned and fretting as they sparkled. Farden could imagine them wailing and crying at the plight of their silver cousin, as she tumbled slowly through the sky. But moons heal. She would be whole again soon. Farden shook his head at his abstract mood. Anything to distract him from his impatience.

It was then that he felt a sudden warm breeze on his cheek. He heard the sails crackle behind him as they billowed outwards. Farden moved to where he could look down on the deck. There, below him, standing just a few feet from the base of the mainsail, was a trio of blue-tunic mages. They were silent and still, yet they had their arms raised to the white sails above them. Farden could see their clothes flapping and their hair shivering. Wind mages. Beloved of all sailors, and now of a certain Written. Farden smiled. He could already feel the ship starting to move. The sound of the mirror-sea splintering underneath the keel was like music to his ears. Finally.

Farden sauntered back to his railing and poured himself one last drop of wine before bed. It was on nights like these that the never =mar used to call to him. The bottle gurgled at him as he poured. *At least he had his alcohol*, he thought. Small mercies.

A sailor came to man the wheel behind him. Farden nodded to him, but they didn't speak. It was only when another man came to the stern, a man in armour and a cloak, that the quiet, moonlit hissing of the waves was broken.

'Fine night,' said the man, gruff-voiced. He had a deep Arfell accent.

'That it is,' replied Farden, looking him up and down. The man looked like a Written. Farden could tell by the way the man lounged against the railing, oozing confidence, a confidence that only came from the feeling of a Book in your skin. Farden noted his grey hair, though it could have been the white of the moonlight, and the unique sparkle in the armour that covered his chest and legs. Scalussen, no doubt. Farden stared at the man's face. 'Do I know you?' he asked.

'You did,' the man replied. 'A bloody age ago.'

'Efjar,' ventured Farden, unsure. His visitor nodded.

'The Iron Keys. Vice's old regiment. First year.' Farden bit his lip as a name tried to form itself in his mouth. The man beat him to it. 'Gossfring.'

'Gossfring!' Farden blurted, like a cork escaping a beer bottle. 'Gods, that was an age ago. I didn't recognise you.'

Gossfring smiled. 'I've aged something terrible, I know. I remember the days when the whores wouldn't know which one of us to swindle first, so dashing we were. Ugly bastard I am now,' Gossfring chuckled. 'But I tell you, if you think I'm ugly, you should see Korti. Got a face that would make a mirror cry. Hah. He's here too, y'know. And Shol. And Enf the Boot. But I hear your memory ain't what it used to be. On account of the…' Gossfring waved a nondescript finger at Farden's face.

Farden turned back to the sea. 'Yes.' Rumours were like diseases. Caught from the last person who had it until it comes around again, when the first person is either dead or immune. 'Well.' It was all he could say. Nevermar was a curse word to the rest of his kind.

Gossfring held up his hands. 'Hey, I ain't judging, Farden. I'll leave that to the younger mages.' He tapped his nose. 'They whisper, but I know it's only temporary, see?'

Farden turned back to the man with a quizzical look. 'Temporary? Are we talking about the nevermar, or my decision?'

Gossfring shrugged. 'A decision is it? A choice? Either way. It don't matter. No hero of Efjar can banish their magick for good, not after what I saw him do to the minotaurs. Ain't possible. You'll see, in the desperate times we're in. It'll fight its way back out,' he said, and it looked as if that was all he had come to say. He adjusted his cloak and half-turned to leave. 'We just wanted you to know it's a pleasure having you back with us. There may be a few who doubt you, but for us vets... well, once a Written, always a Written. Tough life it is. Makes you do tough things. Things no man can explain. Things no man should need to explain.' Gossfring chuckled then. 'Ramblin', aren't I? Anyways, that's all I wanted to say. Enjoy your wine, Farden.'

Farden nodded a goodnight to the man and watched him leave. It was a while before he moved, deep in thought over Gossfring's simple wisdom.

When he finally did move, he reached for the bottle and let its mouth hover over his empty glass. A single drop of wine dribbled from it, and then he tilted it back. He held it up to his eyes and the silver moon and swilled the dregs of it around. 'Hero,' Farden muttered to himself and the wind. Gossfring's words swam around his head.

Farden dangled the bottle over the railing and let his hand grow limp. The bottle landed in the ship's wake with a splash, lost to the inky, silver-lined blackness. Even though his eyes had lost sight of it, Farden aimed a hesitant hand at the sea and the unseen target. He strained so much that his fingers bent to claws, and the tendons stood out like bones on the back of his hand. For a long time, nothing happened. Then, just as he couldn't stand the pain in his head any longer, a puff of flame burst from his palm. It was a little sputter, a cough of fire, something a candle might be proud of but nothing more. To Farden it was a fountain of flame. An onslaught. He clenched his hand as the magick burnt him, and bit his lip. He felt guilty, then, for a moment, for trying to resurrect his magick, after all those years trying to kill it.

But maybe Gossfring was right. 'Desperate times and all that,' he told himself, thinking of the door in the Arkathedral. Elessi was still in danger. He hadn't saved her yet. *Besides*, Farden lectured to himself, *perhaps it would be different*. Perhaps he wasn't a curse any more. Perhaps he was something new, or something very old.

In the darkness, there might have been a smile on his face. *Hero*. He had been called that before.

He had forgotten how much he liked the sound of it.

Chapter 4

"Ships have a curious relationship with the sea. The sea both loathes and loves them. A fickle mistress, she. Caressing the keel one minute, dashing the bow against the rocks the next. That is why we must pray to Njord, and pray that his sea remains a kind lady."
From the diary of Captain Rasserfel, in the year 801

'Up!' the sergeant bellowed. A score of sweating bodies pushed themselves off the scrubbed deck. 'Down!' came the shout, and the bodies kissed the wood with their noses. 'Halfway up and hold it!' The sergeant swaggered through the rows and lines, tapping arms with his boots. He could see their arms shivering with the tension. 'Hold it!' he yelled in their ears.

At the far corner of the group, one of the men sagged and crumpled to the floor. The sergeant cast him a look, mouth poised to bellow, and then thought better of it. He turned away and let his lungs loose on the others instead. 'And up again!' he shouted. At the edge of his eye, he spied the man slowly but surely pushing himself back up.

It was the mage. The one who had come aboard at Krauslung with the Arkmage and the Written. The one who had spewed his guts down the port side not a minute out of the harbour. He was a sweaty wreck if the sergeant had ever seen one, a feeble and exhausted mess, but by Njord, he had the determination of an iron bar.

'Up! Down! Up! Down!' the sergeant yelled his orders in

quick succession. The soldiers and sailors bobbed up and down like flotsam on a wave. In the corner, the man crumpled to the deck again. The sergeant pinched the bridge of his nose and sighed.

※

Farden was tired. His body was screaming. His mind was the only thing still capable of moving. He thrust at the deck with his palms but his body refused to move. He rolled onto his back and lifted a hand to shield his eyes from the sun. Somebody grabbed his wrist and dragged him out of the exercise squad and into the sweet shade underneath the bulwark. He squinted up at his saviour. His uncle.

'Tsk. Know your limits, boy,' Tyrfing tutted, as he passed him a wooden cup of cold water.

'You haven't called me that in years,' Farden wheezed. 'When are people going to learn that I really, really hate being called that?'

Tyrfing shrugged and turned back to watch the others train.

It was a fresh morning, the kind that makes the teeth ache if breathing in too sharply. The kind where the sun sits behind a veil of constant misty cloud, teasingly warm. The kind where the sea is a lazy blanket of grey-blue, where ships rely on wind mages and the momentum of the day before. A day neither here nor there. Half-asleep and plodding. Just like their progress.

The sails had pushed them far in the night, past the eastern shadow of Albion and the western reaches of Halôrn and Emaneska, almost into the Rannoch Sound.

Farden lay on the deck and watched the sails puff and shudder. When the ship leant the right way, he could even see a lone and stoic figure in the crow's nest, eyes fixed on the east.

When his lungs had quenched their exhausted fire, Farden sat himself up and got to his feet. The training squad were still going. The men were shirtless, the women almost, and the Written only just covering their backs with open tunics. They jumped and sprawled, jumped and sprawled, all to the barking of the sergeant. Farden moved to join the squad again, but Tyrfing put his hand on his nephew's chest. 'Not today. You're done.'

'I'm done when I can't stand,' Farden snapped. He looked down at his feet and then back to his uncle. 'And it looks like I'm standing.'

'What's got into you today? You seem...' Tyrfing began, but then trailed off. Now that he had asked the question, he understood. The bottle from the day before. The still-receding effects of the nevermar. The fight to come. He couldn't blame him.

Farden began to unbutton his shirt. 'Why aren't you joining in, hmm, old man?'

Tyrfing gave him an acidic glance. 'Those days are long behind me.'

'Surely you can just shapeshift into a stronger, younger body.'

Tyrfing shook his head, and as he did so, his beard turned a darker shade of grey, the wrinkles faded from his face, and his eyes began to sparkle. He looked as Farden remembered him. 'Like this?' he asked. 'Why pretend? Shapeshifting is like painting an old wall. You can make it look better, but it's still the same old wall underneath,' he smiled, fading back to his old self. He coughed then, and turned away to cough at the sea. There was a persistence in his uncle's coughing that concerned him. Farden frowned, and left him to it.

Stubborn as always, the mage joined the end of the squad, to the sound of a few titters from nearby sailors. He glared at them and then began to jump and sprawl with the others. He barely made it to a half-dozen before his body told him no, and promptly gave him cramp in both legs to make its point. He held himself off the floor, and grit his teeth against the pain. *Damn that nevermar.*

A hand patted him on the shoulder. Farden looked up to find

Gossfring standing over him, open-shirted, scarred, and smiling. The young white-haired mage from the day before stood behind him, expressionless and vacant. 'Perhaps it's time for some sword practice, Farden. I remember you as quite the bladesman,' he suggested. 'Perhaps you can show Inwick here some moves she don't know.'

Farden wiped away a river of sweat from his face. The offer was an escape route, and as much as it stung Farden to take it, he did. He shakily pushed himself to standing and left the squad to its exercises, following the others to the forecastle. Loki was there with Whiskers, sitting on the steps and listening to Ilios snore. The god was twiddling his tiny flute around his finger.

'Here to provide some percussion?' chimed the god. He was quickly discovering his dislike for the sea, mainly due to where he had chosen to sit. Occasionally, an ambitious wave would spray over the bow, soaking both him and the rat. Loki would grunt and wipe the seawater from his face, muttering darkly under his breath. Whiskers didn't seem to mind.

'Swords?' Loki asked, at the sight of the training blades in Gossfring's hands. A sweaty Farden nodded.

'You seen Farden swing a sword before, lad?' asked Gossfring in a loud voice. He swung his training blade experimentally, testing its weight. The dull blade hummed around him. It was quieter at the prow of the ship. Most of the sailors were aft, watching the training, high above in the sails, or asleep, rocking back and forth in their hammocks below.

Loki didn't try to hide his displeasure at being called *lad*. 'I haven't had the pleasure,' he icily replied. 'Though my good friend Heimdall did tell me a rather bloody tale of Farden and a young Albion noble, a young noble who rather foolishly decided it would be wise to challenge him to a duel. Am I telling it right? Over a seat, of all things, wasn't it Farden? At a certain Duke's table?'

'That's enough, Loki,' said Farden, wincing.

Gossfring winked at the younger mage, Inwick. 'A noble, eh? So, what happened next? I smell a story.'

Loki scratched his head with his flute. 'You know, I don't recall the rest. Farden?'

Farden sighed. 'I put a sword through his fancy dancing shoes.'

'Which ones?' asked Loki.

'Both of them,' Farden said.

Gossfring chuckled at that, and tossed the mage a blade.

'How callous.' Inwick gave them all a disapproving look. Farden examined the woman as he twirled his blade. She stood straighter than straight, as if the meat of her had been wrapped around an iron rod. It was plain to see that she was of old-stock; of a traditional family, mage born and bred. Farden remembered the sort from the School. Everything about her was smart. Her hair was a long shock of white, tied back in a tight tail. Her hands were folded behind her back. Her boots were like black mirrors. The model of military neatness. There wasn't a stray hair on her head nor a speck of seawater on her clean tunic. Only a single bead of sweat marred her perfect appearance.

Gossfring passed her a sword. 'After you then ma'am,' he said, settling back into a defensive stance.

Farden had expected something more sedate from such a groomed and polished woman. He couldn't have been more wrong. Inwick attacked like a forest fire, a whirling dervish of blunt steel and accuracy. It was shocking to watch. Gossfring barely managed to fend off of her blows. Each one came closer and closer to touching him. He managed a single swing before she swivelled around and caught him across the throat.

'Told you,' he grunted to Farden, as she released him. 'Fastest we ever seen. Save for Undermage Modren and you, mind.'

'I can see that.'

'Try your luck,' Gossfring replied, chuckling. 'I think you two will be a good match.'

Farden stepped forward. The look on Inwick's face was that of cold invitation, as though she had spent all her life training to fight a legendary beast, and finally, here it was, face to face with her at last. Farden wondered if she wanted to lop his head off as a trophy.

Farden balanced the blade lightly on his shoulder and sighed. The sweat still dripped off him. His body was tired. The Written dancing back and forth in front of him was young, fresh, and ready. Skilled, too. But he had one small smidgeon of comfort. One small fact that made Farden as calm as a summer lake. There was one skill he hadn't abandoned during all his years of exile, just one…

…Killing things. With a sword, no less.

'After you, then,' Farden grunted, blade still perched on his shoulder.

Inwick looked momentarily confused. 'Are you going to adopt a stance, or not?' she asked.

Farden just shook his head. Gossfring took a wise step back and winked at Loki. The god looked on, intrigued.

Common courtesy would have dictated that a gentleman, even during a polite duel or practice, be gentle and courteous with a lady opponent. But Farden was no gentleman, and Inwick was not the average lady. She lunged at him, vicious even with her blunt blade, and Farden sent her spinning with a giant counterstrike. It struck her off balance, and once he had tripped her with the blade, Farden was quickly at her throat.

Inwick looked up, sprawled on the deck, utterly bemused. 'Unfair,' she hissed. 'You didn't…'

Farden shook his head. 'Fighting *is* unfair, lady mage. The age of respect and fair-fighting died a long time ago. I'm surprised they didn't teach you that at the School.'

Inwick didn't reply. She simply got to her feet, looking for all the world as though she were about to stride away. But it was then that she swung her blade, aiming high, for Farden's head. Luckily, he saw it coming; he knew he had bruised more than her elbows and knees.

This time, Farden barely kept her at bay. Inwick swung with everything she had. Left, right, up, down, the blows rained like hailstones in midwinter. Farden parried and blocked, his arms weak but his form strong. Only battle and murder can teach a man to move like that, and Farden had seen his fair share of both.

A full minute of furious exchange passed before he saw his opening. He whacked out at her leg and was rewarded by a shout and then a blow to the shoulder. Farden growled and pushed back. Blows now began to connect with muscles and bones. Swords clanged together like anvils and hammers. A small audience had clumped together. The duel was suddenly becoming a battle of endurance and sheer will.

'That's enough, you two!' Gossfring warned. He could see the shining lights under Inwick's tunic as she ducked and danced. He was about to step in when she aimed a huge downward strike at Farden. He hopped back as the blade hit the deck and showered sparks over Loki and Timeon. Farden didn't bat an eyelid. He put his foot on Inwick's blade and kicked with the other, nearly snapping her wrist as he kicked her hands free of its handle. He slowly and gently lowered his sword, now notched and bitten, to rest on her neck. She flinched as if it were hot.

'Best of three?' he whispered, offering a hand. To his surprise, Inwick grasped it. She didn't say a word, she simply shook her head and went to stand by Gossfring.

'Maybe we'll practise again later,' he said, with a surreptitious nod of approval to Farden. As he led the slightly bemused Inwick away, she could be heard whispering.

'I thought you said he was half the man he used to be?' An elbow in the ribs silenced any more of that conversation.

With a smattering of applause, Farden sauntered to a clear section of deck and began to practise his old sword forms, twirling his battered blade in all sorts of cartwheels and somersaults. He was a blur. A tired, and shaky blur, but a blur nonetheless. Something fresh ran through his veins.

'There's the old Farden,' smiled Tyrfing, watching his nephew.

'Yes,' hummed Loki, distracted. 'The old Farden indeed.' He was busy patting the smouldering patches on his cloak where Inwick's sparks had fallen. All around his feet and legs, little black cinders hissed and died.

☙

Afternoon fell, swiftly chased by evening, and soon they were both nipping at the heels of the sun as it drowned in the blackness of the horizon. Nuka had driven the *Waveblade* and her crew hard throughout the rest of the day, barking orders and laying about with stiff ropes. As night fell, the ship was clearing the Rannoch Sound, a section of sea below the curving claw of Albion's northeastern limits. Nelska and Hjaussfen lay due north, and the *Waveblade* sped towards them both.

Evening found Tyrfing in his modest cabin, surrounded by his armour and other shiny objects. A brace of axes lay up against his bed. A shield lay in complex pieces on the cabinet behind him, surrounded by little tools and implements. The Arkmage ignored them all. He was at his desk, poring over a book, and no ordinary book for that matter. The fringes of its thick pages were a bloodshot red, while the paper itself was a pale, wan green. The colour of seasickness, or sun-kissed lichen. Its cover was made of thick copper, bound in brown leather.

Merchants had an unofficial rule: *if something was heavy, then it was worth a pretty penny.* This book fitted that rule. It weighed half as much as a desk, and it had cost more than a few pouches of gold. And yet, the strangest thing about it was that it was completely, utterly blank. There was not a scribble to be found in any of the pages. Not yet, anyway.

Untouched and uninked, the green pages were spread open before him. Tyrfing's quill hesitated above them, waiting for something. A single droplet of black ink quivered at the nib of the quill, hovering, ready to go to work. It didn't have long to wait.

As Tyrfing stared down at the empty page, a line of thin script began to scratch its way across it, as if scrawled by some ghost wielding an invisible quill. Tyrfing didn't look the least bit shocked. He waited patiently for the phantom scribbler to finish his words before reading, lips mouthing them.

TYRFING, ALL IS SEEMINGLY WELL HERE. MALVUS IS STILL WAITING TO CLOSE THE JAWS OF HIS PLAN. THE CITY IS TENSE. THE BODIES HAVE BEEN BURIED AND THE MESS OF BATTLE CLEARED AWAY. HOW FARES THE VOYAGE?
D

Tyrfing touched his quill to the page, under where the last message had finished. As he wrote, the ink vanished the moment it touched the paper, as though the quill was bone dry. Tyrfing had to concentrate hard on his imaginary letters:

AS QUICKLY AS POSSIBLE. SHE IS IMPOSSIBLY FAST. NUKA TELLS ME WE SHOULD ARRIVE BY MORNING. FARDEN CONTINUES TO BE POSITIVE. IT'S ALMOST AS IF A NEW FARDEN FELL WITH THE DAEMONS. HOW IS ELESSI?
T

And so the strange conversation went.

ELESSI IS STILL MOCKING DEATH. MODREN HAS GROWN EVEN MORE DESPERATE. HE STRANGLED ONE OF THE HEALERS TODAY. THE JEASIN WOMAN MANAGED TO CALM HIM DOWN BEFORE THE POOR MAN HAD THE LIFE SQUEEZED OUT OF HIM. WE NEED TO HEAL ELESSI, AND QUICKLY. IF WE DO NOT, I FEAR WE SHALL LOSE BOTH OF THEM.
D

AND OF THE HAWKS WE SENT TO TOWERDAWN?
T

NO WORD FROM THE DRAGONS, OR OF <u>HER</u> EITHER. SHE HAS GONE NORTH, I KNOW IT. TO EITHER THE SCATTERED KINGDOMS OR THE ICE FIELDS. GODS ONLY KNOW WHY. MAYBE TO SUMMON AN ARMY WHERE WE CANNOT REACH HER.
D

THAT WORRIES ME DEEPLY. WE HAVE TO CATCH HER, BEFORE IT IS TOO LATE.
T

THAT I LEAVE TO YOU, FARDEN, AND THE OTHERS. I HAVE EVERY FAITH IN YOU.
D

In the privacy of his cabin, Tyrfing winced. His quill bent to the page once again.

SOMETIMES I WONDER WHERE THIS ENDLESS FAITH COMES FROM. PERHAPS IT'S A NEFALIM THING. IT'S MISPLACED, FRIEND. I'M NOT WHAT I USED TO BE. YOU KNOW THAT BETTER THAN ANYBODY. WE NEED MORE TIME, MORE MEN, SHIPS, DRAGONS. ANYTHING...

T

IT IS A FAITH WELL-FOUNDED, OLD FRIEND, IN EXPERIENCE AND TRUST. YOU ARE MORE THAN CAPABLE. AS ARE THE MAGES. UNTIL YOU GET TO NELSKA, YOU AND THE CREW OF THAT SHIP ARE ALL THAT STANDS IN HER WAY. IF YOU CANNOT SUCCEED, THEN NOBODY CAN, AND WE MAY AS WELL WAVE THE WHITE BANNER NOW, AND PRAY THAT MY FATHER ORION AND HIS ILK WILL SHOW US WHAT LITTLE MERCY THEY HAVE...

There was a pause in the phantom scribbling. Tyrfing went to reply, but realised Durnus hadn't signed his initial. Perhaps he was fetching more ink. Tyrfing used the pause to wonder how in Emaneska a blind man could write so legibly. He must have been using one of the trusted servants to read for him. Brave, considering Malvus' deep pockets. Not that he had a choice.

Soon enough, Durnus' scribbling began again, hesitant this time, unsure. Broaching a wounded subject.

...HAVE YOU TOLD HIM YET?
D

Once again, another wince. Tyrfing put down his quill and rifled through his grey hair with sweaty fingers. In was in that uncomfortable moment that there came a rap at the door. Tyrfing quickly scribbled a large and underlined NO. on the page and then quickly flipped to an empty page, knowing full well Durnus' sibling book would flip too.

'Come,' Tyrfing called, and in walked Farden, fresh from walking around the deck, by the looks of his ruffled hair.

'Are we going to the captain's table, or not?' he asked quietly. There seemed to be a slight hint of dread in his voice, almost as if the last two words were two shaky fingers clinging to an escape ladder.

'Yes, we are. One minute,' replied Tyrfing, waving for his nephew to enter. Farden sagged a little and shut the door behind him. 'I'm talking to Durnus.'

Farden looked around, befuddled. 'How?'

'Using an Inkweld.'

'Inkwhat?'

'Weld.'

'Well what?'

Tyrfing rubbed his furrowed brow. 'Just come and see, you infuriating bastard.'

Farden did as he was told and wandered over to the desk. His hands were deep in his pockets, sullen like the rest of him. 'It's blank,' he said. 'And green.'

'Watch,' Tyrfing muttered, dabbing his quill in the nearby pot of ink. As he wrote Durnus' name and the fact that a certain nephew was now in the cabin, Farden leant close to watch the ink sink into the paper. It left no trace save for the fine scraping of the quill's nib. For a moment nothing happened, and then a line of script wrote itself across the page.

JUST AS I WAS RETIRING TOO. WE SHALL TALK MORE SOON.
FARDEN, YOUR UNCLE WILL FILL YOU IN ON ELESSI.
GOODNIGHT, GENTLEMEN.
D

Farden had to admit he was impressed. He even found himself waving goodbye to the open book, and the distant Durnus, as if it were a scrying mirror. 'Very useful. Though I imagine a few hawk-pedlars will be irked by being put out of business.'

'This and its partner are the only ones I've ever seen, and they cost a pretty pouch of gold.'

'How much exactly?'

'None of your business. Privileged Arkmage information.'

'Worth it?'

'I'm not outside in the cold waiting for a hawk, am I?'

'I suppose not.'

'To dinner then, and enough of this conversation.'

Farden nodded, trying to hide his reticence to follow his uncle out of the cabin. Dinner meant people. People meant conversation. Conversation meant Farden having to respond. All Farden wanted to do at that precise moment was curl up into a tight ball and let sleep kidnap him. He was tired from a long day of practice. His body was on fire again but this time it had a glimmer of the good sort about it. Of muscles worked to aching. Of blood and body ridding itself of old poisons. The only blessing about the very mention of dinner was that it carried the prospect of food. Now that, Farden did want to partake of.

Before they entered the Captain's cabin, Tyrfing slung a look over his shoulder and tutted. 'Put a smile on your face, Farden. Your gloomy expression won't make this ship go any faster,' he said, finishing his reprimand with a harsh cough.

Farden tried anyway.

※

Roiks was deep in the midst of a story when they sidled into the captain's cabin. He had his hands raised, as if the punch line was a cudgel he was about to slam into the table.

'... and then, right, Sheps comes down the tavern stairs all sheepish like, with an eye as dark and as hollow as a whirlpool at night. Got a trickle of blood from his nose too, right down to his lip. So I says to him, "Sheps! Why the shiner, lad? Didn't she take kindly to a fine bit of sailor?"'

Roiks paused to stifle a snicker of laughter. The others around him had heard this story before and yet they were still chortling behind loaded forks and calloused hands. Stories like that are like fine wines; they get better with age and air.

'So then Sheps pauses at the bottom of the stair, all frosty-eyed, like I just pissed on his leg. Then, all of a sudden, he cracks a smile, bloodied as it is, and begins to laugh. "Boys!" he announces, all proud and beamy, "let's just say that fine maiden was more of a sailor than I!"'

Roiks slapped the table then, sending his beaker tottering around his plate. The two nearest him began to guffaw with laughter. 'Turns out the maiden that ole Sheps caught winking at him was naught other than a rather comely-looking blacksmith's 'prentice from Manesmark, and had a twitch of his eye no less, from the sparks and the soot, see? So imagine this poor lad's surprise, when he begins to get tired, already cursed with a feminine face, and in a manly sort of profession to boot, been a long day at the forge-fire, his eye is causin' him trouble, some sailor leering at him all night, he takes a wander up to his two-copper room for the night, snuffs the lantern, beds down, all comfy-like, only to suddenly find slithery ole Sheps sashayin' into his very bedroom, pants already half 'round his ankles, cock happy as a flagpole, and gibbering on about sending his vessel deep into port! He was lucky to only get a black eye and a bloodied nose by my reckoning!'

The cabin crumpled into a wheezing, teary-eyed mess of laughter and smattered applause. Nuka was doubled up and red-faced. The rest of the crew were much the same. Even Lerel was in the tight grip of hysterics, coughing and spluttering, being the only one unfortunate enough to have boldly taken a mouthful of her supper right on the cusp of the punchline. Roiks laughed the hardest and longest, banging the butt-end of his knife against the fine tabletop over and over again, mouth wide and cackling, chest heaving with strangled air.

'Dear me,' gasped Nuka, face red. He turned around to the two men standing beside the door, smiles straying onto their lips. Even Farden's. He quickly got to his feet in the presence of Tyrfing. As did every other man and woman at the table. 'Please, Arkmage, Farden, sit.' The captain gestured to a brace of empty chairs that sat on opposite sides of his table.

The company at the table was comprised of the *Waveblade*'s officers. The first mate was a narrow man with a wine-reddened face and plenty of grin to share in his spade-like face. Hasterkin was his name. He was bald save for a stripe of red hair around the back of his skull. The second mate was of course Lerel, dressed in a smart shirt and ship's trousers. She had wine in her cheeks too, and gave Farden a knowing smile as he sat down in the midst of the group. He hadn't bothered to take off his cloak.

The other five gathered around the captain's table consisted of a middle-aged woman with hazy, wine-addled eyes, the ship's healer by the looks of her robe; the captain of the soldiers and mages, a plain but muscular Colonel by the name of Tinbits; the third mate, Gabbant, a very tall and balding gentleman with a thin pair of spectacles balanced on the bridge of a protuberant nose; Roiks, utterly drunk; and Nuka's own personal cook, a silent sort of fellow whose mind and eyes was far away and contemplating dirty dishes. The gods were nowhere to be seen.

With a click of the captain's fingers, the servants came forward with a pair of steaming plates. Showing his hunger, Farden seized his cutlery quickly. It was a stew of some sort. Thick, creamy, with chunks of shark, celery, and carrot. There was a pile of Paraian rice on the side, the orange sort, and a wedge of bread so thick and wide, Whiskers could have used it for a mattress. Farden tucked in with a will while Tyrfing nodded to Roiks.

'Funny story, from what I caught.'

Roiks bobbed his head up and down. ' 'Pologies for the crudeness your Mage.'

Tyrfing cracked a smile. 'None needed, bosun. I was a soldier once, don't forget. I've heard worse. Anyway, I'm in need of some laughter. As you can probably imagine, the magick council don't tell many stories like that.' There was a round of laughs from around the table, then a small silence as everyone went back to their food and half-empty glasses. The servants reappeared with more wine. Farden gulped at his. It was strong stuff. Ship-brewed. Salty sweet and with the kick of a mule. Farden found his stomach liking it a little too much. It was already creeping towards his head.

Roiks waved a dirty fork at him. 'Speaking o' stories. Spotted you training with that white-haired mage today, Farden. Looks like these old stories we keep hearing about you might just be true.'

Farden forced a smile. All he could think of was his room, his stark, lonely room. It was fine company at the table, but he simply wasn't in the mood for people. The fatigue and the withdrawing nevermar were still pummelling him. 'I wouldn't know much about those,' he said, between mouthfuls.

'All those Written talk about is you,' said Lerel.

Farden forced another smile.

'I don't think I've ever seen so many mages in one place. It's no wonder I've been having headaches, then,' mumbled Gabbant, contemplatively.

'You been havin' headaches, mate, because you're so much taller than the rest of us. Higher up. Thinner air,' chuckled Roiks. Gabbant shrugged and smiled.

'Gabbant's got a point. Been getting many a complaint of headaches and nosebleeds. Many of the men aren't sleeping right, either,' said the healer, at the lower end of the table.

'If that's all they're experiencing, Shia, then I'm happy,' Nuka said around a mouthful of his food. 'We aren't about to start chucking mages overboard.' He grinned.

Tinbits rubbed his chin. He seemed the quiet and calculating sort. 'I'll have my mages suppress as much as they can.'

Tyrfing nodded. 'As will the Written. And so will I.'

'So are we making good time?' asked Farden, nipping at the heels of his uncle's words. The table flinched at the sudden change of subject. Nuka nodded, but was too busy chewing to answer. Lerel did it for him.

'She's at top speed right now. Can't you feel it?'

Farden shook his head.

'Course he can't, Lerel, he's a landstrider,' chuckled Roiks.

'How much longer until we reach Nelska then?'

Done with his food, Nuka leant back and folded his hands over his ample belly. 'We'll strike coast in the morning,' he said.

Farden seemed pleased enough with that. He went back to his stew and attacked it viciously, leaving the others to joke and talk. Roiks launched into another story that had the cabin in stitches within minutes. Farden and Tyrfing couldn't help but laugh along with them. The bosun was a born comedian.

Once the tears were wiped and the smiles put away, the conversation once again turned serious. This time it was Colonel Tinbits who instigated it. 'If I might ask a question, your Mage, why do we suppose the dragonriders have been silent these past few months?'

Tyrfing covered his mouth with a napkin as he coughed again. 'In all honesty, we do not know. Perhaps our hawks simply aren't getting through. Storms. Wild wyrms. Anything.'

'But it's been months now.'

Nuka nodded. 'Well, we'll see in the morning.'

The talking died for a moment, leaving space for the sounds of chewing and sipping and the gurgling of busy stomachs.

Roiks was drumming his fingernails against the edge of his

plate. 'So,' he finally said, 'what else does the north hold for us, besides saving the Undermage's lady wife? The sailors have been talkin', see. About those daemons that fell from the sky, so I 'ear. And that girl too. They're saying this voyage has got somethin' to do with them and her.' The chairs around the table creaked as the others leant a little closer to hear the answer. The ship had been alight with rumours and speculation. Word had it they were sailing to war. Nuka had been silent on the matter. The captain glanced at Tyrfing, and he nodded.

'War, ladies and gentlemen, and plenty of it,' announced Nuka, puffing out his barrel-like chest.

'One ship for a war?' asked Hasterkin.

Gabbant mumbled something. It might have sounded like 'Fool's errand,' but he was wise enough to keep it under his breath.

'Against the girl?'

'Against the girl,' replied Tyrfing. Farden was still busy with his stew, stabbing at vegetables and stirring it into an angry swirl.

There was a pregnant pause. 'And the daemons?' Roiks finally said it.

Nuka nodded. 'And the daemons.' The bosun bit his lip.

'Well,' Gabbant said with a sigh, 'that'll be a story for the grandchildren. Should there be any.'

Roiks saw his chance to lighten the mood. He chuckled drunkenly. 'We all know you better than that, you ole git. Nobody at this table likes his wenches more than you do, save for me, that is.' Hasterkin and Tinbits began to laugh. Roiks wagged a finger. 'I'll wager there's more than a few little Gabbants runnin' 'round Krauslung, mark my words.'

'Now there's a sobering thought,' snickered Lerel.

Gabbant scratched his balding pate. 'You're telling me.'

'Better get you two some more wine then. Here we go, ma'am!' Roiks chortled, sliding a bottle towards Lerel. She grabbed it eagerly. Roiks took a sip of his own wine. 'So who is she then? This girl?'

Nuka flashed him a look, and Roiks realised he had pried too deeply. He was about to change the subject when Tyrfing answered.

'She's Vice's master plan, Roiks. The one foretold by the Lost Song.'

'The depressing old poem?'

'None other.'

'Knew I never liked that old dirge,' Gabbant grumbled.

Tyrfing nodded. 'She was born to tear the stars out of the sky, and she can do exactly that. As Krauslung found out so very recently. "One to which the stars succumb, and bring Ragnarök upon the earth." That's her.'

'Ragnawhat?' Hasterkin asked.

Shia the healer tutted. 'Don't you know your lore, man? The end of the gods. The end of Emaneska.'

'Not if I can help it,' growled Farden, around a steaming mouthful. He had been so silent they had almost forgotten he was there. They could barely see his face under his hood, which was still stubbornly pulled over his face.

'But she's just a girl,' croaked Nuka's cook. He had been as silent as Farden.

Tinbits tapped his glass on the tabletop. 'You should have seen her on the Manesmark hill. That's no ordinary girl.'

'Daemon, more like,' muttered Lerel.

There was a sharp squeaking noise as Farden shoved his chair back. 'And she'll die like the rest of them,' the mage whispered as he made for the door, stew firmly in hand. 'If you'll excuse me...' he began, but he didn't finish. The sound of the door shutting was explanation enough.

'My nephew is tired from a long day,' Tyrfing elaborated, staring at his bowl. He coughed and put a fist to his mouth again.

'Long day for all,' Nuka replied gruffly. The others took their hint, and set about pouring drinks and fiddling with cutlery.

If anybody could be trusted to lighten a mood, it was Roiks. He clapped his hands together and put his elbows on the table. 'Now then,' he began, a smile already beginning to curl, 'did I ever tell you the tale of young master Gabbant here, and the stray donkey?' Gabbant groaned, and Roiks slapped his hand on the table. 'No? Well then, allow me to elaborate, gentlemen and lady.'

It wasn't long before he had the room wheezing and crying.

Chapter 5

"Politics - Can't live without 'em, and you can't kill 'em."
Skölgard proverb

A bank of sea-fog dared to pour through the gap in the harbour wall. Its fingers tickled the ships and massaged the oily, lazy waters. Soon enough, the city was wrapped in its soft, dewy embrace, muffling the night sounds. It was a perfect evening for whispering.

Down by the docks, the air was hazy enough with the belching of the tavern chimneys. With the sea-fog, the world had been turned into a blurred smear of orange and black, nothing quite solid, nothing quite real. A few people wandered to and fro, walking as if their eyes weren't working properly, arms out straight and stiff, feeling for obstacles and edges. Their shadows made an odd sight indeed. Every now and again there would be a muffled thump, and a wail, or a curse. The fog smothered all.

'By Njord, it's cold tonight,' whispered a figure, slouched against a corner. A green and black shield rested against his knee, glistening with dew. He seemed to be talking to himself, or perhaps to the fog, and for a long time nothing answered.

'By any god, it is,' finally came the reply, from a man with his back to the very same corner. There was no need for hoods, with the thick fog, but still this man insisted.

'Have you got what I want?' asked the first.

There was a metallic thud as something heavy and wrapped in cloth landed next to the man's shield. 'Every last coin, as we agreed,' replied the second. He leant closer to the edge of the corner. 'And what of the men? Have you done what I asked?'

'I have,' came the reply. 'They're fed up. Low pay and poor futures will do that. Terrible combination. I could barely stop them from griping at me. I got twice the number of names you wanted. I should be asking for double.'

'In that case, I shall count myself lucky.'

'That you should.'

'Careful, Colonel. Only a hot forge lies between a pile of coins and a blade. They are of the same stuff, after all.'

There was a rustle. A knife was reached for. 'You threatening me?'

The subtle squelch of lips sliding over teeth. 'Of course I am. Remember, that coin at your feet is not a bribe. It is compensation.'

'Compensation? For what?'

'For living the rest of your life knowing the Copse could have you excommunicated and executed for treachery, at any moment. You have friends in high places, Colonel. High, and very dangerous places. Dangerous friends.'

There was a silence. The sort reserved for when cheeks drain, mouths hang agape, and hearts sink into places where only other organs tarry. The sound of realisation. 'You couldn't.'

'Could I not? Think of where I will be in a few hours.'

The colonel bit his tongue for a moment. Then, with the creaking of leather, he bent down and picked up the bag of coins. It was heavy indeed. He tucked it firmly under his jerkin before he lifted up his shield. He nodded in the direction of the sea. 'Where have they gone?'

The hooded man hummed. 'North, so my ears tell me. After that girl, and her daemons too. Fool's errand and a one-way voyage, if we are lucky.'

'Hmph. And what, may I ask, happens if it's not?'

'Then you, Colonel Jarvins,' said the man, 'will be leading the army that greets them.'

The man called Jarvins swore he heard a chuckle. 'And what of Arkmage Durnus?'

There was another silence. 'Will you be... er, *removing* him?'

Silence again. 'Hello?'

But no reply came. Colonel Jarvins peeked around the corner and found that his employer had faded into the fog. He spat, cursed, and promptly faded himself.

※

Durnus gently let the book fall to a close with a thud and thumbed at his tired eyes. Strange, how his eyes were bereft of the luxury of sight, yet still managed to ache as if they had spent the whole day hard at work. Strange it was, and irritating.

Durnus waved his hand to the servant standing by his side and dismissed him. The man bowed and scuttled away. He hadn't understood a thing of what he had just witnessed, but no doubt it had been very odd. Ghostly books and vanishing inks. Probably wasn't natural in his eyes. No wonder he left as quickly as he could.

As the door clicked softly shut behind him, Durnus got to his feet and began to feel his way to a cabinet. It wasn't often he felt the need for wine, but tonight he did. With a sigh, he uncorked a bottle with square edges and felt for a glass. He listened to the wine gurgling. *One. Two. Three. That will do.* He tiled the wine back and set it on the side.

Old habits die the hardest, and even despite fifteen years of being blind, Durnus' was to wander to the windows and stare out at his city, imagining the slope of its countless roofs, its cobbled capillaries and veins. Occasionally he would even wander onto his balcony and lean over as if he were watching his people.

As the old Arkmage pressed his forehead against the cold glass of the window, he mentally churned his distant counterpart's words over in his head. One stuck out like a thorn, snagging at him: *No.* Of all the words they had traded, that, and its punching stubbornness, was what made Durnus sad.

Time, for immortals, can only be measured in what others lack of it. Disease and age held no sway over Durnus. The sun could set and rise again and it meant nothing. Another day in a sea of thousands. These days, time was only apparent to him when others were running out of it. Modren and Elessi, for example. The shortest of marriages, and now she lay in bed, swiftly running out of time. Tyrfing too, and his unwillingness to tell Farden the truth. Farden's daughter and her surge to the north. Soon it would be all too late, and that is a strange thing for an immortal to feel. Only in these senses was he painfully aware of time, of every single second that inexorably slid past, slippery and elusive. For all his mastery of magick and mortality, it was painful how useless he was against time.

Durnus drank his wine quickly, as though it were in danger of evaporating. Soon he found himself nudging noses with the bottom of the glass. He poured himself another and went back to the window.

After an hour of staring into nothing, there came a knock at the door, then a creak as it opened. Durnus barely noticed it. Four glasses of wine will make anybody distracted, even immortal Arkmages with the hearing of a god.

'Anyone in 'ere?' called a voice, finally rousing Durnus from his thoughts.

'Who is that?' he challenged, wine in hand.

'Jeasin.' Ah, the woman Farden had brought from Albion. The blind one. The courtesan, so the others had tactfully put it. The whore, in other words. *What was it with Farden and women?* 'The servants said you were in 'ere,' she muttered. He could hear her shrugging.

Durnus nodded. 'That I am. And to what do I owe the interruption from a lady such as yourself?'

More accustomed to the stunted vocabulary of Tayn, Jeasin wasn't used to such formality. It was why she had found Farden so intriguing in the first place. His accent and his words. Normally, if a person spoke like that, then they were Dukes, or lords, or nobles, or rich, or something of that sort, and therefore utterly untrustworthy. She was having a hard time shaking that preconception. 'You sound busy. Mayhaps I'll leave you to it.'

Durnus called out just as she was closing the door. 'Would you like some wine?' he asked.

Jeasin shrugged again, borrowed clothes rustling, and mumbled something that might have been a yes. Durnus took the click of the door shutting for his answer. 'Four steps forward, mind the chair. Two to the right. Forward three,' Durnus recited, as he felt the ridges and edges of the bottles. 'Red, white, blue, or purple? Or gold, if you are that way inclined?'

'Wine. Colour don't matter to me.'

'Gold it is.'

Jeasin followed the Arkmage's instructions. She soon found herself at what felt to be a dresser, and soon enough a glass of wine was placed in her hands. 'Don't think I've ever met another blind person before,' she said, absently.

'Is that a good or a bad thing?'

'Different, I s'pose. You know your way around. That's useful. This place is so big I don't dare leave my room.'

'Is that why you came to mine?'

'Can't talk to walls.'

'Lonely then.

'Didn't say I was lonely. I said you can't talk to walls.' She sounded offended.

Durnus chuckled softly. The wine was making its way from his stomach to his head. 'Farden warned me you had a temper,' he said.

There was a clink as Jeasin found a table to put her wine on. 'Rich, coming from that bastard.'

Durnus was intrigued. This woman sounded almost like Elessi, in the way she spoke of Farden, and it wasn't just the accent. 'The marital status of his parents during his birth aside, how did you come to follow him here?' he asked.

Jeasin laughed. 'Follow? No. *Dragged* is more like it. Didn't 'ave a choice.'

'Dragged? I find that hard to believe.'

A snort. 'How well do you know that mage?'

The Arkmage put his chin on his knuckle. 'I knew the one that went away better than he knew himself. I knew his uncle too. The Farden that came back,' Durnus paused, 'I haven't made my mind up about him yet.'

'Well, he ain't like any man I've ever known. And I've known a lot,' replied Jeasin, unabashed as always about her profession.

Durnus leant back in his armchair. Before he'd returned, nobody had told stories of Farden. He was a sore subject. They had just mumbled and shrugged him off. The old Arkmage smiled. 'Tell me about him then,' he said, sipping his wine and keeping the bottle close.

'Well, the Farden that I know is a strange sort. Used to come by once a year maybe. Then twice. Then once a month. He was comin' to the cathouse for six years before he asked for me. He was gentle, I s'pose, compared to most. Quiet, too. Think he said 'bout four words to me in the whole evenin'. Part of me just thought he was just satisfyin' a curiosity, you know? Like most of the other men. Want to know what a blind girl was like to fuck, pardon my cursin'. Thought I'd see him just the once, but then he came back the next day.

Then the week after that, and the more he came back, the more he would say. A word here and there, just as he was leavin'. A whisper or two. Askin' me about the house and its girls. What I liked, what I didn't. He was a regular, soon enough. I used to find him waitin' downstairs with the other girls. His hood would be up and his face down, just waitin' for me.'

'For what?'

' 'Til I'd finished with whatever man I was with.'

'Ah,' Durnus cleared his throat, 'patient, for Farden.'

Jeasin sipped her golden wine and nodded. This old man seemed to want to hear the story, so she went on. 'Generous too. Paid well, he did. Other girls used to try to get a piece of the action. He weren't havin' any of it. I once heard him turn down three at a time, for the price of a song as well. He just kept starin' at the floor and shakin' his head, just waitin' for me. So it went for months and months. Sometimes the Duke...'

Durnus raised an eyebrow. 'Duke?'

Jeasin nodded. 'Kiltyrin. Whatever Kiltyrin wanted, Farden would do. I never asked much. Don't want to know too much. The guards that came to the house blabbered enough that I never 'ad to. Those pillocks don't know what tongues are for,' she paused here. She seemed to notice the stillness in her listener. 'You didn't know 'bout the Duke?'

'No.'

'Do you w...'

'Carry on.'

Jeasin shrugged and settled back into her own armchair. 'You don't need eyes to see bruises. I could tell by the way he walked into the room sometimes. You must know what it's like. Cracked rib 'ere. Broken finger there. Whole arm once. Barely said a word to me that day. He was the Duke's man, if you know what I mean. There were plenty of other men, but he was the Duke's *man*. The little blade in his boot. Came out to play quite often too. Sometimes he was away for weeks at a time. Didn't see him for six months once. Came back with a bag of coin so big I could 'ave used it for a pillow. I actually did, for a while. He's partly how I bought the cathouse outright. Became the molly.'

'Molly?' Durnus asked. 'I have to admit I am not the most familiar with courtesan parlance.'

' "Call a whore a whore, but treat her like a lady." That's what the old city watch master used to say. He kept his word too, for the first few tankards of ale. I make no apologies for what I am,' Jeasin shrugged again. 'Molly's a mother cat. Head of the cathouse.'

Durnus nodded. 'I see.'

'Kiltyrin. You know him?'

'Unfortunately.'

'Then you know?'

'Know what?'

Jeasin sniffed. 'Mayhaps you don't then. Not much to tell as I didn't see it 'appen. I'm just here because of it.'

'What, woman? What?'

'Farden killed the Duke. Finally snapped if you ask me.' Here Jeasin shuffled uncomfortably in her seat. 'Though part of that might be a little of my fault,' she confessed. Durnus seemed to be waiting for her to press on. She sighed. 'A cathouse ain't without its troubles. Mine wasn't any different. Rowdy men. Drunk men. Poor men. Thievin' girls. An' jealous wives to boot. The usual. I used most of the coin I got to bribe the guards and keep 'em happy. I've never told Farden, but I think he 'elped, in a way. Men knew not to talk about him, let alone get in his way. Knowin' I was his favourite girl gave us a little protection.'

'So how is Farden murdering the Duke your fault?'

'I'm gettin' to that. So, Farden came back from a job one day. Quiet as you like. When he left, there was a man waitin' outside my door. Bald man. Spoke a bit like you do. Suspicious sort. He had a proposition.'

'Which was?'

Another sigh. 'He wanted to watch Farden and me, when he came back to see me. I thought he was like that, you see. More interested in dogs, than cats, we used to say. I said yes. Sounded like he worked for the Duke, an' he paid me in jewels.'

'Jewels?'

'A pile. Enough to set a pair of guards on the door and feed the girls for a year without me workin'. It was everythin' I'd ever wanted for them. Protection. The Duke's favour.' She almost sounded wistful.

'Then what?'

'So Farden came. The man watched through a little gap in the wall he'd made. An' I never saw him again.'

'Why?'

'Who knows. Never told me.'

'What happened to Farden?'

'He was gone for weeks. I assumed he had another job from the Duke. Apparently they tried to take his armour. Duke wanted it for himself. And they did it too. Nearly killed Farden in the process, strung 'im up in a tree and stabbed 'im with a spear, so that Loki said. Somehow he survived, and the next thing I know I've got an unconscious guard captain lying on my floor and Farden blackmailin' me. Forced me to leave my girls, he did. Said the guards would blame me for harbourin' him.' Her tone grew harder. 'Fucked me over. Sorry.'

'I do believe it sounds like it was you who did a bit of the fucking, so to speak.'

Jeasin snorted, but she didn't reply. She knew he was right. 'Perhaps I did.'

Durnus took a deep breath. Maybe he hadn't wanted to hear

this after all. 'And here I was thinking he had become a simple hermit by the sea.'

'He was that too.'

'I can see now why he did not want to divulge any of his past,' he mumbled, swirling his wine. He swirled a bit too vigourously and spilt some on his sleeve. 'His bloody, murderous past,' he added, wincing at the lump that had formed in his heart. It made sense, in a way.

'He likes to keep his secrets, that mage does. Kept all of it from me for more than ten years. Maybe it's the wine talking, but I'd always dreamt of endin' up here. Krauslung. Or Essen. Or Kroppe. Any of the places the men used to talk about. Anywhere but that bloody island and its Dukes. Maybe Farden did me a favour, in a way.'

Durnus sniffed. 'I know the feeling.'

'Something tells me that you actually do…' Jeasin hummed.

'I had another life once, before this one,' Durnus began, and then finished with the same breath. 'And that is a story for another time.' He drummed his nails along the rim of his glass. He had suddenly been struck with an idea.

'Suit yourself.'

Durnus shuffled to the edge of his armchair. Jeasin could feel him coming closer. She held her wine close. She could smell him. He smelled of tiredness and dust. Of thick cotton robes and wine. 'Now, young lady,' he said. 'I would bet good coin that you ran a few hustles in your time? Hmm? A con or a swindle here and there? That is what whores do, isn't it? When they are not whoring, of course.'

Jeasin sensed something behind his words. 'We've been known to dabble,' she replied coyly.

'Good, good,' said Durnus. 'Why play fair, when you can play dirty?'

Malvus was in high spirits. Leaving the sea-fog to hug the gates, he strode into the Arkathedral with a slight spring in his formal step.

Years of planning. Barrels of coin spent. Months of coercing and pulling the tiniest of strings. Working his way to the top of the Copse, and now to the twin thrones. By all logic, his tongue should have been worn to a stub. More so than any other council member.

Politics, like most things, could be compared to war. The battleground was the well-trodden marble flagstones of the great hall. The quarrelling factions the sides of opinion and allegiance. The arsenal of weapons were rhetoric, magniloquence, facts, rumours, lies, and the tongues that delivered them. Some weapons were heavy and bludgeoning, like the trusty mace. Others were like daggers, subtle and sinister. And, like war, politics were far from fair. Sides could be bought, blackmailed, persuaded. Everybody had a weakness. He had seen that from the start.

Wars are fought for one purpose only. Never mind causes and injustice, or even greed or land. Rubbish. Wars are fought to be won. They are not fought to be lost. And Malvus liked winning. He was close, he could feel it.

Tonight it felt as though he were storming the final stronghold.

Malvus approached the Evernia guardsmen that were standing on either side of the formidable gates. They were watching him closely. He nodded almost imperceptibly as he passed between them, and with a heave, they swung the gates shut and locked them with one of the great iron bars.

Council Malvus took the steps two at a time. He barely noticed the levels and floors passing him by as he jogged to the tip of the Arkathedral, where his chambers lay waiting. The Arkathedral was almost empty at that time of night. Even the servants were heading to bed. A few sleepy-eyed feasters were waddling back to their rooms, holding bulging stomachs and grinning at the memory of wine. They smelled of perfumes and silk.

Malvus strode to his door and stopped mid-pace. His foot dangled in the air, yet to find the floor. His hand hovered in front of the door, yet to find the handle. His door was ajar. He felt for the little sickle-shaped blade that was tucked under his belt. *Could Durnus be this underhanded?* he asked himself. He had once pondered simply killing the Arkmages off. Quietly, of course. An unfortunate accident perhaps. But no, it was unspeakable to execute an Arkmage, never mind both. Besides, it would have been too obvious, what with his tongue. It would turn his own followers against him, and the city too.

As he pushed the door open and strode into the candlelight, Malvus flicked the blade from its sheath and held it ready. His rooms were empty, dark. He padded around, cautious, knife held at the ready. But he needn't have bothered. It was in his bedroom that he found his intruder. It was a woman, a blonde, all alone. She was sitting in a chair next to his expansive bed, entwined in shadow. The maids had lit the candles some time ago and now they were beginning to sag in their cradles.

'To whom do I owe this rather unexpected pleasure?' Malvus said. His voice sounded loud in the silence.

The woman turned her head, and Malvus recognised her as the blind woman he had seen at council, with that halfwit Farden. Guests of Farden and his uncle, so it had been whispered. Malvus knew to pay attention to whispers.

'Does a name matter?' she replied.

Malvus shut the door behind him. He didn't lock it. Not yet. 'So what shall I call you then, woman? I think it is only right that I know the name of my intruder.'

'Call a whore a whore,' smiled the woman, with a casual shrug.

Malvus raised an eyebrow. He had thought as much, from the way she held herself. The way she dressed. 'I don't remember requesting a whore.'

Jeasin turned to the window and away from Malvus. 'I'm blind, Council Barkhart. They say that when you're born without your eyes, the gods make up for it with other things.'

'Such as?'

'I can smell a tavern from a mile away. In fact, I can hear one below in the streets. I know there's fog in the air tonight; I can smell its damp. I can taste the salt from those docks, where I can tell you've been. S'on your clothes.' Malvus let the eyebrow fall. Jeasin raised her sightless eyes to seemingly look at the high, arched ceiling of his grand room. 'And I can smell the danger in this old place too. Stinks of it.'

'Danger? Of what?' Malvus lifted up his dagger.

'Change. Something I feel certain people aren't going to like. Like that Arkmage. And his lapdog, Farden, for example.' She said the last name with a face that wanted to spit.

Malvus smiled. He would have caught himself but the woman was sightless. He needn't have cared. Releasing his grip on the sickleblade, he strode to the side of the bed to look at her, to take her in. Despite her bedraggled hair, her simple, borrowed clothes, she was attractive enough. Blonde locks. Curled. Eyes of blue, green maybe. Hard to tell by the candles. Not the finest he had ever had, no, but attractive enough. She was of Albion stock too, by her accent and cheekbones. A foreigner. He reached out and raised her chin up with a finger. She didn't flinch. 'Perceptive, aren't you? And what is it that you want from me? Why my room, and not another's?'

'I heard you in that hall of yours. I recognise a man in charge when I hear one.' Jeasin rubbed her finger and thumb together. 'They've always got the deepest pockets.'

Malvus wrinkled his lip, withdrawing her hand. 'A common

beggar, then. You came here for my coin.'

'My only price tonight is a promise from you, Council.'

'That sounds expensive. Promises usually are. A promise of what then, whore? I'll bite.'

'Just your protection, for now. Maybe a room in this Arkastle or whatever you call it. Fancy myself a lady of its court, maybe. If there will still be one, when you've finished.'

Malvus sneered. This was a woman he could understand. Direct. Selfish. Clever. 'Self-preservation. I see. You feel the mountain sliding out from under you, so you want to find a sturdier footing.'

Jeasin nodded. 'Sounds about right to me.'

'Clever girl.'

'I try,' Jeasin said, getting to her feet and turned to face the councillor. With a smile and hands that moved with the confidence of practice, she slipped the straps of her dress from her shoulders. 'I have your word then?'

Malvus said nothing. He simply went to lock the door.

Chapter 6

"The Smiths and Pens of Scalussen were a ruling class in their own right. Not quite lords, born into land and power. Nor were they kings or queens, with royal blood passed down from vein to vein. No. Theirs was a hierarchy and position based on skill and skill alone. Theirs was a democracy of ability and wisdom. The finest Smith and Pen would ascend the ladder of authority, ruling until usurped by another. A perfect system? Perhaps not. Jealousy was also forged in the fires of Scalussen, in time. But that is true of all hierarchies."
From the writings of the infamous, and anonymous, critic Áwacran

Fog had swallowed the north too, in one giant gulp.

It was the cusp of morning, and it was as though the *Waveblade* floated on the edge of a half-dreamt world. Featureless, smothering, the fog was thicker than a stew. Even the crow's nest had been partially swallowed by it. Those standing at the wheel had to squint to see the bow. There was nothing to guide them save for the distant, muffled hiss of a beach, and the faint shadow that gave the grey some precious depth. Had it not been for the murmuring and slapping of the waves at her keel, the ship could have been flying through a dream.

'Fog-giants,' murmured one of the nearby sailors. 'They'll clobber us to bits. This is how they hunt, you see. They run ships aground and then have their way with them.'

'No such things,' hissed Roiks, from the step above him. Every whisper seemed loud on the deck of the silent ship. The whole crew could have heard a mouse cough.

The sailor turned, wide-eyed and earnest. 'There is, I say. My cousin's ship ran aground near Belephon. They were tinder in minutes. Said great fists formed out of fog and smashed 'em to splinters. No survivors.'

'Then how did your cousin come to tell you that story, hmm?' That foxed the sailor. 'Well...'

'Pipe down!' Nuka grunted from the wheel and all fell silent save for the waves, the creaking of the ropes, and the breathing of the sailors as they stood by, ready for anything. Tyrfing had the mages on deck, just in case.

Farden was standing at the railing of the stern, looking back at their bubbling wake as it disappeared into the fog. A length of knotted twine unravelled behind the ship, bejewelled with water droplets. Farden followed its brown length through the gap in the railing and onto the ship, where it slowly unwound from a little wheel. It squeaked as each knot left it.

'Eighty-seven,' whispered Gabbant, as he bent over the table that Lerel was poring over, maps and scraps of parchment spread out in front of her in no discernible order. She furiously scribbled down a few calculations with one hand, while the other gently wandered across a map of the Nelska coastline.

'Three points to port, Cap'n,' she called, and Nuka flicked the wheel.

Farden didn't dare ask how she knew where they were. Their process looked far too intricate to disturb. Though the air was cold, a little bead of sweat had gathered on Lerel's forehead. It sounded as though she hadn't taken a breath in at least a minute.

Farden shook his head and wandered to the steps where Roiks and a handful of sailors stood ready for orders. They were whispering earnestly about something. Nuka was too busy to chide them again. Farden couldn't help but listen in.

'Wreckwitch.'

'What?'

'Wreckwitches. Siren bitches who draw ships into rocks with wind and fog, then once they've floundered they come aboard and drink the blood of the crew.'

'Nonsense!'

'It's the truth.'

'About as truthful as an Albion merchant, you are.'

'Well, this ain't natural fog, lads, so what is it?'

'Who knows.'

'Almost as if something don't want to be seen.'

'Njord's balls, lads, we're in league with the Sirens. Naught to fear from them.'

There was a moment as one of the sailors looked up into the fog. 'Sure about that, bosun?' he asked.

An eerie silence came and went. It was broken by the sound of Roiks snorting and then spitting something over the side. 'Sure as a loaded die, lad. Now pipe down so the Cap'n can hear himself think,' he ordered, and the sailors said no more. Farden turned to his left where his uncle stood behind Nuka and the wheel. He had been listening just like everybody else. The two mages swapped a look, one that ached with sudden suspicion.

There couldn't have been a more inappropriate time for a dragon to roar, but it did, somewhere high and lost in the fog, leaving them with its rumbling echoes. Every neck craned. Every eye turned upwards. Nuka handed the wheel to nearby Hasterkin and stood next to Tyrfing. Farden had to step closer to hear the captain's hushed words.

'How long exactly did you say it was that the Sirens have been ignoring your hawks?' Nuka mouth in the Arkmage's ear.

'Ignoring is a strong word,' breathed Tyrfing, 'but several months.'

'I'm not one to put weight in the pockets of the superstitious sailor stereotype, your Mage, but I think it would be wise to...' Farden lost the rest of that sentence to Lerel calling another direction.

'Another point port!'

He turned back to find Tyrfing nodding. Nuka put his fingers between his teeth and blew hard. Farden had never heard a whistle so piercing. 'To quarters!' came the order. It was as if the whole crew had been simultaneously bitten by something with very large fangs. The deck erupted into a fountain of activity. Men scampered into the mast to tuck sails. Hatches were battened. Sheets of thin armour were slid across the scattered skylights. Men poured into the decks below and then promptly poured back out again, weapons in their hands. Rolled hammocks and blankets were shoved against the bulwarks. Water mages went to and fro, soaking the decks and the flanks of the ship. Pulleys rattled, ropes squeaked, and somewhere deep inside the ship cogs were turning.

Farden moved to the nearby railing. To his fascination, he saw the armoured hull peeling apart. Rows of hatches were beginning to creep open underneath the circular shields that were bolted to the bulwarks. In jolting increments, the wooden hatches were cranked and levered up and up until they all sat at a high angle. Crossbows and arrowheads began to peep out from behind chain-mail curtains. Some were held by the ship's soldiers, some slid out on their own runners. It was a marvel of military machinery. Every inch of it screamed Tyrfing.

The Arkmage in question was running back and forth along the aftcastle, watching his mechanical marvels twitch and click. He was close to climbing the mizzen mast when Farden caught his arm. 'Is this really happening?'

Tyrfing looked around. 'Precautions, nephew.'

Farden winced. He trailed in his uncle's wake as he hurried down the steps and under the mainmast. 'Inwick! You and another, up to the crow's nest! Heim...' Tyrfing caught himself just in time. He grabbed Farden's wrist. He wasn't surprised to find it firmly armoured. 'Find Heimdall,' he hissed.

Farden didn't have to. 'There,' he said, and pointed to the bow, where Heimdall was standing on the bowsprit with Loki. Ilios was still on his platform, but he was now wide awake. He and the gods were staring straight up into the impenetrable fog.

A great stillness fell over the *Waveblade* as the last rope was tied off and the last hatch raised. The entire crew fell silent as mice, listening only to the slapping of the waves beneath them, the cotton echoes of the fog, waiting, but for what they did not know, though most suspected it involved wings, and teeth, and claws. Some crouched, staring into the sky and the rigging. Others hunkered down and muttered prayers to Njord and Evernia and to whomever else was listening. Only Lerel spoke, giving headings to Nuka, and even she whispered. The *Waveblade* was as still as the fog it pierced.

A long howl from far above sent the crew into a fresh state of muttering. Anybody who had ever heard the roaring of a wild wyrm or dragon knew what it meant. Hunting call.

'Silence!' hissed Tyrfing, from the bow, the air close, like a jealous lover.

Farden was still pacing about, incredulous. He raised up his hood, as if he hoped the shadow of it would make his urgent eyes shine brighter. 'Are you seriously expecting the Sirens to attack us? Have I missed some snippet of insanity while I was away?' he mumbled to his uncle.

Tyrfing ignored him. 'Heimdall? Ilios? What can you see?'

Heimdall was squinting. 'Four of them. Cream-white. Curled horns. Nails like crumbled rock. Northern dragons.'

A memory bubbled up from nowhere. 'Lost Clans,' Farden

said. He remembered saw-blade claws and lava-rock eyes, a silent dragon and a haughty rider's grin. *Lord of the Castle of the Winds...*

Tyrfing looked at him quizzically and then nodded. 'Too far south to be a simple hunting run,' he bit his lip. 'Any more?'

Heimdall scanned the sky, making all the others look up as well. 'None. Not a flash of colour in sight. Though this air, this fog,' he paused then. 'It is not natural.'

Another roar echoed through the grey fog, closer this time. Half the crew ducked instinctively. Shushing whispers flew across deck. Ilios warbled from the corner of his beak. Heimdall murmured the translation. 'Male. A big grey and no rider. He seems to be chasing something.'

No sooner had the deep words left Heimdall's mouth than a distant patch of fog blossomed orange. The whooshing sound of flame and the splash of some unfortunate seabird drifted by shortly after. Ilios growled as softly as any gryphon could.

'Something is wrong,' this from Tyrfing.

Farden sighed, laden with many thoughts. 'I think you're right.'

With a nod to Heimdall and Loki, the two mages crept back to the aftcastle. Tyrfing whispered orders as he passed each man. 'Silence now. Not a noise,' he urged.

Roiks was still trading hearsay on the stairs with another sailor when they passed him.

'I hear a dragon can spy the heat of a man's heart, and 'is breath too.'

'That ain't true. They would have come down on us already.'

'True it is.'

'Roiks,' chided Nuka. 'Silence.'

Roiks threw a rough salute and fell silent. 'Aye, Cap'n.'

Tyrfing, Nuka, and Farden bent their heads together. 'Roiks is right,' said Farden.

Nuka made a concerned face. 'About our hearts?' he asked.

Tyrfing shook his head. 'No. But they can sniff out magick. It's why the wild ones hunt it.'

'I've got several scars to prove it, if you'd like to see,' Farden offered.

Nuka waved a hand. 'Then, begging the question, why aren't we aflame this very moment? We must be a beacon of magick with all these mages aboard.'

'Must be this fog. Heimdall said it wasn't normal.'

Silence, but for the fog, the creaking ship, and for the roaring circle of dragons above.

Farden rubbed his nose. 'We need to go ashore.'

'What, all of us?'

'No, just a few. You and I. Heimdall maybe. To see what's truly going on here,' said Farden. Tyrfing made a face at his suggestion. Farden narrowed his eyes at him. 'Spit it out, uncle.'

'I agree with going ashore, but with all... to be honest...' Farden's eyes got narrower. Tyrfing let the words tumble out. 'I don't think you're fit enough to come, Farden.'

As Farden opened his mouth to speak, there was a whoosh of wings overhead. A dark shadow skimmed through the fog, dragging wind behind it. It was so close it worried the pennant at the tip of the mainmast.

The *Waveblade* held its breath. The silence in the dragon's wake was almost painful in its severity. Teeth clenched like vices. Fingers strangled cloth, rope, and railing. Abdomens clenched and brows furrowed. A gryphon poised itself. Breath lingered in the darkest parts of lungs, burning.

Just as the ship was teetering on the cusp of exhaling, somebody foolish dropped their sword.

The peal of the blade striking an iron shutter was enough to wake even a Krauslung drunk. There was a screech, almost of delight, as the dragon heard the clang and clatter through the fog. A dark shape wheeled and flapped. There was a treacherous moment in which the whole crew hoped the dragon was not a foe after all, instead some benevolent emissary sent by the Old Dragon to guide them into port. That concept was quickly and universally eradicated as soon as the first spout of curling flame flirted with the iron point of the bowsprit.

Nuka let his lungs and tongue loose. 'Forward ranks, fire at will! Wind mages, get us moving! Roiks, give that overgrown lizard the full prickly glory of our broadsides when I turn her. Let's show this beast what steel tastes like!' he yelled, as he spun the wheel as far over as it would go. The *Waveblade* lurched to do his bidding.

Tyrfing whirled around to order Farden to get below. Much to his horror, he found his nephew standing calmly with his arms crossed and his boots untied, laces trailing tauntingly.

'Don't you dare…' he gasped.

'Looks like you don't have much of a choice in the matter, uncle,' Farden shrugged, and before Tyrfing could even flinch, he was kicking off his boots and hopping frantically towards the nearest railing.

'Stop!' Tyrfing shouted, leaping after him. But it was hopeless.

With a kick of his feet, a mock salute, and one last grim look at the icy water, Farden hurled himself overboard, leaving nothing but his boots wobbling on the deck.

'Man overboard!' A woman's voice. Probably Lerel. It was the last thing the mage heard before the ice-cold sea knocked the air from him.

The words he heard next were very clear indeed.

'You're a dim-witted, cretinous, obtuse, ignorant, blunt-nosed *fuckwit*, Farden, and that's all I will trust myself to say at this moment in time.'

'You forgot stubborn,' Farden spluttered. It wasn't often in life that a man gets to involuntarily punctuate his words with sea-water. This, unfortunately, was one of those times. Farden had experienced one before and from what he remembered, it hadn't improved much. He retched and spat.

Farden was dropped on the shingle like a sack of dead bones. Tyrfing stood over him and swung his arms in a circle to warm them up. He winced at the cold that was trying its hardest to penetrate his chest. 'What were you thinking, boy?' he wheezed.

'Of a way to get you and I ashore.'

'Well... you certainly did that,' Tyrfing spat sand from his mouth. He pressed his hands to his armoured chest and pressed hard. Within a few brief moments, steam was coming from his wet robe. Farden waved his hands and slapped his own chest, his tongue too cold to get the words out. Tyrfing rolled his eyes and knelt by his nephew's side. He spread a hand over his ribs and pushed down. Farden winced as the magick stung him. The heat was intense, like the fire burnt at the centre of his bones.

'See? This is why I wanted you to stay behind. You're still on the verge of exhaustion. You can't handle magick. Not to mention the fact that you're about as good a swimmer as a boulder troll,' hissed Tyrfing. He looked around. The fog was as thick on the beach as it was on the sea. The world around them was monochrome; a canvas of wet slate, granite, and fog. Even the tide-abandoned seaweed had been dyed a charcoal grey. It was about as welcoming as it was warm. 'And what exactly was your plan, anyway? Now that we're here? Why just the t...' His questioning came to an abrupt halt when they heard a commotion somewhere out to sea, muffled by the fog. The two mages turned to listen as there was a deep thud and a roar. Silence followed and they both frowned.

'We need to get off this beach,' Farden coughed. He put his red-gold fists against the stones with a clank and pushed himself up. He couldn't hide the fact that his arms shook with the effort and the cold.

'If the rest of your plan is as well-thought out as that, I cannot wait to hear it.'

'Sarcasm does not become an Arkmage.'

Tyrfing grunted, and shed his soaking white robe. The armour underneath glittered in its intricacy. Farden chose to keep his cloak on. Despite the spell, he had to fight to keep from shivering as he waited for his uncle to stow his unwanted clothes under a slab of granite. Hearing the frantic drum-roll of chattering teeth, Tyrfing looked up. Farden was going a paler shade of blue. He almost looked like Durnus. His scars stuck out, pink and livid. Wet hair clung to his face like the tentacles of some dishevelled, black squid. Tyrfing shook his head. 'You're not ready,' he muttered. Farden threw him an acidic look.

'For what?'

A sigh. 'Anything.'

Farden simply sneered, and began to trudge up the beach. He moved as quietly as his feet and the shingle would allow. He soon heard his uncle catching up. His steel sabatons played dull notes on the stones.

The peculiar thing about fog is that it is a canvas for the imagination. The mind paints its own monsters on its grey wisps. Tendrils become claws. Whorls become faces. Shadows of cliffs and rocks become crouching enemies. Ambushes. Marauders. Dragons. Farden glared at each and every one of them, but nothing came. They all faded as the fog swirled.

Only when another dull boom rumbled through the fog did Farden turn around. He hesitated. 'Do you think...?'

'No, no I do not. That ship was built to fight daemons. A few dragons should be manageable,' Tyrfing replied tersely. His tone was a concoction of uncertainty and anger, the latter directed at the former and at Farden for causing it.

It was a long and silent walk that took them to the sheer cliff-face that marked the edge of the beach. The mountain rose up out of the wet boulders and splintered shingle without so much as an introduction or a gentle angle. In places, it actually lent out past the vertical, making little hollows and miniature caves for the fog to linger in. Farden and Tyrfing looked around for some sort of a path, or a road, or anything that would lead them somewhere civilised. No luck.

Tyrfing crossed his arms. 'Now what?'

Farden scowled and pondered the question for a moment. He then dug into his cloak pocket and produced a copper coin, bitten by a sliver of green rust on one side. Tyrfing rolled his eyes. 'Scales, we go left, Arkathedral, we go right,' decided Farden.

'It's such a treat to see sheer tactical brilliance in action.'

Farden glared. 'What's your problem, uncle?'

'Your impetuosity, for one.'

'I think you'll find I'm the only one doing what's necessary. I'm doing what we came here to do.'

'You're doing the first thing that came into your head, nothing more. Like the same old Farden.'

Farden's reply was sickly in its scorn. 'Well, I wouldn't want to disappoint. Everybody likes a bit of nostalgia.'

Tyrfing tried to summon some patience. 'Just toss the damn coin.'

Farden did so. With a chime, the coin rose, and fell, and Farden held his palm out for his uncle to see. 'Scales. Left it is,' he said. He turned and walked away before Tyrfing could venture a reply.

For half an hour they walked with the cliff at their right shoulders. The wet rock undulated between sheer and intrusively angled, but at no point did it show any sign of a doorway or stairwell.

Nor did the beach show any sign of transforming into a road or path. At some points, the mages had to crouch and shuffle along like ducks to avoid banging their heads on overhangs. The worst element of it was that the fog refused them any sense of distance or time; they wandered on in a bubble of featureless grey, the cliff-face their only hint of actual progress.

Farden's thoughts had been stewing while they walked, and now they were coming to the boil. As they emerged from under yet another section of overhanging granite, slick with moisture and bedecked with rotten moss, Farden turned on his uncle.

'Do you know what the problem is?'

Tyrfing looked a little startled to say the least. 'Are you saying there's only one?'

Farden ignored the retort and stuck to the scripted tirade he had been working on for the past ten minutes. 'Nobody is giving me a chance. Nobody trusts me to make a right decision for once. The ideas I have are always the foolhardy ones, the impetuous ones. Whatever Farden suggests must be wrong. Same old Farden.'

'That's not true. If it were, Farden, we wouldn't be in Nelska this very moment. This was your plan, to come to the Sirens for a cure. Not ours.'

'And I would place good coin that you're already regretting listening to me.'

'That's not true…'

Farden cut him off. 'I came back because Albion was killing me. In fact, the more I think about it, it actually *did* kill me. I came back to make amends and yet all I seem to be making is trouble again. Have you seen the way the younger mages look at me? Most of them don't see a legend, they see a legendary failure wandering the decks. A Written who gave up his Book. Who made mistake after mistake and now expects the world to pay for it. I bet they've all figured out my connection with Samara too,' he hesitated as he spoke her name.

He still couldn't get used to it. 'They judge me before I've had a chance to open my mouth. And you're no different uncle. If you had been the one to jump from the ship first, you would have been leading the way, being the heroic one. But me? I'm stubborn and impetuous. I'm condemned before I even act.'

'Do you blame us? A sabre-cat can't file off its teeth and go gallop with the deer, Farden.'

'I thought you said I'd come back from Albion a different man.'

'Some of you has, some of you hasn't. Most of you, Albion has stolen. Changed you into gods know what, I don't want to know. Thankfully, that Farden seems to be fading away each day that passes, and I can see more of the Farden that exiled himself. But you left a rash, stubborn, angry man. A great mage, but a broken man. Now the mage part is broken too, and the rest of you with it. My apologies if that sounds harsh. I thought you might appreciate the truth.'

Farden didn't. 'Broken things need fixing, uncle,' he said.

'And when have you ever seen something broken fix itself?'

Farden clenched his fist. 'I guess we'll have to see, won't we?' he said, and as he spoke those words, something hardened inside him, wrapping his new-found clarity in a shell of ice and steel. It could have been called resolve, even ambition. It was harder than both.

Tyrfing watched his nephew stride off. 'I hope we will,' he said. He flicked a droplet of sea-water from his nose and turned towards where he imagined the sea to be. 'Farden?' he said, tentatively. No response. 'Farden!' Tyrfing hissed.

Farden was already turning around, wagging angry fists. 'And another thi...'

'Shh!'

'What?!'

Tyrfing jabbed his finger in the direction of the sea, where, nestled in the fog barely a pebble's toss away, the forked end of scaly yellow tail lay coiled in the shingle. It wasn't moving. A simple streak of colour on a dead canvas.

The mages instantly began to creep towards it. Bent double, they shuffled across the stones. Tyrfing kept his hands low and at the ready. Farden could do nothing but boldly reach for a nearby rock.

They came to a halt a few paces from the tail. They could now see a dark, still shadow at the end of it. Not a sound came from the beast. Not even a snore. Farden gingerly reached forward and placed his hand on the tail's yellow fork. It was as large as a shield, but limp as a rotten fish. Now they were closer, they could taste the musty smell in the air. Far from pleasant.

Farden shook his head. 'Cold,' he mumbled. Tyrfing sighed, and stood up. He went to examine the rest of the beast. The poor dragon lay sprawled on its side in a crater in the shingle. One of its legs was broken, snapped and baring bloody bone, and groping awkwardly for the sky, wherever that may be. Its mouth was open, its ochre tongue hanging limp and useless. A pair of legs lay trapped under its bloody neck, where a ring of telltale holes punctured its thick scales like an ugly necklace. Tyrfing respectfully shut the dragon's great eyes as he walked around the beast's head. On the other side, only the rider's head remained visible. A Siren of course, a young male at first glance. He too was bruised and bloodied, the face twisted in great pain. Golden scales decorated his purple lips. A stub of a whitewood arrow stuck from his neck.

'Cold indeed.'

Farden cast a wary eye upwards. 'I think I know what is going on here.'

Tyrfing caught sight of something metallic and reached for it. He tugged a sword from underneath the Siren's body and tossed it to Farden. The mage caught it awkwardly in his numb fingers. 'You'll need this, then, if I get your meaning, nephew.'

Farden thumbed the blade's edge. 'It looks as though Elessi may have to wait a little longer,' he said, trying to ignore the worry that sentence caused him.

※

The dead dragon may have been the first, but it was not the last. Stone-faced and silent, the mages followed a trail of murder along the beach. There isn't much that can tug at a heart like a dead dragon. The extinguishing of creatures so majestic made their chests ache. It made them feel guilty for it, but every time they came across a carcass, they prayed it wouldn't be a dragon or a rider they knew. They were spared that, at least. Every dragon, six, no more, no less, were strangers to them. Guilty, but no less angry. Tyrfing and Farden closed eyes and patted scales as they passed.

There was also nothing like a dead dragon to stir something bloodthirsty inside a man. The mages stalked the mist like ravenous beasts, begging for something culpable to come stumbling out of the mists and meet their swords. They didn't have to wait long.

'There,' Tyrfing pointed, as they crouched behind a large boulder. Farden followed his uncle's finger to a gash in the cliff up ahead. Stairs had been hewn from the granite. The higher they went, the deeper they had been cut. Whatever lay at the top of them was a secret that belonged to the fog.

Without so much as a word, Farden got up and marched forwards, sword dangling by his side, dripping cold dew. Tyrfing mumbled something that could have burnt the ears from a grizzled soldier, but he followed nonetheless. Choices were not high on their list of possessions.

At the foot of the stairs, somebody had stacked a trio of torches, bound and wrapped to keep off the cold air and the wet. Farden removed one of his gauntlets and felt their wrappings. They were barely damp; the fog had scarcely touched them. Fresh, very fresh indeed, almost as though somebody had stacked them there within the last hour. Farden slid his gauntlet back on and began to take the rough steps two at a time. Tyrfing followed once more.

Two steps at a time might have been a little ambitious, even despite Farden's anger. The steps were tall, and the going steep. It didn't take long for his body to start complaining. A tired body doesn't like steps at the best of times, but when the aforementioned steps are endless, irregular, and more slippery than a pile of eels, the body complains a little louder. Farden was soon panting. His legs were aflame in minutes.

'Rest, you ignoramus,' Tyrfing chided. He would have taken the lead, but the rock had grown narrower. He looked back to find that the ground had somewhat disappeared. For all he could tell they were a thousand feet in the air.

Farden shook his head. 'Don't have time.'

'Elessi isn't going to…'

A cough rang out from somewhere above them. A cough thick with phlegm and a lifetime of pipe-smoke. Farden and Tyrfing froze. Silence. Had they been heard? There were no voices, no shouts, no bells nor alarms. Just the aching knowledge that somebody was nearby, hidden in the grey. Farden held his sword tight.

Suddenly the somebody began to walk. Up or down, they couldn't tell. Armoured feet clanged rhythmically on the black granite steps. 'Coming or going?' mouthed Farden. Tyrfing closed his eyes and strained to listen. Farden bit his lip. He looked up, where the stairs faded into the fog, grey teeth, chewing on wool. Steep and slippery… There was only one thing for it. Farden held his sword with both hands and then began to climb as fast as his sore legs could manage. It would only be seconds before he was heard, with his boots stamping so loudly on the wet stone, but seconds was all he wanted. All he needed.

Tyrfing went to shout but quickly caught himself. He could do nothing but watch as his nephew sprinted up the steps and flung himself into the fog. There was a second of silence, then a clang of metal and a muffled yelp. 'Farden!' Tyrfing called as loud as he dared. The second dragged into two, then three, then ten. Ten seconds is an age to those that count it.

Tyrfing was just about to charge forward when he heard a scuffle. He caught sight of a body flying down the steps towards him. The Arkmage barely had time to duck as the corpse sailed over his head and down to the rocks below. A couple of seconds passed before there was a wet crunch.

Farden came sauntering down the steps a moment later, a splash of blood on his left shoulder. The blood was so bright it was one step from orange. 'Lost Clans indeed,' he said, looking around for something to wipe his sword on. There was nothing but rock.

'I hope you're thinking what I'm thinking?'

Farden nodded, eyes glazed. 'A coup.'

'It looks very much like one.'

'Well, it looks as though finding a healer is not going to be as easy as we first assumed.' Farden grit his teeth, making his jaw creak.

Tyrfing looked back towards the sea. 'What's your plan?' he asked, quietly.

Farden raised an eyebrow. 'I say we sneak into this mountain, find out what has happened to the dragons and what these Lost Clan bastards are up to. We help if we can. If not, we find ourselves a healer somehow, some medicine, and we get out again. We come back with reinforcements later. Once all of this...' he waved his hand in a circular motion, so casual, to encompass their state of affairs, '...is finished.'

'Fine,' Tyrfing agreed. Farden couldn't help but relish that sign of confidence. 'Nuka will keep the ship out of sight so long as the fog lasts. If it lifts, he'll have no choice but to leave. We'll be on our own.'

Farden put his legs to the steps once again and put his sword through his belt. As they stared silently at each other, they wondered at the glaring gaps in his simple plan. How would they find a healer? How would they make it up to the peak without being noticed? Was there even a healer left alive in Hjaussfen? How would they escape? They were questions asked in each man's silence. And yet, both knew that only walking forward would actually find the answers. 'Then we will have to be quick about it after all, won't we, uncle?' Farden finally said, daring a wry grin.

Tyrfing nodded. There was a glint in his eyes too. A hint of something only an Arkmage that has been forced to languish in a marble throne for a decade and a half could feel, when abruptly faced with danger. Tyrfing cleared his throat with a wince and a wet cough and then nodded. 'That we will, nephew,' he said.

Chapter 7

"Do I resent being blind? Does a prisoner resent his bars, his chains, his punishment? Perhaps. It depends on whether the prisoner is guilty or innocent. I was guilty of inaction and fear. My blindness is my punishment. But, as any prisoner will tell you, some punishments are easier than others. Some days I hardly feel blind at all."
From the diary of Arkmage Durnus, written in the year 901

Jeasin awoke suddenly, as if she had forgotten she had fallen asleep. She tensed, blind eyes blinking, feeling the soft cotton of the sheets, the smell of the room, of dead candles, velvet, leather. A man. Jeasin licked her dry lips. The warm sensation on the back of her arm told her it was morning, but only barely. Early sunlight. She could hear footsteps clacking on the marble in the hallway. She put out a hand and found the other side of the bed empty and cold.

Perfect.

Jeasin sat bolt upright and tucked the blanket around her as a makeshift dress. She listened, as hard as her sharp ears could, for any hint of breathing, or watching, or waiting… company of any sort. She couldn't feel the prickle of eyes upon her; she had become very adept at sensing that in her time in Tayn. It had helped in ways she couldn't begin to list.

Sweeping her legs from the side of the bed, she placed them on the warm floor. The sunlight had been there too. She stood up, blanket-dress trailing behind her like a cape, and went to the door. She put her back to it and held one bare foot out, as if testing the edge of a precipice.

Eight forward, said a voice in her head. Durnus' words from the night before. Jeasin tread a deliberate line, toe to heel, across the floor until she counted eight.

A dozen to the right, came the next order. Jeasin turned and mouthed the numbers.

Twenty-one to the left. Stop. She stopped.

Turn right. She turned.

Hands out. Jeasin's knuckles nudged something solid, wooden, and ornate. Her fingers traced the notches where the carpenter's chisel had bitten. Her nails caught on the nodules where the varnish had dried in the gaps. The cold of the hinges and edges. *Take what you can find.*

Jeasin found the empty lock where the key should have been and stamped her foot. Malvus had been careful. She should have expected that. Not one to waste time dithering, she began to feel across the desk, pawing for a quill, a pin, or a... Jeasin grabbed the sliver of a parchment knife and jabbed it into the lock, as deep as she could. She jiggled it left, then right, then up. Something clicked, and she wiggled it some more. All those childhood nights spent picking the precious lockets of the other girls had finally paid off.

Paid off they had, but it still took no less than ten minutes of nail-biting, frantic, blind jabbing to get the lock open. It crunched as it gave up on its secrets. Jeasin stumbled forward as it gave way. She heard a sharp ping as the parchment knife lost its tip. She heard something tiny fall to the marble and skitter into a corner. She winced; she didn't have time to go looking for it. Malvus could come back at any moment.

Delving into the drawer like a mole into dirt, Jeasin used both hands to explore. It was all parchment: letters maybe, notes, she had no idea. Her eyes failed her spying. *Take what you can find!* she told herself, and with a shrug she began to fish out ream after ream of dry and wrinkled parchment. Her finger grazed a thick, waxy seal and she quickly traced it, intrigued. Its contours brought a very strange look to her face. She felt it again to make sure. It had to be…

There came a shout from the hallway and Jeasin flinched. She gathered together her pile of papers and frantically tapped them on the desk to keep them from flying out of her hands. Tossing the parchment knife back onto the desk, she quickly felt her way back to the bed and found her dress with her toes, crumpled and abandoned on the floor. Jeasin shuffled into it as quickly as she could, muttering to herself as she hopped and wriggled. 'Bloody… Arkmage's… Problems. Not mine,' she hissed to the empty room. Seconds later she was at the door and combing her hair into some sort of semblance with her spare fingers. More shouts echoed down the corridor outside, muffled orders and yells. Jeasin's heart was fluttering. There was nothing else she could do but wrench the door open and hope for the best. She had tried at least.

It was then that a strange thought came wandering through her mind. It was simple, treacherous in its timing. *What was she doing?* Why was she even helping this old Arkmage? Some relative of Farden's, a strange old man she didn't know, whose room she had wandered into the night before, on some notion of company? A lonely impulse to share a space with the only person within a hundred miles she had something in common with: blindness. Now she was spying for him, potentially risking her life, all for a simple promise. Jeasin couldn't remember the last time she helped somebody without some smidgeon of payment. It wasn't in her blood to do so. Not in her habit.

Malvus had even said it. *She* had even said it, for gods' sakes, ruse or no. Something was about to envelop this Arkathedral, and the side she had stumbled onto had already been marked as the losers. Durnus had called it a coup. She didn't know what that meant, but it had the smell of bloodshed about it. It sounded like something a Duke would do.

Ruse or not, Jeasin's night with Council Barkhart had just bought herself a rather shiny ticket to safety. She felt the weight of the papers in her hand and pulled a face. They might as well have been a fire to throw that ticket into. *What was she doing?!*

She didn't owe these people her safety. That was it. The treacherous thought had swallowed her mind in its full gelatinous glory. Jeasin gripped the doorhandle as if her fingers were fused to it. She half-turned back to the desk, and bit her lip.

'Fuck it,' she hissed. She didn't owe them anything, so why couldn't she shake the sudden feeling of guilt?

❦

They were polite enough to knock, at least.

When the guards came for him, Durnus was standing in the very centre of his room. His hands were folded behind his back. His face was calm. He had his best robe on. He had smelled them coming for him. All eagerness and sweat and shiny silver coin in their pockets.

Part of him wanted to send them all flying from the windows, trailing fire and screams. That would show Barkhart the true power of an Arkmage, he thought, the true reason they held the thrones. But such an act would also seal his own political fate. The Arka had tasted dictatorship before, under Vice, and they would not suffer it again. Malvus would have all the proof and cause he needed to legitimately dethrone him and Tyrfing. Dead guards on city streets tend to do that. Going calmly at least came with a sliver of something he might have called a chance.

They marched into the room in pairs. Malvus had sent a dozen for him. Their short spears were low and levelled and their armour polished to perfection. Some looked worried, while others looked victorious, even contemptuous. They surrounded the Arkmage with a circle of spears, and then a man stepped forward to take his hands.

'Arkmage Durnus,' he announced, in a loud voice. 'Your presence is required in the great hall.'

Durnus raised an eyebrow as he felt a hand grab his arms. He heard the clink of metal. He could smell the familiar scents of a certain brand of pipe tobacco, conjoined with lashings of a dubious perfume. Up until now, they had been the scents of a loyal and faithful man. Stressed, over-worked, but faithful. Or so Durnus had thought. Stress, it seemed, could bend the strongest of steel with time and pressure. 'Colonel Jarvins,' Durnus said, with a sour look, wondering what his price had been. Rumour had it Jarvins had an ambitious wife, with dreams far above that of a guard's status. 'And am I refusing to attend?' he asked, meaning the irons.

Jarvins shook his head. 'It's for your safety. And for ours, your Mage.'

Durnus felt a cold loop of iron encircle each of his wrists. Too cold to be natural. There was magick in the metal. 'So be it,' he said, and with that, the Arkmage Durnus was marched from his rooms.

Step after confident step, they marched him across the marble floors. Durnus could hear the occasional gasp of a servant. The grim nod of others. The smiling teeth of council members standing by. Durnus grit his teeth and held tightly to his calm. With every step and passer-by the urge to resist became greater and greater. The guards must have felt the fire in him; he could tell from their steps that they gave him a pace or two of extra room. The iron around his wrist became colder.

Soon enough he was brought to a halt. They were still a few corridors from the great hall, standing at what Durnus guessed to be Modren and Elessi's door. He made a wry face. They must have been brave indeed. No surprise then that he now heard the breathing of another dozen guards, maybe a score. No chances were to be taken with a grieving Undermage.

'Ready?' asked Jarvins. Durnus wondered if he were talking to him, but a grunt from the other guards told him different. He stared straight ahead and waited for the chaos to unfold. He knew Modren would not go as quietly as he. Politics were last on his list of what he cared for at the moment.

Durnus did not have to wait very long at all.

As the guards formed up in pairs before the door, shields at the ready, somebody reached for the doorknob. His fingers had barely graced it before it exploded outwards, with all the ferocity of a slingstone. It slammed into the chest of the nearest guard and floored him with a clang and a surprised 'Oof!'

The heavy door came next, bursting from its hinges in a flash of light and black smoke. Still in one entire piece, it flew from the doorway and introduced itself to the first rank of guards, smashing them against the opposite wall. Modren stood in the door's charred wake. Ice spun around his left hand. His right had become the colour and texture of the marble itself.

'Treacherous bastards,' he spat. He saw Durnus standing nearby, and saw the spears that had suddenly leapt up to tickle his pale throat.

The guards had already picked themselves up and formed a wall of shields around the doorway. This was the Evernia guard after all, highly-trained and clad head to toe in powerful anti-magick armour, armour Tyrfing had helped to perfect. Unfortunately, they were the finest guards within a thousand miles. Sadly, they weren't the most loyal.

'Kill the spells, mage,' ordered Jarvins. He had splinters in his hair.

Modren bared his teeth like a dog. There was a dangerous moment, but at last he did as he was told.

The order came. 'Clap him in irons.'

'The hell you will, Jarvins, you snake...' spat the Undermage. Fire ran along his arms as a threat. But it was no use. Half a dozen spears were held to Durnus' neck again. He growled, and put out his flames.

Jarvins gestured to his men, who wrestled Modren's arms behind his back. 'Council Barkhart's orders, I think you'll find,' said the colonel, almost conversationally.

'I don't take orders from worms.'

Jarvins smiled. 'You do now.'

Side by side, Modren and Durnus were marched through the golden doors of the great hall and pushed to their knees. A huge crowd of council members were waiting for them. Every single one of them was wearing a smile that Modren longed to burn from their faces. He struggled and writhed like a criminal facing the gibbet.

Malvus was standing at the foot of Evernia's statue, calm, collected, and as happy as could be. He was wearing a long coat of red and grey, complimented by a white shirt and black trousers with creases so sharp they could have drawn blood. His thin black shoes were polished to glorious mirrors. He drummed his nails on Evernia's marble dais while he savoured every inch of the scene in front of him. For some reason, there was a battered old warhammer leaning next to him, but for the moment it was ignored. Malvus brushed a lock of waxy hair from his eyes and raised his hands. The crowd behind him murmured excitedly. 'Shall we?' he asked with a smile.

There was a loud chorus of, 'AYE!' from the crowd. It made the mages' blood boil, but only Modren let it show.

Malvus swept a long length of sand-coloured parchment from the statue's base. It was so long that he walked ten paces toward the mages and most of it still lingered between Evernia's feet. With a supercilious smile, he held it up for everyone in the hall to see. Edge to edge, it was covered in the scribblings of a thousand different hands, in lines of names and ink-stained X's. Malvus held it up like a trophy, like the head of some defeated general.

'I shall keep this brief,' he intoned. He tossed the parchment to the floor in front of Durnus and Modren. The Undermage stared at it as though it were a diseased rat. Modren mouthed some of the names to himself.

'What is it?' asked Durnus.

'A list of traitors,' muttered Modren.

'This,' interrupted Malvus, 'is a petition signed by the city, by high-ranking mages, sergeants, lieutenants, and colonels, by School instructors, appointed magick council members, renowned merchants, property owners, and of course, the people themselves. Why? Well, according to the founding writings of this council, we, as the majority, have the right, nay, the *privilege* to call for the abdication of Arkmages should they be judged unfit to rule.' Malvus gestured to the parchment snaking along the floor. 'It appears that the people and their appointed have spoken, dear sirs. It appears you are most unfit indeed.'

Durnus kept his chin high. 'And they are the richer for it, I am sure.'

'How much does it cost, exactly, to buy that many scrawls, Malvus?' hissed Modren.

A rustle of chuckling ran through the crowd and the guards at the door. They knew the truth, they simply didn't care. Every single soul in that great hall knew they simply had to recite the lines and play the part. The city would be none the wiser, like an audience to a play. There would be no peeking behind the scenery. It was a farce. A comedy of traitors. The Copse was having its day.

Malvus wisely avoided getting too close to the red-faced Modren. He whispered in Durnus' ear instead. 'Less than you might imagine, let me tell you that,' he grinned, then stood and turned in a swift movement, managing to flick Durnus in the face with his coattails as he turned.

'And so,' he announced to the hall, 'It gives me the great

honour to announce to this city, this country, and its armies, that Arkmages Durnus and Tyrfing no longer have the right to their thrones or to their titles. The title and position of Arkmage is hereby suspended from this day until this council, acting on behalf of the people, finds a suitable replacement or alternative. This council has spoken!' There was a deafening cheer as Malvus finished speaking. He swaggered back and forth past the statue. Those near enough clapped him on the back, laughing and grinning. He smiled through wily lips.

With a flourish of his coattails and the squeak of boots upon the marble, he raised his hands to his crowd. 'And who shall steer this council true until such times as a worthy replacement can be found?'

'Malvus!'

'Malvus!'

'Malvus!' came the shouts, the sickeningly eager shouts. Modren glared fire and brimstone into every eye he could meet. Durnus stared sightlessly at the floor while he waited for the noise to die away.

When it did, Malvus was there, standing over both of them, hands on hips. 'Fortunately for you, the city has decided that execution would be a step too far. At least for now,' he chuckled, and then gestured to the guards. 'Take these failures to the prison. Toss them somewhere dark and cold, where they can reflect on their crimes of neglect and greed. And take that maid of theirs too. The sick one. She can share her husband's fate,' he ordered.

It was fortunate that Malvus called for the guards the moment he did, for his mention of Elessi sent Modren into a flaming rage. A literal flaming rage. He thrashed and he lunged and he kicked and he spat, and all the while his clothes and skin sputtered into deep orange flame. His eyes were mad, his threats and shouts just guttural barks, like a wolf set ablaze.

Malvus was startled to the say the least. His calm composure cracking for just a moment, he stumbled backwards and almost tripped over his own shoes. He smoothed his coat with his hands as Modren was hauled away by half a dozen guards, fire charring the marble beneath him. 'As if we needed more proof!' he yelled. More cheers came from the council.

Only Durnus remained calm and still. He was pulled to his feet by his shackles. The guards gave him a moment to speak before they hauled him away. Malvus strutted around him. 'Any last words, Durnus?'

'Many. But only a few shall suffice,' he said, in a voice as brittle as an autumn leaf, yet as cold as the winter it dreaded. As Malvus came to a sneering halt in front of him, Durnus somehow managed to fix him with a glassy stare that raised the hairs on the nape of his neck. Durnus continued, speaking only to him. 'I pity you, Barkhart. Your glory will be as fleeting as the morning frost. There will always be a schemer like you, you see. They could be behind you, in your faithful crowd. They may be in the city below. They may even be a thousand miles from here, so far blissfully unaware, but they will come, one day, and challenge you. They will flock to usurp you. Undermine you with tongues and coinpurses, like you have done to Tyrfing and I. They will see a stone that needs kicking from the mountaintop. A bare neck ready for the blade. Trust me, they will come, and when they do, you will know your errors. Good luck, I say.' Durnus chuckled then; a single, condemning snort that rattled Malvus more than any laugh or a threat ever could. Only the future that the seer showed him, spoken over tea-leaves that morning in the cobbled street, allowed him to cling to his confidence. Malvus quickly waved the guards away and Durnus was hauled away by his elbows, heels sliding across the marble. He kept his misty eyes on Malvus until the golden doors were shut in his face.

Another mighty cheer went up from the council then, accompanied by an eager rattle of applause and back-clapping.

Malvus turned and strode purposefully towards Evenia's statue. With a heave, he seized the old warhammer and swung it onto his shoulder. He marched into the crowd and they parted like water before a sharp keel. Hands patted him on the shoulders as he walked by. Laughing words of congratulations swirled in his wake. Malvus didn't say a word to any of them.

When the crowd fell silent, Malvus stood in front of the twin thrones, so still he seemed frozen to the marble. Several minutes he stood there, as the whispers began to build yet again. One man stepped forward, peeling away from the crowd, and raised a curious finger.

'Malvus?' he asked. 'Are you...?' His question trailed off as Malvus began to move. He raised his hammer high into the air, as high as his arms could reach. It teetered for a moment, clasped by white, stretching fingers, and then it was brought down with an ear-splitting crack, colliding with the very centre of the twin thrones. A half-shocked gasp went up from the council. The rest flinched at the noise and watched, wide-eyed, as Malvus brought the hammer down and down again, in great furious swings. Marble chips and milk-white dust flew like sea-spray. The guards ran forward and then floundered in hesitation, unsure if this was a step of treachery too far. None dared stray into the arc of the swinging hammer. Malvus was sweating now, somehow speeding up, not slowing down. The hammer-blows rained as though he were a seasoned blacksmith. The tendons stood out on his rolled-up forearms like cords. He grunted and hissed with every strike, grinning through the dust, a rabid dog.

Within minutes, one half of the twin thrones was a battered, obliterated mess. It lay on the floor in chips and chunks, a mound of featureless disarray. Unmatched craftsmanship, smashed and scarred to nothing. Panting, Malvus paused for a second to admire his work, and then with one last swing, he split the nearby Underthrone in half. Its broken back fell onto the floor, spitting marble as it split again. The warhammer fell with it, cast aside with a loud clang and left to wallow in its own destruction.

The council watched with wide eyes as Malvus took to the scarred steps of the remaining throne. He took his time, nudging broken marble aside with his toes as he took each glorious step. Had he been facing the council, they would have seen a smile on his face so wide that they would have feared for the safety of his cheeks. Then, at the summit, with a clap and a rub of dusty hands, Malvus Barkhart turned and slowly sank into the seat of the throne. Many years abruptly culminated into that one act of gravity. His heart thumped.

All was achingly silent in the great hall. Malvus stared straight ahead, waiting, drumming his dusty, marble-bitten nails. Then, one by one, the council began to drop to its knees. Malvus' smile got even wider. 'Ring the bells!' he ordered, with a laugh. 'Ring every bell! Let the city know what it has done today!' *What I've done today*, though this was to himself.

Chapter 8

"No better guise than a shapeshifter's hide."
Latter section of an Albion parable

Hjaussfen was an exercise in darkness. Darkness, and a stench only a rat could savour. The mountain fortress was as quiet as a graveyard, and in more than one place, it played the same role.

The precarious stairs had delivered them straight into the windowless bowels of the mountain. It was pitch black save for the occasional stubborn torch. It was a mercy in a way. There had been fighting there. The vicious sort. The fruits of it lay sprawled and twisted in corners. The darkness did its best to give the corpses an inkling of respect. Whatever had happened to the mountain, it had happened quickly and brutally. It sparked fresh prickles of worry and fury in Tyrfing and Farden.

The mages crept between storerooms and servants' quarters, steam-starved baths and abandoned guard posts. The long stairs had taken their toll on Farden's legs and now he had fallen behind Tyrfing. He didn't seem to mind; the Arkmage was like a master thief, thoroughly in his element, tiptoeing back and forth, darting and probing. He let his magick flow into both light and shadow, illuminating the darker paths, but wrapping himself in shadow at every corner and junction. The spells flowed out of him like wine from a skin. It was effortless to watch, but irksome too. Farden scrunched up his face more than once. He tried a spell, just once, out of curiosity, but his body still wasn't ready. The magick stung him, a blinding headache came and went, and so he left well enough alone.

To the untrained eye, the deep reaches of the mountain fortress might have seemed bloody, but abandoned. The guard on the stairs had proven to them otherwise. As did the occasional echo of voices or footsteps, the smattering of fresh crumbs by a bench, or the drag-marks of some bloody altercation, still tacky to the touch.

'This is making my blood boil,' hissed Farden, as they passed a figure curled around a splintered door-frame, displaying the sort of disturbing stillness that only a corpse can. The mage's voice sounded foreign in the silence.

Tyrfing nodded as he peeked around a corner. His blood had been boiling since the beach. 'Stairs,' he breathed.

'What?'

'Stairs. They'll take us up.'

Farden felt strong enough to take the lead. His sword was out and low, barely grazing the granite floor. Tyrfing strode behind him, hands out, dangerous.

As they set foot to the wide, simple stairs, they heard an echo murmur to them. Something from the levels above, like the rustling of a great tree, or a giant snake shuffling along. Uncertainty was a painful thing, in moments like that. It made the breath catch at the back of the throat. Tyrfing stifled another cough as Farden moved on ahead.

The source of the murmuring was soon discovered: Feet. Hundreds of barely-covered feet walking in a silent line. The mages watched them from the top of the stairs, down the length of a long corridor, dark except for its distant end, where shadows and their owners shambled along in droves. Soldiers, their armour and mail glinting, telltale, in the torches they carried, marched alongside them. Even at that distance, the mages could see them shoving and pushing their captives along.

'Reminds me of a Krauslung we liberated, a long time ago,' muttered Farden.

'At least we have no Vice to fight.'

'No, just the entirety of the Lost Clans.'

Tyrfing shrugged as if that truly didn't worry him. 'Let's go.'

Go they did. As quietly as their boots and armour would allow, the two mages sprinted down the corridor as the tail of the train of captives passed by. Two soldiers were bringing up the rear. By the time they felt cold, metallic hands and a blade slide across their throats, it was already too late for them. Once their cloaks and helmets had been pilfered, they were quickly and quietly stowed in a dark doorway. Their comrades were too busy haranguing the captives to notice.

Tyrfing and Farden donned the helmets and slung the cloaks over their shoulders. While Tyrfing kept a wary eye on the soldiers up ahead, Farden reached out to gently grab the skinny arm of the rearmost captive in the sorry line, an older man with a long waterfall of silver-blonde hair. Gentle Farden may have been, but the man still yelped like a stung hound.

'Shhh!' Farden hissed as quietly as he could. Tyrfing ducked as one the soldiers looked back down the line.

'I'm sorry,' gasped the poor man, screwing his eyes shut. 'Whatever it is, don't hurt me!'

'Pipe down,' Farden whispered in his ear. The mage shook him lightly, and gradually the man cracked open his eyes. There was no fist hovering above him, no blade tickling his chin, just a man with a face from the mainland, an Arka man by his paleness. The helmet only covered his brow and his cheeks. It was plain even in the tepid torchlight. The Siren's eyes widened, and he opened his mouth to accommodate the enormous smile that was spreading across it.

'Thank Thr...!' he cried, too loud for comfort. The mages

winced. Farden clapped a hand over the man's mouth and shoved him back into the line. The other Sirens around them were none the wiser. They glanced fearfully over their shoulders. All they saw were two soldiers in helmets; the light was too bad and their hatred too strong to notice any different.

The soldiers, however, had heard the noise over the shuffling, murmuring procession of feet. One of them broke off and stood aside, waiting for the line to work its way past him. Farden saw the figure lingering ahead, passing time by whacking random captives with the flat of his sword blade. There were bars of steel riveted to the mail on his shoulders. Some sort of rank.

Farden's chest tightened under the pressure of the distinct lack of options. The corridor was doorless, windowless, and straight. He leant close to his uncle, eyes still on the soldier ahead. 'Erm,' he began.

'Hold tight,' came the order.

Farden frowned. 'Hold tight to w...' Tyrfing clamped a hand on his shoulder and a searing pain delved into his body, making his face convulse and his arms shake.

'Stay still. Keep walking,' Tyrfing hissed in his ear. It was all Farden could do to nod and not cry out. As the soldier drew near, the pain faded just enough to allow him to stop gurning. He kept his mouth shut and his hands clamped around his sword, waiting for the inevitable havoc to unfold, as it surely would.

It would have been a sore understatement to say Farden was a touch surprised when the soldier fell in alongside them, calm as a cobble. Farden kept his head forward, looking instead with his eyes, straining so much they ached. Tyrfing's hand was still gasping his shoulder in a grip that a troll would have been proud of. Tyrfing's armour had completely faded in colour. In fact, it didn't even seem to be the same armour any more. It was a pale shirt of dirty mail, complete with a tabard bearing the device of some clan. Farden flicked his eyes down at his own attire and found he was wearing the same. His Scalussen armour had completely disappeared. Farden wiggled his left hand into view and saw that it was scaled, and grey. Despite the pain, Farden smirked to himself as he recited a bit of Albion nonsense in his head. *No better guise than a shapeshifter's hide.*

'Giving you trouble?' asked the Lost Clan soldier, aiming a kick at a nearby captive. His accent was thicker than the ice he hailed from. So thick it was almost another language. Unperturbed, Tyrfing took a breath, and replied in an accent every bit as thick. Farden had to hold himself from laughing with joy.

'Not a bit, sir. Not a bit,' grunted his uncle.

'Make sure you keep it that way. Don't want a riot on our hands.'

'No sir.'

From the corner of Farden's eye, he could see the soldier lean past Farden to examine him. He nodded but kept his eyes straight.

'New recruit?' he asked Tyrfing, noting the hand on the shoulder.

The Arkmage nodded quickly. 'Green as they come. Too many bodies for one day,' he said.

'Hmm, blood-sick. We all got it at some point, didn't we?' hummed the soldier. 'Well,' he said, talking to Farden. 'You toughen up, you hear? We don't want any pale-scales making liabilities of themselves.'

'No sir,' Farden replied, as loudly and as boldly as he could. The pain strangled his voice.

He heard the soldier nudge Tyrfing before he left. 'He'll soon get used to it. After what I hear Lord Saker has planned.'

The name was a ricochet of an arrow, bouncing around the inside of Farden's skull. *Saker.* There it was: the name that had been tickling his memory for the past few hours. *Saker.*

'Oh yes?' Tyrfing asked, but the soldier was already walking back down the shuffling line, tapping his scaled nose.

'Oho yes,' he chuckled, and that was that. 'You keep these ingrates in line, you hear?'

'Yes sir,' chorused the mages.

Once the soldier was out of eye and earshot, Tyrfing dragged his hand from Farden's shoulder. Farden felt a strange weight lift as normality came flooding back into his body. It wasn't without its own brand of pain. It was like having a sword pulled out once it had been driven in. Both hurt, each in different, sickening ways. Farden wheezed as he watched his grey hands fade back to red and gold. He could feel his face contorting and shedding its scales. Farden wiped a drip of sweat from his brow with a shaky hand.

'Does it feel like that every time?' he gasped as the final dregs of pain evaporated.

Tyrfing shook his head in a nonchalant sort of way. 'You get used to it.'

Farden didn't bother asking how. He tapped the captive Siren on the shoulder and the man slowed his pace. He was wise enough to remain calm this time, and facing forward.

'Who in the name of Thron are you?'

'Passers-by,' said Tyrfing.

'We came to speak with the Old Dragon,' Farden replied.

The Siren snorted. It was a cold sound, hard as flint. 'Then I wish you the very best of luck.'

'Why?'

'Last I heard, he was being held in the great hall. We haven't seen him in a week. They say Saker and his Fellgrin killed him.'

'Why? What happened here?'

The Siren shrugged. 'I'm just a cook. What should I know of the whys and hows? One day was normal. The next, the Lost Clans are at our gates, begging for sanctuary against the snows and the ice.

Towerdawn gave them the shelter of the lower slopes. Gave them grain, breads, water. Before we knew it, they had taken the mountain for themselves.'

'But why? You must know.'

'I told you, I'm a cook, not a soldier. And that has kept me safe so far, so I'm not going to start acting like one, if that's what you've come for.'

Tyrfing leant forward. 'What are they doing with you?'

'They march us back and forth. Make us work the kitchens.' The Siren shrugged. 'If you ask me, not much has changed.'

Farden put his hand on the back of the man's head and twisted it sharply to the left, where a man's broken body lay in a doorway, a twisted picture of death. A smear of something brown and flaking painted the door behind him. 'Save for the hazardous working conditions…?' Farden whispered.

The Siren wrinkled his nose. 'We keep our heads down and our scales in one piece. Do what we're told. They give us beds, food, clothes. Treat us fine, save for the occasional beating. Could be worse,' he said, drawing a few stares from the others in the line. Their colourful eyes were as sharp as pins.

Farden shook his head. 'I suppose it could. There could be more spineless lizards like you amongst this sorry bunch,' he said. There were murmurs of agreement from the back of the line. The man's scales flushed a paler shade.

'Well…' was all he could stammer. He looked down at his shuffling feet and said no more.

Tyrfing leant close to his nephew. 'I think it's time we made our exit. Before they expect a rescue.' His words may have had a cold edge, but the Arkmage was right; the stares from the others were becoming desperate. Elbows nudged. Lips mumbled. Something about a pair of saviours.

They were not in a position to be saving anyone, never mind

in any great quantity. Not yet.'

Farden nodded and sidled away from the line. With his eyes he tried to convey to the Sirens that they would return, just in case any of them began to try to run or shout. Luckily, they seemed to understand, and under the wincing gazes of a score or so, Farden and Tyrfing slipped into the darkness of another stairwell.

※

Farden stood in the milky light of the fog-strangled day. With one hand he pinched and rubbed at his eyes. With the other he held himself up against the glass of the window, trying to act casual, fresh. He was anything but. *Could this mountain have any more stairs?* he inwardly gasped.

'Ready?' Tyrfing was hovering nearby.

Ready to keel over. 'Absolutely. Let's go.'

'Good man.'

And on they went, padding even softer than before, as if the air was thinner as well as brighter. There were fewer shadows here, thanks to the thick windows that punctured the walls. Fewer shadows, but fewer places to hide.

Farden found himself peering down side passages and out of windows. His bearings were nowhere to be found. 'When was the last time you were in Hjaussfen?' he whispered.

'The anniversary of Towerdawn's coronation.'

Farden pulled a confused face. 'When was that?'

'Five years ago.'

'How much of this rabbit warren can you remember? Do you know where we are?'

'There must be a thousand miles of corridor and hallway in this mountain, Farden. I doubt even the oldest dragons have seen every one of them.'

'Hmph,' Farden sighed. He took a moment to gaze out of a nearby window, smeared with dust. It was at that precise moment that a pale dragon skimmed the mountainside, flashing past the glass. Farden leapt back, his sword almost falling from his hands. But the beast had already vanished into the fog. 'Too close,' he muttered.

Tyrfing took the lead, and they walked one behind the other, sidling along the hallway like crabs along a tideline. 'How are you feeling?'

Farden rolled his eyes. 'I wish people would stop asking me that.'

'We'll stop when you start feeling better.'

'I do.'

'This family has never been good at lying.'

'Had enough practice.'

'Hmm,' Tyrfing said no more.

'I feel tired. Like I spent the whole of yesterday exercising.'

'Funny, that.'

'Apart from that, my wounds are healed. My headache seems to have given up on me. The nevermar seems to have gone.'

'Hmm,' his uncle hummed again. 'Sounds too soon to me. Do you feel weak? Dizzy?'

'Only when I stand up.'

'Memory?'

'Coming back. Slowly,' Farden replied, wondering if that was a good thing or not.

'Magick?'

Farden tapped his teeth together in thought. 'Long gone.'

'And how that upsets me, to think you might have eradicated it for good. I hope you're wrong.'

'So do I,' Farden unsure if that was a lie or not. He was still so torn over the thought of his magick. Old habits. They're an inch from immortal at the best of times.

The mages crept on, and as they crept, they turned to making up their minds about the mountain and its madness. It was a coup, pure and simple. The Lost Clans had come to claim the warmer climes, the palace of the Old Dragon, the finer half of Nelska. Farden wondered why. From what he remembered, and that was patchy at best, the Lost Clans were not bitter about their northern habitat, nor their southern cousins. He wondered what had changed in the last decade and a half. Then he remembered Saker, and the look in his eyes as he had talked of the Old Dragon, of Farfallen. There had been no respect in them. Farden remembered a feast with dancing, witches, and boxing. He thought of Farfallen laughing and drinking and felt a pang of hurt flash across his chest. *Damn memories*, he cursed inside his head.

'Either it was a small force that took Hjaussfen, or they're all holed up in the palace,' muttered Farden, changing subject for himself.

Tyrfing snorted. 'Luckily that's where we're headed.'

Farden prodded him as he passed to take the lead. They had found yet another stairwell, and took the stairs as quickly as they could. 'I'm being serious. The mountain doesn't feel invaded. It feels abandoned.' Farden was right. Apart from the contingent they had met in the lower levels, and the occasional echo of something distant, Hjaussfen was silent and empty. Almost eerie.

Tyrfing nodded. 'A lot of Sirens have been forced to the mainland or Talen due to the ice. The Long Winter hadn't given up on the north as easily. Even at the coronation the crowds were thin. The dragons were few. Painfully so. Durnus always said that Towerdawn had inherited a dying breed.'

'That makes me sad.'

'Let's hope this coup isn't the first nail in their coffin.'

'Not if we can help it.'

Tyrfing pulled a wry face and shook his head. 'Farden,' he said, 'we're here for Elessi. Keep that in mind. Save the maid and the world first, like you said. Then you can think about the Sirens.'

Farden didn't reply to that. He was too busy walking straight into a slumbering guard.

The eerie silence was shattered in a moment, trodden to dust. Farden fell head over heels with the guard, armour crashing onto the stone. Their armour was somehow entangled, mail caught on plate. They thrashed and flailed but neither one broke free. It was one of those moments in a fight where all technique and skill evaporates and all that is left is vicious, desperate thrashing, where both parties know that only one will emerge alive.

The guard knew it all too well. He came awake in seconds. Farden's sword had already slid away across the stone. He recklessly pounded his opponent in the face with one hand while trying and failing to peel himself free with the other. The guard was shouting something garbled, trying to seize Farden by the throat. Leather gloves soon found an unprotected neck. The mage suddenly found himself being strangled. Farden kicked and hammered with all his might, but the guard refused to budge. He gripped even tighter. Farden's armoured finger found an eye socket and plunged into it. The sound he elicited was akin to a wolf howling around a mouthful of broken crockery. Farden pressed and pressed, deeper and deeper, until, just as the blood was beginning to run, the man let go. As he rolled away, Tyrfing found his gap, and despatched the man quickly with a shimmering hand to the face.

Farden gingerly touched his throat. 'And just to think,' he wheezed. 'You almost stayed on the boat.'

'You're welcome.' Tyrfing eyed the corpse grimly. It was an ugly sight, face caved, a bloody mess of white gristle and wet crimson. He sniffed and recoiled. The guard had soiled himself in death. Such was battle. 'We need to hide the body,' he said, though he didn't make a move to do so.

'We don't need to do anything else but disappear. You could

have heard that struggle from the summit. We need to leave,' Farden replied, getting shakily to his feet. As if to prove him right, the sounds of marching feet began to echo down the hallway. Tyrfing and Farden groaned. 'See?'

Tyrfing waved a hand. 'I see alright. This way!'

They scuttled off in the opposite direction of the approaching noise, as softly and as quickly as they could manage. It didn't take long for a shout to hurtle down the corridor after them. It just made the mages run faster.

They took the first left they could find, and then the next right, and so on, zig-zagging through the granite depths as fast and as erratically as they could. When they finally stopped for breath behind a door to a modest bedroom, they found themselves wrapped in silence again.

'Let's not make that mistake again,' Tyrfing said. Farden nodded, still massaging his bruised neck.

It took them over an hour to worm their way up, one level at a time. Slowly but surely, the fortress granite paled into the palace marble. The corridors lifted their rafters and shuffled their walls aside. Windows became stained and grander. Torches became more frequent. The rooms they spied grew larger. Soon they found themselves creeping through a Hjaussfen they remembered.

It was plain to see that the mountain's lustre had flaked. Call it age or neglect since the coup, but the palace lacked some of the glow Farden could vaguely remember. Perhaps it was the distinct lack of bustle, or dragons. Whatever it was, it was sad to see.

Unfortunately for the two mages, the higher they climbed into the mountain, the more numerous the soldiers became. Soon they were running out of places to hide and rooms to duck into. It was only a matter of time before they stumbled across a guard post, or a banquet hall full of unfriendly individuals. Now and again they caught sight of a Lost Clan dragon and its rider. They sauntered about the hallways, leaking a confidence that only such an existence can summon. The riders all wore bearskin, leather, and bare chests, even the women. They looked decidedly tribal, in their furs and skins, with their rings of leather-bound teeth around their necks. The dragons were typical of the northern breed; shorter, stockier, with dark eyes and scales like knotted wood. They were the colour of wet clay, muddy snow, ivory, or thumbed charcoal. Such a contrast to the rainbow hues of the Hjaussfen dragons. Farden couldn't help but eye their curled horns and claws as they tread the marble floors.

Soon enough, they came across another line of sorry prisoners being shepherded along. These were cuffed and chained with iron. Farden peeked out from an alcove as they passed. They were riders by the looks of their scales and colourings. More than a few of them looked badly beaten. Every so often, one would turn a head and look back the way they had come, wearing a face so uncomfortable and pained that Farden could almost taste it himself. The soldiers flanking them would bark something and jab a stick at them, and the rider would turn back. It could have been a trick of the mage's ears, but he swore he heard something roaring somewhere in the mountain. There were echoes of hammers too, and shouting. A cacophony muffled by the rock.

'There,' Tyrfing whispered, as they peeked out from their alcove.

Farden squinted. 'Where?'

Tyrfing pointed to a diamond-shaped opening in the wall a few hundred yards up ahead. 'That archway ahead leads up into the nests. In the great hall.'

'Are you sure?'

'Not entirely, but we will soon find out,' Tyrfing replied. Another roar echoed through the halls, punctuation for his words. 'We're definitely getting close.'

That they were, and that meant soldier after soldier strolling past their hiding place. They were nestled tightly behind a pillar and a broken door. Nobody spared it a glance, but the hall was long, and open, and the soldiers too frequent to provide them with a gap. They waited, and then waited some more, but the soldiers and patrols kept on coming. Farden was busy watching the left. He was squinting like an owl. He thought he had just seen a witch.

'I think there's only one thing for it,' muttered his uncle, watching the right. 'We can't come this close and fail now.'

'For what?' asked Farden, but he'd already realised. He shook his head. 'Oh no, not again,' he moaned.

'Just hold your breath when it starts and then breathe slowly and calmly once it's finished. These spells sink better into a relaxed body. It's like warm clay. More malleable.'

'Thanks for the tip,' Farden grimaced. He rolled his shoulders and clicked his knuckles, as if that would help at all. 'Fine. Do your worst.'

'Hold still,' Tyrfing reached out to hold his nephew's shoulder. Farden grit his teeth as Tyrfing's hard fingers grabbed him. It felt as though a bag of hot coals had just been strapped to his shoulder. The pain came, just as before, stayed, and then receded to a level that was just about bearable. Farden looked down at his hands and noticed the scales there were different from before, a shade of dusty lilac. They were slender too, compared to his usual. Farden looked down to see what clothes his uncle had clad him in this time, but found his view blocked by something protruding from his chest, something inside his cotton shirt. Farden frowned, confused. As he raised his hands to query the obstructions, the realisation dropped like a stone.

'You made me a woman?!' he hissed, whirling around.

'Keep your voice down!' Tyrfing warned. He had taken his soldier's form again, exactly as before.

Farden's lilac scales were turning violet. 'Do you really think this is a good time for jokes?'

'Even the Lost Clans would be less suspicious of a woman, Farden. The quicker we get across, the quicker I can turn you back.' Tyrfing looked his nephew up and down and cracked a little smile. 'I have to say, you would have made a very ugly niece.'

'You better hope I never get my magick back,' Farden warned, struggling half-heartedly against his uncle's grip. He was stuck fast. The more he moved, the more the spell hurt. 'Turn me back now!' he winced.

'It's done now. On your feet, madam,' Tyrfing ordered. Farden had no choice. He winced as they got to their feet. Tyrfing took the sword and gently nudged him forward. 'Ladies first,' he smirked.

Farden brandished a finger. 'I swear to the gods…'

'Shut up and head down. Act miserable,' Tyrfing whispered in his ear.

No problem there, thought Farden, as he shuffled across the corridor. Tyrfing played the part well, shoving and waving the sword about. Few of the soldiers they passed batted an eyelid. One paused to look Farden up and down, licking dry lips, before sauntering on. Just another prisoner, shambling through the halls.

It took them a long minute to reach the alcove and its stairs. The closer they came to it, the louder the noises became, a clamour of roaring and grunting, the bell-pealing of iron and hammers. As soon as they were safely tucked into the alcove's shadow, Tyrfing released his nephew. Farden tottered around as his body twisted back into its normal state, armour and all. He patted his chest. 'Thank f…'

'Shh,' Tyrfing held up a hand. A crooked shadow was coming down the stairs towards them. Tyrfing grabbed Farden again and thrust him forward. The mage yelped as the pain struck him a third time.

'Morning,' grunted the soldier, over the din, as the prisoner and her guard came into view.

'Morning,' replied the guard, in a gruff voice. The soldier held up his torch as they passed. He gave the female a lingering look as she went by, eyeing her ample chest. She shot daggers at him. With a shrug, and a dirty chuckle, he went on his way.

Farden grit his teeth as his uncle released him again. 'Could I get a little warning, next time?' he hissed.

'Feeling sick?'

Farden closed his eyes. 'Very.'

Tyrfing nodded. 'It's all in the mind. That spell doesn't really twist the body so much as the brain. Instead of altering your bones and muscles, like true shapeshifting, it tricks the eye into seeing something completely different. Hence why your armour disappeared and your clothes changed.'

Farden rubbed his sweaty forehead. 'This really isn't the time for lectures, uncle.'

'Sorry,' he answered. 'I...' An ear-splitting roar cut his sentence in two. The two mages barely swapped a look before bounding up the stairs to the nearest nest.

Like most of the nests in the hall, it was unoccupied. Strewn with brittle, pale straw and pine needles, the going underfoot crackled as they crept towards the gnarled edge of the rock-hewn nest. They stuck to the shadows, keeping their faces out of the light. A hundred torches blazed below. They shuffled slowly to the edge and peered down into the great hall.

A difficult sight greeted them with open arms.

Below them, sprawled in a circle on the cold granite floor, were five dragons. They lay prone and uncomfortable, with their legs splayed at odd angles. While their tails thrashed and beat the stone, their heads remained perfectly still, lying within inches of each other. It took Farden and Tyrfing a few moments to realise why.

Iron collars. Great, heavy iron collars that were being bolted and molten into holes in the granite around the dragons' necks. It was a miracle they were staying still. Farden suspected it had something to do with the fact five riders stood nearby, with five knives to their scaled throats. One stood above the rest, a woman with golden hair and scales. She held her chin high, but her eyes were firmly fixed on the only dragon who was not struggling to be free, the big red-gold male. Towerdawn. His tawny eyes were fixed on his rider, Aelya. Farden could only wonder what they were saying to each other in their private silence.

It was then that Saker himself swept into the hall, with his captains at his back. Even from a distance, Farden could see the smugness on his face. His many teeth flashed in the torchlight. He drank in the scene for a moment before gesturing to one of his soldiers. He beckoned for something, and then moved to stand by Towerdawn's head. He flicked one of the dragon's horns with his finger. Farden could see Towerdawn's scales ripple with anger as he bared his row after row of fangs. Saker laughed. A cold sound, like the hammers on the iron.

As he knelt down to whisper into Towerdawn's ears, a gang of soldiers and soot-blackened workers shuffled into the hall, weighed down by something heavy and cumbersome. It took them a few moments to manoeuvre it into view, and then it was shown to the mages and the hall in all its ugly glory.

It was a throne, but not like any throne Farden had ever seen. Not grandiose. Not ornate. Instead, it was made completely out of iron. Its makers had given it a cursory polish and file, but nothing more. It shone dully in the light. The strangest aspect of it was its legs. It had long, thick legs, far longer than they rightly should have been.

Saker seemed pleased enough with it. Thrilled, even. He patted the Old Dragon on the head and then leapt up spryly, jabbing his fingers at the floor. The soldiers and workers shuffled forward, arms shaking and veins popping.

Although it took them a while to manhandle it into position, it didn't take long for the throne's ghastly purpose to become apparent. There was a reason Saker was so content with such an odd throne, a throne with such long legs. Why? The mages saw it now. It had been forged to sit on top of Towerdawn's huge collar. It was a pure, cast-iron insult. A slap in the Old Dragon's scaly face. Humiliation, wrought and forged.

As a pair of wooden steps were carried in to flank it, Saker couldn't have looked more eager to climb them. They were barely on the floor before he was striding up them, chest bared and furry coat-tails snapping behind him. With a flourish, the Lord of the North claimed his new throne atop the Old Dragon's golden head.

Farden boiled with fury. His face was a shade so red that Tyrfing half-expected the straw beneath them to burst into flame. His fingers clutched desperately at the rock. Tyrfing didn't blame him. He eyed the glittering knives at the riders' throats. 'Easy, nephew,' he muttered.

Farden simply growled in reply.

Saker was looking around as if addressing a royal court, head held high and a tight smile to show a sliver of his needle-teeth. In actuality, his audience was a meagre one. Aside from the gaggle of workers, a score or so of his soldiers and captains, and the five dragons and their riders, there was scarcely a soul in the great hall. A few dragons lingered in the upper nests. Pale, sleepy things. Juvenile wyrms. A handful of riders stood by a fireplace, watching their lord with grins. Saker may have looked like a king, but his kingdom, for the moment, looked like the swollen population of some eccentric village.

Saker rapped his knuckles on the arm of his throne and looked at the dragons prostrate at his feet. Yellow, blue, black, green, and gold. They lay like a colour wheel. Every single one glared great daggers at him. Saker almost seemed to enjoy it. He tapped his foot on the Old Dragon's collar. 'If only Farfallen could see you now, *kafflechs*,' Saker spat something foreign. 'He would be mightily displeased.'

Chuckles from the bystanders. Farden wanted to gut them all.

Saker tapped his throne again. 'Now the beauty of this arrangement is simple,' he paused to cross his legs and shuffle into a more comfortable position, like some tavern storyteller, spinning yarns for his supper. 'Your claws and limbs are bound. Your tails soon will be. Your wings are useless. You have yet one weapon left at your disposal.'

The blue dragon, Farden didn't recognise her, hissed at this. Something bright and molten dribbled from the corner of her mouth. Saker pointed, delighted. 'Exactly!' he announced. 'Fire.' He got to his feet and slapped a hand against his chest. 'Any one of you could burn me to a cinder this very moment, but you would kill your Old Dragon in doing so.'

Saker was painfully correct. The dragons had realised the fiendish design the moment their heads had been pinned to the floor. They were bound by more than just stout iron. No dragon could blow fire at Saker and miss, but no dragon could miss Towerdawn in the process. Scales were little defence at such close range. Towerdawn's snout was only mere inches from the others'. It was a dastardly design. Saker looked extremely pleased with it.

Towerdawn looked at his dragons one by one. They all had a pained look in their jewel-flecked eyes. He bared his great fangs and struggled as much as he could, but the iron pinning him to the granite held fast. Saker's throne barely wobbled. 'Ingenious, isn't it? Old beast?' he smiled.

'Unlike you, I am not above sacrificing myself for the good of my people,' Towerdawn hissed. It was hard to talk with his jaw pressed so tightly to the ground. 'My dragons will do what is right.'

His dragons, however, flashed him looks of defiance and sorrow. Towerdawn's great heart sank.

Saker leant back in his chair. He looked infuriatingly comfortable. 'Something tells me otherwise, Towerdawn. Your dragons are bound by honour. We Clansmen are bound by something a little stronger than that.'

'Like greed?'

Saker kicked the dragon's collar. 'A desire to survive, *kafflech*.'

There was a rumble as a trio of Lost Clan dragons sauntered into the hall. One was huge, a burnt brown colour, with spines that curled like goat-horns. The one beside it was a fish-scale grey. She glistened wetly when the light caught her. Shimmers of blue and green ran across her flanks, like a mackerel. The last, and the one that led them, was a lithe black dragon with veins of red and orange mottling her skin, like lava seeping through granite cracks. Her horns were painted red. She had thin little slits for eyes, the colour of sulphur. This was Saker's ride. Fellgrin, the cowardly cook had called her. Her forked-tongue smile certainly lived up to that title.

Saker nodded to her and she came to sit by his side. She casually rested a saw-bladed claw on the Old Dragon's golden head, and tapped it rhythmically.

'Have you found the fog-brewing trouble-makers yet?' Saker spoke aloud, addressing the other dragons.

'No, lord,' answered the huge brown male, barely understandable in their strange accent. 'Not a sign of them on the slopes. They must be inside the mountain. Perhaps holed up in the old springs. We found the ship in the fog too, but we lost sight of it. Turneye chased it, but he has yet to return.'

Not too far away, in one of the nests, two mages flinched and shuffled backward a little.

'You lost it,' came the reply, not so much a question as a damning fact. Then Saker waved his hand. 'So be it. Ships do not bother me as much as accursed wizards do,' spat Saker. 'Get Kass and her witches on it. If your useless noses can't sniff out the magick, then perhaps their finches can. Wherever they're hiding, we shall dig them out.'

The mackerel-grey dragon piped up. Her voice was thin and high like a skald's pipe. Odd, for a creature of that size. 'And when we find them, lord?' she asked.

Saker ran a hand across his ridged scalp. 'Toss them from the summit, do what you will with what's left.'

Fellgrin muttered something, and Towerdawn growled as her claw went a little too deep. Saker nodded and tapped his foot on his throne. 'Save us the trouble of finding your wizards, old beast, and we may just spare them the fall.'

'I have lived far too many years to not know a lie when I hear one,' Towerdawn replied. Fellgrin jabbed at him with her claw again. The Old Dragon roared. It was hard to see, but she may have drawn blood through his scales. In the nest, Farden raised his head slightly so he could get a better view. He squinted at the Old Dragon. Something wet and golden tricked down Towerdawn's neck. Fellgrin swung her canary-eyes in his direction and he quickly ducked back down, hoping the shadows had held him.

Fellgrin growled and Saker got to his feet. He adjusted his fur jacket and jumped from the throne. He landed on the floor with a clap of hard boots. 'I'll find them myself,' he barked, and swept from his hall. His small entourage followed him. Even the riders were led away, still firmly at knifepoint. Only the five dragons and the slumbering wyrms remained.

Farden didn't waste a second. He scrambled upright and down the side of the nest. The rock was roughly hewn, and there were plenty of handholds, but even so, he had to drop a level or two to the granite below. He landed hard and stumbled, but he managed not to break anything save for his pride. His tired legs yelled at him as he scurried across the open hall to the dragons.

They had heard boots on the stone. Their eyes swivelled madly as they tried to see who was approaching. Not a single one of them, Towerdawn least of all, expected to see a ghost striding into their tight little circle. 'Of all the saviours Thron could have sent...' he gasped.

Farden smiled. 'I know. You're stuck with me.' He prodded at the green dragon's collar, making the beast growl. He recognised him now. It was Glassthorn.

Tyrfing had caught up. 'I think what the Old Dragon means is that he is surprised to see you,' he whispered.

Farden shrugged. 'I get that every time I look in a mirror,' he said. He knelt by Towerdawn's huge head and looked deep into his russet-gold eyes. The similarity between those great orbs and Farfallen's took him aback. Towerdawn tasted the mage's emotion. He tried on a comforting smile.

'It is good to see you,' he said in a low voice. 'Even under such circumstances as these.'

Tyrfing knelt down by the Old Dragon's head. He tested the collar, poking, prodding, rattling it until he was satisfied of its secrets. 'What happened here?'

Towerdawn sighed. 'The Lost Clans have been bitten hard by the Long Winter. They came with their hands out and their tails tucked between their legs, and we believed them. Every lie. Gave them pity. Fed them. Housed them. But they didn't come for shelter, or for help. They came for our home, our springs, our breeding grounds.'

Each dragon growled at the mention of their sacred grounds. Even the riders were barely permitted to tread the soil of a breeding ground. It was the desecration of a breeding ground that had caused the Arka-Siren war many years before.

'The snows and ice had driven them south, onto our borders. What we didn't know was that the last of their grounds had been lost to a glacier. A terrible shame, in any dragon's eyes. And so, they came here for ours.' Towerdawn bared his teeth. 'And I let them in. With open wings, too. They said the snows had driven them south. That they needed supplies for a little while, and then they would move on. I should have read Saker's heart a little better, but he's wilier than a snow fox. Bitter too. Centuries of jealousy and discontent have led to this. We should have expected it.'

'It's not the first time in history that a kingdom has been ambushed like this,' Farden offered.

Towerdawn fixed him with a pained stare. 'It is for us.'

'I think I can get this open,' hissed Tyrfing, eyeing the collar.

'Do it,' ordered the Old Dragon. Tyrfing seized the rough metal with both hands and held his breath. It wasn't long before he was blushing a shade of crimson. Soon enough his hands began to glow. The metal began to blister, and Towerdawn set his jaw against the pain.

'Where are the other dragons?' asked Farden, distracting him.

'Sealed in our prisons.'

'And the riders?'

'With them,' Glassthorn answered. 'The distance aches.'

'What about the wizards I heard Saker mention?'

The great blue dragon chuckled through the gaps in his sharp teeth. 'We were caught off guard, but they weren't quick enough to catch us all. Some of the wizards and a few of the soldiers escaped. They've been driving Saker mad ever since, which is one small morsel of satisfaction. They're the ones behind this fog.'

'Impressive.'

'And the only ones keeping the Clans from completely destroying our last breeding grounds.'

More growls from the dragons. Farden tried to help Towerdawn by pushing his neck away from the spitting, glowing collar. It was like shoving against a wall, one of muscle and scale. Tyrfing was drowning in concentration. His hands that throttled the collar were now white-hot. The iron was slowly, but surely, relenting.

Glassthorn rattled his own collar and shackles. 'Can you help with these, Farden?'

Farden couldn't help but make a face. 'Er...' he began. 'Not right now,' he muttered. Glassthorn gave him a quizzical look, but said no more. Towerdawn distracted him with questions. He could smell the lack of magick in the mage. It pained him.

'We know why we are here, but what about you? Did they send a hawk? Are there others?'

Farden turned back to the Old Dragon. 'No, and no. It's a long story, Towerdawn. One that I don't think we have time for,' he said, eyeing the bubbling metal.

'One minute,' Tyrfing gasped.

Farden eyed the nests above and the doorways. They were too exposed, too few. He lifted his sword onto his shoulder and crouched lower. '*She* has reared her head.'

This time, there were no growls, no baring of teeth, just the hot whooshing of a collective sigh. 'She brought three daemons down on Krauslung. We killed one, let two escape. Now she's heading north for more magick.'

'Do you mean to intercept her?' asked the big blue male.

'Not yet, but we will,' said Farden, squeezing his teeth together before continuing. 'Elessi was hurt in the battle. One of the daemons cut her with his claws.' He made a rough gesture to where she had been hurt, drawing a line down his neck and chest. It was an honest sort of gesture, indicating more than just a wound. 'Now she's hovering on death's doorstep, and we don't know how to save her.'

'Daemontouched,' whispered Towerdawn. There was a sharp ping as part of the collar cracked under the searing heat of Tyrfing's hands. The air about his shoulders wobbled.

Farden nodded. 'We need your help.'

Towerdawn groaned. 'We are not much of that, under the current circumstances, mage.'

The big blue shook his spines. 'No cure for that sort of

wound, mage.'

Farden eyes went wide. A crack had appeared in his plan, and was getting wider by the second. The idea that they had come all this way for a shake of a scaly head and a handful of commiseration had just entered his mind, and he didn't like it. Not one bit 'Surely there must be something? In the tearbooks maybe? The healers must know something!' he asked. '*Something?*'

'To be daemontouched, Farden, is to know death.'

'But she is still alive!'

'Yes, for now…'

'Almost done!' Tyrfing hissed.

'… but sadly not for long.'

Farden clenched a fist. 'There has to be a way!'

'Did you not hear me? How do you cure death, Farden? Impossible. Once you've seen the other side you cannot come back.'

Farden punched the granite. He couldn't meet the Old Dragon's gaze. He looked instead at the cracking, glowing collar, so painfully close to his neck. Char-marks were beginning to appear. Flecks of molten iron decorated the dragon's scales. 'No. I promised him…' Farden started to say, but he didn't get much further.

It was at that moment that a loud clapping echoed throughout the hall. A slow-paced, sadistic *crack-crack* of mocking hands. Footsteps played their own rhythms alongside it, and the scraping and shuffling of claws and scales provided the percussion. Farden and Tyrfing turned to face the music.

Saker stood in the nearest archway. A shadow draped itself across the middle of his face, giving him the look of a court jester, daubed and painted. He was smiling like one too, all needle-teeth and thin lips. His yellow eyes matched those of his dragon, standing very close behind him. Behind them stood a score of riders and clansmen, weapons being worked free of their scabbards and sheaths. Above, the crunching and rasping of feet and claws could be heard. Blunt snouts poked into the light.

    Farden heard the whipcrack of fireballs bursting into life behind him. The dragons on the floor growled in unison. The mage could do nothing but raise his sword and point at Saker as the air began to grow hot, and uncomfortable.

Chapter 9

*"Blood, fire, eggshell, tears,
tell the wyrm your deepest fears.
Shadows, hunger, snow and stone,
let the bond sink into bone.
When it's done, two days of silence,
mind in turmoil, blood in violence,
take wing and breathe the highest airs,
the bond is forged, an iron pair."*
An old Siren bonding poem, for the riders and their dragons

Farden's neck was beginning to burn. He could feel it. Like one of his carved candles, he could feel his neck melting. First the prickling, then the sweat dribbling under his collar, and now the sensation of his skin roasting. How ridiculous. His uncle's spells would cook him alive before anybody in that blasted hall dared to move. He shook his head. *Here he was, yet again*, he said to himself. *Between a rock and a bloody sharp blade.*

With an exasperated sigh, Farden lowered his sword and shrugged his tired arms. 'Well, what are you waiting for?'

Saker took a ponderous step forward, a theatrical cat, stalking a bunch of mice. 'I was hoping you would give me an excuse, mage, to finally test your famous mettle.' Behind him, Fellgrin growled something incomprehensible. Saker nodded. 'But judging by the fact you hold a sword in your hand, and not a spell, I imagine I will be disappointed.'

Farden bent a finger towards him. 'You could come a little closer, and we'll see how disappointing I can be,' he replied.

Saker let his smile die. 'Why have you come here?' he snapped, the muscles across his chest shivering like a plate of eels.

In answer, Tyrfing kicked a piece of iron collar across the floor. It dribbled molten metal as it skittered over the flagstones. 'Why do you think, Saker?'

Saker narrowed his yellow eyes at the iron. His calm and sneering demeanour was slowly peeling away, scale by ash-grey scale. 'I imagine your visit had something to do with daemons falling from the sky, but it seems that you've become distracted by matters that don't concern you. Typical of you Arka.'

Farden took a step forward. Everybody in the hall tensed. Somewhere in the shadows of the nests, bowstrings creaked. He decided to try something a little different. 'How about a trade?' he suggested. Saker tilted his head, intrigued. Farden knew he couldn't help but entertain him. The Lost Clans were nomads. No nomad could refuse a good bargaining.

'I'm listening.'

The mage smiled. 'You don't need an excuse to test me. You know that. We know that. Let's not treat each other like idiots. My offer is this. You give me and my uncle an hour with one of the Sirens' best healers, and we'll leave. Alone. We won't interfere with whatever greedy little empire you're trying to build,' Farden offered, waving his hands at the bound dragons. 'We'll get back in our ship and turn around.'

'That's it? An hour with a healer, and you'll leave,' Saker snapped his fingers, 'like that.'

Farden shrugged. 'We didn't come for them,' he said, glancing back at the five dragons. He could feel sulphurous eyes on him. *In* him. Fellgrin was trying to read his mind. He winced. This was no gentle reading of his thoughts, as Towerdawn had done, but rather a bludgeoning, body-weight slam against his thoughts, a raw scraping against his brain. Farden tried his best to keep her out. 'We have our own problems,' he added.

'Farden!' Tyrfing hissed. The dragons growled. Towerdawn bared his teeth.

'Shut up,' Farden waved his hands at them.

Tyrfing's spells turned a dark shade of orange. The heat they threw off was fierce. Farden almost had to take another step. 'You spineless bastard...' his uncle shook his head.

'I came here for Elessi, not to get stuck in some civil war!' Farden shouted. He turned back to Saker. 'My offer stands. Let us have a healer and we'll be on our way.'

Saker rubbed his scaly chin. Fellgrin lowered her mighty, horn-riddled head to his shoulder. It alighted there as softly as a feather. Saker cocked his head as if to listen to something, and yet all the while, she just kept staring at Farden. The mage could almost feel her razor-claws gouging the inside of his skull. He grit his teeth and tried his hardest to resist, to push back. He thought of betrayal, of lies, of nothing; he dredged up every single memory of his blades falling for the Duke, anything to keep her at bay.

The silence ached around them. After a minute, Farden broke it. 'What do you say, Saker?' he asked. 'Do we have a deal?' Saker lowered his hand to his sword-hilt. Fellgrin lifted her head and let the verdict tumble from between her teeth.

'He lies,' she rumbled.

'Kill them!' bellowed Saker.

Farden felt his ears pop as his uncle's spell enveloped him, diluting the sudden roar of snarling action to a murmuring din. It is in such rare moments that time slows, dripping by with all the haste of treacle. Farden watched, momentarily dumbstruck, as black arrows bounced from the very air in front of him. Ripples spread from where they struck, snapping in two, or spinning to the floor like twigs in a gale. He could feel the heat of his uncle's spells slide past his ear, blinding him as they flew across the hall. Behind him, he could feel the rush of air as Towerdawn tore himself free of the half-molten collar. Beads of orange iron scattered like raindrops. A river of hot fire poured across the floor. Farden watched it all.

'Farden!' the shout shook the mage from his stupor. He hadn't frozen like that in decades.

'You good?' Tyrfing yelled.

'Never better!' Farden grinned. He flourished his sword as a brave clansman ran forward through the flames and smoke, axe raised and howling. Farden strode out to chop him down to size, but before he could even get near, Glassthorn's tail swiped him into the wall. Farden clenched his teeth. He could do nothing more than wave his sword. Fire swirled, keeping the rest at bay.

There was a mighty roar as Towerdawn seized the collar of the big blue male in his jaws and bit down hard. The iron crunched and whined. The blue dragon began to push and buck, slamming his neck against the metal. It took seconds for the iron to crumple, and suddenly the blue was spitting fire of his own. Towerdawn joined him, spewing a fountain of flame at the dragons above. The heat of the fray was terrifying. Tyrfing punched the air and lightning flicked from nest to nest. Over the sound of the cracking and booming, screams could be heard. 'They will kill you, if you stay!' Towerdawn hissed between breaths, fire sputtering around his teeth.

'What about you?' Tyrfing shouted.

Towerdawn shook his head. 'They will keep us as trophies. You need to go, while you still have a choice.'

Tyrfing nodded. It was the truth. 'Farden!' he yelled.

'What?' Farden yelled, still trying to find something to introduce his sword to. The fires were too intense.

'We're leaving!'

'Already? I was just starting to have fun!'

'Get moving, nephew!'

'And Tyrfing?' rumbled the Old Dragon, in the deepest of voices, just as they were turning to run.

The Arkmage turned. 'Yes?'

Head to the library, if you can.

All Tyrfing did was nod.

Masked by the blinding fire and the growing smoke, with the sound of roaring, of flames, of shouting, and of arrows burying themselves in scales ringing in their ears, the two mages fled from the hall.

❦

Farden was first into the wide corridor. It was emptier than a drunk's wineskin, for now at least. As he moved to hug the wall, sword low and ready, he found his uncle's hand on his shoulder. It gripped him hard, and pressed him against the stone. Farden turned to find Tyrfing staring at him with an angry look in his eye.

'Tell me that was just a ruse,' he snapped.

'What?'

'Tell me what you just said in there, about leaving the dragons behind, was a ruse.'

Farden tried to shrug himself free but Tyrfing held fast. His uncle's fingers had the consistency of steel. Farden rolled his eyes. 'You heard Saker's dragon,' he said. It was an answer, but then again it wasn't. It was the best kind.

Tyrfing's grip relaxed. 'I did,' he said, as if reminding himself. Something caught in his throat then and he turned away to cough it out. Farden surreptitiously rubbed his shoulder as he watched his uncle convulse. Farden sighed.

'Are you finished? There's an army of angry dragon-riders behind us.'

Tyrfing wiped his hand on his cloak and took the lead. Threads of light swirled absently around his crooked fingers.

Farden looked back as something crashed and roared behind them. He frowned. 'Where are we going?' He still had to shout over the noise.

'The library!' A memory of trawling through endless piles of useless books came floating back to Farden. He groaned. The words *hopeless* and *mission* scampered through his head in quick succession. 'It's not too far, from what I remember!' Tyrfing yelled, already sprinting down the corridor.

※

Three stairwells, several fiery, bloody encounters, and a score of bodies later, a breathless pair of mages stumbled into the dusty mouth of a corridor that led to the library. It was dark there, too dark for their fire-blinded eyes.

'A little light?' Farden called, and Tyrfing quickly obliged. Rays of white light reached out into the shadows. Farden saw their problem almost immediately. He raised a finger, pointing into the dusty gloom before them. 'Erm...' was all he could say.

Where the ornate doors of a grand library had once stood guard, a wall of grey rubble and boulders had now taken their place. The end of the corridor looked as if the mountain had swallowed it, and then vomited it straight back up. Rock, impenetrable and solid.

Tyrfing rubbed his blood-spattered forehead with the knuckles of his fist. 'Don't say it,' he snarled, eyes closed and deep in thought. 'Don't say anything.'

Farden looked around at the smooth walls that had escaped unscathed and intact. 'This is the right corridor, isn't it?' he asked.

Even as he voiced the question, little features began to ring bells in his memory; the shape of the columns, the low ceiling, even the dragonscript scratchings of some thoughtful stonemason, giving directions, an arrow pointing straight towards the rubble. Farden scratched his head, frustrated. 'Would you like to go back and check with Towerdawn?' he ventured, sourly.

His uncle didn't answer. He was busy racking his brains, and quickly too. The trail of bodies they had left behind was no doubt being followed. They had minutes at most.

Farden stalked up and down the hall, aimlessly prodding bits of loose rubble and wreckage with the tip of his sword. A broken spear lying in a bed of its own splinters. A shoe with a bloody cut across its toe. A shield with a mosaic of dust and dents across its grey face. The cracked blade of a halberd or axe. A stray bit of cloth, burnt to a memory. 'What a mess,' he remarked. 'Cave-in, do you reckon?'

'Has to be.' Tyrfing cracked open an eye and followed the grooves of claws and the scars of spells across the walls. 'Over-zealous wizards, maybe. Now be quiet. I'm trying to think what I might have missed, before we get cornered.'

Farden kicked out maliciously at a cracked stone and watched it bounce off the wall of rubble at the dead end of the corridor. It struck with a thud. A rather hollow thud, come to think of it. Farden raised an eyebrow. Not the sound one expects from stone striking stone. 'What have we here?' he mumbled to himself.

'Shh!' his uncle flapped his hands, muttering to himself about escape routes and riddles.

Farden padded softly to where his stone had skittered to a halt, just at the foot of the rockfall. He peered closely at the rubble, at its nobbled contours, its deep, bloated veins of mica, at the dust that coated it. It certainly looked like rock, but what was rock that didn't sound like rock? Farden raised his sword and prodded one of the boulders with its tip. The blade sung dully as it kissed the rock.

Much to Farden's shock, the boulder twitched under his blade. A bright, flame-orange eye, almost as big as his fist, popped out from the stone, no more than an inch from his sword-tip. It squinted, staring straight up at him. There was an awkward, utterly confused silence.

'Erm...' Farden began, but he wasn't given a chance to finish. With a scraping roar, the entire rockfall unfurled in a whirlwind of dust and crunching stone. Grey limbs flailed. Teeth flashed. Something strong and clawed wrapped around his waist and wrenched him inwards, sucking him into the swirling blur of rock and darkness.

Before he could even think to kick or scream, Farden abruptly found himself face-down on a cold and red-stained floor. He blinked, once, twice, to make sure he was alive. Apparently he was. Farden began to grope for the handle of his sword but his hand found a boot instead. He looked up, head still spinning, to find a muscular Siren staring down at him, a spear-butt raised ready to knock the daylights out of him. The Siren was about to strike when a gruff voice barked out an order. 'Stay your hand!'

Farden was quickly and roughly rolled onto his back. He found himself gazing up at a scarred face. One from a dream, long ago, when Farden had been a different man. The face spoke. 'By Thron. It *is* you.' Hands the size of hams grabbed him by the scruff of his cloak and dragged him into the air. Farden was so bewildered he didn't even struggle. Confusion was to be expected after being swallowed by a wall. Farden blinked owlishly at his saviour.

Eyrum smiled as widely as his freshly-bruised face would allow. The Siren looked a distinct and painful mess. His one good eye was bloodshot, the scar across his bad one knotted and taut with age. There was a blue-green pattern of ugly bruises running down his cheek and neck, the signatures of fists, or boots, or both. A tooth at the corner of his mouth looked decidedly loose. The Lost Clans had clearly had their way with him. Farden wondered absently how many of them it had taken to subdue this giant.

Eyrum gripped the mage's shoulders. 'Gods be blessed. You're alive. And well, by the looks of you. By what Arka magick have you managed to stay so young, mage? Or are you a ghost of a dead man?' he asked.

Farden managed to gather enough of his wits together to form a reply. 'No, I'm perfectly alive, despite the rumours and the best attempts of many,' Farden replied. He tapped his vambraces. 'And no magick the Arka know of.'

Eyrum looked pleased. 'We thought you dead,' he muttered, leaning closer, as if it were an admission he didn't feel happy making.

Farden patted his thick arm. 'Apparently it's not that easy,' he said, and cracked a smile to ward off any more questions. 'Where's my uncle?'

There was a sudden and familiar scraping noise, and Eyrum pointed to something behind him. The mage looked around just in time to see the rockfall spit his uncle out onto the floor. The Arkmage landed hard on his chest, air driven out of him, face scrunched up into the very picture of confoundedness.

Farden watched as the strange pile of boulders revealed its true form: a long, lithe dragon that had coiled itself into an impossible shape, and wedged itself in the door. He watched the beast unfurl and stretch, its colouring changing from the stony-grey to a deep, charcoal black. It blinked its orange eyes and raised a claw to the visitors. 'Well met, and good wishes,' hissed the dragon, from behind needle-like teeth. 'Shivertread, at your service.' He looked between the two mages. 'I believe you knew my mother, Havenhigh?'

'We did,' answered Farden, nodding slowly. He could see the family resemblance now, especially in the barbels hanging from the dragon's jawline, as though he were part-carp. He was lithe too, like his mother, and he had her colouring. He was young though, little more than a wyrm.

Behind them. Eyrum let out a long sigh. 'Too young,' he

rumbled. There was a muttering of sadness through the crowd of soldiers behind them. 'Killed by the Clan.'

'And they are paying for it, pint by pint,' Shivertread eyed the floor at Farden's feet, which was a dubious shade of reddish-brown.

'Not fast enough for my liking.'

The black dragon turned his head, tasting the air with his long grey tongue. They could hear distant voices shouting. 'More are coming.'

Eyrum curled his bloodied lip. 'Keep them at their guessing, Shiver, while we have guests. Blood can be spilt later.'

The dragon tapped his fangs together. His breath rattled in his throat, but he knew Eyrum was right. 'Fine,' he said, before quickly resuming his position. The dragon slipped in between the archway of the door and curled his tail and limbs about him. As he rolled himself into a tight, and dangerous, little ball, scales scraping on the stone, his wings pressed outwards to wedge him against the walls. Once he was in place, his scales began to fade through the spectrum of blacks into a dirty, dusty grey that perfectly matched the stone around him.

'Why have I never seen a dragon do that before?' asked Tyrfing. He stared hard at the pile of rocks in the doorway, trying to identify the component parts of a dragon. He was having a tough time doing so.

Eyrum shrugged. 'Shivertread seems to be the first. Do not even ask me how he does it. Not even his mother knew,' he said.

'They say his egg used to change colour too,' mumbled one of the nearby soldiers.

'That it did,' Eyrum hummed. 'But that's a story for another day. Come, mages, let me introduce you to our new abode.'

The old library had been transformed into a fortress. A fortress of books and dusty shelves but a fortress nonetheless. With Shivertread acting as guard and gate, the countless books and tomes of the library had been piled into extensive barricades and makeshift walls. There were even arrow slits in the thicker ones. The stout oak bookshelves had been gently toppled over to make secondary defences and rough barracks for the soldiers and riders. Farden counted them in his head. A paltry three dozen of them at most, with possibly more under the bookshelves or hidden deeper in the dark, cavernous room. It was hard to see in the gloom.

There were others there too, in the dusty shadows, shuffling to and fro, or standing stoic and sombre. Farden could hear the crying of little children being hushed and soothed. A few elderly women were absently flicking through a pile of works, sharing words with wizards. One man standing close by looked like a farmer. He was still holding a pitchfork. Sirens of all sorts, not just riders or soldiers. The lucky and the leftovers.

'Is this all that's left?' asked Tyrfing.

'All that we could gather. We haven't left this room in three weeks,' Eyrum sighed, and began to lead them a rather un-merry path through the twists and turns of the barricades.

'What about food?'

'Dwindling.'

'Arms?' This from Farden, as he sniffed the air. It felt close, still, and stale.

'What we carry. A few spare staves made from bookshelves. We've been trying to make arrows but it's slow going. Square wood does not fly straight, as our resident fletcher says.'

Farden stopped to stare at a group of wizards. There were four of them sitting in a square, tucked away behind a toppled desk, illuminated by sagging candles. Two had their eyes open, though just barely, while the other two had theirs closed, scrunched up in deep concentration. Even at that short distance, Farden could see the veins standing like cords on their necks and foreheads. Tyrfing came to stand at his side. 'Feel it?' he asked his nephew. 'Their magick?'

Farden shook his head. All he felt was tired. He took a few

steps towards them.

'I would not interrupt them, Farden,' Eyrum warned. Farden waved a hand, but kept on walking, drawing wary stares from the two resting wizards and the nearby soldiers.

There were open books lying in the wizards' laps. Their pages glistened with sweat in the candlelight, their edges thumbed with grime. Farden bowed to them, and the two wizards politely returned his gesture with a pair of nods. Farden moved to the large window behind them. The glass had been blackened with soot and covered with rags to keep up the ruse of a cave-in. Farden knelt down to rub a miniscule section of the soot away with his little finger, making a little window for himself. All he could see was swirling grey.

Tyrfing broke the silence 'So these are the fog-brewers Saker was talking about,' he muttered.

'A week solid, they have been casting. Keeps the Clan confused and got our ships away safe to Talen. There are eight wizards in total. They take it in turns.'

Farden couldn't help but whistle. 'I imagine they do,' he said.

'Farden?' Tyrfing cleared his throat. Farden turned and saw his uncle pointing to a sorry-looking group of people further into the library. They were huddled around a single whale-oil lantern. Each one of them sported a bloody bandage of some kind. Heads, fingers, arms, legs, ribs, ears… each had something. A single wizened old man was edging around their circle, doing the best he could.

'A healer,' Farden said, quickly getting to his feet.

Eyrum frowned. 'Are you hurt, mage?'

'Not me,' Farden shook his head. 'Elessi.'

Eyrum followed them with a quizzical look on his face.

Farden marched up to the old healer and put his hand on his arm as gently as his urgency would allow. The old Siren was still startled nonetheless. 'Old man,' Farden leant close. 'I need your help.'

The Siren looked him up and down. There was dust in his

wiry black beard. Flecks of blood sat on the shoulder of his robe. 'I am sure you do, son, but so do these others. I am afraid you will have to get in line,' he said, his voice a cracked rattle of parchment. He went to move on but the mage held him back, shaking his head.

'No, no, I don't need your bandages, I need your advice. Your knowledge. My friend in Krauslung has been attacked…' he paused here, suddenly very aware of the number of ears around him, '…by a daemon. Now she refuses to wake up and our Arka healers are clueless. They've never seen such a wound before. I need to know how to help her and I am hoping that you Sirens have the answers.'

A few of those in earshot began to snigger and nudge each other. Daemons, how preposterous! Even Eyrum had to grimace at their mention. Tyrfing glared at each of them in turn.

The old healer's lips quivered as he fought not to smile. He looked around. 'It is kind of you to try to stir up some humour in such a dark situation, Arka, but unfortunately you're wasting my time,' he said.

'And you're wasting mine, old man. I am deadly serious.' Farden held him a little tighter. He stared deep into his scale-rimmed eyes, as though trying to physically push the truth into the healer's face. The healer's smile gradually faded into a grimace.

Tyrfing piped up. 'He is indeed,' he said, turning to Eyrum. 'Vice's legacy. *Her.*'

'So it's true?' Eyrum asked, still unconvinced. The Arkmage nodded soberly. 'Well, she picked a fine time to rear her head.'

'She has her father's timing,' Farden muttered over his shoulder. He turned back to the healer. 'The Old Dragon told me that to be daemontouched is to know death. I want you to tell me he's wrong.'

The healer squinted. 'Are you sure it was a daemon, son?'

Farden was growing very tired very quickly. 'Trust me, old man, an entire city watched three of them fall from the sky,' he urged.

He turned around to look at Eyrum and his men. 'Why is this so hard to believe? You're Sirens. Some of you must have been with us when we fought the hydra.'

A rider by Eyrum's side spoke up. 'I was. But that was different. That came from the other side. Daemons, they're…' he made a jab towards the ceiling with his finger.

Farden blew an exasperated sigh. He turned back to the healer. 'Can you help my friend or not?'

The healer's face twitched as he thought. He was very aware of the iron look in this mage's eyes, and of the tight grip he had on his thin arm. It took him several moments before he was able to shake his head. 'There is no cure for those who are daemontouched. I'm sorry.'

'Then where are your colleagues?' he demanded. The old man made a limp gesture to the back of the room.

'They will say the same.'

Farden was already striding across the library. 'We'll see!'

'Farden!' Eyrum and Tyrfing called after the mage, but he was already interrogating another healer, this time a sharp-nosed, middle-aged woman in a smart, but blood-smeared, tunic. She was already shaking her head by the time the others caught up. Farden's hands were slowly curling into fists.

'I heard you with Insillir and I will tell you the same. There is no cure, mage,' the healer was saying.

'You Sirens are supposed to be the finest healers in Emaneska,' Farden snapped. He kicked a nearby wall of books. 'You have more history at your scaly fingertips than Arfell can dream of, more knowledge, more experience, and you're telling me there's no cure?'

The healer crossed her arms. Her face was stony. 'That is exactly what I am saying. No amount of shouting or kicking will change that. I have sick people here, give them some peace and quiet, man.'

'Ridiculous!' Farden began to tear the books from the top of the makeshift wall. Book by book he ripped through it, glancing at titles as he dug. 'You're telling me that all this is useless?'

'Farden!' Tyrfing barked. Farden ignored him. He wheeled on Eyrum instead. 'Do the wizards know anything about daemons? Anything? What about the dragons?'

'FARDEN!' yelled Tyrfing. The library went deathly quiet save for the muttering of the wizards in the corner. Farden looked as if he would explode into flame at any moment. He quivered with anger. Everybody was staring at him. They were slowly shaking their heads.

'I refuse to believe that there's no hope,' Farden growled. 'There has to be something...' His boots squeaked as he turned on his heels and made for the very depths of the cavernous library. A few soldiers made half-hearted attempts to stop him but he shrugged them aside. Tyrfing rubbed his forehead.

'You know where he's going, don't you?' asked the big Siren.

'Mhm,' hummed Tyrfing.

'And can he read dragonscript?'

'Not unless he learnt it in Albion.'

'Albion? So that was where he was?'

The Arkmage sighed. 'It's a long story, my friend.'

'We have to go after him.'

'Mhm.'

They found Farden exactly where they knew he'd be: in a dark and dusty corridor at the back of the library, hidden by a narrow arch and some equally dusty steps. Farden had snatched a lantern from somewhere. He was busy scouring the hallway's thick oak shelves, staring at the gnarled spines of the countless tearbooks that lined them. They filled the shelves like forgotten jewels, stacked side by side. Every one of them sparkled in the light. Sapphire blues rubbed shoulders with dun coppers and flame-reds. Dusty emerald tones squeezed in between jet, quartz, and rare pyrite. Farden glared at each and every one of them, as if they holding secrets and refusing to divulge them. Farden reached up to grab a particularly thick one, but Eyrum stamped his boot loudly.

'Keep your hands to yourself, mage. This hallway is a graveyard to us. Only our scholars can touch the books.'

Farden's fingers stopped dead in their tracks. They clawed at the dusty air, frustrated. 'What of Farfallen's? Surely that…'

Eyrum held up a hand to interrupt him. 'They gleaned whatever they could from that tome long ago, Farden. If there was a cure, they would know. Stop torturing yourself with hope.'

Farden slammed his hand against the butt end of a shelf. The solid bookcase didn't even rattle. 'I promised him,' he hissed. 'I looked right into his eyes and *promised him.*' He winced as a dull pain spread across his chest.

'Modren will forgive you,' Tyrfing offered. It was all he could say. His eyes wandered over the tearbooks, wondering, like his nephew, whether there was a secret hidden in their pages. He didn't show it, but he too had a pain in his chest.

'How can you be so calm about this? So accepting? It's Elessi we're talking about,' Farden scowled.

'Futility, nephew. I don't like this any more than you do.'

'You don't sound too concerned.'

'You heard Towerdawn in the great hall, Farden. To be poisoned by a daemon is a death sentence. There is no cure for death. Elessi is slipping over to the other side, and we're powerless to stop her.'

Farden scrunched up his eyes as he listened to his uncle's words. He put his head against the oaken shelf and wrapped his hands around the back of his neck. Failure lapped at his mind like a hungry sea at a shoreline. All he could see when he shut his eyes was Modren's face, and the look that had passed between them in that marble corridor. All he could see was Elessi cleaning his wounds the day that he had come back from Carn Breagh, the way she had dabbed and prodded with her cloths. The mage let his forehead roll back and forth across the wood. He knew the others were watching. They kept silent out of respect.

When he finally stood straight again, the mage didn't know what to say. He raised his eyes to the ceiling and let his hands slide across his neck, as if he were about to strangle himself...

Farden froze. His fingers pressed against the knot of a scar running around his weathered neck, probing, poking, remembering. Of cold waters and pebbles, of a fingernail ship and a screaming figurehead. Of the pushing, always the pushing. The mage shook his head. 'No,' he said. The word was a pebble being dropped on the flagstones.

'No?'

Farden wagged a finger. 'No,' he repeated.

'No *what*?' asked Eyrum.

'There's still hope.'

Tyrfing was on the verge of throttling his nephew. He was more stubborn than he remembered. He didn't think it possible. 'Farden, just let it go.'

'No. You're wrong. Wrong about curing death.'

Tyrfing tried to stay calm. He threw up his hands. 'Please, enlighten us. What do you know that we don't?'

Farden had begun to smile like a madman. 'The truth. You *can* come back from the other side. Believe me.'

'And how can you possibly know that?'

'Because, uncle,' Farden took a breath, 'I think I've done it.'

Tyrfing was about to reply when he saw the look in his nephew's eyes. Despite his smile, his pupils were like flint. Serious. Unflinching. There was a hardness in them that only truth can buy. Farden brought his face very close to his uncle's. So close he could feel the heat of his breath on his cheek. So close they almost touched noses. 'I can bring her back.'

Before Tyrfing could even absorb Farden's words, he was off, jogging down the corridor, his boots throwing up little puff-clouds of dust. 'Where is he going now?' The Arkmage strangled the air.

'I dread to think,' Eyrum grumbled, utterly bemused. 'But I think it's best to follow.'

The hallway curved and wandered deeper into the mountain and its gloom. They followed the shine of Farden's lantern as it bobbed along ahead, splashing urgent shadows across the bookshelves. They flanked them like the walls of a glittering canyon, caught in the mist of floating dust motes and abandonment. There was a reverence to the hallway's state, like a graveyard, as Eyrum had said. Except here, the gravestones were memories and the tomes that held them close.

Farden had found the end of the corridor. He was in the middle of trying to hang the lantern's handle on the wrist of a marble statue of an angry-looking Thron. Eyrum grunted with displeasure at the sight of the mage's lack of deference. A statue it may have been, but it was still his god. Farden left the lantern dangling from one of Thron's muscled arms and turned his attention to an ornate pedestal that rose out of the dust. Tyrfing stood by Farden's side and stared at the giant tome that rested upon it, open and blank.

Eyrum did not look happy to be there. 'What do you know of the *S'grummvold*?' he asked gruffly.

Farden spread his hands over the pages, his fingers leaving tracks in the dust. 'The Grimsayer?' he asked, remembering its name. *How could he have forgotten this was here?* 'That it shows you dead things.'

Eyrum muttered something dark and disgruntled. He stood like a wall behind them, arms crossed and bruised face unsure.

'What are you trying to do, Farden?' asked Tyrfing.

'I'm trying to find Elessi.'

'If I remember rightly, she's in Krauslung.'

'Her body may be, but we know the rest of her is slipping to the other side. Call it her ghost, her soul, whatever. I will find out with this. If its not too late, I can find it and bring her back...'

'*How* exactly, Farden?'

'I don't know yet. I've got an idea,' Farden couldn't help but swallow at that thought. 'Hopefully I'm wrong about that.'

'So, what? You're going to drag her... her *soul* back from the other side by the scruff of its neck, back to her body?'

Farden flashed him a grin that many might have assessed as maniacal. Underneath that grin, the same clarity he had felt in Krauslung enveloped him. Clarity so crystal he felt as if he moved too fast something would snap. It made perfect sense. 'If that's what it takes, then that's exactly what I'm going to do.'

'By Thron. Shiver must have thrown you on the floor harder than we thought,' Eyrum groaned.

Tyrfing was beside himself. 'Can you even hear the words coming from your mouth?' he gasped. Farden was far from listening. He was leaning over the book now, squinting at the blankness of its pages.

'Show me anyone,' he whispered to it. For a long moment, nothing happened. Farden bit his lip. Tyrfing moved to grab his nephew by the collar and drag him bodily back to the library, back to sense and reality, but to his surprise, it was Eyrum that stopped him. The big Siren caught the Arkmage's hand and silently shook his head. It was then that the Grimsayer began to glow.

Two lights, like little orange fireflies, slid from the depths of the tome's spine and floated into the air. Their tails were like threads of flame, weaving shapes and patterns behind them. They were brighter than Farden remembered, bigger too. He passed his hand gently through them and watched them roll and frolic. 'Show me anybody,' he repeated.

The pages slapped his hand as they flew past. They stopped as abruptly as they had begun, and soon enough the twin lights were weaving a figure as tall as a man's hand, directly over the centre of the book's spine. The figure was a tree troll of some sort, with arms and legs of broken branches and pine brush. Moss trailed from its head and arms like rags. It looked fearsome, yet sad. Dead.

'When I first found this book, I asked for Durnus. In fact, I asked for Ruin, and the book couldn't give me a straight answer at the time,' Farden said. Something whispered in the darkness as he talked. Only he seemed to notice.

'Farden is right. The Grimsayer will only show the ghosts of those who have passed to the other side, those who have left this mortal world. Dragons, Sirens, Arka, daemons, beasts… they are all kept within these pages. Everything that has ever died and will come to die.'

Tyrfing wore a stern face. 'You Sirens have kept very quiet about this,' he said.

'It is not a power that one should brag about.'

Farden was talking to the book again. 'Show me Elessi.'

The book replied with a flick of pages. Entire sections as thick as thumbs turned themselves over in great big flaps and thuds. The book was nearing its end when it suddenly stopped. The lights began to weave, though this time they were uncertain of themselves. They would take it in turns to stutter and flash, scrawling a lock of curled hair here, the angle of an elbow there. The onlookers squinted and peered as each feature became apparent. Even though the image never seemed to quite reach completion, and despite it flickering like a wind-harried candle, it was easy to see that it was Elessi. She looked serene and calm. The lights flicked back and forth, constantly adjusting her feet.

'She's walking,' Farden muttered, realising what the lights were doing.

It was easy to see that despite his frustration, Tyrfing was spellbound. 'Walking where?'

The Grimsayer answered with a muttering heave and then a solid bang as the entire weight of the book slammed on Elessi's head and fell open at its very first page. Even before the dust had cleared, the lights quickly went to work, drawing their subject. This time it was not a creature, not a person, but thin spires of rock arranged in little crowns and circles of five or four. They reared up from the page like the spines along a dragon's back. There were nine clusters of them altogether, spread haphazardly across the page. Some lay broken and smashed, while others were wrapped in moss and upended. Only three seemed perfect. A memory tugged at Farden. He couldn't quite pin it down.

'What are they?' asked Eyrum.

'I feel I should know, but I don't,' Farden replied. The Grimsayer rustled its pages. It was a very disturbing sound.

'Gates to the other side perhaps. Like elf wells,' Tyrfing suggested.

'Maybe. Whatever they are, Elessi is going towards one.'

'Well, perhaps this book can enlighten us on where the nearest one is,' Tyrfing thought aloud. He prodded one of the brighter clusters of stone with a finger. 'One like this.'

Eyrum sighed. 'The Grimsayer does not wor...' he began, but his words failed him. The Grimsayer apparently had other ideas. The lights began to zip and flutter across the page, drawing a mountain, their mountain, then a shoreline running and flying southwest, almost faster than their eyes could follow. They saw the fortress of Ragjarak, then icebergs and the mountainous waves that crashed against them. Soon the lights were drawing flat, sweeping lines of blank ice fields and bold hills, frozen waterfalls and trees trapped in an armour of snow. As the lights began to trace the jagged lines of foothills and colossal mountain crags, they stopped. While one kept the scenery at bay, the other flit about almost lazily, as if tired, sketching a ring of five thin monoliths.

Farden turned around to look at the big Siren. 'Apparently it does.'

'Eyrum!' a shout barrelled down the hallway. It was swiftly accompanied by a dull boom. 'We've company!'

'Blast it all!' Eyrum snarled, before sprinting back up the corridor.

Tyrfing was already running after him. 'Come on, Farden! We'll be needed.'

Farden nodded and instinctively checked his armour. His fingers grasped his vambraces and he froze. 'I'll be right behind you!' he lied, turning back to spread his hands over the Grimsayer's first page instead. He licked his lips. 'Show me the ninth,' he whispered to the lights. 'Show me the last knight.' The lights hesitated, unsure of what to do. 'Show me the ninth Scalussen knight! Come on, show me where he is.' Farden tapped the pages eagerly as the lights momentarily shivered, but it was just that; a teasing little flutter. They swam back and forth in a slow figure-of-eight. Farden could imagine the little things shrugging at him.

'Farden!' shouted his uncle.

'Agh,' Farden grunted, unable to tear himself away.

'Move!'

'I'm coming!'

There are moments in a person's life where the mind experiences an extraordinary moment of thoughtlessness, of pure action, as if the clouds have opened and the sunlight has poured in. For that brief moment, muscles are given the freedom to do what they do best, to move, and the mind can only sit back and watch. Ethics, morals, judgement, they are all barged aside as undiluted instinct comes sprinting through. This was one of those moments for Farden.

The mage slammed the Grimsayer shut and drove his arms

under its scaly cover. He could feel his back twinge in protest as he heaved, but he ignored it. There was a crackle as the book was forced to face its own weight. Farden begged for it not to disintegrate. He pulled it tight to his chest, arms out flat, and waddled backwards. *Heavy* was not a word that did the big tome justice. Even with his elbows at his ribs the book still nudged his throat.

'What in gods' name are you possibly doing now?!' Tyrfing bellowed, seeing the shape of the silhouette running towards him.

Farden barged past, toting Grimsayer and all. 'Who knew a book of ghosts could weigh this much!' he yelled as he passed. The Arkmage was flabbergasted at the sheer audacity of it all. He slapped a nearby bookshelf with rage.

'*How* are we possibly related?' he shouted in utter despair.

Farden had already disappeared behind a winding corner, but his retort came back just fine. 'I've been asking myself that for years!'

part two
of ghostgates

Dead Stars - Part 2

Chapter 10

"The Scribe is a curious man. Suspiciously old in my mind. Longevity comes at a cost, so they say, and I see no cost to him, save for the burden of torturing our hopeful mages with his needles, and I would hazard a guess that he enjoys that. Some whisper that he drinks daemon-blood, that that's what keeps him alive, like in the old eddas and tales. Rubbish, I say, preposterous. Daemon-blood doesn't exist. You'd have to find a daemon first..."
Excerpt from Arkmage Helyard's diary, found after his death in 889

'Two sixes. One blade.'

Roiks lifted his hand to smite the table in outrage, a long drawn out *F* sound hovering on his lips. 'Fffffff...' he began, but the female company changed his mind, '...fffbloody hell, woman. How do ye do it?'

'Luck?' Lerel chuckled.

Roiks scowled. 'Tricks, I say. Magick and the like. I 'eard about you and that Arkmage.'

'A bitter loser, Roiks, as always,' Lerel winked. A veritable hill of wooden coins, all painted different pastel hues, sat in front of her. Around it her winning card hands were spread, fanned out, each a little trophy, so the conquered Roiks and Loki could count how many times they had been so coldly and swiftly trounced.

'What about you, sir?' Roiks nodded deferentially to the

hunched-over god sitting on the opposite side of the little table. He had no idea what Loki truly was. To him, he was simply an important guest aboard the *'Blade*. Renowned scholar. Perhaps the exploring type. Foreign diplomat maybe. He certainly looked foreign. He smelled it too. If there was one part of his body Roiks was said to be glowingly proud of, it was his long and crooked nose. The crew said he could sniff out land at a hundred miles. It was the prime reason behind his nickname: "Sharknose," an epithet Roiks was not entirely opposed to.

This Loki smelled of dust and earth, like road mud on old leather boots. He smelled like the cargo holds of the Paraian merchant dhows they sometimes traded with, of resinous wood that'd spent a decade or more soaking up the scent of spices and spilt oils. Foreign to the core.

Loki had his hands and dog-eared cards deep in his lap, below the table. He stared at them with narrowed eyes, silently calculating their worth and his chances. This was another new thing to him; cards and gambling, and he had quietly admitted to himself on the third round that he liked both intensely. Even though they gambled with humble wooden chips, Loki found the whole experience quite exciting. It suited his curious, cunning mind, tested his new-found intrigue of reading the expressions of humans. Gods were not used to such things, of course. They did not play games. They did not gamble. What treasures or currency could they have possibly wagered with, up in the darkness of the sky? All that gods have is time. Nobody likes gambling with time.

Loki shuffled in his seat. He hummed for a moment, as if thinking, and then brought his hand onto the table. He flicked a look at Lerel as he did it; the woman had won nine straight rounds already. 'Two sixes and a black mule,' he confessed.

Roiks thumped the table again.

With a wide grin, Lerel began to drag the rest of the wooden coins towards her mountain, looking very pleased with herself indeed. 'I should start playing for real money.'

'Gods, woman. You sure you ain't a cheat?' Roiks demanded in mock horror.

'Bosun Roiks,' replied Lerel, mimicking his expression, 'dare you to accuse a superior officer of cheating?'

'No ma'am! But I will ask a question. How'd you get so good?'

Lerel shrugged. 'Practice,' she said. It was an honest answer as any. She'd grown up on the dusty streets of Paraia. Cards could earn a clever girl a pretty coin. And coin meant food.

Loki had been shuffling around in his chair, as if he was sitting on a splinter. He readjusted his cloak and tapped the table. 'Another round.'

Roiks chuckled. 'You want to take another round of embarrassment?'

Loki looked to Lerel, who was busy relishing the thought. 'Perhaps beginner's luck takes a while to warm up?' he suggested, tapping the table again. Lerel began to push his pile of coins back into the centre.

Roiks sighed. 'Then I'm glad we ain't playin' fer real coin.'

The first round went to Lerel, as expected. When the second went to Loki, the others simply assumed it was an accident on her part, sympathy maybe. The third wiped Roiks from the game. He pushed all his chips to the centre after slyly glimpsing Lerel's hand. He put so much of his coin into beating her that he completely forgot about Loki, who trounced both of them with a solid three blades.

Fourth, fifth, and sixth also went to Loki. Then a seventh. Lerel did her best to win the eighth, but Loki soon had the ninth too. Each time, his cards were near-perfect. Roiks, sitting back on his chair with his arms neatly folded under each dubiously-smelling armpit, eyed the game with hawk's eyes. 'Beginner's luck, eh?' he asked of

Loki, as Lerel sniffed. The god was still hunched over the table, hands in his lap.

'Must be,' Loki flashed a white smile.

Roiks squinted. 'Might I ask, sir, what land it is ye hail from?'

'You may,' replied Loki, buying time to think. 'Albion.'

'Ah,' mused Roiks. 'Couldn't tell from the accent, see. I'd of said Hâlorn, sir. Like your dark-eyed friend. The one that's taken a likin' to our crow's nest.'

Loki nodded as his cards were dealt. He swiped them from the table and cradled them in his lap.

Roiks leant forward and jabbed the tabletop with his pointy elbows. He flashed a glance at Lerel, who was busy squinting at her cards. Loki had already placed his cards back on the table when he looked back. Roiks eyed them carefully, noting the lack of dog-ears and scratches. They looked pristine, in fact, not like a deck that had been shared round a ship's crew once or twice. A sailor's fingers weren't the kindest to cards. 'What've ye got, Lerel?' Roiks asked.

Lerel took a moment to hum and whisper to herself. She swapped one of her cards out, and smirked, rather unintentionally. She flipped her cards over. 'One eight. Two bloody crowns.'

'A fine hand!' Roiks slapped Lerel heartily on the shoulder, almost ploughing her head into the table. 'One that's mighty hard t' beat, if'n you ask me,' he added, flicking a look at the god.

'That it is,' Loki muttered.

'Man's got to have something downright special in his hands to beat that. Suspiciously special,' Roiks grinned.

Loki palmed his cards and checked them again, just to be sure. He kept them right there on the table, so Roiks could see for himself that there was no foul play. 'And might I enquire why you asked after my origins?'

Roiks winked at Lerel. 'Some folk tell of a land where no man ever cheats. They don't know how, see? No man lies, and no man cheats.'

'Sounds perfect, Bosun,' said Loki, crossing his arms, 'but a little fictional.'

'That it does.'

'And what would be the name of such a place?' asked the god.

Roiks raised an eyebrow. 'I forgot a long time ago. Shame, really. But I know it ain't called Albion, and it ain't called Hâlorn. Plenty of cheats come from there.'

'Is that so?' asked Loki.

'Aye,' Roiks replied. 'That they do.'

Loki snorted. He turned his cards over with a careless flick. It was a pitiful hand: one three and a pair of green cudgels. 'Well, if you know one, Bosun Roiks, then perhaps you could point him in my direction, so that he could teach me. G... men like me don't know how to cheat,' he said, staring the sailor right in the eye. Even as he spoke, he was sliding a pack of cards from his lap and back into the pocket he had fished them from. Cards identical to the ones they were playing with... if a little less dog-eared.

Roiks eyed the god for a few seconds, and then burst out laughing. 'Beginner's luck it is then,' he brayed, slapping the table and making Lerel's coins jump. Roiks reached deep into his breast pocket and brought forth a chubby cube of metal. It was a die. Each of its six faces was puckered with red spots. He pinched it between finger and thumb and held it up for all to see. 'Now I was born at sea, and there are plenty of cheats out here for the playin',' he said, as though he were speaking to the die itself. He rolled it towards Lerel. It clattered across the wood and then landed on a six with a clunk. 'Always lands a six. A loaded die it is. A mage put a charm in it for me many years ago. Treated me well in many a tavern and through many a late night I'll tell ye that fer free. My lucky die.'

Loki was about to ask how magick made something lucky when something caught his eye. Something fluttering outside the window of their cabin, something dark against the grey that still clung to the ship. 'Hawk!' he cried.

And a hawk it was. The poor thing was scrabbling madly at the spray-stained glass. A Siren hawk. It had a bell on one foot and a tiny scroll tied to the other. Roiks rushed to open the window for it and it flapped its way in. With a keen screech it circled the room once and then flapped onto the table, tapping its claws on Lerel's pile of wooden coins. Roiks wriggled the tiny scroll free from its leg. Its job now done, the hawk began to preen.

Roiks read half-mumbled, half-aloud. Loki and Lerel caught little snatches of the message. '...trouble... fighting way out... main harbour... south and 'round the... mists lifting... bloody hell...'

Loki cocked his head to one side. 'Is that part of the message?'

Roiks tossed the scroll onto the table. He made for the door. 'Think it should've been, sir. This needs to go to Nuka *now*,' Roiks rattled off a reply. He was already halfway gone by the time he finished. The door slammed with a thud.

Loki reached for the scroll and read it quickly for himself:

SIRENS IN TROUBLE. LOST CLANS TAKEN OVER. FIGHTING WAY OUT. ESCAPING NORTH TO MAIN HARBOUR. MEET US THERE. BE READY TO FIGHT YOUR WAY SOUTH AND AROUND THE HEADLAND TO GO NORTH. BE QUICK. MISTS WILL BE LIFTING VERY SOON.

'Hmm,' was all Loki could say.

'What is it?' asked Lerel, already on her feet, eyes wide.

Loki went to stand at the open window. He ducked his head so he could look at the sky. The mists were already fading. The high sun, now a bright patch in the heavens rather than a lost rumour, was busy burning them away. The sounds of waves slapping the shore and the mewing of frightened gulls grew louder by the minute. Loki craned his neck even further. It might have been a trick of the paling mists, but there were great shadows circling above, dark and dangerous.

'Looks like we're going north,' said Loki, nonchalant as could be.

ॐ

Books and fire make truly ugly partners. Theirs is a brief relationship. Passionate, true, but in the way that a fight or a battle is passionate. A whirlwind romance, as destructive as both, like the hot chaos wrought by a wife discovering a cheating husband. They should be kept wholeheartedly apart, for the better of themselves and the bystander.

But sometimes, romances such as this cannot be avoided.

With a roar that was pinched into a scream, Shivertread burst from the door-frame in a cartwheel of fire and flailing wings. A cloud of flame and smoke chased him as he barrelled into an overturned bookshelf. The solid oak shattered like brittle glass. The dragon writhed in the wreckage as men and soldiers scattered. Books and splinters flew in all directions, falling prey to the pools of fire that had flooded the entrance of the library.

They had been found.

Clansmen poured through the door like rats squirming through a hole in a sinking ship. They brandished shields, spears, and burning torches. They chanted as they charged forward to tackle the ranks of Sirens, chanting words of hate and fear in their own private tongue, in their own fearsome rhythm. A dragon marched behind them, plodding forward in a way that didn't speak of laziness, nor ponderousness, but of sheer size and muscle. It had barely managed to squeeze its wings into the corridor. Fire poured from its grinning jaws as it spewed a jet of scorching flame into the library. It spread across the ceiling like a second lick of paint; first yellow, then black and sooty as it died. The air became thick and tough as the fire consumed what it could. Screams and yells from the people joined the clatter of feet and the roar of battle. The library was suddenly a living, writhing thing, caught in the throes of panic.

Eyrum was suddenly in the middle of it all, dashing through the labyrinthine defences they had spent weeks fortifying. Half of it now smouldered. The clansmen were tossing their torches as far into the library as they could. It was disastrous. Nothing encouraged a lick of flame like piles of books whose business it had been to keep as dry as possible for the last thousand years.

'Form up! Arrows! Wizards! Dragons!' Eyrum barked orders like a rabid dog as he sprinted in a zigzag towards the entrance. He swiped aside a flaming torch as it flew at him. He batted it to the floor and stamped it to death. 'Get some water on these books!'

There was a sudden collective hiss as scores of jugs and tankards doused the defences. It was followed swiftly by a clash of metal as the advancing clansmen collided with the spears of the Sirens. Shivertread was in the middle of it all, spinning around like a crazed beast, full of claws and teeth.

Eyrum could already see the outcome of this bout. Barely three seconds at the front line and it was already painfully obvious. He could feel it in the furious movements of his men, the jab and twitch of desperation. He could feel it in the heat burning his skin. Hear it in the crackling of the books and pounding of feet. The enemy was flooding in faster than they could hold them. It was becoming bloody and vicious around the doorway. The clansmen were pinched between fierce opposition from the front and eager comrades pushing in from behind. As men fell dead or trampled, some actually began to climb the grotesque pile of the fallen so that they could leap the defences and break through.

Eyrum grit his teeth and ran one of them through with his

spear. He yanked his spear out of the man's chest with a squelch and a scream and snarled. He hadn't had the time to fetch his infamous axe. What he wouldn't have given...

'Fall back to the second line!' he yelled, and heard his order echoing through his men. The wizards unleashed a barrage of light and ice to keep the clansmen at bay while the soldiers retreated. Thin, slender women darted to and fro with knives, casting spells that flashed with blue and green light. Screams followed them as they poured through a gap in the book-walls. Witches. In the smoke and steam, their little finches could be seen flitting about, pecking at anything they could find.

'Forward in the centre!' came an eager shout from one of the sergeants. Eyrum cursed and was about to countermand it when there came a sound of cracking whips, of panicked cries and yelling. Great orbs of light began to detonate with light and fire between the shelves.

An Arkmage had come to the rescue.

Eyrum dashed to the centre of their retreating line, dragging men with him as they ran. Together they formed up behind Tyrfing as he waded into the fray. He shimmered with light and blue fire. There were two wizards now at his side. One had an arrow through his neck, but he staunchly ignored it. They were holding books at arm's length and repeatedly slamming them shut. They closed with thunderclaps and bursts of lightning.

It was a brave display, but in the end, there were simply too many.

The invaders ferreted out the weaknesses in the defences and managed to pincer the centre of the library. They struck at the rear, where the dragons had been left to fight. Fire bloomed in the smoky gloom. A great wail echoed through the library as a dragon roared. There is a certain roar that only a dragon in a certain situation can make. It is not pleasant. It comes with nails in the heart. The Sirens fought like the possessed when they heard it, and for a moment the tide was turned again.

Farden stood on the right flank. His foot was firmly pinning the Grimsayer to the floor, and he battled with the best of them. His sword was blooded three times over, and he had to resort to a two-handed grip to keep it from slipping. He hacked and parried, slashed and sliced as the clansmen kept coming. While his uncle summoned whirlwinds, Farden was one himself. He stabbed at throats and slit arteries, scored bones and severed limbs. Screams and blood bathed him. A line of dead people queued at his feet.

Tyrfing and Eyrum were soon driven to his side. The centre had been lost, and they were now falling back into the very depths of the library. The lines of battle had been scattered and smashed to pieces; the fighting was anywhere and everywhere, and by the gods it was brutal. There was one sliver of mercy, however, and that was the fact that the entrance the library was now fully aflame. Fire had consumed the walls and lines of books and shelves, and in a kindness, had created a wall of defence against any reinforcements.

'We need to get out of here!' Farden shouted, in a brief lull in the tumult, one of those awkward moment in battle where one notices amongst the roar the groaning of the half-dead, the sluggish crawling of the wounded, and slow drip, drip, drip of blood. The moment where the smell hits, and lingers. It is in these moments that horror treads.

But these men were veterans. They shrugged it aside like ash on the shoulder.

'That we do!' shouted Tyrfing.

There was a sour look underneath the blood spatter on Eyrum's face. 'As do my people, mages.'

Tyrfing looked shocked. 'We would never sugg...' he said.

Eyrum cut him off. 'We have been tunnelling an escape route. We've had to be gentle and slow, using the old ways of dragon-fire to bore a hole into the rock and down to the mountainside. It was why we had the wizards make the fog.'

'Is it finished?'

'Almost. Nothing a hammer and muscle cannot finish.'

Farden slapped the Siren on the back and then bent to drag the Grimsayer from the floor. He could have sworn it whispered something in his ear as he lifted it on his shoulder. It was hard to tell in the roar of battle. 'Muscle you have plenty of, my friend. Let's go!'

Eyrum led the mages through the pandemonium to the very back of the library, where the Sirens had begun to prepare their final stand. Bloody soldiers and wizards had formed a line across the furthermost alcove, between the rock and a blackened window. Wives and children huddled behind them, weeping. The rest had gathered what weapons they could find. Even the farmer was there, with his pitchfork levelled. He almost skewered Eyrum as he and the mages jogged out of the fog.

'Is this it?' Eyrum demanded, knocking the pitchfork aside with his spear. He made an ugly, fearsome sight with his gnarled face all bespattered with blood. A few of the children whimpered. Eyrum paid them no heed. 'Is this all there are?' he demanded again. A few of the soldiers answered with nods and murmurs. 'Then get them into the tunnel, and smash your way through, as planned. You, and you,' he said, pointing to two burly soldiers, 'take the hammers.' He pointed to a trio of thick hammers that had been left leaning against the near wall. They were huge, iron-headed beasts, made for crushing. Eyrum reached for the third and left his spear in its place.

'Where is your ship?' he turned on the mages.

'In the fog. South, probably,' Tyrfing answered.

'If we're taking the same route, then we'll need it in the harbour.'

Tyrfing pulled a face. 'Have you got a hawk?'

They found their hawk in a nook that had so far been spared the carnage of the fighting. That said, it raged painfully close. So close in fact, that while Farden and Tyrfing were seeing to the hawk, Eyrum stood a dozen paces away, calling to his soldiers, and breaking the skulls of any clansmen that ventured near. The sounds, sporadic like punctuation to his shouting, were nothing short of sickening. There would be a gruff yell from Eyrum, then a clatter of boots. Then, a split-second of silence as a cursory identification took place, then a great whoosh, ended by a muffled yelp and a wet crunch of bone and face as they met iron and momentum.

Farden had counted twelve so far. Blood was beginning to pool around his boots.

Tyrfing was talking to a nervous, greying Siren that was hobbling back and forth, tending to his frightened hawks. His wispy grey hair was like a wild shrub. It seemed to explode in all directions. He never seemed to stop moving, not even for a second. Farden recognised him, but he couldn't put his finger on why.

'I don't care which one. Just a fast hawk for a fast message!' Tyrfing was blurting.

The old Siren was wringing his hands and staring over at Eyrum, who was busy twirling his heavy hammer as if it were a willow branch. He didn't seem to hear the Arkmage. 'Old man!' Tyrfing clicked his fingers in front of his face.

'My hawks,' he stuttered, 'they aren't used to such conditions. Fire. War. We miss our tower.' More wringing of the hands. Tyrfing shook his head and snatched a scrap of parchment and a quill from the nearby table. It was soiled with hawk-mess.

Farden stepped in. He grabbed the old Siren's hands and shook them gently. 'The finest and the fastest, which one is he?'

'It's a *she*,' the man seemed to drift out of his frightened reverie a little. 'Always a she.'

'Well, which one is it?'

The man turned to his hawks, all three of them, and stroked the head of the middle one. She was a small beast, a darker shade than the others, with a white chest and two thin feathers, like that of heron's, trailing from her head and down across her back. Her hood covered her eyes, its bells jangled as she moved. 'She is.'

Tyrfing finished his message and rolled it up without even waiting for the ink to dry. 'We'll use her then,' he ordered, holding out the little scroll like a flaming poker.

The old man hesitated. 'Dragons,' he bit his lip. 'They've been catching my hawks. They eat them.'

Farden pushed him gently towards the table. 'She's better off out there than in here!'

'Quickly!' Tyrfing waved the scroll.

There was a scream from behind them as Eyrum missed his mark, but only by a little. The following screams, those of the Siren finishing his work, were unmentionable. The three bystanders tried their level best to ignore them.

'Fine!' said the Siren, as he deftly twirled a scrap of twine around the hawk's leg. He lifted her hood and fastened its bell to her other foot.

'Farden, the window if you please!' Tyrfing yelled. Farden swiped a smouldering book from the bloody floor; a heavy tome that had a cover made of polished mahogany. He looked at the row of blackened windows behind the table.

'Any in particular?' he asked.

'Just throw the godsdamned book!' came the startlingly loud reply.

Farden threw it as hard as his tired arms could. There was a sharp crack as the book met the windowpane. Only one could win, and the book sailed out into the grey, leaving a gaping hole and shaft of bright light in its wake. The fog was fading indeed. The old Siren ran to the window, hawk on his arm. 'A ship, you say?' he asked Farden.

'That's right!'

The Siren whispered something urgent in the bird's ear and then held his arm up to the smashed window. 'Fly!' he shouted, and the hawk sprang from his arm. Gone. Snatched by the air.

Farden turned to his uncle. 'What about us?'

'We stay until the Sirens are safe, and then we make for the *Waveblade*.'

Farden flashed him a look that wore the frayed edges of disbelief. With a grunt, he picked up the Grimsayer. 'You make it sound so easy.'

'I'm learning from you.'

The two mages quickly made their way back to the back of the library with Eyrum and a gang of soldiers in tow. The smoke and heat were becoming unbearable now. The fires were spreading at a rapid rate, leaping from shelf to precious shelf. Most of the clansmen had all but retreated, lost in the maze of burning defences. A pitiful few Sirens limped out of the thick smoke to join them, Shivertread and a few remaining dragons in tow. One of the other dragons had fallen. Another was still fighting.

The sound of hammering fell silent as they reached the rear of the library. Now the escapees were pouring into the tunnel as fast as they could. The smoke vied with the dust for a space in their lungs. Coughing was rife; the sharp slapping of its echoes against the freshly carved rock sounded like a macabre applause, congratulating their escape.

Only Eyrum, Farden, and Tyrfing stayed behind. They were busy dealing with a few clansmen who had stumbled upon the escape. They fought them savagely, though the smoke made their ferocious movements seem dreamlike and sluggish. Eyrum could barely see the tip of his hammer, just its steel shaft and the whorls in the smoke it made. Every other moment he felt the wet thud as it collided with something unlucky. Tyrfing and Farden were his flanks. One cast sharp, deadly spells at anything that dared come his way. The other had his bloodied steel, staying still with one foot on a giant of a book.

Farden spat blood. A fist had caught him in the mouth. 'We need to cover their escape, otherwise we'll be fighting all the way down the mountainside!'

Tyrfing looked up from his casting. 'What would you suggest?'

'You two are the ones with the hammer and the spells. Cave the tunnel's mouth in,' Farden snapped.

'And what about us?'

Farden shrugged. 'Windows?'

Tyrfing looked horrified. 'It's sheer mountain out there.'

'Not all of it. It's scree below these. I saw when the hawk escaped.'

There was a roar somewhere in front of them, and in the grey darkness of the library they saw a great explosion of flame. Dark shapes were momentarily painted against the smoke. Many, many, dark shapes, the light turning them ghoulish and twisted. The three dashed to the nearest window.

'You'd best be right, nephew.'

'Check for yourself!'

Eyrum uttered a guttural roar as he took his hammer to the nearest windowpane. Light poured into the alcove, showering them and the dirty floor. The men shielded their eyes, wincing. The colour of the blood and gore that drenched their clothes and skin was suddenly very, very red.

Whilst Tyrfing put his fist to the rock arch of the tunnel, whispering intently to himself, Eyrum and Farden looked over the splintered edge of the glass. 'See? Scree.'

'*Sheer* scree,' replied Eyrum pointedly.

'Scared?' asked Farden. He was.

'Never!' Eyrum laughed then. Such an easy laugh. Farden

didn't care if it was false. It gave him a little courage.

The ear-splitting sound of cracking rock made them duck for cover. Tyrfing's spell had broken the wall in a hundred different places. All it took was a tap from his dusty knuckle, and the mouth of the escape tunnel imploded, sealing itself solid with a puff of thick grey dust. The Sirens were safe. 'Ready?' he shouted.

Eyrum nodded. 'As we'll ever be. My suggestion is not to look.'

'I'll take that advice.' Tyrfing nodded. He stretched out a hand towards the black window. A gust of wind sighed around them and blew the remaining glass and dust out into the air.

As the three readied themselves to jump, Tyrfing turned to his nephew. Farden had sheathed his sword, and was now holding only the blood-spattered Grimsayer, cradled in both arms. 'I don't envy you, Farden.'

'Why's that?' he asked.

Tyrfing pointed to the cumbersome tome. 'With the weight of that book, nephew, you'll drop like a boulder.'

'Well, taking into consideration your iron stubbornness, and Eyrum's sheer mass, I think I will take my chances,' he replied acidly, a little smile pulling up his cheek. There was something of a chuckle from Eyrum. How odd it was, that the more dire the situation, the more fun they had to poke at it. Such was the way of dire situations. Why make them even direr? Farden was about to place a wager when they heard the zip and clatter of arrows behind them.

'Well, can't stand around chatting all day!' he yelled as he sprinted forward. He took the window-ledge in one great leap, and sailed out into the fading grey of the morning light like a most ambitious boulder indeed.

When a person jumps from any great height, there is a moment where the world lies to them. It whispers to them a great and awful falsehood. It comes the very second that feet slide from rock or ledge, and lasts just that brief moment before reality takes grip. That moment where wind and treacherous momentum collude to convince the person, miraculously, that they can fly; that they could do this all along, yet never knew. It is that thin sliver of a moment before the heart begins to climb into the throat, and the face, previously grinning wide with downright elation at this discovery, begins to fall as fast as the rest of the body. Gravity strikes. The lie becomes apparent. Hope falls like a rock.

Farden enjoyed his brief lie. He had to admit it; he fell hook, line, and sinker for it. His mighty leap had thrown him far from the mountainside, and for one sweet, grasping handful of seconds, he flew, legs pedalling frantically through the cold, misty air, one arm clutched to the Grimsayer while the other flapped like a wing. What a sight he must have made.

Then the realisation came crashing down. Literally.

Farden fell like the weight he was. Groping at the sky was as futile as trying to catch the moon, but he tried anyway, clawing and scratching at nothing as he plummeted. He heard the grunting *whump!* of the two landing beneath him. A flash of pride came suddenly as he realised he would have won his wager, and then the impact jolted it from his mind.

His legs crumpled and his arse took most of the landing. Luckily, his cloak had bunched up in the fall, and managed to make quite a cushion between his rump and the scree. The severe incline helped too. He almost lost the Grimsayer as he bounced and rolled.

The three cried out as they slid and bounced down the slope, still falling, but being connected to the ground didn't make it seem so dangerous. Farden grit his teeth and stuck his legs out like tree roots, but they skittered over the top of the scree, futile against the speed he was now gathering. He could do little but grimace, and watch the world slide upwards to meet him.

Ahead of him, Tyrfing met a rock and flew over it with a yell and a crash of armour on the other side. Farden rolled to avoid the same fate. Eyrum was sliding down on his belly, whether by clever design or sheer unfortunate luck, Farden didn't know. He was somehow steering with his hammer, using its weight to slow him down. Farden's eyes flicked to the Grimsayer and considered doing the same, but thought better of it.

Arrows began to ping and ricochet off the rocks and scree around them. Farden ducked as he heard one flit past his ear. It sliced a line across his cheek and buried itself deep in the cover of the thick Grimsayer. 'That was too close!' Farden shouted to himself, a little wide-eyed. He could have sworn the book muttered something cantankerous, but with the roar of the sliding rock and wind it was too hard to tell. The arrows faded as quickly as they had come; the men were falling too fast to offer much of a target. Farden felt as if they were already halfway down the mountain. Despite the ripping of the scree and the pain in his legs, he almost let his grimace turn into a grin.

Almost.

From below, Tyrfing flashed him a quick look. 'Erm, Farden?!' he yelled.

'What?!'

Tyrfing could only point.

Below them and fast-approaching, was a ledge jutting out of the scree at a sharp angle. It wasn't so sharp as to stop them, but sharp enough to cut the slope in twain like a black, granite saw stuck halfway through a grey bone. The real heart-tugging, aspect of it was that the slope appeared to fall away soon after it, into complete and utter thin air. A cliff. No doubt about it.

'Shit,' was all Farden could stutter.

Eyrum slammed his hammer shaft into the rock in a spray of shale and pebble. Tyrfing's hands shimmered with green light, tugging at the passing rocks. Farden breathed a sigh of relief as he drew level with them, but as he slid quickly passed them, he began to flail and shout. He tried to dig his heels in but his knees buckled under the strain and speed. He reached out to Tyrfing with his spare hand, but he was already too far past him. Tyrfing's eyes grew wide as he watched his nephew plummet toward the ledge. Tyrfing tried to pull him back with a spell, but he didn't have anything to brace himself with. Those sorts of spells, even for Tyrfing, needed sure footing and solid ground. 'Farden!' he yelled, futilely, as if his words could halt him. He grabbed and pulled, but he just fell faster.

'Uncle!' Farden shouted. His mouth became a silent scream. Eyrum tried to reach him with the head of the hammer, but he was too far ahead.

Farden reached the ledge. There was a sickening moment as the sound of Farden's fall changed from the hissing roar of tumbling gravel to the solid scrape of rock, then cold silence as he was tossed up and out into thin air. Once again the world lied as he hovered at the apex, just before gravity bit into him. Farden had somehow managed to turn in mid-air, and he threw a wide-eyed and ashen look back at his still-sliding friends. To his credit, he was still hugging the Grimsayer.

And then he fell, with a scream so high-pitched he would later regret it with blushing cheeks. It was partly why he didn't hear the keen whine of golden wings above him. The other reason was due to the other sad fact of falling: that the faller will almost always look down to see his doom rushing up to great him. So it was that Farden's eyes were glued to the jagged fingers of rock below him, completely oblivious to the huge golden dragon swooping down to snatch him from his fate. It was only when Towerdawn's sharp talons slid under his arms did he snap out of his fear-stricken reverie. He felt a lurching jolt as the dragon flared and beat his wings. It wasn't a moment too soon; Farden managed to spit on a jagged tooth of cheated rock as Towerdawn pulled him up. He flashed the dragon a joyous grin. 'Not this time,' he whispered to himself. The Grimsayer in his arms rustled in the wind. It sounded like the book was sighing.

'We are not out of danger yet, mage!' boomed Towerdawn from above. He took a breath and blew a great trumpeting roar. Farden heard the voices of other dragons somewhere above and behind him echo the call. He looked up to see Tyrfing and Eyrum in similar positions. Eyrum was tightly held in the grip of the big blue dragon from the great hall, while Tyrfing was in the grip of lithe Shivertread. He swayed from side to side as the charcoal dragon swooped and flapped, a little less practised than the other dragons.

It was then that he heard a different sort of roaring. Farden threw a quick look over his shoulder and spied a multitude of dark shapes chasing them, blowing fire and smoke as they flew.

Towerdawn growled. 'Hold on tight, Farden.'

'And the same to you, Old Dragon!' Farden gulped as Towerdawn hugged the jagged mountainside, wings flat, limbs and mage tucked close to his scaly underbelly. It was all Farden could do to lift his legs to his chest and hope for the best. He could have sworn that his cloak slapped the railing of a balcony as they rocketed by, stomach-churningly close to the ground.

Towerdawn led his meagre swarm, five dragons in total, west and down through the rolling, hollow foothills of grey Hjaussfen. As the snow-spattered terrain levelled out, the dragons hurtled under the arms of cranes, skimmed thatched rooftops, and careened between watchtowers, sparing only inches for their wingtips and tails. But these dragons had been born on this landscape. They had spent a thousand years doing this for fun and training. They knew every twist, turn, and roll like the back of their scaly claws.

The Lost Clan dragons didn't.

Farden grinned as he heard an almighty crash from behind them. He caught a glimpse of two dragons tumbling to the ground, half a watchtower in the process of collapsing on top of them. There was another boom as a farmhouse exploded in a writhing mass of stone, thatch, and wings. Each roar was like a fanfare of justice being served.

In a blink of an eye they were swooping down toward the sea, where the volcanic granite of the mountain fell away to wind-carved and hollow cliff. Farden found himself praying that their scroll had reached Nuka in time, praying to whomever was listening. It was the first time in a decade and a half he'd allowed himself to pray to anything.

Before he knew it, they were diving over the granite spines of cliff edge and down to meet the sea. The cold, salty air slapped the mage in the face, chilling him to the bone. The mist had receded to the edges of the harbour's bay, and there, wreathed in its fading tendrils, was a glorious sight indeed: the *Waveblade,* in full battle-sail and slicing through wave after wave with its glittering bow.

'There!' cried Farden, even though Towerdawn had already seen her. He couldn't help it.

⁂

Loki drummed his nails on the varnished railing. The shipsmiths had spent far too much of their effort on varnishing this boat, he had decided. The wood under his pale fingers was so varnished, in fact, that it appeared as though it had been wrapped in thick glass. The dark wood was a blurry creature, living under it. *What a waste of time,* he thought to himself. It was already tarnished by the salt.

Heimdall stood behind him, as stoic and as silent as ever. His tawny eyes were roving the frothing feet of the black cliffs, the sheer walls of rock standing bravely against the cobalt sea. They were draped in the remnants of the morning's mist.

'Any sign?'

'Not a soul.'

Loki raised an eyebrow. He licked his lips and shuffled closer to the older god. 'Such a human expression,' he mumbled.

'Hmm?'

Loki dared to speak a little louder. 'Such a human expression. *Not a soul.*'

Heimdall slowly shook his head. 'That it is.'

'Blind to the truth, as usual. There must be plenty of souls, even in this barren armpit of the world. Am I right, brother?'

Heimdall tore his eyes away from the distant cliffs and turned them slowly on Loki. He was narrowing his eyes at the sea and its waves, watching their white tips burst as the wind caught them. 'You know the answer to that already, Loki. Why do you ask about such things?'

'Oh, no reason. Jealous of your eyes, as usual. I wonder what it would be like to see the rivers of them, streaming across the landscape.'

Heimdall turned his gaze to the land again and sighed. He didn't often watch the dead, in the ashen hues beyond where magick lingered. He forced himself to now. Little figures, wispy like the mists, trailing around the roots of the mountain. 'They do not so much stream as limp. Trickle even. A sad sight.'

'No doubt,' Loki was drumming his fingers again. 'And are there many?'

A silence, perhaps while Heimdall counted. 'Thousands.'

'So many.' Loki sounded almost wistful. 'How unfortunate it is that we have to live off prayer, instead of...'

Heimdall's voice was like a brick striking a bell. 'It is beyond forbidden. You know that. I should have you punished for the very mention of such a thing.'

The god held up his hands, pulling an innocent face. 'I'm only thinking aloud.'

'Well, think of something else. Their souls are sacred, to be untouched.'

Loki sniffed. 'Isn't that what we built them for, to power us with prayer? Why should their souls be any different? The daemons lived off them.'

'We are not daemons,' Heimdall growled. 'You would have the humans be simple tools then? Beasts of purpose, like their cattle are to them?'

'Isn't that what they are?'

Heimdall frowned, looking somewhat pained. Disappointed perhaps. 'They are much more, Loki. I had hoped this venture would have taught you that at least. Come now, you have tasted their food, their wine, slept in their fortresses, seen their power, even sampled their games, so I hear. How can you compare them to cattle?'

Loki thought about it for a moment. 'Shallow trivialities. Such accomplishments are distractions, when they could be so much more.'

Heimdall let anger flash across his face. Loki couldn't miss it. 'Not souls to be harvested, as I believe you are suggesting. Blasphemy, Loki. No, you place too much stock in what they *should* be, when you miss what they already *are*. Look at them. Look at this ship. They have become powerful creatures in their own right, even capable of killing daemons on their own. We should be proud of them,' Heimdall lectured, gruffly. 'You are such a young god, Lightbringer, and a rash one at that. You judge these humans by the many, not by the few. These few will save the world,' Heimdall turned his head to the south and east. 'Even if the many are foolish enough not to thank them for it.'

'And yet they refuse to pray to us, or pray to false gods instead.'

'Not all of them. You've felt the desperation in those that still do. They more than compensate for those that have turned their backs,' Heimdall corrected him.

'It's still not enough. Killing daemons should be our job,' Loki muttered.

Heimdall growled again. 'What has gotten into you?'

Loki waved a hand. 'I feel like a spectator, not a god. They show little respect for us gods. You say that they will save the world? Even now, they trifle with saving a maid over killing the One, as we've ordered.'

Heimdall shook his head and sighed. It sounded like the wind wandering through the sails. 'The stars have little sway over the cogs of this earth now, whether we like it or not. You would do well to remember that, Loki,' Heimdall admonished him. He watched Loki's blank, emotionless face for a moment before walking away. Whatever he was thinking, he was hiding it well.

As the older god left him to his own devices, Loki muttered far beneath his breath, far enough that even Heimdall would have trouble to hear it. 'We'll see,' he said.

A shout rang out across the deck, shattering the silence. 'There! To the starboard! Dragons!'

'Archers and bolts at the ready! Mages!' Lerel bellowed from the wheel. All across the ship, the creaking and clanking of a hundred bows and ballistas joined the pop and roar of spells bursting into readiness.

'Hold!' Nuka ordered. He had a strange contraption tucked tight beneath a bushy eyebrow. A spyglass, he called it. It was formed of slices of crystal stacked in a neat long line, thinner at one end, and thicker at the other. Some were coloured a malted yellow colour, while others were delicate, and as transparent as the air. They were held in place by four thick brass rods and a liberal dash of thin wire. It looked like something Tyrfing would dream up.

In this case, he had.

'They're Sirens!' yelled the captain.

'An' they got a whole party of the grey ones on their tails,

Cap'n!' shouted Roiks, from high up in the mainmast, waving a spyglass of his own.

'Wait for my signal!' bellowed the captain.

The dragons dove down to meet the foaming tips of the waves, fast and low. Nuka clamped his spyglass to his eye again. He could spy dark shapes dangling from the talons of the nearest three. 'Tuck that for'ard sail in!' he roared. 'And be quick about it! We've got bodies incoming! Give them some room to land, there! Get that gryphon out of the way!' The orders were rattled off like sling-stones. Ilios didn't need to be told. He had scampered amidships before the words had fully left the captain's mouth, almost as if he had known they were coming...

Towerdawn led the five dragons in a line. He roared and trumpeted as they drew close to the ship. The Lost Clans dragons were no more than half a minute behind them, already snapping at their tails. One by one, Towerdawn first, the three dragons swooped down and dropped their cargoes on the bow of the *Waveblade*. They landed with yelps and shouts, but they landed safe all the same. Little mercies.

Just as the Lost Clan dragons were bearing down on them, jaws splayed, fire crackling in their throats, the last two dragons flapped hard, up, up, and over the mast grazing its pennant with their claws.

It was perfect timing.

'NOW!' Nuka roared, and the *Waveblade* let fly.

A wall of arrows, bolts, spells, and even a spear or two exploded from the ship, flying straight into faces of the oncoming dragons. Two were killed instantly with heavy ballista bolts. The others collided in a flailing effort to escape, and were picked off at will as they tangled, writhed, and roared. Fellgrin was amongst the pile, battering spells and missiles aside with her huge wings and thick scales. As the others crashed into the cold, dark waters, already dead or dying, only she and one other managed to escape, scrambling over the wave-tips in an effort to flee. Towerdawn and his dragons were quickly after them, barely sparing a parting word for the ship and her crew.

'We will see you in the north!' cried the Old Dragon, as he sped after Fellgrin and the other, teeth gnashing and fire boiling around his teeth. Eyrum saluted them with his hammer.

As the splashing died and the bodies sank, Nuka strode across the crowded deck, heartily clapping shoulders and hands, bruising many in the process. He was already bellowing at the mages and their Siren friend. 'By Njord's frozen arse, you have either the worst timing, or the very best! Only the gods could tell.'

Farden was bent double, hands pressed to his shaking knees. He looked up, grimacing. 'The very best, I think, on Towerdawn's part.'

'Winds be damned, mage, you're whiter than a virgin, and bloodier than a butcher's floor. What in Emaneska have you been doing?' he asked, eyeing the gore splattered across their clothes and hands. 'Or dare I ask?'

Farden was still trying to regain his breath. It had been snatched away by the wind. 'Mountain-climbing. Dangerous activity.'

Lerel came running up. She spied the Grimsayer resting like a boulder on the deck. 'What's that? Could you not find a bigger book?!'

Farden shook his head at her. 'I couldn't even begin to tell you.'

'Well, you can try at dinner!' Nuka clapped his hands. 'So, are we successful?'

Farden couldn't answer. Tyrfing did so on his behalf. 'Not quite, Captain.'

Nuka winced, and bit his lip. 'Ah. North, then.'

'North it is.'

Nuka leant forward. 'North to *what*, may I ask?'

'The answer to that, Captain, lies with *them*,' said Farden, jabbing a finger towards the stern. Nuka's eyes walked the length of the mage's outstretched arm and hand, following it across the crowded, silent deck, to two silent figures standing by the ship's wheel. Two gods, faces vacant, eyes narrowed. Looking innocent, for all the world and its heavens.

Farden was already marching across the deck.

1561 years ago

Beautiful.
It would have been, in any other circumstance.
A hundred thousand lights, all aglitter, creeping towards the city like a horde of fireflies. Rivers and streams of them flowed and surged across the ice. Lines and clusters of them, moving in waves and currents. A hundred different armies from a hundred different lords.
Halophen had been right.
Emaneska had come for the Nine.
'They said it,' panted Chast. He had been talking like this for hours now. The others were swiftly tiring of it. 'They said they'd come, and we didn't believe them. Just kept on going about our business. As if we were kings ourselves.'
'We are kings.' The words surprised even Korrin, and they had leapt from his own mouth. five years had gone by since the desert, since his sword had tasted the neck of King Halophen. The Nine had been busy indeed. Quashing rebellions in the east. Hunting warlord kings in the south. Breaking the back of depravity across Emaneska. People had cheered them. The Smiths had praised them. Emaneska had praised them. They were untouchable. Righteous. Powerful. Conquering. They were like kings, in their own right. They had all thought it, at some point or another. And it was about bloody time somebody said it out loud, *Korrin thought.*
'We are kings,' he said again, drawing frowns from Balimuel and Gaspid, his closest friends of the Nine. 'Are we not?'
'Korrin, the farmboy...' Estina was muttering. Korrin stamped his foot on the marble of their Frostsoar balcony. 'This is our castle.'

He waved his hand over the black veins of the city below. Spots of orange and yellow burnt here and there, where the fire from the catapults had landed. 'Our city.' He rapped a knuckle on his breastplate. 'Our crowns.'

Gaspid rubbed his goatee, making the glittering metal of his gauntlet rasp against it. Standing in the orange light of the gathering armies, their armour looked like molten rock, like shimmering lava. 'A crown doesn't make a king. Actions do,' he intoned, wisely.

'You're damn right, Gaspid. And look at all that we've done over the last five years.'

'My my, is this the same Korrin, the quiet son of a pig farmer?'

Korrin frowned at Balimuel. 'I'm just saying what we're all thinking.'

'He's right,' Lop said, gazing out at the encroaching hordes. 'But look where it's led.'

'What are kings, if not conquered?'

'Korrin is right,' Balimuel growled. 'We are kings, every one of us, and we should act like them.'

Estina got up from her rock and raised her visor. 'What are you saying Balimuel?'

'I'm saying we should go down there and protect our kingdom.'

'But the Smiths ordered...'

'There won't be any Smiths, if we do not.'

There was a silence then, and in that moment a roar blew in from the south, borne on a hot wind, unnaturally so for the icy north. A roar of fire and iron, of steel and straining wood. The Nine turned to face it. A hundred lights flashed in the dark, sparking bright in amongst the firefly torches. Thunder then, of a hundred catapults lurching, hurling their fiery missiles high above the city, so high they almost came level with the Knights' gazes. Thunder struck as they crashed down on the city, fallen stars of chaos and flame. Fires sputtered and flashed in the streets. The wind brought the Knights snatches of screams, of crying.

Korrin stood. *'I'm not going to sit here and watch. That's not what we were made for.'*

Chast was biting his lip. *'Have we ever fought so many?'*

'No,' Balimuel chuckled. They could always rely on him to make light of any dire situation. It was his way. His huge shoulders held a lot.

'Maybe it's time we truly put our armour to the test.'

'But it's the armour they came for.'

Korrin clenched his fist, and felt the metal shiver and pop around his knuckles and fingers. He watched as another swarm of fireballs rose into the sky, each a shard of the approaching dawn, making the sky glow orange and furious red. Thunder rolled again. Screams followed. *'They'll have to try harder than that,'* he said, and then marched for the door.

The others traded glances. Balimuel reached for the handle of his sword. *'Our little Korrin, indeed,'* he smiled.

Chapter 11

"His world is afloat on ambition and dreams,
Long nights of ale spent sharing his schemes.
The world is his oyster all wrapped up in shell,
But my dear, oysters need catching, and his live in Hel."
Excerpt from 'Lark and Lady,' an old comedy originally thought to be penned by Billo the skald

'I have spent a long time and a lot of coin sowing the seed of doubt in this city, and now it is harvest time,' Malvus said to the stained-blue window. It painted the city below a cobalt blur.

The good Colonel Jarvins, or rather, the new *General* Jarvins, given his most recent accomplishments, stood behind him, admiring his new armour. It had come straight from what had been left in Arkmage Tyrfing's rapidly disassembling forge.

'And what are the crops of such a harvest?' Jarvins mumbled. The armour had come with several epaulettes, and his wife, immensely proud of her husband's sky-rocket to status, and no doubt hers in the meantime, had insisted on sewing several bright red ribbons to it. For burnished gold-green armour, the colour clash bordered on vomit-worthy. He hadn't the heart to rip them off just yet, but he was tempted, as he flicked them back into their rightful place.

Malvus, or rather *Lord* Malvus, as befitting his new status, turned around wearing a little hint of surprise on his face. 'Well,

well,' he remarked, grimacing once more at the dreadful sight of the gaudy red ribbons. He slid a dagger from his pocket and marched up to Jarvins. The general tensed as he saw the blade, but Malvus was not after him. Only his ribbons. He caught them with a sigh as they twirled to the floor. At least he could claim it was the Lord Malvus' orders. 'Now that is sorted, an answer to your question,' Malvus said, striding back to the window.

'The crops, or rather the juicy fruit, of our harvest are many. Taxes. Power. Expansion. Adoration, and the freedom to rule this city as I see fit.'

'You mean the Marble Copse. As the Copse sees fit,' Jarvins pointed out. He himself had been a member for many years now. The Copse's attitude appealed to him, a man who had spent half a decade policing the finer debaucheries of the magick markets.

'Jarvins, I *am* the Copse now,' replied Malvus, with a tone of icy exasperation.

Jarvins cleared his throat. 'Right you are,' he said, biting his lip. 'So, how are we going to harvest these fruits?'

'All in good time. In fact, ah. Here we are,' Malvus smiled as he heard the echoing thud of the hall's doors shutting. Three men were walking briskly towards them. Two held their heads and noses high, confident and eager smirks curving on their lips. The third at the centre held his head straight and formal. His strides were military-crisp and sharper than a winter wind. The creases in his shirt and cloak looked as though they could cut like daggers. His face was blank, a shadow of unease hiding there. Toskig had heard the good news, just like the rest of the city. He had heard the bells and seen the protests turn to parties in the streets. He had heard the sound of change on the wind. As for how good this news actually was? He had yet to fully decide. For the moment it sat with Toskig like a cold stone in the stomach.

'Ah, fellow victors.' Malvus welcomed them with arms held

wide. As the two council members came to a shuffling halt, Toskig stamped his feet and came to attention. He even saluted. Malvus received it with a curt bow, his armour and long cape rustling. The others had to privately admit that the new Lord of the Arka made a grand sight; all wrapped in golden mail and fringes of black, with a cape of soft grey that stretched to caress the floor behind his leather shoes. If clothes maketh a man, then these made Malvus look like a king. He knew it too, judging by his effortless smile, his glint in his eyes. He gestured for the men to sit on a nearby bench. The councils did as they were told. Toskig remained standing. Jarvins hovered in the background, trading glances with him.

'The fruits incarnate, Jarvins. Council Draun, Council Brothniss-Parr, and Sergeant Toskig, thank you for joining me on this fine morning. I trust your celebrations ran long into the night?'

Draun chuckled. He was a wicked willow of a man, thinner than a beggar's lips. His bony face was puckered with two beady eyes, and his nose ventured outwards like a beak. 'And long into the morning, Barkhart,' he said. His voice was narrow and dry.

Jarvins clicked his tongue. '*Lord* Malvus,' he corrected.

'Lord. My apologies,' Draun sniffed, looking uncomfortable.

'Accepted.' Malvus waved his hand in a little circle. He was enjoying playing this new role. 'And Brothniss, how were the streets?' he asked the second man, looking him up and down as he spoke.

Brothniss-Parr was a plain man. Plainer than parchment. He was of average build and average height, not too muscular and not too thin. His hair was neither short nor long, and hovered in the nether regions between black or maybe brown. His face was, well, a face… in fact, he had no features worth noting save for a black mole hovering just below his left eye. Apart from that, he could have been lost in a crowd at a moment's glance. 'Electric, m'lord. Most of the citizens held their celebrations right on the cobbles. Taverns turned inside out.

Markets opened late. The city had quite a time of it, for the most part,' said Brothniss.

'What do you mean, for the most part?'

'There were a few that did not partake of the revelry. The Temple and the Remnant caused a little trouble,' Brothniss explained. By his side, Toskig murmured in agreement. He had spent most of the night making sure such "trouble" didn't escalate into anything more serious. The city was like metal left on the anvil, so beaten, so hot and so passionate, waiting to be carefully moulded and shaped. He knew it would snap if not treated so. He abruptly realised Malvus was looking at him.

'Your Ma...' he caught himself just in time '...Lordship.'

'Sergeant Toskig,' Malvus said, with that glint in his eye. 'I hear from Manesmark that you can make a recruit piss himself with little more than a handful of words.'

Toskig nodded. 'It has been said, my lord, but never proven.'

Malvus took a step forward. 'And you, Sergeant, are the only one I am unsure of.'

'Unsure, my lord?' Toskig frowned. His hands were held stiffly behind his back. Military man to the core.

'Where do you stand on all of this?'

'All of what, my lord?'

Malvus waved his hand to the broken thrones behind him. Half the rubble still had to be cleared away. Toskig bit the inside of his lip. It was not a sight he was proud of witnessing. 'All of *this*. The Arkmages dethroned. The Copse taking control. This shift of power. This change? I would hear your opinions.'

The Copse. Toskig had heard that name several times in the night. The new council. Toskig let his tongue loose. 'Well, it depends,' he said.

Malvus looked intrigued. 'On what?'

'May I be honest?'

'You may.'

'It depends on what you intend to do.'

Malvus smiled then. A sympathetic, understanding smile. Perfectly practised. The kind that Modren would have fought not to stave in. He went to another bench and picked up a stack of waiting parchments. Some looked old, while some looked very new. All of them had been sealed with the red wax of the School hawkeries. He handed a few to Toskig and Jarvins and let the men read. They were formal letters of complaint. Some anonymous, others signed by familiar names. Toskig even found one from himself, addressed to Tyrfing. He mouthed the words as he rehearsed them. Words like *unacceptable*, or *dire situation*, or *simply too many*. The echoes of yesterday's cheers rang in his head, cheers of the instructors and mages drinking to change. He pulled a wry face.

'I take it you recognise these?' Malvus asked of Toskig. He nodded. 'Good.'

'Lord Malvus, forgive me being blunt as a spade, but what am I really doing here? Why not talk to Captain Haverfell? He has been far more outspoken about this…'

Malvus cut him off with a question. 'Are you happy with the current state of your army, your School, Toskig. Are you proud of it?'

Tosking frowned again. There were two soldiers inside him. One whispered of treachery, loyalty, and other such guilt-ridden words. The other spoke proudly about the way things used to be, of the way things should be. Toskig looked to the splintered throne behind Malvus. What was treachery when there was nobody there to betray?

'No.' Toskig's tone was flat.

'You've been a soldier in the Arka army for, what? Sixteen, seventeen years?' Malvus feigned ignorance. He knew exactly how many years Toskig had been soldiering. He had done his homework.

'Twenty-six my lord,' Toskig said, as his chest swelled.

Jarvins nodded and made a scrunched-up face of approval.

'Twenty-six,' mused Malvus. 'And in all that time, did you ever think the army would be in the state it is now?'

Toskig opened his mouth, unsure of what words to fill it with. Malvus filled it for him. 'An army bursting at the seams with underpaid and undervalued men and mages, nudging shoulders with newcomers, farmboys, *pretenders* who take up your precious space, time, and coin. An army that has lingered in its barracks for fifteen years An army untried and untested, carelessly forced to fight against hellish foes the likes of which we have never seen.'

Toskig had to nod. All his gripes and complaints had just been delivered neatly on a silver platter. The proud soldier ground its teeth. The loyal one held its tongue and blushed. The fight on the hill had been a shambles for his recruits. Most of them had lost their nerve and crumbled under the pressure. A paltry few had barely managed to cast a small spell or two. The rest lay in crowded graves, high in the Manesmark slopes. Those graves would have been even more crowded had it not been for the spit and verve of the veteran companies around them. A decade and a half stuck doing patrols and guard duty will give any veteran an unquenchable thirst for battle. Toskig knew this better than most.

Lucky. That's what they'd been.

Malvus smiled and walked to his stained-glass window. 'Look at what depths the Arkmages have brought us to.' He was talking to everyone now, not just Toskig. Malvus knew he had the big sergeant thinking. He would crumble like the rest had.

Malvus looked through the glass, turning the city yellow, green, blue, and red with little movements of his head. 'A shadow of our former selves, whore to anybody who wants to practise magick, a crowd of penniless bickerers. Over-taxed. Under-valued. We need direction.' Malvus took a breath before delivering his killer line. He had already rehearsed this several times that morning. 'And that is where you four can help me.'

'Us?' Jarvins spoke up. He was no actor. He delivered his line flat, barely making it sound like a question. It did its job.

Draun and Brothniss quickly stood up to join Toskig. 'Us?' they chorused.

Malvus pointed at each one of them in turn. 'I am putting you four in charge of turning this city around.'

The two councillors looked at each other with grins. Malvus could almost see the coins glinting in their eyes. Toskig stood a little straighter. 'I want taxes levied on the magick markets. If they want to trade in Emaneska's finest port, then they need to pay the tax for the pleasure. Draun, this is your responsibility. Brothniss, I want these bickering factions calmed or silenced. Their usefulness has faded. They can believe what they wish, as long as it falls in line with the Copse's creed.' Malvus delivered his plans like punches to a gut. 'And yes, you will be compensated handsomely for your work.' The grins of the councils widened.

'And what of me, my lord?' gruffly asked the sergeant.

Malvus broke into a smile. 'Now, Toskig, how would you like to see your army returned to its former glory?'

Toskig's throat was dry, but his nod was sure. 'Very much so, Lord Malvus.'

Malvus stared Toskig straight in the eye. 'Then it's yours to command.' The captain's eyes went wide, and Malvus leant closer. 'These farmhands and peasants don't deserve the magick they wield. The common man has dabbled in the matters of magick for too long. They deserve a sword and a shield, nothing more. If they want to be paid, then let them fight for it. Do you not think, Jarvins?'

'Absolutely.'

'Toskig?'

'Yes, my lord?'

Malvus walked forward and put his arm around the sergeant's

ample shoulders. 'I want you to build me an army I can take to war, Toskig. An army that can make the Arka into the power it can be.'

'War, my lord?' Toskig looked. 'Against whom?'

Malvus smiled along with Jarvins. 'Why, *General* Toskig. Against everyone.'

※

'How is she?'

'Colder than ice. Stiffer than a board.'

Durnus shook his head.

'Can you keep trying?' Modren pleaded.

Durnus hesitated. 'This spell is dangerous, Modren. I have only dared to use it once, and that was on Farden, a long time ago,' he said.

'Just do it.'

'Hmph,' Durnus sighed. He stretched his hands out again and felt Elessi's cold and clammy forehead. Her hair was tangled, the texture of straw. Durnus felt a stab of iciness in his veins as he felt the heat flow from him. His fingertips burned.

But it was no use. After a few seconds he let go, and rubbed his fingers together. 'That is all I dare to use, Modren.'

'Fine.' Modren slumped back against the wall. He felt almost as blind as Durnus in the gloomy dark of the cell. Their only light was a tallow candle that sputtered fitfully in the corner, and a narrow shaft of pale light that poured from the barred grate in the door. It fell directly on Elessi's face, making her skin seem even paler, if that were possible.

His wife was the living dead, and Modren hated it.

There hadn't been a single flutter of an eyelash. Not a hint of a mumble. Even when the soldiers had moved her to the cell, she hadn't stirred. The only thread of hope that Modren could cling to was the faint and sporadic thumping of her heart, and the even fainter breath that he could watch mist his armour. That was all he had left. Even that was slipping away.

Their surroundings were no solace. The damp holes were good for two things: confining miscreants and growing mould. Durnus had barely managed to keep Modren from exploding when they had brought Elessi in, late the previous night. Many a prisoner had caught their death in those dank surroundings. It was all Elessi needed.

'We have to get out,' Modren said, for the tenth time that hour.

'As I have repeatedly said, Modren, be my guest. You know as well as I do who built these cells, and what spells still bind them.'

Modren got up to challenge the doors again, but all he managed was a sour grimace and scowl as he stared at the faceless door. 'They've never had to confine a pale king before.'

'I have already tried.'

'Try again.'

'Modren,' sighed Durnus, his patience wearing thin. 'Enough. I cannot take any more of this.'

'Of what?'

'Of this futile griping. Our current circumstances are these,' Durnus gestured to the darkness around him. 'I dislike them as much as you do, but I cannot change them one iota. Be calm.'

'You try keeping calm when it's your wife on the slab,' Modren muttered darkly to himself.

'What?'

'Nothing.'

There was a grim silence in the cell, filled with only breathing and the creaking of the Undermage's knuckles on the bars. A moment filled with quiet desperation, swirling with frustration.

'What of that woman? The blind one?' Modren asked, from between his teeth.

'Jeasin?' Durnus sighed. 'I do not expect her to materialise any time soon.'

'Another casualty fallen to Malvus' guile.'

Durnus contemplated trying to get some sleep. What else was there to do in confinement such as this? Sleep, and wait. Wait, and sleep. The poor excuse for a cot in the corner of the room could only sleep one, and most of its dirty hay had gone to keep Elessi warm. Durnus didn't quite relish the thought.

'How did this happen so easily? So suddenly?' Modren hissed, staring out of the bars. He could see a trio of soldiers milling in the distant hallway. Their slouching, armoured figures were framed by the elusive daylight. 'How did he get away with it?'

Durnus grimaced. 'It has been brewing for years, right under our very noses, like mould under floorboards of an old house, rotting away the foundations until one day it all comes crashing down. Malvus saw his chance and took it. We were too preoccupied with greater evils to notice.'

'It sounds all very neat when you put it like that.'

'Well, it is. Neatly done on Malvus' part. He has played his hand very well indeed. Using the discontent of the masses and the greed of the ambitious,' Durnus quietly replied, trying to mask his true contempt. He had cursed himself repeatedly for letting Malvus manoeuvre them like this, for tipping them from the throne so damn easily, so *succinctly*. He had never even expected it.

Malvus throttled the bars. 'You speak as if it's just a pile of coin in jeopardy, instead of a country and a pair of thrones.'

'All that matters is stopping Farden's daughter. And Elessi of course,' Durnus added, as he felt Modren's hot eyes on his back.

Modren was about to reply when a shadow darted in front of the bars of the grate, interrupting the shaft of dim daylight. He quickly pressed his nose between them. 'Who's that?' he hissed. To his surprise, a sheaf of papers slapped him in the face.

'Here!' hissed a female voice, rife with urgency.

Modren barely had hold of the papers before they were rammed through the rough steel bars. 'What in gods'…?'

'Jeasin?' Durnus' ear pricked up at the sound of crackling paper and the urgent voice.

'Count yer lucky stars I've still got a scrap of conscience in me, Arkmage. Here's what you asked for,' snapped the voice, unmistakably Jeasin. Before either of them could say anything she was gone, marching past the guards with a wave and a sly nod. They didn't stop her, and she disappeared from view.

Modren held the crumpled pages up to the narrow beam of light. 'Looks like she delivered after all,' he muttered. Durnus had gotten to his feet. He felt for Modren's shoulder. 'Will any of it help us get out of this godsforsaken hole?' Modren asked.

Durnus shook his head. 'I will not know until you read it to me, mage. Get to it.'

Modren squinted at the scribbled lettering. It was spidery, faint too, thanks to a rushed hand and cheap ink. 'Spare no expense, Malvus, why don't you?' muttered Modren as he leafed through the pages, trying to make sense of them. He caught little snippets and read them aloud:

' "Yet another day, and yet another magick market poisons our streets with its greed and undeserved filth…" blah blah blah. "Magick has long been squandered by the common, undeserving man. Magick is for the master, not for the peasant in the field. It is time this Arkathedral ruled with the iron fist it used to…" gods, this is Marble Copse through and through.'

'What else?'

'Diary entry, diary entry, waffle, waffle, feckless bullshit. Deluded grandeur…' Modren paused as he flicked to another page. A word, or rather a name, caught his eye very quickly indeed. 'Saker?'

'*What*?'

Modren read it aloud.

> MALVUS,
>
> I TRUST THIS MESSAGE FINDS YOU COMFORTABLE IN YOUR NEW SURROUNDINGS.
>
> THE SHIP AND ITS CREW WILL BE DEALT WITH, AS REQUESTED. YOU SHALL CONSIDER IT A FAVOUR TO BE RETURNED LATER. I WILL TAKE THE MAGE'S HEAD AS A GIFT OF OUR ALLIANCE. WHAT A TROPHY IT WILL MAKE.
>
> I WILL NEED A MONTH OR TWO TO SECURE MY POSITION HERE, THEN WE SHALL BE READY TO MOVE EAST, AS PLANNED.
>
> HAVE YOU HEARD FROM THE DUKES? THE RUMOURS SAY KILTYRIN HAS LOST HIS MIND. WODEHALLOW IT SHALL BE. ONE DUKE'S ARMY IS BETTER THAN NONE, AND THERE WILL BE MORE FOR THE TAKING.
>
> WHAT OF THE FALLEN ONES?
>
> UNTIL THEN,
> SAKER, LORD OF NELSKA.

Modren looked up from the letter. 'Well, fuck me...' he muttered.

Durnus sought the coolness of a nearby wall. He silently began to curse himself again. 'That man has his eyes set on more than just my throne,' he replied. 'And it appears the Copse has deep roots indeed.'

'And the ship?'

Durnus rubbed his eyes. 'The *Waveblade*,' he nodded.

'And what's this "Lord of Nelska" business all about? What is going on, Durnus?' Modren crumpled the papers in his fist.

'If only I knew, Modren,' Durnus could barely talk. For the first time in his life, he felt truly, truly blind. 'If I only knew.'

Modren turned to look at the pale face of his wife, framed by the shadows of the bars and the papers in his hand. Very slowly, he began to curl his fingers to a fist. Durnus didn't say a word as the Undermage began to pound on the door. He let him pound until his knuckles bled. Until the bones began to splinter. He would have done the same, if he wasn't so numb himself.

Chapter 12

"As a land, Dromfangar, without a shadow of a doubt, is simply bloody boring. There, I've said it."
An excerpt from Wandering Wallium's bestseller 'Travels in Emaneska' - first printed in the year 882

Desolation was the business of this land. A hundred miles it stretched, in every direction the compass had to offer, barren as the mind of a fool. Its skin was endless dust and tawny shrub, occasionally puckered by the picked-clean bones of creatures that had ventured their luck on the wastes, and failed. Deer, sabre-cat, cow, donkey, man; it was a land where even the maps walked in circles. Only the buzzards and gulls dared to brave it.

Them, and two stubborn women.

Perhaps stubborn wasn't quite the word. *Eager*, was more apt. One was eager to please. The other was eager to stay alive. So it was that Samara and Lilith tread the Gordheim wastes.

They had been silent for a day or so. Hokus and Valefor had visited them twice since the mountains. The first time they had appeared from the smoke of their meagre campfire, giving Lilith quite the fright. The second time they had had the decency to wait by a waterfall, idly turning the water a filthy rust-colour with their claws as they had delivered their directions and orders to hurry. Their complaints were simple. They were not moving fast enough, and

Samara was painfully aware of it.

The girl looked back at Lilith. She was in the middle of negotiating a patch of dried brambles. She was wobbling back and forth as she tried to avoid the finger-sized barbs. Samara shook her head. The years in the wilderness had made the seer hardy, but at the same time they had taken their toll. Every mile that the wastes offered them, the slower her feet moved and the more her chin rested on her chest. Every mile north.

To Lilith's credit, she hadn't made a sound. Not a word of complaint had passed her lips in the last two days. She had soldiered on with quiet resolution. She may have slowed, but she hadn't stopped. Her face was an unwavering mask of iron determination.

But it was exactly that: a mask.

Underneath the facade, Lilith was slowly but surely crumbling away.

'Come on, old woman,' called Samara. Something resembling either impatience or pity made her scrunch up her face. 'By the time we reach the Spit it'll be dark.'

Lilith nodded and momentarily increased her pace. She tugged her cloak free of the bramble and trudged across the sandy earth towards her young companion. She spared her a quick look. Samara was looking fresher than ever. The only hint of the long miles they had travelled was the thin film of dust and road-grime covering her clothes and face, painting her a sandy grey. Samara was barely sweating. Her hair wasn't tangled or greasy. She walked like her feet had never known a blister. Her breathing was light and the wind had even caught her humming something a mile or two ago. Such were the benefits of being young, and daemon-blooded. Lilith shook her head and just kept moving. She distracted her aches and dark thoughts by counting the clanking sounds her heavy pack made.

The pine tree was a monstrous, lonely thing. They had spied it twenty miles back. Such a huge and vertical thing was hard to miss on such a flat, barren wasteland.

It must have been a practical joke of nature, or of some wisecrack god, to put such a giant tree in such an empty place. The tree must have been a hundred feet tall at least, leaning at a slight angle to the east like a solitary tower with questionable foundations. It was a pine tree through and through, with a sharp point and gently sloping sides. Its needle foliage was a dark, dark evergreen, almost black in the places where the sun couldn't reach, and it was bristling with gnarled, mahogany cones the size of a man's head. A few that had fallen littered the dusty earth like forgotten boulders.

They had smelled the tree from a mile away; it gave the wasteland breeze the sickly-sweet smell of thick, dripping resin and warm wood. It mingled surprisingly well with the sulphurous stench of the two daemons lounging against its enormous trunk.

Samara marched towards them eagerly, while Lilith did her best to keep up. She counted her blessings as she walked. There weren't many to count. A spot of shade, courtesy of this lonely tree. Maybe a rest. Some food if she was lucky. Having the daemons in plain sight rather than having them explode out of a campfire. Thin comfort, Lilith sighed quietly to herself.

When she arrived at the tree, Samara was just getting up from her knees. The daemons smiled when they saw Lilith. They had taken to goading her mercilessly about her abilities as a seer, her age, her slowness, and, most disturbingly, how rotten she would taste when they finally ate her. It was the subject of her impending doom, and that subject alone, that was the reason behind her dark mood, and her crumbling resolve.

Hokus rubbed his hands. 'Well, Valefor, if it isn't our favourite fate-juggler. You almost looked surprised to see us.'

'Never trust a seer who's surprised to see you, Hokus.'

Valefor 'How right you are, brother.'

'I'm surprised to see you standing still and waiting for us for a change, rather than ruining my campfires,' Lilith replied acidly. At a sharp look from Samara, she quickly added, 'my lords.'

The two daemons shrugged at that. She was poor sport today.

Samara smoothed the dust from her knees. Her hair was reflecting the green tinge of the light falling through the pine. It gave her a haunted look. 'How are we doing?' she asked. The question, so high-pitched in her young voice, veritably begged for approval. Samara couldn't help but notice it herself. She inwardly cringed.

Valefor snorted smoke. 'Terribly,' he said. 'You are days behind the others, and they are supposed to be chasing you.'

'It will not do,' Hokus shook his head. He sounded angry. 'Our plans cannot wait for mortal feet to tread. He grows impatient.'

Samara nodded. She couldn't help but feel her burden grow even heavier at the mention of *him*. 'Well...' she ventured.

'Well what?' Hokus snapped, biting off a flash of flame in his blast-furnace mouth.

'Is there a faster way we could travel? A ship? A dragon? Anything?'

'She catches on quickly, does this one.'

'For her age.'

'She has our blood in her, after all,' Hokus nodded. He looked to the south and east, where a faint strip of darkness smudged the horizon. Mountains, cloud, or a forest maybe. 'The growing magick is calling to the dark places of this world. There are things burrowed in the earth that escaped our fate. Things that have been forgotten and lost. Some have already answered its call. They head north, like you.'

'*Things*?' asked Lilith, unnerved.

Valefor sniggered. 'We have a few ideas.'

'Like what?' asked Samara, intrigued.

'Walk until the sun sets. Make a fire. There is a hill, to the north. We will meet you there,' instructed Hokus. Lilith inwardly groaned. The daemons made scraping noises as they hoisted themselves off the tree. Where they had been leaning, great char marks and resinous bruises tarnished the red-brown trunk.

'What are you going to do?'

'The magick has its call. We have ours.'

'It has been centuries since the presence of daemons have been felt. Already, creatures are coming to pay their respects.'

'Choosing sides, so to speak,' Valefor smiled as he sent a pine cone tumbling with a vicious kick. The parts that didn't wither into splinters soared high into the open grey-blue of the barren sky. 'Nature is always first to choose. That's why the gods were so eager to master it.'

Hokus nodded. 'Even now I can hear the rustling of rocks, the chattering of teeth and nails, drawing near.' Lilith stared out into the wilds, as if she could spot these chattering, rustling beings. There was nothing to be seen, but the daemon's words still sent a little shiver up her arched spine. 'Sunset,' he ordered. Samara bowed as they turned to walk away, then instantly began snapping twigs from low-lying branches.

Lilith waited until the daemons had gone. For some reason, they had taken to walking instead of disappearing in a cloud of smoke and ash. She wasn't sure which she found more disturbing, the power of their spells, or the casual, brazen way they plodded across the wastes, leaving burning footprints in their wake.

'How can you trust them?' Lilith sighed. She didn't care to whisper. If the daemons could hear the chattering and rustling of unnamed horrors from gods knew how many miles away, then no amount of whispering would help her.

Samara shook her head. 'Not this again, Lilith,' she hissed. 'I told you, they're flesh and blood.'

'Fire and ash, more like,' replied the seer. 'They have it in for me. I can tell. It's fine for you. They need you. You're useful. I'm surplus to requirements. They'll be rid of me as soon as it bloody suits 'em.'

Samara shrugged. 'Not my problem,' she said.

Lilith scowled. 'No, 'course it ain't. You're fine.'

Samara dropped her bundle of sticks and turned around. Her hands were glittering with frost, turning an artic blue. She pointed a finger clad in ice. 'You sound as if you want out, Lilith? Had a change of heart? Going back on your promises to Vice?'

Lilith couldn't help but look back the way they had come. She licked her dry lips.

'No,' she said, quietly, defeated. Fate was a hopeless beast. She cursed herself again, for the hundredth time that week. Why had she ever looked? 'No, I ain't. Just seems as though I'm getting the worst of it, is all.'

'Well,' Samara began, but she trailed off before she could think of anything to say. She let the ice on her hand melt away and went back to her stick-gathering.

※

All things considered, Lilith needn't have kept pace, but she did so to keep Samara happy, or quiet. One of the two. In all honesty, she still cared about the girl's fate, even though she had come to realise that her own was truly sealed. She resigned it begrudgingly to some sort of motherly instinct. She had spat a great globule of phlegm in the dust when that thought crossed her mind.

As the sun died its slow death, they came to a low and lonely barrow mound, ringed by a crown of brambles. Samara hacked her way through them with her hands and a couple of spells, clearing the way for Lilith. She strode to the top of the barrow and stamped the top of it as Lilith had taught her. Even in the wildest parts of the world, barrows weren't very common. They were hasty graves built for the most hated of enemies. It was a true punishment, as it refused the dead the pyre they needed to set their souls free, to set them on the path to the other side. A burial in the cold earth forced a soul to roam the wilds as a ghost, pleading with the living to burn their remains and unshackle them. It was a cruel art, saved for the cruellest.

The barrow seemed sound enough. Most were old and had a tendency to cave in under any sort of weight. That sort of thing wasn't a danger for most. Even the hardiest of explorers seldom dared to camp atop a barrow. Ghosts could be bitter beasts.

As Lilith began to build the pine twigs and branches into a fire, Samara walked in circles around the barrow, looking for the hulking shapes of Valefor and Hokus. They were nowhere to be seen. 'Is there any food?' she asked, as her stomach rumbled audibly.

Lilith nodded and the girl came to sit by her side. She dug through her pack as Samara put her hands to the fire. She soon had the dry twigs crackling, and the cool air began to smell like burning resin.

Lilith turfed a cloth-wrapped packet onto the dust. The cloth was cold to the touch; another of Samara's spells. 'The last of the venison,' she announced. Samara had brought down a stag during their journey through the Össfen foothills. That was the thing about fire spells: not only could they catch dinner, but they could also cook it at the same time.

Samara unwrapped the meat and dangled a slice of it over the flames. If there was one thing she had learnt from her years traipsing the wilderness as a child, it was that she hated cold meat. Lilith was not so picky, and she began to wolf down her slice with alacrity. The day's trudging had given her a powerful hunger.

As Lilith ate, Samara pondered the silence. Walking made the brain churn, and the last ten miles had made hers think about Lilith. The momentary shred of pity she had felt for the old crone earlier had soon blossomed into a full-blown tapestry of sympathy. Samara wasn't used to such a thing. She'd tried to ignore it, but it stuck fast. It confused her. It made her uncomfortable.

Once she had gobbled down her venison, she rubbed her hands on her cloak and cleared her throat. 'So,' she said, lunging into the question she had wanted to ask since the pine tree. 'What's wrong with you?'

Lilith looked up, a little surprised. She was busy sewing up a hole in her sleeve that a bramble had ripped. 'I might ask the very same of you, girl. Can't remember the last time you asked me such a thing.'

Samara just shrugged. 'I want to know. There's something wrong with you, that's for sure.'

'Such tact, girl.' Lilith shook her head, and coughed up two words she too had been nursing since the pine. 'I'm dying,' she blurted.

'So? You've been dying for a long time,' replied Samara, matter-of-factly. There was no venom in her words. Just plenty of fact.

Lilith jabbed herself with her needle as she turned to scowl at her. 'Not in that way, girl, not in the way that we're all dyin', in the way that I am *going* to die. Soon enough.'

Samara cupped her chin with her hand. 'Is this about Hokus and Valefor again?'

'No,' Lilith snorted. She knew the end, and it was not at the end of their claws.

'Then what? How?'

'Don't matter. Just that it happens soon,' she muttered. 'Nothin' to cry about. Made my peace with it,' she lied.

Samara shuffled around to the other side of the fire so she could face the old woman. The fire did different things to each of their faces. Samara leant forward to watch the light play amongst the cracks and canyons of Lilith's wizened skin. Lilith looked up and watched how the flames softened Samara's, how it smoothed it and made her look even younger than she already was. How it turned her eyes a russet orange.

Samara shook her head, remembering several wine-addled evenings of Lilith muttering to herself. 'So it is true. You did look at your own death.'

Lilith looked into the flames and said nothing. That silence last for almost half an hour. Samara didn't bother to press her.

As the darkness grew thick and oily around them, Lilith began to make herself comfortable. With grunts betraying how sore she truly was, she wriggled around until she had found a hollow in the dust, and then positioned her pack under her head. All the while she kept staring into the flames. It was only when she pulled a small flask from her pocket that Samara piped up. 'Do you think that's wise? They'll be here soon. We'll be moving on,' she said, her voice sounding loud against the crackling of the pine twigs.

Lilith grunted some more. 'I ain't drinking myself to a stupor, girl, just warming myself up. S'cold on these wastes,' she replied. There was a musical popping sound as she thumbed aside the cork of the flask. The sharp tang of mörd escaped.

Samara didn't feel the cold. Her magick was growing stronger with every mile they travelled northwards. She could feel it filling her veins again as before. It kept her thoroughly warm. She watched as Lilith took a few sips from the flask, winced, and took a few more. Her wrinkled lips puckered with the taste of the stuff.

'Want a bit?' Lilith noticed how the girl was staring. She waved the flask in her direction, mindful to keep it away from the fire. It was a well-known fact that the only thing that could start a fire faster than a fire mage was a drop of mörd.

Samara wrinkled her nose, but took the flask anyway. She sniffed its contents and then immediately regretted it.

'It'll set fire to your belly,' Lilith coaxed. She had never let the girl drink before, but what's the point of knowing the pyre is drawing near and not letting a few morals slip?

'You say that like it's a good thing.'

'Trust me, girl. Sometimes it's the only thing that let's you know you're still alive.'

Samara felt another little pang of pity at that reply. Damn emotions. Samara shrugged and took a swig. It probably wasn't the best idea to take such a bold mouthful, but she did nonetheless, and it was all she could do to swallow it before it burnt a hole in her mouth, never mind her belly. She coughed as she tried to take a breath.

'Good, eh?' smirked Lilith. She waved her hand for the flask but Samara didn't give it back right away. She pinched the flask between her knees and reached for the knife at her belt. She tugged it free and, holding her hand over the mouth of the flask, dragged the blade across her palm. Dark blood sprang to taste the night air, and as she clenched her fist, drops of it began to dribble into the flask. Lilith watched the whole process wide-eyed. She had thought that she had tasted the last of that blood. She raised herself onto her withered arm and shuffled closer to the fire. Samara kept the blood flowing for a long minute or two, and with each tiny drop, Lilith leant that little bit closer, until she was lying almost in the fire.

Once Samara was finished, she held out the flask to Lilith. To her surprise, the seer didn't snatch it, like she had always done, but instead reached out slowly and let her hand linger on the flask before she took it, brushing Samara's fingers. It was a moment that neither of them ignored, but neither of them could mention. To Samara, it was a gesture of pity, of new and confusing sympathy. To Lilith, it was one that meant she could face the north on her feet, rather than on withered knees. It meant everything. 'Thank you, girl,' she mumbled.

'You're welcome,' Samara replied, her voice equally low. It was a trade of words they were far from used to.

Lilith put the flask to her lips and tipped its end toward the sky. She gulped it down as quickly as she could manage. Both the mörd and blood stung her, and she had a hard time deciding which was more painful. Within moments, the flask was drained, and Lilith sighed as she dropped it on the ground. She closed her eyes, letting the heat swirl around her stomach. The blood began to make her twitch and flinch, but the strong mörd had also numbed her somewhat, so she simply lay there shaking, rather than doubled-up and wretched as normal.

After several minutes of convulsing, Lilith began to moan, like a sleeper caught in a dream. It sounded like the drunken moans that Samara had heard through many a rainy night as a girl. She decided to venture a question.

'Did you look, or not?' she asked, quietly. Lilith took so long to answer that she was about to ask again, only louder, when the seer sighed softly.

'I did,' she said, words slurred just a little.

'When?'

Another sigh, as if the words were tough to get out. 'You were jus' a baby. Barely a year. Growing so fast though. Never seen a babe grow like you did.'

Samara pressed on. Maybe it was the mörd, maybe the blood, maybe Lilith had simply stopped caring about the answers, whatever it was, Samara had questions to ask. 'And how many babes have you seen?'

'More than you think, but always one less than I'd like,' Lilith answered cryptically, making Samara pull a confused face. The seer groaned then as a wave of cramp spread across her body. Samara wondered if her timing had been a little awry. She turned around to scour the sunset-washed landscape, but there was nothing for miles. Not yet.

'Why did you look?'

Lilith smirked between pained grimaces. 'Would you look, if

you 'ad the power to?'

'No. I don't need to, do I?'

Lilith shrugged. 'Well I did. Us mortals can't help but wantin' to know the end of a story. People don't like doubt and they don't like fate, either. That's why they came to me in their droves, askin' me to read their futures with my stones. Half the time I just told them what they wanted to hear and only that. First thing a seer learns is that you can be ruined by knowin' everything.'

'And that's what ruined you?'

'Didn't want to end up like all the others I'd seen over the years. Didn't want to end up drowned, or stabbed, or crushed by a rock, or fallin' out of a third-storey window onto a butcher's cart. Didn't want to be another future, so I made sure mine was as long as possible. That's what ruined me, girl, if you have to ask. That and a powerful thirst for wine.'

'So you found Vice?'

'Came across a book in my younger days. Scholar from Arfell didn't have enough coin to pay for his readin', so he paid me with a stolen book. All he wanted to know was the name of a girl that worked in his library, so I obliged him. Said it was valuable anyway. Before I could sell it I wound up readin' it.'

Samara nodded along. 'Let me guess. It was a book about daemons, or blood, or something?' she ventured.

Lilith smiled, eyes still blissfully closed. 'All three, girl. Imagine my surprise when my stones soon found me a pale king so close, in my very own city. Almost killed me he did, when I first approached 'im, but I think he saw somethin' useful in me. Vice put me to use over the years for his various little schemes, and he kept me just as alive as he needed me to be. His own future was hard to read, being as powerful as he was, but he seemed happy with what I cast for him, thank those bastard gods,' she said, with a dry laugh. 'He taught me all about them too, and you.'

Samara pushed on, trying her luck. 'So what did you see? In your own future?'

Lilith's smile turned upside down at that. 'None of your business, girl. That future's mine an' mine alone. Keep your nose out.'

'But you already told me it was death. What happens?' asked Samara, as blunt and as tactless as a spade to the face, like any young, inquisitive person can be.

'Why, so you can help?' replied the seer. 'You've never cared. Why start now?'

Samara wrapped her arms around her knees as she leant forward. 'Don't know,' she said. It was an honest answer. 'Why not?'

Lilith scoffed. ' 'Cause I've seen that moment many times, girl, and even though I can't read your fortune, I know you ain't in any way a part of mine. Not even you and all your magick can change that.'

Samara pouted. 'Suit yourself.'

'I will, thank 'ee,' replied Lilith. A moment passed.

'Are you sure?' Samara asked.

'About what, girl?'

'About you. About dying?'

Lilith opened her eyes and squinted at the night-bruised sky, as if reading the twilight's stars. 'Sure as nails.'

'Why won't you tell me?' Samara pleaded, like a child asking for a sweet.

Lilith stretched across the dirt, searching for a warm patch. She didn't answer for a while. She groaned and grimaced again as more pain flitted through her body. She pulled her hood down over her face so that all Samara could see were her lips. They were already looking less-winkled. It was then that she began to talk. 'It happens in the north. The far north. I'm wearing clothes just like these. Black boots, rope belt. I'm running. I'm covered in snow, dirty, bloody snow. There are black rocks all around me. Cracked ice. Then *he* appears.'

Lilith shivered, as she had done in the privacy of darkness many a time before.

'Who?' Samara flexed a fist. 'I can stop him, whoever he is,' she stated.

Lilith shook her head. 'Not this one. Not this time. He belongs to another, an' I already seen to that.'

Samara didn't know what to say. All she could do was wonder at the strange little ache that had developed just above her stomach. It was an odd sensation. She frowned at it, tucking her chin under her cold arms. Several minutes passed before she realised she could blame the old venison, and so she did. She watched Lilith as she curled around something square and thick in her pack. 'So what does that make that? Our collection of skins? Is it a... what do you call it? Your legacy? Is that the word? You can't even look at it,' she asked.

'That's the word alright, dear.' Lilith smiled with red lips. 'It used to be insurance, for when this was all over. But now there ain't no point. I won't be coming back, and nobody wants it that can save me. So it's a legacy indeed. For posterity.'

'What does that mean?'

Lilith shrugged. 'Vice... your father... said it once. For the future, he said.'

Samara was busy rubbing her chin against her arms, agitated, confused. 'Just tell me who. Who does this to you?'

'Don't change a thing if I tell you. Told you, I've already seen to his end. Don't you worry.' There was a tinge of regret in her voice then.

'And you're sure the stones are working right this time?' Samara leant forward.

A little and rare smile appeared on Lilith's face. 'Like I said, girl, sure as nails. I seen enough futures come true to know I'm right. Stones never lie, and I've asked them enough questions to know it all,' she whispered. Lilith closed her eyes then. The mörd was fading.

Her face was a scrunched-up picture of discomfort and twitching pain. Her body had begun to shake as if she were deathly cold. The withered hand wrapped in her folded sleeve was fidgeting.

An hour passed this way. Samara stared at the flames and tried to decipher her irritating new emotions, while Lilith fell into a fitful sleep, enduring the borrowed blood burning through her old veins. Night fell on the wastes, black and cold. Only a thin, broken fingernail of moon gave them any light, save for the flames of their fire. In the distant south, a black shape of a pine tree sat against the night sky.

For wanderers, travellers, explorers, and the downright lost, there is a constant confusion in the fact that the more barren and emptiness a landscape is, the more numerous and worryingly vocal its nightlife is. Samara had spent her life in the wild, but she could never shake the feeling of trepidation when something hairy and fanged howled uncomfortably close. She had always said it was her human side shivering; a sliver of something ingrained from the ages of darkness, when humanity had gathered around campfires and whispered of monsters. She eyed the black shapes skittering across the landscape, using her spells to watch them as clear as day. Foxes, rats, owls, voles, jackals... they all crawled from whatever hole they had made their nests in, and came to cry and hoot and whine to the night. There were other things out there too. Samara could feel bigger eyes upon them. Unnatural eyes. Fires and barrows. A combination that made ghosts lick misty lips.

Samara saw them moments later. The two shapes strode across the landscape like actors striding onto stage. Where they walked, the things of the night scattered. Fearful yelps echoed across the plain.

Samara nudged Lilith with her foot and the seer snuffled something derogatory and altogether foul. She slowly came awake, still halfway into a strange dream. 'They're here,' said Samara, calmly and quietly. Lilith heard a slight nervousness in her voice, like that of a favoured servant hearing the sound of a king's boots on the stairs. Trembling, Lilith pushed herself upright. She winced at the pain that flitted through her limbs. The blood was still at work. 'Where?' she asked, squinting past the flames. She could hear the thumping of their feet striding up the incline of the barrow. Samara fell to her knee. Lilith did the same. Valefor came first out of the gloom, grinning like a fiery jester as usual, and then Hokus, narrow-eyed and curious.

'Do I smell blood?' he asked, without so much as a greeting.

'That you do, brother,' confirmed Valefor, sniffing the air. His nostrils flapped. 'Daemon-scent.' Reaching out a single claw, he gently lifted Samara to her feet by her chin, and then tapped her arm. Samara opened a hand, where a faint welt of a cut could be seen, already half healed. Valefor flicked a glance to Lilith, who was still kneeling, swaying back and forth. 'I see,' was all he said.

Hokus growled. 'What use you still see in her escapes me, cousin.'

'She,' began Samara, unsure. She raised her chin. 'Has served me... *us* well so far.'

Hokus waved an arm. 'So be it,' he said, reaching into the fire and grabbing a handful of burning coals. Clutching them to his charcoal lips, he blew hard, making them glow white hot. 'We have found you transportation,' he said, between breaths.

Samara looked around. The glare of the coals and their little fire had made it difficult to see anything beyond the summit of the barrow. 'Where is it?'

'*What* is it, would be more appropriate,' Valefor chuckled. 'Show them what we've dragged from the depths of the forest's caves, brother.'

Hokus nodded. He drew his hand back, the one that held the coals, as if to throw a punch at the moon. Then, with the quietest of grunts, he hurled the coals down the slope of the barrow. They landed in a flash and hiss of sparks, scattering like coins out of a torn purse.

The two beasts standing at the foot of the barrow snarled in reply.

Wolves. Two enormous wolves. The flash of the coals lit their maws for the briefest of moments, but it was all that was needed. Yellow teeth and huge ice-white eyes. The mere sight of them was enough to stop the hearts of lesser creatures. Even Samara flinched. Lilith fell to the ground, prostrate on the stubbled grass, shivering.

Uttering low whines, the wolves began to pad up the slope in the gentle, yet terrifying way that wolves do: legs bent and fluid, effortless, head low and moving not an inch with the motion of the paws. Eyes fixed like nails welded to steel.

They stopped just short of the daemons. Even Hokus and Valefor, in their current size, looked puny beside them. Easily taller than a man, the wolves were wide and long like a cow, with thick, shaggy coats and tufted ears. Their claws were so large they could have been fashioned into doorhandles, their fangs polished and whittled into dirks. These creatures had a smell about them, like old leather, of dusty fur and hot, rotting meat.

'What are they?' asked Samara, breathless.

'Fenrir,' grinned Valefor, obviously enormously pleased with their find.

'They're massive...'

Valephor made a shocked face. 'These are small, for fenrir. The elves used to breed them much, much bigger,' he said, wagging a claw like a lecturer.

'I hate to think,' mumbled Lilith. She had gotten to her feet, and now stood on shaky legs. Her fear had faded quickly once she had remembered her earlier thoughts. All the same, one of the fenrir growled at her, and she stumbled backwards.

'They can smell the blood on your breath, seer,' said Hokus. He clapped his hands together and the colossal wolves flinched. 'Ready?'

Samara pointed at the creatures. 'How do we... er... How are they going to...'

'You ride them.'

'*Ride* them?' Lilith spluttered.

Hokus glared. 'Problem with your ears, old woman?'

The seer had the cheek to bob a curtsey. Samara blamed the mörd. 'They're just fine, thank 'ee,' Lilith replied.

Hokus glared a little more. 'Every question you let dribble out of your leathery mouth wastes more of our time. Gather your things. You ride north,' ordered the daemon.

Samara went to it with a will, hoisting her pack over her shoulders and putting the fire out of its misery with a few quick stamps. In the darkness, the volcanic veins and cracks in the daemons' skin glowed a faint orange, giving them just enough light to see by. The thin moon did the rest.

As Lilith gathered up her cloak and her pack, Samara stepped up to face the nearest, and largest of the fenrir. Its breath was like the breath of a forge. It stank of decay and death. The fenrir growled, throat rattling, as she reached up to touch the fur hanging around its chin, but it didn't move. It had its orders. Samara twiddled the fur between finger and thumb and made a contented little noise. 'Soft,' she mused, and with the help of Valefor, she lifted herself onto the back of the giant beast. The fenrir's shaggy coat made a perfect saddle. Thick enough to dig heels and hands into. Thick enough to keep the bones from being jarred. Samara let her hands sink deep into the warm, shaggy fur and gripped tightly.

Lilith was struggling to climb her fenrir. Her pack was heavy, her hand still withered despite the blood. The beast snarled as she slipped for the third time and tugged too hard on its coat. An impatient Hokus finally pushed her onto the fenrir's back, muttering something about excess baggage. His claws strayed close to her neck, but he held himself.

Once their cargo was firmly aboard, the fenrir lifted their

heads to howl at the sliver of moon. It was a skin-prickling harmony, one that undulated as the two howls intertwined, both piercing and deafening at the same time. For just a fleeting moment, the wastes were silenced for miles around.

'We will meet you in the north. The fenrir will know where to go, and where to wait,' Hokus instructed, as the huge beasts began to paw at the dirt.

'We have several other engagements,' replied Valefor, looking southwards.

'How do you get these things moving?' Samara asked.

Valefor winked. 'Like this,' he said, as Hokus clapped his claws together, making a sound like a whip-crack. The fenrir burst into life. One giant leap took them from the barrow to the flat earth, and then they were off, galloping across the wastes, nipping at the heels of the wind.

Chapter 13

"Power may rest in the hands of the gods, but defiance is a man's business."
Words from the writing of the philosopher Winble Narn

Questions. The ship was veritably aflame with them.
Where did the dragons go?
Why had the Lost Clans attacked?
Is the Old Dragon still alive?
How did they escape the mountain?
Where are we going now?
How are we supposed to sleep in these crowded conditions?
What are we going to do with all these women and children?
'Where do the dead go?'
The whole table looked up at that. Forks dangled, hesitant, in front of open mouths. Knives rested mid-slice on the porcelain plates. Every eye turned on Farden. The mage met only one pair, those of a dark and tall man that his uncle had insisted the others refer to as "Heim". The god-incognito was sitting silently in front of his untouched plate, smiling politely and somewhat uncomfortably.

'Where do what now?' Roiks repeated. Despite Nuka's covert kicking, he had been recounting a ribald tale concerning a lifeboat and several young, innocent maidens. Gabbant, Colonel Tinbits, and Hasterkin had been mid-guffaw. Now they simply stared, laughter dead, mouths half open.

Farden's question had been simmering within him all afternoon, bubbling and boiling like a stew, working its way up to his lips. His interrogation of the gods had been thwarted by his uncle. Loki and Heimdall had quickly made themselves scarce. Farden had been forced to keep quiet, for the time being, under threats of being tossed into the briny deep, Grimsayer and all. Farden had spent the rest of the afternoon helping to house the stranded Sirens, or thumbing through the Grimsayer and simmering quietly to himself.

Now the question had boiled to the top. It wasn't the best timing. All the others knew of "Heim" was that he was a quiet, slightly odd, keen-eyed aid of Arkmage Tyrfing's who wasn't too keen on his food.

'You heard me,' replied Farden, still staring directly at the tawny-eyed god.

'I do not know what you mean,' answered Heimdall, in a low voice. His eyes flicked around the table, finally resting on Captain Nuka.

'You four,' Nuka said, pointing to Roiks, Gabbant, Hasterkin, and Tinbits. 'Dismissed.'

Roiks immediately got to his feet. He knew the captain well enough to feel the edge to his tone. Even though he wasn't the ranking officer, he shepherded the others quickly to the door. 'Right. Dinner on deck, lads. You 'eard the ole captain.'

It was a moment's work on the bosun's part. Moments later the door was shut and the clomping of boots quickly faded into the corridor beyond. The ship pitched and rolled on a wave before anybody spoke.

With a clearing of his throat, Tyrfing put his knife and fork down and rested his elbows on the table. He looked to his nephew and nodded. 'It seems that my nephew wants answers.'

'So it would appear,' Heimdall replied. 'It would also appear that he does not have the patience to wait until after dinner.'

Farden let himself bubble over. 'You're all sat here like nothing is wrong. If Modren were here, instead of me, he would be marching across those waves on foot, instead of sitting here, eating and laughing and pretending that nothing is wrong, like today never happened. You're acting like Elessi is at home, darning her new husband's socks,' Farden scowled. 'Well, she isn't. And let's not mention my beloved daughter, heading north as we speak. What about her, eh? We all seem a little bit too relaxed for my liking,' he said, drumming his fingernails slowly on the table.

'Now look...' began Nuka, readying his fork to punctuate his points with little jabs, but Tyrfing cut him off cold.

'He's right,' said the Arkmage. By his side, Lerel raised an eyebrow. Nuka frowned. Farden, face blank, simply listened as his uncle went on. 'Farden is the only one around this table that actually seems to know what in Emaneska is going on. I can hardly believe it myself, and he'll forgive me for saying that, but it's true. I also know he's got a plan, and even though I suspect it will be the downright maddest plan I've ever heard, I want to hear it. You came here to help us, Heimdall. You can do that by answering his questions. He's not the only one who wants to hear the answers,' he said, shuffling in his seat. He glanced at Farden out of the corner of his eye. His nephew was nodding. Tyrfing shrugged. If there was one thing their family wasn't good at, it was apologies.

'What exactly happened in Hjaussfen?' Lerel raised the other eyebrow.

'Let's just say we reached an understanding,' said Tyrfing. His little speech over, he began to cough. He hoarsely excused himself and went to stand by the window.

Heimdall folded his arms. 'Your questions then, mage?'

Farden leant forward. His exterior was expressionless, but inside he grinned a little at his minor victory, and at his uncle's words.

It warmed him in ways he hadn't felt in years. 'I'll ask again. Where do the dead go?'

'You mortals already know full well. The other side.'

'Yes, but by what path?'

Heimdall pushed his plate forward and let his elbows occupy its space. It was odd to see a god make such a human movement, as simple as crossing arms over a table. 'You think your maid is on this path.'

Farden nodded. 'I do.'

Heimdall shook his head. 'Then I shall not tell you.'

Lerel and Nuka pulled similar faces. Tyrfing was about to interject when Farden held up a hand. 'Let him speak. I know what he's going to say,' he said, enjoying the looks of "do you?" radiating from the others at the table. Farden settled back in his chair and motioned for the god to continue.

Heimdall fixed the mage with his tawny stare. 'I have been patient with you. We,' he motioned to the ceiling and the sky beyond it, 'have been patient. We have watched you chase the salvation of your dying friend across the sea in the hope that the path to that goal was entwined with the other, more serious path. The path we should be treading, as was explained to us in Krauslung.'

'Forgive me, sire, but you're talking in riddles,' Nuka bowed his head, reverent as any.

'And avoiding my question.'

Heimdall waved his hand. 'I have let you waste enough time trying to save the maid. It is time we do what is most important, and kill your daughter, Farden. Before she brings the whole sky down upon us.'

Farden rubbed his stubbled chin, absorbing the words. He nodded slowly. 'I see,' was all he said. The others held their breath, half-expecting the mage to throw his chair against the bulkhead, or storm off in a rage, but instead he pulled back the sleeve of his cloak and let his armoured forearm fall on the table with a thud. He pointed at the glittering Scalussen metal and watched Heimdall's eyes take it in. 'You're a god that sees a lot of things,' he said. 'Have you seen this before?' Heimdall didn't answer. Farden went on. 'I know you have. A god like you, a *watcher*, if I heard Loki right, doesn't forget things like this.' Here he flicked the metal, making it sing. 'Especially something that has godblood in it, whatever that may be.'

The eyes of the room slowly swivelled from the vambrace to the god.

Had the god ever tired of being a god, then he could have sought a lucrative career in gambling. His face was deader than deadpan. Unreadable. Still, there was something in his silence that betrayed him.

Farden tapped his vambrace again. 'My next question then, seeing as you're unwilling to answer my last. What exactly is godblood?'

'I would have thought the clue was in its name,' Tyrfing suggested.

'As would I. But I have it on good account that gods, or rather ghosts, don't bleed,' replied Farden, remembering his altercation with Loki on the beach. 'You could say I know first-hand.'

Heimdall stayed silent and still and staring. Farden's eyes did their best to hold Heimdall's heavy stare. He held it for as long as he could while he spoke. 'You brought me back from Albion to fight my daughter, and I intend to do exactly that. Whatever emotions I had for her were lost that day on the hill, when I saw what she did, and the smile on her face as she did it. Nobody understands the gravity of the situation more than I do. And whatever reservations you have about me, us, bury them. We've earned the right to be trusted. No more secrets. Not now. Not when we're so close to the end,' Farden said, calmly and slowly. He wasn't a born speaker, but his words were tough and true.

For a long while, Heimdall didn't answer. It was only when the silence was becoming unbearable that he sat back in his chair, making it creak loudly under his weight. 'The Allfather demanded that you be punished for your insolence, after what you did to Loki. He is a young god. But a god all the same,' he said, quietly. He saw the reaction of the others. 'Ah yes. They do not know you struck him.'

Farden lifted his chin. 'And I would do it again, too,' he said, making the others pale.

Heimdall continued. 'I have watched you longer than most, Farden. Longer even than our sister Evernia. Watched you tarry and squander your gifts and duties. I remember when Evernia called for help, I doubted you in front of all the gods. I proclaimed you unfit to carry responsibility on your shoulders.'

Farden raised his chin. 'And now?' It was like asking the hangman if he could see the knot.

Heimdall let the politest of smiles tug at his mouth. 'Even a god can be wrong, at times,' he said. 'But I think your uncle is right. We came here to help you.'

'So my questions?'

Heimdall looked to the wooden ceiling. 'It is a fine night to taste the air, do you not think?'

So it was that Farden, Heimdall, and Tyrfing ended up on deck. Lerel and Nuka stayed behind to see to their unfinished plates, citing hunger and something about ignorance being bliss.

Heimdall was right: it was a fine night to taste the air. Salty and ice-cold, it stole the mages' breath away as they climbed the stairs onto the quiet deck. Night had taken the sky, and the stars were on watch. In the east, a waxing moon held court. Its milky light turned the wave-tips into mercury and silver as they reached and bowed before the ship as it sped east and north around the Nelska cape. Sailors and soldiers went about their evening business quietly, smoking pipes and murmuring in low voices. It had been a long day indeed. All were tired.

The three went to the prow, where Ilios lay curled up, yet awake, in his usual spot. The wind was playing with his feathers. He eyed them curiously as they approached and sat on the steps beside his head. He raised a tufted ear when he saw the huge, gnarled tome that Farden placed on the deck.

Heimdall had remained standing. He folded his arms behind his back and stood in front of the mages like a soldier at ease. 'You asked of godblood. Why?' he asked.

'When the second daemon attacked us outside the Spire, it saw my armour and hissed that word at me. Then it left. Quickly too.'

Heimdall was intrigued. 'That is interesting, if unexpected.'

'Farden seems to think there is something about the armour that will help fight the daemons, and his daughter,' explained Tyrfing. 'He wants to find the rest of it.'

Farden scowled a little at his uncle. 'I was getting to that bit.'

'Well,' said Heimdall, 'if what you say is true, Farden, you may be right.' The mage barely resisted the urge to punch the air.

'So what of the rest of it? You must know where it is.' Farden was trying hard to hide his excitement.

'If only it were that simple, mage,' said Heimdall. 'I know where it was last. I do not know where it is now.'

'How delightfully cryptic.' Farden ran his fingers over the perfect ridges of his armour. 'So this wasn't part of the reason you wanted me to come back?'

'An added bonus, it would seem. If we are abandoning secrets, then the real truth is that we did not know about this.'

'There seems to be a surprising amount you gods don't know.'

'We're gods. We're not perfect,' said a familiar voice. Heimdall turned around to find Loki standing in the shadows by the iron-wrapped foremast.

'Evernia's favourite saying,' said Farden. He was surprised

that he could remember that. Clarity he may have had, but his memories were still frayed. The nevermar hadn't left him yet.

'Join us, Loki. Even you have not heard this story.'

Loki moved from the shadows without making a sound and went to stand by the railing, beside Tyrfing. A dark shape slid from the inside of his cloak, slithered down his leg, and then scampered across the deck towards Farden. The mage didn't even flinch. He held his hand out and Whiskers ran up to his shoulder, where he nestled into the mage's neck. 'I thought I had heard all the stories,' Loki muttered.

'Looks like we're not the only ones the gods keep secrets from,' Farden nudged his uncle. Tyrfing nodded stiffly. He couldn't help but notice Loki's jaw clench.

Heimdall began to pace up and down. His voice was low, rough as gravel. 'Loki and Evernia are both right. We gods are far from perfect. We have been known to make a mistake, or two, in the past. Mistakes like the ones being worn around your arms and legs, Farden.

'In the years after we dragged the daemons into the sky, humanity grew and flourished faster than we could have ever imagined. We watched you from afar as you built kingdom after kingdom, forging the beginnings of empires. The Arka settled. The Sirens prospered. The first inklings of what would later become the Skölgard grew hungry. I believe you call this time the Scattered Kingdoms. Well, with kingdoms come kings, with kings come greed, and with greed comes war.

'While these skirmishes and minor wars raged, the monstrosities left behind in the wake of the daemons and their elves continued to breed in the dark places of the world. I watched them all, and from above, I realised the world looked very much as we had left it. A dangerous, vicious place, full of darkness and war.

'When the Allfather called for a solution, you were barely a notion, Loki. This is why you have no memory of this. We all swore a silence on the matter.'

'On what matter?' Farden interrupted.

'Patience, mage,' Heimdall told him. He paced some more before he continued. 'We decided that if we were unable to protect the world we had left behind, then we would need to create something that could. So it was that we came to the smiths of Scalussen, a city high at the Spine of the World, populated by peaceful, wise, and gods-fearing people. We bade them to make us suits of armour to which we could lend our powers, what little we had. At that time the world was rife with prayer, and we were stronger then than we are now. It took all our power, gathered for almost five hundred years, to summon enough wherewithal to spill one drop of the Allfather's blood into the Scalussen forges, and it took all the smiths' skill to bind it to the metal that they drew from it. One by one, they forged nine suits, for nine warriors of their choosing. It took a decade to summon them all. I watched them arrive from every corner of the world. Some eager. Some skilled. Others both. Warriors and hopefuls all. The smiths and their pens called their names and they came.'

'The Scalussen Nine,' Farden said. 'I have chased their legacy for years.'

'As have many, and for one reason only. Not the warriors themselves, not coin, not fame, but the blood we spilt on their metal. *That* metal, Farden, that you wear. You know what power I speak of.'

'Life,' Loki whispered, staring at the mage's vambraces.

'Exactly,' grunted Heimdall. He quickened his pacing. 'Of course, we were foolish to assume that the world would accept our efforts. We imagined these Nine as guardians of peace, fighting for the gods and the people as protectors, forever watching over Emaneska as we should have been. And they did, for a time. Wars were interrupted. Elf wells were destroyed. Creatures thrown back into the shadows. The darkness was pushed back just a little. We had succeeded.

'But soon enough, it was greed that muddled our efforts. Word spread of suits of armour that had been wrought by the gods, and soon enough every king and warlord with an army to their name came marching north. Scalussen and her lands were besieged for a long and terrible year, and slowly but unavoidably, the Nine fell, one by one. I watched as the remaining knights threw themselves into the volcanoes of the Spine, to keep the armour from falling foul of greed. All but one.'

'One? Only one escaped?'

'Only one. Wounded, he fled Scalussen, leading the fight away from the people and the ruined city. He shed his armour as he fled. A pair of vambraces here. Greaves and gauntlets there. He buried them in the ice and snow as he ran, in the hope of keeping them lost. Finally, he disappeared from my view, seeking refuge in the mountains. Like the kings and lords that chased him, I looked for days, weeks, even years, watching for any sign of him and the armour. I have looked for centuries and never found him. The rest of his armour was lost with him. By some twist of strange coincidence that baffles even the best of us gods, Farden, you have the only pieces known to man or I,' said Heimdall. 'It was one of the reasons Evernia put so much faith in you.'

'How oddly convenient,' muttered Loki.

'Call it blind stubbornness, and luck,' Farden replied, touching something around his neck.

Tyrfing spoke up. 'Wait a minute. How can you, of all gods, Heimdall, just lose somebody in the mountains? Your eyes see beyond things we could only hope to understand.'

'They do, but there is one place I cannot see. Only once place he can be.'

'Where?'

'Hel, Farden. The darkness between this world and the other side. Where the path of the dead leads.'

Farden was almost halfway to his feet, excited, or incredulous, or angry, or all three at the same time. 'You knew this all along? You knew where the Scalussen armour was *all along*?'

Heimdall held up a hand. 'On the contrary, mage. You speak of it as if it were a cave that one can simply wander in and out of. It is the realm of the dead, Farden. One must be dead to journey there.'

Farden was already halfway through the Grimsayer, hands spread and fingers drumming eagerly. 'What was his name?'

Heimdall hesitated, sensing another distraction on the horizon.

Farden pointed a rigid finger at the blank page of the Grimsayer. 'His name, Heimdall?'

'It will not help,' the god insisted.

Tyrfing slammed the deck with the flat of his hand. 'Give it to him, before he pops a vein.'

'It was Korrin.'

'Korrin,' breathed Farden, and the Grimsayer came to life as it had done in the library. Ilios whistled low and cautiously as it went to work. Twin lights like orange fireflies arose from the dusty paper while pages flapped and whirred past, too fast for any eyes but Heimdall's.

With a thud of heavy pages, the book came to an abrupt halt, lying as still as a gravestone. The lights began their weaving. Farden leant forward, years, decades, and more culminating in every flick and frolic of their tails. He veritably shook with anticipation. No Elessi. No Samara. Only Scalussen occupied his mind.

A pair of feet appeared, armoured in achingly familiar metal, then a pair of legs, then a chest, shoulders, arms, and then finally a head. The lights fell back as if to admire their work, and the onlookers basked in the soft orange glow of the young man lying sprawled across the page, as if slumped against a wall. He flickered in the same way that Elessi had.

Farden's eyes widened to saucers. 'Fuck me. He's still alive!' he gasped, drawing a dark frown from Heimdall. 'He's been alive for all these years!' Farden scrabbled to get closer to the image, so close that his nose almost touched it. His wide eyes devoured every inch of Korrin's remaining armour, every ridge, every curve, every plate that covered his head, chest, shoulders and upper arms. It was simply, undeniably beautiful. Every inch like Farden had dreamt and more. He had to stop himself from reaching out to touch it.

'That can't be possible,' Tyrfing said, awed. His eyes were almost as wide as his nephew's.

Heimdall crossed his arms, as if Tyrfing hadn't listened to a single word. 'Of course it is,' he rumbled.

Farden grabbed the sides of the Grimsayer as though he were throttling the life from it. It hissed as he slid it along the deck, closer still. 'Where is he? Where can I find him?'

Farden barely managed to retrieve his fingers before the Grimsayer slammed itself shut and then flicked to the very first page. A familiar scene began to fly across its pages then, of ice and trees and frozen mountains, of snow and of nine rocks clustered in a circle, pointing at the sky.

'By the looks on your faces,' Loki said, looking at Tyrfing and Farden, 'I'd say that you two have seen that place before.'

'Well, I'd be lying if I said I was expecting that,' Farden took a deep breath.

'You know this place?' Heimdall asked.

Farden nodded. His nails were nervously drumming on his vambrace. His knee jogged up and down. 'It's where Elessi is,' he said.

'That's a ghostgate,' Loki blurted. Heimdall shot him a glance, and then sighed.

'Loki is correct. There are a few still left in the world. You have encountered one once before, Farden, in Albion.'

Farden clicked his fingers. The mental itch he'd been clawing at died away. He remembered now. 'When we went back to the

Arkabbey.'

'Ghostgates are doors for the dead, made when the world was young, made before we fell from the sky,' Loki piped up again. 'They are like the holes in a gutter, for souls to flood through.'

Tyrfing frowned. 'A charming metaphor.'

Farden slapped the deck with his hands. It was all so simple. 'Whatever it's called, it's where I'm going.'

'No, mage,' Heimdall boomed. 'Your business is with your daughter. Your path leads to her, not the maid, nor to your own greed.'

'Even when I can use it to fight her? That makes no sense.'

'There is a reason that armour is better hidden away, lost.'

Farden got to his feet. 'Are you saying that I'm unfit to wear it? I'm not warrior enough, like Korrin?'

'It takes more than a sword to make a warrior, Farden.' The god chuckled here. 'It matters not. It is inconsequential. You cannot retrieve it, just as you cannot retrieve your maid.' His smile faded as he saw the hot glint in Farden's eye. 'And for that, I am sorry.' The word sounds alien in his mouth. He had never apologised to a mortal before. 'You will pursue Samara. All else can wait,' Heimdall instructed. He looked to Tyrfing, expecting him to nod, but the Arkmage stayed still. He looked torn.

Farden clapped his hands and grinned. 'Well,' he said. 'You can do whatever you damn well please, Heimdall. I'm going north to that ghostgate. You're more than welcome to stop me, if you can.' Farden just stood there, smiling, while Heimdall simmered like a distant storm.

Heimdall stared out from under his bushy eyebrows. 'I am beginning to agree with the Allfather on the subject of your punishment,' he rumbled.

Farden raised his hands to the dark sky. 'I'm waiting,' he called. Tyrfing couldn't help but wince at the blasphemy of it all. Farden stood there in silence, like a parched farmer waiting for rain, glaring at the night sky. 'I said, I'm waiting!' But nothing happened. No punishment came, and Farden shrugged.

As he bent to pick up the glowing Grimsayer, he flashed both Heimdall and Loki a dark look. 'I've been punished enough,' he grunted, before sauntering back to his room.

When Farden had disappeared into the gloom, Tyrfing tapped his hands on his knees. He coughed once, twice, grimaced, and then ran a hand through his beard. 'Looks like this story finally has its hero,' he mused.

'What?' Loki asked.

'Nothing. Just something Durnus once said to me,' Tyrfing mumbled. He ruffled his gryphon's ears before standing. He bowed to the gods, trying to add a little deference to the situation, and made his excuses. 'Speaking of Durnus, I better go and relay the evening's revelations. I bid you both a good night.' He left, leaving the gods to listen to the soft thumping of his boots as he receded into the creaking darkness of the deck.

'What did he say?' asked Loki, irritated at how confused he was.

Heimdall was glaring at the sea. 'Nothing,' he replied, and went to go stand by the railing.

❦

Farden found his bed thoroughly occupied. Lerel was curled up like a cat, half-lost beneath the blanket and pillow. Farden quietly shut the door and rode the sway of the ship to the bedside table. The Grimsayer barely fit, so he wedged it on its end. He could have sworn he heard it mutter. Perhaps it was the creaking of the *'Blade.*

Farden felt the weight of tiredness pushing down on him. He perched on the end of the bed and let Whiskers tiptoe down his arms into his hands.

'What a day, old boy,' Farden whispered, with a shake of his head. The rat stared up at him with his expressionless black eyes and twitched his whiskers.

What a night too, he sighed. What revelations. Farden's head swam through a sea of emotions he couldn't begin to fathom. Excitement, fear, worry, elation. They mattered little. All that mattered was the piercing, crystal determination that had once more settled over him, the clarity as sharp as a diamond. For once, Farden knew exactly what he was doing. He could taste the end, whatever that was.

Whiskers ran his paws across his face and chattered to himself. Lerel shuffled around in her sleep, moaning something. Both the mage and the rat turned to look at her.

Farden frowned. 'She's taken up my whole bed,' he muttered, then smiled. He reached out and tucked the blanket over her. She was still fully dressed. He wondered how long she had waited for him.

He placed the rat on the foot of bed. Whiskers curled up there, and didn't move, watching Lerel carefully. There was something about her that the rat was wary of. Farden didn't blame him. He probably sensed the feline in her. The mage ruffled his tiny black ears, tinged with silvery grey. He slid off one of his vambraces, and wedged it under a pillow so Whiskers could crawl inside it.

With a sigh that was as shallow, yet as deep as any sea, Farden got to his feet. He dabbled with the idea of crawling into bed with Lerel, but he shook his head. Something about her reminded him of a time with Cheska.

Cheska. His sweetest enemy. He couldn't wait to forget her. Besides, Lerel was fast asleep, and his clarity couldn't afford to be clouded. Farden stretched out on the smooth floor instead. He was dead to the world before his head even hit the wood.

She felt no cold.

She felt nothing of the jealous pine needles stinging her ghostly feet.

She felt nothing of the wind, tugging at her misted curls.

She felt nothing.

No confusion, as she tread the sticky loam of the dark, foreign forest. No fear, as the wolves skipped around her, gnashing jaws, as the ravens cawed and scattered in the pines. No regret, no anger, no fear, just a simple sense of *purpose*. To walk. To keep moving. But to where she did not know.

She could only watch as her body moved inexorably forward, bare feet glowing softly as they flowed effortlessly across the dirt and ice and rock.

She could only gaze down as the peaks of the mountains flew by beneath her, as her limbs trailed green and blue alongside the flowing magick, silent and soaring in the wake of the moon. Always moving. Ever north, with the stars shining down on her. Always crisp night. Never warm day. If a ghost can feel anything, anything at all, it is the dull ache of longing for a shred of warmth.

Elessi felt it. She felt it with every mile. But she could also feel it waning. The further north she travelled, the more the ache died away, until she had almost forgotten its bitter touch. *The touch of what?*

With every mile north, she was waning too.

Chapter 14

"There is no other way to describe the inner workings of the magick council than to say it is an eternal and vicious game of chess. And woe betide anybody who tries to take the king, the Marble Copse itself."
Ripped from the diary of Council Fustigan

'These Arka girls can't dance to save their lives,' Jeasin snorted, listening to the shuffle and clomp of the banquet hall around her.

'These women, *whore*,' Malvus muttered sternly, 'are your betters. The cream of Krauslung society. Wives, sisters, daughters, and mistresses of the new ruling class of this fine city. You'd do well to mind your tongue around such company.'

'Fine.' Jeasin shrugged. 'But they still can't bloody dance.'

Malvus allowed himself a small smile, and turned to watch the evening's revelry.

Well, perhaps *revelry* wasn't quite the best word to describe it. The mood in the grand banquet hall was one of smug sedateness. He watched the men and woman calmly wheel around, treading traditional steps to the slow whining of the ljots and keening of the flutes. Everybody was dressed head to toe in the finest clothes the Arka markets had to offer. The new lords and ladies of Krauslung and beyond. Malvus could see it in their pinched smiles and twinkling eyes. He could see it in the grinning whispers as the men passed each other, or lingered at the tables. This was their city now, and they knew it.

And he ruled them all.

Malvus turned to the woman by his side. He looked her up and down, at her borrowed finery, her curled hair, her new, glittering jewellery circling her neck and wrists. She stood there, hip tilted to one side and arms crossed, staring sightlessly at the fine crowds around her. What a proud creature she was. What a hard woman. Malvus liked that. He had noticed the stares of the other women, of the councils' wives and daughters. They wouldn't meet his eyes, but he had seen them glancing at Jeasin. Albion trash, in their eyes. A whore. She didn't belong in these circles. Malvus had initially agreed, confining her company to the nights and to his sheets, but now an idea had begun to form in his mind. An inkling. He smiled again as he considered it. *Every king needed a queen.*

'And what would an Albion courtesan know of dancing?'

Jeasin laughed then. Brash and bold. 'Dancin' ain't about music and banquets. It's about bodies, and how you use it. It don't end on the floor, Malvus. It don't stop when the music does. I know more about dancin' than these sisters and wives ever could.' She winked then. Malvus rolled his eyes. *Confident creature.* He reached for her hand and she let him raise it. He half-expected her to snatch it away, but she was too clever for that. He kissed it, an inch past formally, and then led her to the dance floor.

The crowd parted to let them through, every head bowing politely and reverently. Malvus relished every minute of it, every footfall and step. He held Jeasin on his arm like a prize.

As it turned out, the Arka women didn't know how to dance, and if the glances had been scathing before, now they were positively boiling. Malvus led Jeasin around the floor, letting her spin and swivel, while he watched his newly appointed lords smirk while their mistresses and spouses stared on. A few of the younger women even tried to imitate the Albion woman, raising the eyebrows of the men even further.

Something about Jeasin's dancing seemed to raise the pace of the evening. The skalds in the corner kicked something lively into their tune, and soon the sedate air began to crumble, leading to something altogether informal.

'More wine!' called Malvus, snapping his fingers at a pair of nearby servants. They rushed to do his bidding. Decanters of purple and yellow wine were soon flying about on trays, glugging into half-empty glasses and being swigged by laughing mouths. How quickly it was, that the veneer of refinement flaked away, to reveal the debauchery beneath that only power, money, and an excuse can buy.

Malvus led Jeasin back to the window. Toskig was there, with Jarvins. The latter was slouching against the wall in his new armour, idly watching his wife swan about the room. He had a half-empty bottle of ale dangling from his hand. Toskig clicked his heels as Malvus approached. Jarvins slid a little way up the wall, and saluted with his bottle. Malvus ignored him.

'General Toskig. How are you enjoying the banquet?'

Toskig looked a little uncomfortable. He wasn't used to such company. What he wouldn't have given for a good old tavern, or a mess, with a flagon of foaming ale and a good old brawl. 'Very good, my lord,' he said, stiffly.

'And have you met the good lady Jeasin?' Malvus gestured to the woman at his side, managing to ignore the snort Jeasin made at the mention of *lady*.

Toskig bowed as low as his armour would allow. 'My lady.'

'Pleasure,' Jeasin said. She could play her role at least, when needed. 'You a mage?'

Toskig shook his head quickly. 'No, my lady. Though I taught mages, at the School. In Manesmark.'

'And a fine job of it he did too.' Jarvins gargled his beer.

'Knew a mage once. A Written,' Jeasin began, causing Malvus to raise an eyebrow. 'Farden, you know 'im?'

There was an awkward silence between them, broken only by Jarvins swaggering off with a sigh, off to drag his wife back from the edge of embarrassment, and to find himself some more of that fine, strong ale. Toskig cleared his throat. 'I knew him, yes. Fought with him in Efjar, when I was naught but a recruit. Good man. Even better mage.'

'Yes, well,' Malvus hissed. 'A traitor to our cause, of course.'

'Of course,' Toskig muttered, looking at the floor.

' 'Course,' Jeasin. She knew better than to say anything more.

'My lord!' a shout rang out over the music and the sounds of the hall. Malvus turned to find a skinny boy weaving his way through the crowd, dressed in the livery of a messenger. The boy skidded to a halt, bowed once, twice, even three times before handing the scrap of parchment over, with shaking hands.

'What is this?'

'Message for you m'lord. From a Nelska hawk. Marked urgent, said my master.'

Malvus snatched the parchment from the boy's hands. 'Away with you.'

'Yes, m'lord!' The boy scuttled off.

'Word from the dragons?' Toskig asked.

Malvus flashed him a look. 'In a fashion, General. Nothing you need concern yourself with.' He folded the parchment and slid it deep into his silk pocket. He kept his hand on it. 'I'm afraid I must leave you in the good company of the General, Jeasin. He'll escort you back to your rooms.'

'You mean your rooms?'

Malvus narrowed his eyes. It irked him that she couldn't see his expression. She might have held her tongue. 'Any room will do, as long it isn't this room.'

'An' what if I want to dance some more?'

Malvus smiled a greasy smile at Toskig and then leant close to whisper in the woman's ear. 'Then you can do it in the darkness of a prison cell,' he breathed. 'Or, if you prefer, at the end of a rope.' Jeasin simply turned away, saying nothing. 'I'll leave her in your hands then, Toskig.'

'Yes, my lord,' replied the general, and with that Malvus strode towards the door, urgent and hurried. Toskig watched him go, wondering what in Emaneska to say to such a woman. He'd heard the stories from Jarvins. Everybody had.

'So,' he coughed.

'You 'ungry?' she asked, abruptly.

Toskig shook his head. 'Erm. I ate…'

'I'm bloody starvin',' she muttered, as she felt her way towards the smell of food, wafting on the breeze from the back of the hall. She strode forward confidently, making others get out of her way. She was enjoying this, despite Malvus' parting words. Enjoying the feel of eyes upon her, of the furtive whispers they thought she couldn't hear, of all of it.

Toskig was not enjoying anything. He walked behind her, dodging in between the dancers, trying not to get in anybody's way. A hundred colours of silk and shades of jewellery spun before his eyes. His armour gleamed a little too harshly in the light. The wine had gone to his head.

'Do you need a hand?' he called to Jeasin.

'No,' she flatly replied. And she didn't. She walked right up to the tables, stopping just before them, and began to feel around for what had been left over from the evening's feasting. Toskig watched as she pawed about, collecting things on a dirty plate, like a thief rooting through a box of treasures. A hunk of bread. A slice of cheese. A titbit of ham. Some oiled fish. Only once did she falter, dipping her finger in a bowl of soup. She cursed and kept going. More bread.

More cheese. She must have been starving indeed.

'Finished?' Toskig said, rubbing his stubbled chin.

'Just about,' Jeasin muttered, as she added something greasy and roasted. 'There.'

'Shall I escort you to your room?'

'If you have to.'

'It seems I must.'

'Lead the way then.'

Toskig did as he was told, leading the woman from the banquet hall by the corner of his arm. She clutched the plate in her other hand. The general tried not to wonder where she was going to put it all.

Soon enough, they had escaped the hall, and were walking through the quiet corridors of the Arkathedral, boots and shoes clicking softly on the marble. Glancing through the windows on their right, Toskig noticed night had only just fallen, and the torches of the city were only beginning to glimmer. Toskig stared at his city, at the smoke leaking from chimneys and at the tiny figures below in the orange veins of cobblestone streets. The word *responsibility*, came to mind then. They were his now, in a way. He had swapped two-dozen grubby recruits for the safety of the whole city. No wonder he felt so bewildered, so nervous. A sergeant, in a general's boots.

'Here we are,' muttered Jeasin, pulling him to the right.

Toskig shook his head and pulled her back. 'I'm afraid you're mistaken, my lady. Malvus'... your rooms are higher up. That's the way to the prisons.'

'That it is,' she said, pulling again, but Toskig stood his ground.

The general eyed her suspiciously. 'And what would you want with the prisons?'

Jeasin huffed. 'What do you think, Toskig?'

The general looked over the woman's shoulder and frowned.

A little lump blossomed in his stomach. 'Malvus' orders…'

'…Mean shit. He ain't here.'

'Of course he's not. But there are guards, there are eyes everywhere. Including mine.'

Jeasin put her free hand on her hip. 'It's food, man. Not a key to the door. That's your old Arkmage in there, right? Your Undermage and his wife? Starvin' probably. A little food won't 'urt. You going to tell him?'

Toskig didn't reply. Jeasin sniffed. 'An' here I was thinkin' you were the honest type.'

Toskig frowned. 'You put me on dangerous ground, woman.'

'You were already on it. So am I. Anyone is, where Malvus is concerned.'

'Mind your tongue…'

'I'm gettin' bored of people tellin' me that.'

Toskig sighed. He looked up the corridor, then down it. Nobody. He looked into the hallways that led to the prisons. He could see the guards at the end of it. Loitering by the torches, clacking their spears against the floor. 'Men!' he called. Their heads snapped around and they soon came running.

Toskig took a breath and crossed his arms as Jeasin stepped to the side, plate held behind her back. The two guards trotted up and smartly came to a halt. They saluted, and then glanced sideways at Jeasin. One recognised her; she had been there a few nights ago. *On Lord Malvus' orders*, if he remembered rightly.

'Eyes front, reprobates,' snapped Toskig, in his best drill sergeant voice.

'Yessir!' they barked in reply.

As Toskig began to grill them, demanding unnecessary reports on the state of the prisoners, Jeasin quietly slipped down the corridor, heading straight for the deepest, darkest cell. Her hand trailed on the wall, feeling it turn from marble, to rough stone, then to iron in places, etched with runes and spells.

'Durnus!' she hissed through the grate. 'Old man!'

A face soon appeared, a gaunt face, wrinkled with age. 'Jeasin,' he said. 'What a pleasure.'

'What does she want?' came a mutter from inside the cell.

'To feed us, by the smell of it.'

'And that's all tonight,' she said, pushing the food through the gaps in the grate, piece by piece. She wrinkled her nose at the oily fish as she felt it between her fingers.

'On Malvus' orders again?' said the other voice, that of the Undermage.

Jeasin shook her head. 'No. One of the new generals provided a distraction. Seems to be on your side.'

Modren's pushed his face up against the grate. 'Which general?'

'Toskig?'

'You mean Sergeant Toskig?'

'Yeah, well 'e's General Toskig now. Malvus took a shine to him.'

'And Toskig was stupid enough to accept,' Modren hissed.

'Maybe he just wants to survive, not be locked up in a bloody cell, like you two,' Jeasin shrugged. 'I know I do.'

'Well, thank you, Jeasin. For the food,' Durnus said, quietly.

'This is gettin' dangerous, you know. Sneakin' about like this.'

Modren snarled. 'So's being at the mercy of Krauslung's newest dictator.'

'That ain't my fault.'

'Do you have any news?' asked Durnus.

Jeasin scratched at her head. 'He got a letter. By hawk.'

'From whom?'

'Nelska.'

'Saker then.'

Durnus put his head against the bars, trying not to betray the dark pit of hopelessness that was slowly digging its way into his stomach. 'I can only wonder what he is planning,' he muttered, before disappearing into the darkness of the cell.

Modren gripped the bars. 'Jeasin,' he asked. 'How much do you know about hawks?'

Jeasin raised an eyebrow.

*

The birds smelled foul. She knew that much about hawks. They smelled foul, and they shuffled around on their perches, rattling their claws and making her flinch. Jeasin hated birds. She clutched the scrap of parchment in her hand and edged closer to the nearest hawk.

It screeched and Jeasin quickly backed away. *Curse those mages*, she hissed inside her head. If she had been standing on dangerous ground before, she was now perching on the edge of a very tall and very unstable cliff.

Jeasin bit her lip and tried again. The hawk stayed silent this time. She reached forward and gingerly felt its feathers, cold and soft. The hawk didn't move. She took a breath and reached for its leg, where Modren had told her she would find a little loop of twine. The mage had been right, and her fingers found the roughness of it. While she tried not to think of the sharp beak, inches from her face, she rolled up the parchment with her nervous fingers and pushed it through the loop.

A noise in the corridor outside made her freeze. Boots, on cold marble. She paused, parchment halfway through the loop, heart beating, while she listened to the boots recede.

'Too bloody close,' she muttered, as she pulled the loop tight and tugged it hard. The bird whined. It seemed secure enough.

Jeasin moved to the window and felt for its latch. Gods. *Of course it was stuck.* Jeasin grit her teeth and jiggled it. Still stuck. She pushed harder and it came loose with a stomach-clenching bang. A blast of cold air slapped her in the face, and she winced. Behind her, the birds began to flap and screech. Jeasin flinched again. They were making far too much noise. Jeasin quickly reached for her hawk. Its wings hit her hard in the face as she lifted it from its perch but she hung on grimly, holding it up to the open window.

'The Old Dragon!' she snapped at it, before tossing it out into the night.

chapter 15

"*The wind was a king's daughter once. A beautiful, beautiful girl was she, with a face that could make a daemon's heart melt. But her father the king was a jealous king, a fearful king. To keep her beauty from the leering eyes of men he locked her away in the highest tower of his castle. For years the daughter begged to be let go, so that she might glimpse the face of another man besides her father, and for years the king refused her, each time telling her that next year, she would be allowed. And so the years dragged on, until her nineteenth birthday, when once more she asked to see the face of another man. When the king refused again, the daughter wept and cried like never before. Three days she cried, until finally it broke the king's heart to see her beauty so marred with grief, and so he finally relented.*

The next day the king decreed that all nine cities should put forward a champion, not of sword nor of magick, but of ugliness. One by one the cities sent their champions, and one by one they came, revulsive to the very core. Scarred, disfigured, malformed, they came to stand before the king. All the court but he wilted before their gruesome visages. It took him three days to choose a champion. Finally he selected a quiet young man from the second city, a hideous creature yet pure of heart. The king had him dressed in sackcloth and ashes, and so disfigured was he that the maids needed blindfolds to dress him.

When the king called for the young man, they tread the thousand steps to the very top of the tallest tower together, until at long last they came to the doors of his daughter's room. The king called for his daughter, and thrilled, she came, throwing the door wide open. There, the young man was shown to her, in all his vast hideousness. The young man, so overwhelmed by her beauty, fell to his knees, clutching his heart. The king looked on with a smile, watching his daughter's face curl into disgust at the sight of him. But lo, it was not disgust, but a smile of her own. His face turned to horror as his daughter rushed forward to embrace the young man, kissing him on his twisted lips.

'No!' cried the king in anguish. He cast the young man to the floor, breaking his head upon the stone, and in a moment of rage, he cursed his daughter, there on her own steps. He cursed her face, saying, 'You wish to know the faces of men? You wish to know them? So be it, you may see all the faces you please, but no man shall ever lay eyes upon your beauty, and yet every man will feel your caress.' And in that instant she was turned. Her robes and skin fell away, vanishing from sight until nothing was left of her except the feel of her breath on the king's cheeks, a strong breath, powerful in its force. For the daughter had become the wind, and with her first gust she lifted her father from his feet and hurled him from the tallest tower, lingering only to watch him fall to the rooftops of the city below."

'The Wind and the King' - and ancient fairytale

Melt-water flooded his nostrils, forcing their way into his brain like two daggers of ice, the very definition of cold. The water stung his throat as it sought out his lungs. It flushed them out like old wine-skins. Ice clutched his heart.

His whole mind screamed at him not to breathe. To force it out, not to take it in. There comes a point in a drowning man's final moments where he will scream this to himself over and over, until finally he will relent, and he will grasp at the dangling hope that he could breathe water all along. Farden took such a breath; a deep, gasping breath that would have pulled the flames from a campfire.

But to his surprise, he tasted air on his tongue, and the fluffy cold of snow along with it.

Farden twitched. He pushed out his limp limbs and heard the crunch and creak of barely-settled snow. The snow was a warm blanket compared to the deathly cold of the water. He carefully unscrewed his eyes, wincing as the sharp brightness of the light stung him.

'I thought I was done with all of this...' Farden gargled through the snowflakes. Nobody was around to hear him grumble. Nobody but the sun, and the stars shining through the piercing blue only a winter could own.

One by one they fell. The stars punched the earth, throwing up great columns of snow and rock in their wakes. Farden flinched as the ground shook and the trees cracked. Ten, twenty, thirty, and still they came. Dark shapes began to stand against the white of his dream, leaking smoke and reeking of sulphur.

Farden stood to meet them, and found himself naked against their eyes, wearing only his tattoos for modesty. And they glowed. They glowed like he had never seen them glow before, not even as they had his first night as a Written, when he had crawled, sweat-soaked from the Scribe's doorway, into the arms of the blind healers. Farden held his hands up to the dark shapes and found fire swirling around them.

The dream brought the daemons closer. Hundreds of them stood around him, but they spared him not a glance. They were too preoccupied with a figure standing behind Farden, a figure clad in glistening gold and red. It fit him badly, for the figure was small, boyish, and underneath the visor, Farden could glimpse a pair of small, grey-green eyes. His own eyes, so young and innocent, still untouched by the darkness of his history.

Farden cried out as the daemons reached for the boy. They barged him aside, tossing him back and forth as they rushed in, howling. The dream had taken his voice hostage, and his shouts were hoarse grunts that nobody and nothing heard.

Farden scrabbled forward through the chaos of black limbs and fiery eyes, clawing at anything and everything he could, but his fingers grasped nothing but smoke. When it cleared, the boy was gone. All that remained was a small girl with jet-black hair, standing in the snow. Samara. Her cheeks were rosy in the cold, and her hands were steaming hot. Her boots were half-buried in the snow. Farden tried to grab her, but she shook her head. 'Come and get me,' she said, and the world turned black.

※

Lerel watched the mage thrash around with a mixed expression of intrigue and fear. Farden reached out for the ceiling once more in the way that dreaming people do: feebly, half-realised, as though they were swimming in a vat of treacle. She winced as Farden's head reared up and then came back to the deck with a thud. It seemed to do the trick. Whatever dream he was having was stifled, and he began to snore again. Lerel frowned.

Rolling over onto her back, she put her hands behind her neck and stared at the ceiling, counting the whorls in the stout wood as she felt the ship move underneath her. It took her three tries to get to twenty. Nothing is more distracting than a big rat scampering up and down the foot of the bed. It made her shiver. Farden's rat was an ugly thing. She grimaced at an old memory of eating a rat just like it, the bones squeaking, the hair, stuck on her pink cat tongue… 'Ugh,' Lerel said aloud, shivering again.

Farden cracked an eyelid and found a wooden ceiling staring back at him. No dark shapes. No fell faces. No smoke. No girls standing in snow. No young boy…

Farden flinched and rolled onto his shoulder. The sudden grip of panic faded as soon as he saw Lerel staring back at him calmly, head propped up on one hand. 'There you are,' Farden muttered hoarsely, his throat still asleep. It felt as though he had spent the night shouting.

'You snore like a quillhog.'

'Rubbish. I don't snore. Ask Whiskers.'

Lerel smirked. 'Whiskers can't talk.'

'That's what you think,' Farden said, rolling onto his front. His body ached in a hundred places, and another hundred that he had forgotten existed. It reminded him of how weak his body still was. Farden pushed himself up onto his knees, and pulled a face. 'Why do I have a headache?' he asked, feeling the back of his head.

'You hit your head. You were dreaming, I think.'

'I was...' Farden's expression went vacant, recalling flashes and faces. He sat back on his heels and sighed. He looked up at Lerel lying in his bed and rubbed his grizzled chin. 'So to what do I owe the pleasure of having you in my bed?'

Lerel shrugged. She reached up to flick her dark hair out of her face, betraying her tattoos. 'My bed isn't as comfy as your bed. You weren't using it at the time.'

'Opportunist.'

'Always.'

'So you weren't here for...' Farden bit his lip. As Lerel raised an eyebrow, he heard his words crashing and burning. Too late. 'Er... I mean...'

Lerel sat up. The look on her face was one inch from indignant. 'You must have hit your head hard indeed.' She held her expression for a moment longer, until Farden was about to start sweating, before smirking. 'Well, you'll never know.'

Farden rolled his eyes up to the ceiling and chuckled grimly.

'Breakfast?' she asked.

'I think so. Before I say anything else.'

The wind on deck howled like a wolf, a wolf whose ears were in the process of being torn off. It played tunes on the rigging, whining and groaning in an arrhythmic ballad of foul weather. The clouds were spitting just enough to be irritating, and just enough to make the deck slippery.

Nuka was at the wheel, stoic as ever in his waxed coats and trousers. Heimdall stood beside him, looking for all the world like a statue. Loki was by the railing, simply looking. The sea roared by under his sullen and bored gaze.

The *Waveblade* was stuck, sandwiched between two worlds of grey. The clouds hung over them like a granite atrium, stormy and swirling, while the sea below bucked and roiled and frothed, its waters the colour of iron. The air was cold and winter-touched, as if they were sailing north to another season instead of another land. In the far west, the black knuckles of Nelska were slowly but surely fading into the rainy haze. There wasn't a peek of a dragon to be seen. Not yet.

Eyrum was hopeful though. He stood patiently at the bow with Ilios. The gryphon looked disgruntled by the weather. His wings were arched like umbrellas and he flinched every time the '*Blade* dug into a wave and sent up a fountain of spray. His yellow eyes were narrow and unhappy, but still he seemed unwilling to either leave his makeshift nest or the Siren's side.

'Fine day for a sail,' announced Farden as he led Lerel under one of Ilios' wings.

Eyrum turned around and looked at his new visitor. The mage had his hood up to hide his face from the rain. Strands of wayward black hair had escaped and were blowing about in the wind. His face was pale, stubble hiding more than a few scars, but he looked just as he remembered him from the very first time they had met, in a dining room deep in Hjaussfen. How he had hated him then, for simply being Arka. How wrong he had been.

'A summer's day in Nelska,' remarked the Siren, turning back to the sea. Farden went to stand by his side and both men braced themselves as the *Waveblade* dove headlong into a wave.

'What rubbish,' Farden chuckled. 'Any sign of them?'

Eyrum scanned the skies again with his one eye. 'Not yet.'

'They'll be here soon,' Farden muttered reassuringly. Eyrum barely heard him over the roar of the weather.

'I know,' Eyrum replied.

Farden turned around and faced the gryphon. He wasn't surprised to find Ilios staring straight back at him, eyes narrowed, knowing. 'You know exactly what I'm going to say, don't you?'

Ilios warbled something grumpy.

Farden shook his head. 'What did he say?' he asked Eyrum.

Eyrum didn't look away from the sea. 'I haven't a clue, mage. I don't speak gryphon.'

'He said he was only trying to help,' said a voice, Loki's, from nearby. He had crept down from the aftcastle after seeing them emerge from below. Eyrum immediately bowed.

Farden did no such thing. He eyed the god up and down. He was wearing his usual brown coat, unbuttoned as usual. The weather obviously wasn't bothering him. After all, why should it? What was cold to a ghost, a shadow? Loki flashed a warm smile and waved to Lerel, huddled as she was under the gryphon's wing. Lerel smiled politely but didn't move.

'You speak gryphon, do you?' Farden challenged him.

'Naturally.'

'Naturally,' echoed Farden. 'Well, in that case you can tell him that he isn't helping. If he's concerned with my well-being, then he should know the value of a good night's uninterrupted rest. I've got enough to worry about without his dreams stuck in my head.'

Ilios clacked his beak and squawked.

'I understood that,' Eyrum grunted, hiding a chuckle.

Farden rolled his eyes. 'How are they supposed to help, anyway? Tyrfing told me that you can't see the future any more now that the magick is increasing, so what scraps of it are you trying to show me? What is it supposed to mean? Drowning and being naked in the snow. Rivers full of ghosts. Fingernail ships with screeching vultures for figureheads. What are you possibly trying to show me, Ilios?'

Loki was looking at Farden with a strange glint in his eye. Eyrum had also turned around, wondering what in Emaneska Farden was babbling on about. Ilios leant forward and whistled a low little tune. Loki shuffled forward. 'He says he made you dream about the snow, and Samara, and that he was only trying to help. But he knows nothing about making you dream about vultures or rivers full of ghosts. That was nothing to do with him.'

Farden crossed his arms. 'I don't believe you,' he said, staring flatly at the gryphon.

The gryphon clacked his beak again. He looked insulted. 'You should,' Loki said with a smart look.

'There was a shallow river, and a ship full of... It came down the river and I was dragged away...' Farden mumbled to himself. Ilios shook his beak.

Loki rubbed his clean-shaven chin. The glint in his eye refused to leave. 'You didn't happen to have this dream of yours around the time that I found you in Albion, did you?' he asked.

'Shut it. I know what you're getting at,' Farden hissed. He went to stand eye to eye with the gryphon. 'You're sure?'

Ilios nodded and let out a single wavering note. 'Yes,' Loki affirmed.

'Well,' Farden said, taking a shuddering breath. So it was true. He had gone to Hel. The words sounded preposterous in his head, but he couldn't deny them. He felt a little sick. He hadn't even had breakfast yet and revelations were already falling from the sky. 'At least I know I'm right. And what's coming, I suppose.' *Small mercies.*

'What have I missed here?' chimed Lerel.

Farden pushed his nausea back to where it had sprung from. 'Nothing. Just a bit of clarification before breakfast. Meanwhile, where's my uncle?'

Eyrum grumbled. 'In a foul mood. He seems to be ill, and he can't get hold of Durnus using that scroll of his,' he advised. 'I know a few wizards aboard who would like to see that.'

'Maybe they'll get their chance, if my uncle hasn't burnt it to a crisp already. He below?'

'In the galley,' Eyrum said, turning back to the sea.

'Lerel? Shall we eat?'

'Let's.'

Loki idly gazed at the sky. 'I'm glad I could be of assistance,' he muttered sarcastically.

Farden curled his lip. 'Good. Now you can go back to doing whatever it is you do best. Oh, remind me, what is that exactly?'

Loki smiled the coldest smile Farden had ever seen. It actually made a shiver run down the mage's spine. The god stuffed his hands into his coat pockets and left.

Before they went below, Farden patted Eyrum on his broad back, and then went to place a hand on Ilios' beak. The gryphon was a little confused but he understood the gesture. 'Thank you, I think,' Farden whispered. Ilios whistled and shook his wings as another wave of spray descended on them.

Farden grimaced as he tasted salt on his tongue. The rain was getting heavier. Lerel wiped spray from her face. 'That's our cue,' she said to him, and with that they hurried below.

At the bow, Eyrum turned to Ilios. He was shaking his head. 'Ah, Farden,' he said, spitting sea-water to the side. 'Speaking so to a god. How does he get away with it?'

If a gryphon can shrug, Ilios did.

※

Tyrfing was pacing up and down the corridor outside the galley, pausing only to sip his steaming mug and cough into his napkin. He sounded like a bear with a salmon bone stuck in its gullet. Farden heard the sound from three corridors away, and it made him wince to hear how wet and ragged it sounded.

'Uncle,' Farden called as they rounded the corner to find him wearing a groove in the deck.

'Farden,' said Tyrfing. He wiped his mouth and cleared his throat with a grimace. 'Lerel. Morning.'

'Morning,' Farden replied, studying his uncle. Without his armour he seemed a different person. He looked decidedly grey in the half-lit gloom of the narrow corridor, deep in the ship. Decidedly thinner too, though it could have been the light. His eyes had the weary, red-rimmed look of a man who had been up all night coughing. Surprising, that. 'You sick?'

Tyrfing ignored the stupidity of the question and shook his head staunchly. 'Something I ate,' he answered. It was a poor excuse. They all knew he had an iron stomach. Once, during his first years in the desert, he had eaten the leather sole from a shoe and lived to tell the tale.

Lerel hummed. 'Doesn't sound like you.'

Tyrfing waved them into the galley as another round of coughing took him. It was undoubtedly his chest causing him grief. 'Getting old,' he managed to grunt.

The galley smelled like roasting meat and fresh bread. It was a smell that could have made the tongue dance, had it not been drowning in its own juices. Farden's stomach rumbled appreciatively as the smells wafted up his cold nostrils.

The ship's main cook was as all cooks should be, a jolly man of jolly proportions. Where Tinbits was simply plain and of average build, this man looked like the very dough he was kneading. His head was beaded with sweat from the ovens and his work, and his flat grey hat sat somewhat askew, and covered in flour. It was comforting to see a man who quite obviously enjoyed the food he cooked. It spoke a lot for the food.

'Morning,' Farden bowed. Lerel followed suit.

'Morning!' the cook practically bellowed. 'You're late, for a sailor. And you, ma'am, should know better.'

Lerel raised her hands in mock exasperation. 'I blame him.'

Farden shrugged. 'I've an excuse. I'm a mage.'

'Late for a mage too,' chuckled the cook. He was still bludgeoning the dough with his rosy hands. 'Your kind was up an hour ago. For training amidships. Soldiers too.'

'I see,' Farden hummed. 'So is it too late to break our fast, or is it too early for lunch?'

The cook turned around clapped his hands in a cloud of flour. 'Both, but I've got something for you two all the same. I call it *lunchfast*.'

'Lunchfast?'

'Mid-mornin' snack.'

'Doesn't really roll off the tongue...' Tyrfing whispered from the doorway.

Lerel piped up. 'What about *brunch*?'

The cook looked mildly peeved that he hadn't thought of that. He frowned. 'Don't think that'll catch on, ma'am.'

'Lunchfast it is then,' Farden said. He didn't care about its name, he just wanted to eat it. 'What is it?'

The cook rubbed his hands together and went to a nearby oven. With a flourish of a cloth, he whisked two buns from its hot shelves. He had sliced them in two before Lerel or Farden could blink. Next he reached into a pan and brought out several slices of a pinkish meat, shimmering with grease. He slapped them into the buns, flicked two dollops of a greyish sauce that Farden's nose could only guess was mustard on top, and then squeezed them tight. 'Here,' he said, handing them one each.

Farden sniffed his breakfast. He shrugged off his hood to shed a bit more light on it. Whatever it was, it smelled glorious. Salty, meaty, and greasy, all at the same time. 'What is it?'

'A certain slice o' pig. Bacon, it's called. Came from the ship's pig yesterday.'

Farden mumbled his thanks around an ambitious mouthful. It tasted as glorious as it smelled, perhaps even better.

'You're welcome,' said the cook, tipping his cap and going back to his dough.

Farden and Lerel, enraptured by their sandwiches, wandered back out into the corridor. Tyrfing seemed to have recovered from his coughing, though his skin was still pale and clammy, still as gaunt.

'No healing spell to sort it out?'

'I usually would,' Tyrfing lied, 'but there's a lot of magick on this ship at the moment. Mages are training.' He gestured down the corridor and they began to walk. Lerel in front, face-deep in sandwich, the two mages at the back.

'So I heard,' Farden mumbled.

Tyrfing watched his nephew eat. There was something different about him, something new. 'You look a little better today,' he said.

'I don't really feel it,' Farden grunted.

Tyrfing squinted as he led them down a level and towards the bow. 'No, there's something quite relaxed about you. Last night's revelations, I assume?'

Farden tipped his head from side to side in a way that said yes and no. 'And this morning's,' he admitted. 'Ilios just unintentionally took a big weight off my mind, I think.'

'He does that.'

Farden finished his sandwich and began to lick his fingers clean of grease. Whatever bacon and lunchfast were, he silently swore to make a habit of them both. 'Don't take this the wrong way, uncle, but I can't say the same of you. You look like shit.'

'Agreed,' Lerel chimed in.

Tyrfing nodded. 'I feel it. I spent most of the night trying to contact Durnus via the Inkweld, to no avail. He was silent, and I can't help but wonder if something has happened.'

'He's a pale king, for gods' sake, uncle. He'll be fine. What exactly are you worried about? Samara is heading north. Those two daemons wouldn't attack by themselves. Who else is there?'

'There are other snakes in the grass besides your daughter and her daemons.'

'What, that Malvus chap? The one Modren almost ripped in two? Surely he's all talk.'

'That's all he needs. He uses his tongue like an assassin uses a dagger. You didn't see a lot of Krauslung, Farden; that city is rotten to the core and ready to buckle. All it needs is a careful push. The people have come to believe they don't need things like councils and Arkmages any more. They're moving onto the next best thing, but they don't know what it is. Malvus is in a unique position to give them it. He and the rest of the Marble Copse.'

'Who?'

'Don't you remember? Magick purists, or so it's said. There's been no proof but plenty of talk recently. Apparently they started decades ago under Arkmages Mettelsson and Barnabus. Durnus and I suspect that Malvus has taken the Copse from an inner circle of grumblers within the council to a fully fledged faction that wants to see its beliefs manifested in a Krauslung of their own. For all their talk and pomp, their greed makes them dangerous. And so do their ideas. They'd see the Arkmagehood fall if they could, magick and knowledge restricted to the point of secrecy, a ban on the magick markets, taxes lining their pockets, and worse. They're purists and extremists. They want to return the Arka to some former glory it never had. Idiots.'

Farden wore a vacant look. It was odd hearing his uncle speak about such things, and in such a way. Tyrfing grunted. 'Never mind.'

Farden smiled. 'Tyrfing the politician. The Arkmage. Who'd have thought it? I don't know what to try to believe first; that the hermitic, outcast, Written Tyrfing has taken to the throne of the Arka, or that he shares it with an ex-vampire, daemon halfbreed. '

Tyrfing paused to cough. Farden resisted the urge to clap him on the back. 'We live in strange times.'

Farden whistled. 'And getting stranger by the day.'

༄

The Written had made a home for themselves just forward of amidships, down in the hold where there was room and privacy from the narrowed eyes of superstitious sailors whispering nervous nothings to Njord. They mingled with the cargo, training in twos and threes. Some fought. Some fenced. Some had set up little targets of wood and straw at the far end of the hold and were taking it in turns to hurl ice, rock, or splinters at them.

The three there for a time, wandering between the little patches of furious activity. Tyrfing ran the mages through some drills. Farden and Lerel sat on the sidelines amongst the crates of fruit and fresh water, wearing two very different facial expressions indeed. Lerel's was one of quiet awe, while Farden's was one of blankness, of distance. One might have glimpsed a hint of jealousy there maybe, as his eyes flashed with the reflection of fire and lightning. Perhaps it was longing. *All in good time*, he told himself. It almost sounded like a wish.

Several hours passed in the hold of the *'Blade*, and with every hour that passed, the ship began to rock and buck that little bit more. The ship shuddered every time it ploughed into a wave in ways that would make even the hardiest sailor cringe.

A bell soon tolled throughout the ship, and the urgent order for all hands to batten down the hatches was called. Lerel began to shout orders. The Written and the mages quickly rushed for the stairs. Farden, who had finally given into temptation and joined in with the sword practice, ran alongside them, hurtling through narrow corridors and ducking through low-ceilinged quarters. With every step they took, the roar of a storm grew louder.

Outside, the world had turned a furious black. The sky was a roiling stew of rain and wind, and it battered them mercilessly from the very moment they battled their way on deck. Farden was wet through before he had a chance to think. He hoisted his hood up but the wind forced it down. Hair lashed his face like tiny whips. He grit his teeth and shielded his eyes as he sought the safety of the mainmast. Behind him, Nuka was battling the wheel, Lerel only just reaching his side. Heimdall still stood cross-armed and stoic beside them, looking for rocks or gaps in the storm with his godly eyes. Sailors swarmed the deck like bedraggled rats. The ship mages were already at the railings, trying their hardest to bring the wind into check. They weren't having much luck.

The Written and the mages sprang to help wherever they could. They hauled ropes and slammed hatches shut. Some even scrambled up into the rigging to help drag down the extra sail before it ripped. Farden did his best to help, but whatever task he spied was already in hand by the time he had sprinted to it. He went up to the aftcastle and the wheel, to see if he could help there, but again he was lost in the commotion. As he stood there dumbly beside the ship's wheel, he couldn't help but gawp at the hills of grey water that were rolling past the ship on every side. They towered high above them, looking to crash down upon them at any moment. Farden suddenly felt very small indeed. Small, and endangered.

A flash of lightning split the black sky in two, painting everything a ghostly blue-white for the briefest of moments. It happened so leisurely and silently that half the ship paused amidst the busy chaos, stunned, wondering if they were imagining it. Then there came the ear-splitting crash of its sibling thunder, and a blood-freezing howl as the tip of the mizzenmast was sliced in two. Lightning flashed and sparks flew as the wooden spar, its nest, and its unlucky occupant plummeted into the freezing water. Smoking rigging fell and snarled the deck. Sailors cried out as a shower of wind-blown splinters and sparks fell with it. The *Waveblade* lurched as the tangled, fallen mess began to drag her sideways onto the waves.

'Farden!' yelled Nuka. 'Make yourself useful and hold this wheel. Lerel is needed below!'

Farden dashed to the captain's aid as Lerel sprinted to the deck. Even for a man as strong and as large as he, Nuka was struggling. The ship was turning its flank to face the oncoming waves, whether he liked it or not, and it was all he could do to make it happen as slowly as possible. He was already bent to one knee when Farden seized the wheel. His knuckles turned white as the lightning as he bent his back to it and pushed. Nuka bellowed a strangled order through teeth grit like stones in a wall.

'Axes, Lerel! AXES!'

'We're turning into the waves,' Heimdall warned, his voice somehow calm and low over the roar of the wind and the waves and the rain and the bellowing of the crew. As if to prove his point, the *'Blade* lurched again, and a wave washed over her port railing, knocking a dozen men flat and Nuka to his stomach. Farden fumbled for the wheel as it began to slip and spin. His hands were thrown aside, and he yelped as the wooden handles flew past, rapping his knuckles. *Where were his gauntlets when he needed them?!*

'Grab her, Farden!' Nuka yelled as the receding wave began to drag him away. He scrambled to get upright, but the water and the wind were too much.

Farden watched, horrified, as the wheel began to spin. The handles were a blur. The ship was pitching violently to port as the rudder was left to her merry, sadistic devices. It didn't matter that the fallen mizzen had been hacked away and freed; the ship was now battling its own momentum. The *Waveblade* had just bared her vulnerable side to the onslaught of the waves. In any moment, she could roll, and sink.

It was a nightmare moment.

'Farden, there's a wave coming,' Heimdall said, as clearly as if it were a summer's breezy day and he were inches from his ear. In truth, he was a dozen feet away, his lips barely moving.

Farden looked up and saw it. It was a pure monster. A sheer wall of rippling grey water. It bore down on the ship like an avalanche waiting to pounce.

'Njord help us!' yelled the crew as one.

Not again, was all Farden could think.

'NOW Farden!' screamed Nuka.

The shout ran through his body like a spark, jolting him forward. Without even thinking, he threw his hands into the spinning blur of handles. He half-expecting his arms to shatter, but instead, the wheel stopped dead, his hands firmly grasping two of the handles in a terrifyingly fierce grip.

'Turn her!' came the shout.

And turn her he did.

Farden stamped his feet and pushed with all his might. Strength forgotten and lost surged into his feet and arms as he pushed the wheel up and over. His hands clamped onto the next handle, and the next, and the next, until the wheel was turning. The pressure was nothing short of almighty. His bones were surely close to splintering. He could feel the huge ship bucking and straining against his arms and legs, pushing against his every muscle, but he knew if he stopped to think, he would lose hold of it. Suddenly, Nuka was at his side, and the wheel began to gather speed.

'Wind mages!' Nuka ordered, and down below they sprang to it, filling whatever sails were left with as much wind as they could steal from the storm. Just as the wave came crashing down, the *Waveblade* turned her bow into it, and she rose up with its frothing roar, riding it high into the sky, ready to plummet down once more. Safe, for now.

Farden stumbled back from the wheel, hands and legs half-dead. Nuka didn't have time to thank him. He might have grunted, he wasn't sure. All Farden knew was that he was done. He staggered back and stood dazedly, rain-whipped and wind-harried, in the centre of the aftcastle, letting the chaos swirl around him once more. He caught the eyes of the sailors and mages as they hurried by. They nodded briefly as they dashed past him.

He caught the eyes of Heimdall too. The god was looking back over his shoulder. Farden saw his lips move. His voice echoed in his head.

'Perhaps you are fit to wear the armour of the Knights, after all,' Heimdall said. It sounded as though it stung him to admit it.

It was all Farden could do to keep his smile from breaking into a grin. He must have looked a fool, he thought, swaying from side to side with the ship and the wind, enjoying the feeling of the rain lashing his lips and teeth.

Chapter 16

"Make merry whilst the beer flows."
Old Arka saying

Malvus was wearing the marble thin. His new, expensive boots had long ago given up squeaking on the polished stone; those bits that had protested had been trodden into submission and silence. Still Malvus paced. He paced like only a nervous, impatient man could.

His visitors were late.

'Curses,' he spat, wringing his hands. He tried to remember the last time he had been so nervous, so agitated. 'Calm yourself, Malvus, dear boy,' he told himself, whispering to the wind.

Malvus went to the edge of the Nest and looked down at his shimmering city. It was uncharacteristically quiet, for such an early hour, and for such a city as Krauslung. It was barely midnight. Despite all odds and all its training, Krauslung had managed to drink itself into a slumbering stupor. It was all thanks to the celebrations Malvus had ordered. He smiled. *If you give a man a loaf, he'll thank you kindly. If you give a man a keg of beer, he'll toast you to the morning light.* Malvus had given Krauslung its keg, its excuse. He had climbed even deeper into their hearts. He thoroughly intended to stay there.

Malvus drummed his manicured nails on the marble railing and hummed something tuneless. His new boots tapped a rhythm. He took a deep breath, and that's when he smelled it. Sulphur. Soil. Burning stone. Cooking meat.

Malvus looked down and forced himself to swallow. Tendrils of black smoke were curling around his arms and fingers. Pasting a brave smile on his face, he turned slowly to face the creatures.

He had heard the stories of the battle on the field, and now he saw the stories were true. The daemons, although no taller than seven feet tall, eight maybe, were huge in every other sense of the word. Their mere presence bore down on Malvus like the blunt fist of a hammer. The smoky darkness spread out behind them was so deep it made his eyes ache. One of them was grinning at him, rather disturbingly. 'Gentlemen,' he bravely began, unable to hide the little waver in his voice. 'I bid you most welcome.'

The two daemons looked at each other. 'I have never been referred to as a man,' said one.

'Nor gentle, for that matter, brother,' chuckled the other.

Malvus cursed this most immediate of slip-ups. He stepped forward, clasped his hands together, and dropped to one knee. 'My apologies, lords.'

'That is better, mortal. It took your Siren counterpart considerably longer.'

'I imagine Lord Saker finds it difficult to bow to anyone, even to powerful beings such as yourselves.'

'Flattery too, Hokus. We are being spoilt.'

'Rise, Malvus Barkhart,' the one called Hokus ordered. Malvus quickly did as he was told. He had already figured these creatures out. *Treat them like kings, that was the trick*, he told himself. *Treat them like emperors, so long as they believed you.*

The grinning daemon stepped forward to run his hands over the marble trees that formed the Nest, empty as it was without its gryphon. Wherever his fingers graced the stone, thick black soot-smears appeared. As his brother slowly painted the white trees black, the other daemon questioned Malvus.

'You summoned us.'

'Yes. Saker informed me of your presence.'

'And are we to assume it is for the same reason as Saker?'

'That depends on what that reason was.'

'Are the two of you not in league with each other?'

'We are, in a fashion.'

'Explain yourself, worm.'

Malvus gestured to the city behind and below him. 'This is now my domain. Nelska is now his. We have been plotting our moves together for many years, but our goals have always been separate. I have no interest in that frozen rock he calls home.'

'He insists that you do share a goal.'

Malvus nodded. 'If by that he means power, then yes, we do.'

'War,' said the daemon behind him, his voice sounding closer and hotter than Malvus would have liked. 'Something man and daemon can both enjoy.'

Malvus nodded again. 'The Crumbled Empire is ours for the taking. That was, of course, until you arrived, my lords,' he replied, raising a finger.

'Has our presence disturbed your plans?'

Malvus decided to be bold. 'Yes.'

The daemons laughed then. Even though their mouths glowed orange, it was a cold sound. 'Our apologies, lordling!' cried Hokus.

'We would hate to inconvenience you!' chuckled the other.

Malvus bowed his head and waited until their laughter had died. He could feel a bead of sweat on his hairline, slowly making its way down to his nose. 'Disturbed them for the better, I hope. I saw how you fell from the sky. In that moment I felt a change in the wind. I had the Arfell scholars come and tell me the old stories of you and your kind. The city and its people may believe you gone, and a fleeting threat, but I know what power you have, and have heard what kind of a person brought you here. How much power that takes. I also know that Saker has failed in his task of stopping the Arkmage and Farden, and that they are now chasing that particular person north as we speak, where I assume more of your kind will be falling to meet them. I do believe I am on the right track?' He paused for a moment before continuing, watching their faces. 'I thought so. Well then, if that is the case, then I do believe it is time to choose a side. I wish to choose the winning one. You, my lords. And whatever master you speak for. I believe we can form a lucrative partnership.'

The smaller daemon rubbed his hands. 'Ah, he seeks to profit from our falling, does he not, brother?'

Hokus nodded. 'It would appear so, brother Valefor. And he asks for much. Saker simply asked for immunity.'

Malvus' eyes searched the marble floor. *Curse that scaly idiot.* 'And what did you say?'

The one called Valefor put his snout in Malvus' face. 'We agreed. For now, that is.'

'What was your price?'

'We are but simple beasts, Barkhart,' rumbled Hokus. He had crossed his arms. 'Eradication of Towerdawn's kind. Undivided allegiance. Obedience. Worship. Land, should we need it.'

'I see,' said Malvus, inwardly groaning.

'And what is your offer, mortal?'

'Eradication of magick in the common man. Undivided allegiance. Worship. Land, should you need it. Oh, and an Arkmage.'

Hokus and Valefor both twitched at that word. 'An Arkmage, did you say? They are in the north, as you said,' answered Valefor, suddenly very serious.

Malvus saw his opening and sprinted for it. 'Only one is, lord. The other is under lock and key. As my prisoner.'

Hokus stepped forward. The cracks in his face burnt a hot yellow. 'Which Arkmage?'

'Durnus, the blind one,' said Malvus. He watched as the two daemons traded a long glance. If his years as a merchant had taught him anything, it was to recognise desire when he saw it. The merchant in him rubbed his hands. 'He is yours, if you want him. You can have him tonight, if you please. For a price.'

'Dare you barter with us, mortal?'

'Trade, my lords, nothing more. My gifts, for immunity and the safety of my ventures. My people.'

Valefor grinned. 'You don't look the benevolent leader, little man.'

'I…' Malvus began, but a scuffing sound interrupted him. The daemons whirled around to face the noise, claws bared and smoky wings arched. They found a tall, thin woman standing on the stairs, painted yellow by the light of their fiery glow. She was reaching out, fumbling at thin air. Her eyes were blind. Valefor slid to her side, silent as a zephyr, and held a claw mere inches from her neck.

'Malvus?' Jeasin called. 'You 'ere?'

'I am,' replied Malvus, watching the daemon and his razor-edged claw. 'Stay where you are,' he said.

'What's goin' on? I 'eard voices. And what's that awful smell?' Jeasin asked, looking very confused.

'It's the wind in the city, woman. Go back to your room.'

Jeasin crossed her arms. 'I never 'eard the wind talk before,' she answered.

Malvus stamped his foot. 'The room, whore! Back to it, before I show you what the back of my hand feels like,' he ordered.

'Suit yourself,' Jeasin shrugged. Her bare toes found the lips of the stairs and she slowly retraced her cold steps back into the darkness. Valefor watched her go. 'A blind pet,' he chuckled, once he heard the slam of a door.

'We mortals have our needs,' Malvus shrugged, hiding his relief that Jeasin had escaped unharmed. She was a means to an end, true, but a pretty one. Malvus had grown to like her company, however brief and fleeting it had been in the past few days.

'You were saying... Barkhart?'

Malvus nodded. 'You said I don't look like the benevolent leader,' he said. 'Power lies in people as much as it does in coin and swords. A king isn't a king without his subjects.'

Hokus looked to the starry sky above. 'No, he is not.'

Malvus knew it was time to seal his wily little deal, his future. He tried a smile. 'Do we have a deal, then, my lords?' he ventured, inwardly clenching. His heart beat a frantic rhythm while he waited in the silence for their answer.

Hokus looked to his brother. Malvus could tell they were trading words, silently, in the way that he knew Sirens and their dragons did. It thoroughly unnerved him. After a long and sweaty silence, Valefor winked, and thrust out a black, soot-smeared hand towards the man. 'I believe it is customary for mortals to shake hands on the making of a deal?' he asked.

Malvus nodded hesitantly. The hand was huge. It looked as though it were made of leather, or stone, or both. The claws that waited patiently at the end of it shone dully in the torchlight like burnt steel. He smiled politely, stalling. The daemon's easy smile was worrying. *Just do it,* he told himself. *It's just a hand. A daemon's hand, but a hand nonetheless. Shake the damn thing. Claim your destiny, as the seer told you.* Malvus reached out to grasp it.

He barely noticed the pain at first, as Valefor gripped him tightly.

Burns tended to be like that.

※

Jeasin made sure to shut the door as loudly as she could. She felt for the wall and hugged it, hoping the darkness of the building or the shadow of the stairs would hide her. She held her breath and waited for the silence to end.

'A blind pet,' said one of the strange voices, deep, dangerous, and muffled by the breeze.

'We mortals have our needs,' said a smaller voice. Malvus. Slippery in his tone. She clenched and let her tongue weave a little curse behind them.

'You were saying, Barkhart?' said the other voice. Jeasin suppressed a deep shiver at the sound of it. It was a voice that almost made her glad to be blind. She didn't have to see the sort of beast that uttered it. She knew it was hideous, unearthly. She shivered again and felt her skin crawl. She'd already heard enough. She knew what these creatures had come for.

Gentler than a spider's touch, Jeasin felt for the handle again and stepped inside the tower. She let the door hang ajar, trading the danger of it slamming in the breeze with the risk of trying to shut it quietly. Her feet slapped the marble as she practically flew down the steps to the great hall. She was halfway through the door when the hand caught her.

'Whoa!' gasped the voice. A man's voice. He was surprised, whoever he was. Jeasin wriggled like a fish in his grip.

'Get yer 'ands off me!' Jeasin hissed venomously.

The hand relaxed and let her be. 'It's General Toskig, ma'am. My apologies. Old habits,' said the general, bowing ever so slightly. She could hear his armour clank and the leather squeak.

'Odd habits, if'n you ask me. Do you often go grabbin' at ladies at night, hmm?' Jeasin demanded.

'Not usually ma'am. You startled me. Had I known you were Malvus' woman…'

Jeasin wrinkled her nose, as if a bad smell had bothered it. 'I'm nobody's woman,' she uttered.

Toskig nodded, feeling uncomfortable. 'My apologies again,'

he said. 'It's all still a little bit confusing at the moment, isn't it?'

'Hmph,' was all Jeasin could say, as she tried to move past him.

'Where are you going?' Toskig asked.

Jeasin jabbed a finger in the direction of the doors. 'Our friends are in trouble.'

Toskig winced. 'I told you the last time…'

'I ain't askin' you to help, soldier. I'm askin' you to get out of my way.'

Toskig looked as if he was going to grab her again, but instead he left his hand hovering in mid-air, unsure of itself. 'I can't let you…'

'He's going to kill 'em, Toskig.'

Toskig clenched the dangling hand. 'He wouldn't dare.'

'He's darin' right now. Heard it myself.'

'That is too far,' hissed Toskig. He found himself torn, like old parchment in greedy hands. Old loyalty clashed with new loyalty inside him.

'Like I said, Toskig, I ain't askin' you to help. Jus' to keep quiet,' she said. 'Seems to me you and I are in the same position.' Toskig just nodded. Jeasin prodded him in the chest, and he slowly moved aside. 'You 'old your tongue. I'll 'old mine. Deal?'

Toskig lowered his head. He couldn't even meet the eyes of a blind girl. 'Deal.'

Jeasin darted for the door, hands wildly flailing in front of her. She had learnt her way around the Arkathedral pretty quickly. The Arka liked their wide corridors and their grandiose halls. Made a difference from damp stairwells and narrow alleys. Despite the slimy company, Jeasin was beginning to take a shine to this sort of lifestyle.

And that was the reason why she hated herself at that moment. *Pissing it all away again*, she told herself, as she manhandled the great doors open. The sound of her feet on the cobbles let her know how the corridor twisted and turned. It was empty, by its silence.

Pissing your luck up the wall, as one of her old customers had once daintily put it. That was exactly what she was doing. She'd thought that giving them the papers would have been the end of it, but the old blind man had wanted more. She'd agreed to help, for some strange reason. Jeasin grumbled. She had wormed her way into a position of comfort, somehow at the side of a powerful new ruler, and here she was, racing to liberate one of his most prized possessions. An old Arkmage, who'd had the decency to show her some kindness one evening. Kindness she hadn't tasted in a long time. As she ran, she counted the times in her life she had felt such acceptance, such welcome, in so few words. She flicked out a finger, then two, and shook her head. 'Damn it all,' she spat, as her hands found a bannister.

❦

'Elessi, I know you can hear me. I don't have to ask. I know somewhere, deep...' Modren grit his teeth as they chattered. He closed his eyes and pleaded. '... just come home. Please.'

The Undermage was cradling his wife's head in his weary arms. He hadn't moved in hours. He had just sat there, whispering quiet words to her here and there. Modren's face was dusty and streaked with the path of tears. He had never fancied himself a man for crying. Then again, he had never thought himself a man for love, nor a wife either. Time, that great changer of all. He just hoped he had enough of it left.

'Durnus,' he said, in a cracked voice.

'Mm?' came the distracted reply. Durnus was sitting in one of the corners of the cell with his back to the wall. He was looking up at the ceiling, either utterly engrossed by something or politely pretending he was. Modren suspected the latter.

'Do you, er...' Modren faltered. 'Do you want to say anything to her?'

Durnus snapped out of his trance and looked at the mage. Modren was too tired to wonder how he was staring directly at him.

'I would not know what to say, Modren.'

Modren pulled a hurt face. 'Surely you can think of something. She needs to hear voices to keep her awake, and she's known yours longer than mine.'

Durnus cleared his throat. 'I cannot think of...'

Modren cut him off. 'Well, think harder. Surely you have something to say after all these years?' he demanded. Durnus looked decidedly uncomfortable. It took him a while to answer, letting Modren cool a little.

'I shall say it to her when she is standing in front of me. Alive and well. Is that better?'

Modren nodded. His voice was very small. 'Say that. Tell her that,' he said, and Durnus shuffled slowly over. They both had gone two days without food, giving it all to Elessi. Now, even despite their spells, their muscles were beginning to cramp and stiffen.

'Elessi, I...' he began. He was very conscious how quiet and expectant it was between his words. He had never been good at these sorts of things. Usually it took a few wines to loosen his tongue, or a bit of anger, but he was fresh out of both in that dank hole of a cell. Fortunately, he was interrupted by Jeasin.

'This all sounds very bloody sentimental,' she hissed between the bars of the door, 'but you ain't got time for it. You need to go. Now.'

'I appreciate your fervour, Jeasin, but if you remember rightly, we're waiting on a certain Old Dragon.'

'No, you don't understand. Malvus is up to even more than what you said. He's got visitors, and they've been talkin' about you.'

'Visitors?' asked Durnus.

Jeasin nodded. 'Visitors, and they don't sound human to me.

Deep-voiced things. Smell like…'

Durnus cut in. 'Like sulphur,' he guessed.

Jeasin just shrugged. 'Smelled like rotten egg, to me.'

Modren piped up. 'Are we sure it wasn't just Malvus?' he asked, with a roll of his eyes.

'I should have known. I knew I could feel something. They are shielding themselves well.'

'Who?' asked Modren.

'What?' asked Jeasin.

'The daemons,' he said. *My flesh and blood*, he silently added.

Jeasin pressed her face against the cold bars. 'Well, Malvus made 'imself a deal for his safety, and guess who's the payment?'

'I am.'

'Right you are.'

Durnus didn't look surprised by that. 'Clever man,' he said.

'Where is that bastard dragon when you need him?'

※

'You hear Grintt and the boys got duty in the banquet hall?'

'Mhm,' came the reply.

A sigh. 'Think of all those women, mate.'

'Mhm.'

'Had a servant girl waiting for me too, I did.'

A grunt this time.

'Bet Grintt will be all over her like a rash.'

Not even a grunt now.

'Don't say much do you?' All he got was a shrug. 'Just my luck. Guard duty with a mute.'

The guard knocked his spearbutt against the toe of his boot while he looked out at the glowing city, wrapped as it was in its evening finery or orange torchlight and moonless darkness. The mountains in the distance were like black teeth gnawing at a charcoal sky.

The guard rested his face against the cold window and misted the glass with his breath. Raising a lazy finger, he began to draw, his fingertip squeaking. He was halfway through a raunchy sketch of a certain naked servant girl when something dark flashed across the lights of the city below. Something fast. Something big.

'Hey, you see that?' he flinched, stabbing the window with his finger. He cupped his hands around his face and pressed his nose against the glass, peering into the night. Nothing.

'Mm?' mumbled his comrade.

The first guard's eyes lingered on the rooftops and tiles for a moment longer. Still nothing. The guard sniffed and scratched his cheek. 'Nothing. Just a trick of the torchlight,' he said, as he went back to his sketch. His breath had already faded. His naked servant girl had become nothing but a set of greasy smears. The guard wiped her away with his hand, and that was when he saw it.

Something fast. Something big. A monster of a great golden dragon, plummeting from the sky like a falcon, jaws wide and grinning, its throat already glowing orange as the fire in its belly began to build.

'By Evernia's t...!' the guard gasped, spear clattering to the floor. The rest of his sentence died with him.

The fire exploded through the window and swallowed the corridor whole. Boiling, swirling, clouds of flame, blinding in the peaks of their yellows, bloody in their chasms of crimson. White marble blackened in seconds. The guards were seared to the bone, their armour melted, hair charred, lungs aflame. The fire surged on, hungry for the cells.

The noise came first, the roar of devouring flame and the smash of broken glass. Then the heat, prickly, stoking fear. Then the wind as the air rushed to meet the wall of flame pouring down the corridors.

Jeasin threw herself into an alcove as the blistering surge slammed into the cell door. Modren and Durnus could be heard shouting over the deafening roar.

'Get down!' yelled the Arkmage, recoiling from the door. The iron hinges were already beginning to glow. The door began to squeal, lock spells splintering. Modren threw himself over Elessi as Durnus held back as much of the heat as he could bear.

The Arkathedral prisons were bound with spells written to fight magick itself, to deflect it and crush it. They are some of the strongest spells known to man, designed to hold back mages, Written, even Arkmages, should the need ever rise. Magick is useless against them. Utterly and purely. But dragon-fire?

Everything crumbles before that.

The lock spells snapped, and the door began to crumble with them, their death throes tearing the wood and metal apart splinter by splinter. Durnus pushed forward, squeezing the fire into a maelstrom of heat to melt the metal bolts from the stone. His boots were melting on the hot stone. His robes were beginning to smoke. 'Modren!' he cried, as the door sagged and split. Modren dragged Elessi to her feet as gently as he could manage. He winced as he felt the searing heat on his face. Durnus kept pushing.

As they fought their way into the corridor the flames began to die and recede. Cold air rushed into the blackened warren of cells. Through the smoke they could see charred bodies littering the doorways, splayed up against the walls, mere lumps of charcoal. They could hear bells over the dying flames.

'Jeasin?' Durnus yelled, letting his spell die away.

'Here!' came a coughing. Durnus threw out a hand and Jeasin

came tumbling out of an alcove, clothes half burnt from her back. Her skin was a scorched crimson. She'd been lucky.

'Next time I see that fuckin' mage I'll strangle 'im for gettin' me into this mess!' she was spitting.

'Come on!' yelled Modren. The bells were tolling frantically now, competing with a new sound, the screeching roar of marble being ripped apart and tossed into the sky. Of dragons and frantic claws.

Skidding on soot and charred bodies, they burst into the main corridor, and found a golden dragon grappling with what was left of a marble wall. His claws were painted with white dust. Flame still flickered around his bared teeth. Screams and roars filled the night. Three other dragons flapped behind him, spitting flame and fending off arrows.

'Durnus!' Towerdawn boomed, almost deafening them. 'It's time to leave!'

'That it is, Old Dragon!'

'Climb aboard!' Towerdawn forced the edge of his mighty wing into the corridor, and the mages clambered aboard as quickly as their weak limbs let them.

Once Elessi was safe, Modren turned to Jeasin, hand held out for her to grab. Towerdawn was slowly losing his footing. Arrows clattered off his head. 'Jeasin! Come on!' shouted the mage, but Jeasin wasn't moving. She stood in a circle of rubble, staring about wildly. Her keen ears could hear the sounds of guards and soldiers running to them. She bit her lip. Her new world was crumbling like the corridor.

'No,' she said, backing away. *Pissing your luck up the wall.* The phrase ran through her mind over and over again. No. She could still turn this around. 'I'm stayin' here!'

'You're *what*?'

Jeasin waved her hands. 'I'm stayin' here!'

'Have you gone mad?' Durnus was incredulous.

'I'm no more mad than you two! I've been dragged around

enough already. I understand this place. I've got a chance 'ere.'

'Suit yourself!' shouted Modren. 'Let's go Towerdawn!'

As the dragon wrenched himself free of the broken wall, Durnus stared into the corridor. Jeasin stared right back. They would never have known, but their eyes met then.

'If you see Farden...' she yelled.

'I will tell him!'

Jeasin nodded, and that was that. Jeasin had chosen her path. Its name was Malvus, the ruler of the Arka. A path along a knife-edge, true, but a better path than Tayn could have ever offered.

As the great dragon launched himself from the wall and into the cold air over the clamouring city, Jeasin threw herself into the rubble. She ignored the pain of the broken marble grazing her hip, of the jagged glass scraping at her skin. Then, like a true professional, she took a breath and began to scream.

'Help!'

Chapter 17

"Whales are curious creatures. As old as the dragons and as fickle as the wind, they are seldom seen these days. I hardly find it a surprise. Why should a whale come to sing its song for us, when all it receives in gratitude is a spear in the back. Oil and meat are not worth the silence of its song."
From 'The Edda of the Sea' by Captain Norfumli

It was said that a cup of hot farksa could cure any ailment short of a missing limb. It was doubtful how true that was, but there was one thing it could cure like no other, and that was a cold morning.

The storm had broken in the early hours. The wind blew itself out and the rain had slunk away to the south. A sliver of moon had shown its face in the west; a split-bone pendant dangling in a sky thick with clouds. It played hide and seek with them until the sun chased it away.

With the sunrise came a calm, bitterly cold morning. Breath like pipe-smoke rose from the sailors and soldiers on deck, like steam from a battlefield. The deck resembled one too. The storm had wrought a warlord's path across the *Waveblade*.

'There's a hair in my farska,' muttered Eyrum, darkly. He had spent most of the night making friends with the bottom of a bucket. Like Farden, he was not fond of ships and stormy seas in the slightest.

Farden sipped his steaming hot cup gingerly. He too had been at the bottom of a bucket. 'Better keep that quiet, otherwise everybody will want one,' he whispered.

'You're lucky, Siren. I got a splinter in mine,' Roiks eyed his farska. 'Oh, tell a lie. Sliver of parsnip.' He fished it out with a pair of rope-stained fingers and slurped it up eagerly. The bosun looked exhausted. Deep, dark rings surrounded his eyes.

'This ship looks a mess,' Farden said, eyeing the tangled rigging around his boots and the ugly broken tip of the mizzenmast.

'Give it an hour. I'll guarantee it'll look as though we just sailed though a meadow, not a storm.'

'Mhm.' Farden wasn't so sure.

Eyrum was still trying to get the hair out of his cup. He went to sit down, but as a dark shadow fell over the deck, he immediately stood straight back up. 'What about the ice?' He grumbled.

Farden wore the same disturbed look as the Siren. 'Do we have to get so close to them?' Even though he had grown to trust the *'Blade* and its strength, there was nothing like a tower of ice floating within spells-reach to shake that trust. Farden watched the white giant slide silently past the ship. It was huge. Its glittering tip easily matched the height of the mainmast. That alone made the mage nervous, but what secretly terrified him was that however huge the icebergs were above the water, they were easily more than twice as large underneath it. He resisted the morbid urge to look down at the cold blue of its huge, submerged roots, gnarled and deadly as they were, to see how close they came to the ship. He doubted any ship, no matter how ironclad and huge it was, could hit one and survive. That made Farden sweat beneath his cloak.

'They're goin' to get much closer than that, mister mage. Have no fear,' Roiks waved his hand absently at the northern horizon, where a veritable flotilla of giant icebergs were slowly ambling towards them. Seeing the looks on Farden and Eyrum's faces, Roiks chuckled. 'Relax. Nuka knows what 'e's doing. Used to be a whaler, he did. You always find the best whales up in the iceberg fields. Knows this patch of the sea like 'is head knows a pillow.'

Farden ran a hand across his chin and felt the Scalussen metal grate against his stubble. It was warm from clutching the farska. 'That's hardly comforting,' Farden said. 'I haven't seen him take a wink of sleep since I set foot on this boat.'

'Bah. It's no worse than the Bitches.'

Eyrum didn't know what that meant. 'Is it any better?'

Worryingly, Roiks shrugged. 'Depends if the weather holds,' he said with a grin. He tapped his nose as he walked away, off on the hunt for more farska.

Eyrum had finally retrieved the long black hair from his cup. With a grimace he flicked it over the bulwark and into the sea below. 'Give me a dragon any day.'

᠅

Roiks should have put some coin on his words. The *Waveblade* was shipshape in less than an hour. While half the crew worked like daemons to get the deck cleared, the other half took to the mangled rigging, hacking and splicing it into something functional. Farden and Eyrum did their bit with a pair of brooms and a stomach full of hot farska trying to quell their queasiness.

Even Ilios did his bit. The gryphon vacated his little makeshift nest just long enough to test his healed wings and circle around a few icebergs. He returned with something huge and wriggling in his claws. The gryphon had caught a spotted shark in the cobalt shallows of a hollow iceberg, and had decided it would make a good reward for the crew.

The cooks came up from the galleys to see the thing. Tinbits wasn't quite sure what to do with the wriggling, gnashing thing. The word "lunchfast" was quickly mentioned, and Gabbant finished it off with a vicious tap from his favourite belaying pin.

Of course, nobody knows how to cook a shark better than a Siren. Eyrum led some of his more able-bodied refugees in skinning and gutting the huge beast. Cauldrons were brought up from below and a cooking party was formed right there on the bow. Nuka called a morning's rest for the crew and the soldiers, and ordered Roiks to break out a few beakers of mörd and ale for the fine job they had done.

With the help of a little fire from the mages, the stew soon began to bubble. Mouths began to salivate accordingly. Seats were made out of bundles of sailcloth and battered hatches. One of the Sirens broke out a pair of pipes and a shaky voice. He soon had the crew yelling old shanties and mismatched ballads.

It was a spontaneous morning, and somehow they are always the best sorts of mornings. Only Nuka stayed alone and quiet by his precious wheel, making sure to keep his ship safely along its wandering path between the floating mountains of ice that were now crowding around them. He half smiled, half winced as he listened to Roiks leading the crew in a bawdy song about a donkey and a princess. Some of the Siren mothers turned a little pink at the nature of its lyrics, but didn't complain. They were amongst sailors, after all. Siren or Arka, a sailor's vocabulary is the same.

It took an hour for the shark to cook, but barely a minute for the hungry crowd to empty the cauldrons. Mugs and cups and bowls and ladles swung in like picks to a coal-face, and soon enough everyone was tentatively sipping at their sumptuous stew. It was salty and sweet at the same time, with the sharp edge of the meaty shark and more than a few drops of the Siren *syngur* liquor.

And so the remaining hours of the morning passed by. The sun reached its zenith for the day, but did nothing to warm the air. They were firmly in the north now. There was a bitter edge to the wind, as if it were bringing them a little slice of the ice wastes with every gust.

The crew, the Sirens, the soldiers, and the mages all huddled together in tight circles, not caring a damn for who or what their neighbours were. Such is the magick of hot food and company on a cold day.

Farden managed to sneak away from one of Roiks' infamous stories to bring Nuka a serving of stew. The captain thanked him and licked his lips at the smell of the meaty, salty broth. He hesitated when he realised he had to let go of the wheel. 'Would you, mage?'

Farden pulled a face. 'You sure? What about the icebergs?'

Nuka tapped the wood of the wheel and Farden gripped it with both hands. The metal of his gauntlets clanked against the polished wood and its brass bindings. Nuka smiled. 'After last night, I think you can handle a few lumps of ice,' he said.

Farden felt his awareness of the ship's movements grow. Through the wheel he could feel every dip of every little wave, every twitch of the wind in the half-raised sails. 'I'm not sure *lump* is an adequate word.'

Nuka gulped down his stew, not caring for its heat. 'Just treat them like sleeping bears. Don't go near them.'

Farden smiled. 'Good advice.'

Nuka was watching the men and women below. 'The crew can't believe their luck, I can tell. It's not every day I let them have the morning off. Slackers,' he chuckled. 'But they deserve it after last night. Haven't seen a storm like that for almost a decade now. That's what you get for testing the Nelska cape.'

'How far north have you gone?'

'As far as any ship can go.'

'I see.'

Nuka stretched. 'But this isn't any ship, now is it? Her iron hull will cut through the ice like a boot through a puddle.'

Farden looked a little confused. '*Through...* the ice?'

'What? You thought her iron was just for war? No, mage. This ship was made to break ice.'

The mage still didn't like what he was hearing. 'So we're going to sail *into* the ice.'

'As far as we can.'

'Sounds utterly safe.'

'You'll see,' Nuka yawned. He had rings the colour of tar around his bloodshot eyes. His speech was slow and languid, but his tone was blunt; the night had worn his patience thin. Farden was about to suggest a few hours of sleep when the captain walked to the edge of the aftcastle and tapped his mug on the railing. 'Lerel!' he called. Lerel popped up out of the crowd and began to make her way to the wheel. Nuka turned back to the mage. 'The problem is finding a place for the *'Blade* to break into the ice. You could sail these waters for a hundred years and no inch of them would look the same two days in a row. You see, the ice is constantly either melting, freezing, or sliding off the land. Hence, it's constantly moving. I know these waters better than most, but it's the ice I don't know.'

'Cap'n?' asked Lerel, as she sauntered across the deck towards them. She gave Farden a tired smile, and the mage winked back,

'Where're your eyes, Lerel?' asked Nuka.

'Here,' she said, tossing her spyglass to Nuka. He caught it deftly and put the thinner end of it to his eye, squinting like an owl in the daylight.

'As I thought,' he muttered, handing the spyglass back to Lerel, who also put it to her eye.

Farden squinted into the distance. 'What is it?' he asked.

'Ice cliffs, and nothing but, for miles in either direction,' Lerel answered.

'I take it that's bad?' Farden asked.

Lerel answered this one too. 'It could put us days behind. Here,' she said, handing him the spyglass.

It was lighter than he expected, and sturdier too. He lifted it to his eye and squinted. He could see the ice cliffs glittering, so close he felt he could have thrown something at them. They were sheer, and enormous. Farden grit his teeth. 'That won't do. Not at all.'

They were interrupted by the sound of boots treading on stairs. It was Tyrfing. He looked as though he had just woken up, which in truth, he had. He looked awful. 'What are you three looking so glum about?'

Farden 'We need to f...'

Thump.

It was a solid sound, like the falling of a fat acorn in the loam, except that they were the furthest from any oak or loam anyone can be, and the acorn sounded as though it were the size of a house. There was an awkward silence on the aftcastle. Farden clutched the wheel, feeling the shivers run through the ship as the vibrations died. 'Erm, what was that?' he asked, very quietly. Half the deck had let the noise slip by, unnoticed, deep in their own conversations. The other half looked about, confused.

'Ice,' suggested Lerel, putting her hand to the wheel. She accidentally brushed Farden's gauntlet.

'No,' Nuka shook his head, the tiredness fading a little from his eyes. 'Ice doesn't sound like that,' he said.

Thump!

Another dull echo shook the ship, and this time everybody aboard felt it. A hush came over the *Waveblade*. People either looked to their feet or got to them. A few sailors went to the bulwarks and peered into the slate-grey water below.

Farden looked worried. 'Well, please enlighten us, Captain,' he said, as his hands rattled with the tremors. 'And please don't say leviathan.'

'You're on the right track, mage,' said Nuka. He had a glassy look in his eye, as if a younger man long forgotten had suddenly occupied them. He walked softly, almost gliding, to the railing and looked down at the long, dark shadows sliding under the surface of the water, effortless as dust on the wind. His hand grabbed the wooden rail like a spear. 'Whales,' he hissed.

'Whale!' came a cry from one of the sailors. A murmur ran across the hushed deck, mainly from the old whalers in the crew.

Farden left the wheel in Lerel's hands and went to look, brandishing his spyglass. He had never seen a live whale before. A dead one, yes. Once on a beach in Albion, and once splayed out on a wharf in Krauslung's harbour. Both times he had found them sad, solemn-looking creatures, but that was hardly surprising, given their circumstances.

These whales were smaller and faster than he had imagined. They were a midnight black for the most part, and yet had patches of white here and there. Their fins, tall like the flattened masts of ships, threatened to break the surface with every duck and swerve. They were fast. A trio of them came broadside to the ship and darted towards her, lurching with every strong flick of their wide, flat tails. Just before they struck her iron sides they dove and disappeared into the darkness of the water, rocking the ship with their waves. Farden could hear the dull thump and thwack of their passing tails.

'Sea-wolves!' Roiks shouted over the growing buzz of voices, causing several of the mages to stand closer to the railing.

Farden watched as another four whales darted underneath the ship. They were huge still, but not quite as large as he had expected. 'I thought whales were supposed to be harmless,' he said.

Eyrum was striding up the steps to the aftcastle. 'Until you try to harm them. These are the blackfish. *Orca*, the dragons call them. Forbidden to hunt. Farfallen used to say that these whales had dragon souls in them.'

'Njord's creatures,' said Lerel.

Nuka was counting the whales as they circled the ship. 'Dragon teeth too, if you're ever unlucky enough to find out. Vicious creatures. They even eat their own kind,' he said gruffly, sounding very suddenly like the whaler he had once been.

Eyrum snorted at that. 'Bah. Myth,' he scoffed.

Nuka shook his head. 'I've seen it, Siren. They eat their own kind.'

'They're intelligent creatures. Not mindless thugs.'

'And you're telling me no dragon, no wild wyrm, has ever eaten another dragon?' asked the captain.

Eyrum didn't reply to that.

'Ready the bows!' ordered Nuka. 'Be ready to send them packing!' Farden flinched at that order. He could see a little grimace flash across Lerel's face too.

'Surely they can't hurt the *'Blade?'* asked the mage.

'I won't take any chances. There's a dozen of them by my count, and there's a reason they call them sea-wolves. They hunt like a pack and make waves that can roll a boat over.'

'But this isn't a boat.'

'True, but I'm still not taking any chances.'

Farden ventured a sudden idea. 'Maybe they can help us,' he suggested.

'Help with what?'

Farden scratched his chin. He watched the black shapes circling the ship. Their fins were breaking the water now, like those of sharks. While the others ducked and dove and slapped the ship with their tails, a few others, their white bellies stippled with long scars, stayed a safe distance away. They gently bobbed up and down, pointing their strange sharp noses to the sky. Farden realised exactly what it looked like. Elders, watching the young playing a game. 'You said yourself that we need to find thinner ice for the *'Blade* to go ashore. Who could know better than these whales?'

'I was going to use the gryphon. Or a dragon,' replied Nuka, looking horrified by the idea of asking a whale for help. 'They, at least, can talk.'

'Suit yourself,' Farden shrugged, tucking the spyglass into the inside of his cloak. 'I'm going to go ask for directions.'

'Mage,' warned Nuka, as Farden practically jumped down the stairs. He wove through the crowds of people at the bulwarks, jostling his way to the front. Once there, he took one swift look at the freezing sea below him, grit his teeth, and hoisted himself up onto the railing, much to the gasping of those around him.

'Man over the railing!' yelled a nearby sailor, rushing to grab Farden and haul him back onto deck. The mage just batted him away and kept moving. He was now clinging to one of the stout metal shields that had been riveted to the side of the ship. This particular one was wobbling quite disconcertingly. Farden shimmied down a little further until his feet found the notches of a rough ladder.

'Stop there, Farden!' came Nuka's order.

'No,' Farden replied, a little louder than perhaps he had intended. He stopped in his tracks as the crowd and crew about him bit their lips a little.

Nuka's head popped over the railing. Eyrum's followed. As did half the crew's. 'Nobody disobeys me on my own ship, mage. Get back aboard.'

'Too late now,' replied Farden, cursing himself for being absolutely right.

'You stubborn b…' began Nuka, but he was interrupted by a familiar voice from behind him. It sounded like Tyrfing. Farden could barely hear over the splashing of the waves and the whales. 'There's no use arguing…' he was saying. He was right.

The orca had become curious now. A handful made one last pass beneath the ship, rocking her and making Farden's hands shake, and then slowly, one by one, they began to gather beneath him. Their fins rose from the sea like sharp, black blades. Farden dared to look between his feet and saw one whale hugging the iron keel, staring up at him with a beady black eye marooned in a sea of white skin. It smiled with teeth not unlike those of the shark they had stewed not long ago. Farden's heart was thumping, though he didn't dare admit it. Not even to himself.

'I'll warn you not to get too close, Farden. They're not called killer whales for no reason!' ordered Nuka.

'Be careful!' came another cry, from somewhere in the crew.

Farden couldn't help but stare back at the whale, almost mesmerised. He vaguely remembered a similar look passing between him and a wolf a long time ago, in the forest north of the Össfen Mountains, surrounded by snow and lazy sunlight. 'They look harmless to me!' he called up, trying to convince himself.

Above him, Nuka clicked his fingers. 'Roiks!'

Somewhere behind him a foot stamped and a voice yelled, 'Yessir!'

'On the subject of whales, their habits and their behaviours, who would you pay more attention to? Your captain of nineteen years, former whaler, and all-round nautical authority, or a mage whose legs are as used to the sway of a deck as a pig is to perfume?'

Roiks answered very quickly indeed. 'It'd have to be the first one, sir. You.'

'Right you are,' said Nuka, giving Farden a lingering, sour look. 'Did you hear that, mage? Do as you're told.'

Farden muttered something dark and not altogether compliant. He felt his old curiosity drawing him closer to the water and its sleek, piebald inhabitants. Much to the anger of the captain above him, he climbed further down's the ship's sheer flanks.

The water slid by at a speed that got more and more frightening with every step. One of the whales slid close and blew a fountain of air and steam from a strange hole in his back. It soaked Farden to the skin. He didn't dare spare a hand to wipe his face. He simply held tight, and wondered why he could taste fish.

He vaguely heard the echoes of orders to bring in the sail. A few minutes of clinging later, he felt the *Waveblade* slow slightly. The orca could feel it too. Each of them swam a little closer to the ship, so tightly bunched and so numerous that Farden fancied he could step out and walk to the nearest chunk of ice without getting his feet wet. They swam on their sides so they could stare at the strange pale thing clinging to the side of the wooden, iron beast. Ponderously, they blew great plumes of water and breath. A few of the larger whales, elders as Farden had suspected, swam in circles around the main group.

It was only when the ship came to a near halt that one of them came close to examine the mage. There was a deep rumble from under the water, then a high-pitched whine. The other whales quickly parted like grass in a storm, leaving room for the largest whale to rise up out of the water; a glistening mass of slippery black and white, sporting a fin that was easily as tall as Farden. Its beady eyes were a sharp blue, and there was a pink scar that ran across its blunt nose like a moustache. Deep in its throat it uttered a low and long drone that made Farden's skin shiver. He turned around as far as he could and then, for some reason, as if it were some sort of king that had risen from the deep, he bowed his head. The whale did not move, save for the gentle sway of its fins. It didn't even blink. Farden opened his mouth to speak.

The whale beat him to it.

'A brave one...' it started, its words elongated and dragged out like dough over a hook. It had the guttural hiss of a throat not used to speaking, and yet had the booming resonance of an avalanche. Undoubtedly a male. '...are you.'

Farden was frozen in shock. He could hear the feverish muttering from the deck above. Disbelief hissed back and forth. He managed to form some words. 'Thank you?' he replied.

'Man comes little to us now. Used to sing songs with us. Now avoid us. Hunt us,' replied the whale. He looked to where Nuka stood at the railing. 'We smell the blood on you.'

Farden involuntarily climbed one step higher. With a flick of its tail, the whale moved closer. Farden tried to avoid counting the rows of white teeth lining the creature's pink mouth, but he couldn't help it. Its tongue flicked back and forth. 'What want you? Why you come?'

Perhaps it was the fierce look in the whale's beady eyes. Perhaps it was how ancient and dusty his words sounded. Perhaps it was the shock that he could speak. Whatever it was, Farden felt he owed this creature the absolute truth. And so he told it. Farden nodded towards the ice cliffs in the far distance. 'We're going north to stop a girl from bringing the daemons down from the sky. She means to start a war.'

The whale rolled onto his side to look at the pale blue sky hanging above them. 'Ah, the Othersea,' he said. 'We remember the day its stars were born. We remember the world before.'

Farden felt a sudden wave of dread as he abruptly realised he had no idea which side these whales were on. For all he knew, they were in league with the daemons. Advocates of their return. There was a tense moment, but then the whale turned back to the mage, and shook its head with a splash. 'Fire and sea mix not.'

Farden almost wiped his brow 'Does that mean you can help us?' he asked. 'We need to find where the ice thins out.'

The whale sighed through his strange blow-hole. Farden felt the cold spray on his cheek. 'Felt dark things in water, have we. Old things. Old as us. Old as those on your ship.' There was an uncomfortable silence aboard the *Waveblade* as the crew swapped frowns and confused glances. Tyrfing and Nuka pretended to do the same. The whale flashed a line of teeth. 'We like them not. Fight them, if we need.'

'Yes, but will you guide us to thinner ice? We can fight them with you, but we need to find land.'

The whale ducked his head under the water and Farden heard him singing his question to the others. It was an odd song, made of clicks and squeaks and notes so low that they would have given a dragon a run for its coin.

Soon enough, the verdict was in. The elder raised his head out of the water and clapped his fins on the surface. 'We take you to where sea meets rock. But for us, you must sing.'

Farden grinned. 'Sing?' he asked.

'Sing with us. When Othersea fades black. Like the old years. I smell sea in your blood. Sea and magick. You will sing like ancestors did.'

'You name the song, whale, and we'll sing it,' Farden said, and then he did a bold thing. He reached out a hand toward the whale, drawing further mutterings and sharp words from the deck above. For a moment the whale refused to move. His blue eyes moved from the shiny red-gold of Farden's gauntlet to its owner, and then back again. Then he slipped slowly forward, and lifted the tip of his nose to meet Farden's hand. Even through the metal, he could feel how rough the whale's nose was.

'Felt that metal before, have we,' he sighed, before he slipped back into the icy water. With a slap of his tail that soaked Farden and half those standing at the railing, the whale disappeared under the ship.

'Well, that was certainly unexpected,' Farden smirked as a few of the sailors hauled him over the railing. 'Who'd have thought that whales could talk?'

'If you were one of my men I'd have you flogged,' Nuka glowered.

'Luckily…' Farden started, but the captain cut him off.

'But you aren't, so I'll have to ask the Arkmage to make an exception,' he said, turning to Tyrfing.

The Arkmage crossed his arms and shook his head. 'He has

enough scars,' he answered.

'Lucky indeed,' Nuka threw up his hands and went back to his wheel, rattling off orders as he walked. 'Man the masts, men. Apparently we have some whales to follow!'

Farden watched him go with a concerned face, hoping the man was simply over-tired. He was not the sort of man he wanted to lose as a friend.

'Stupidity, bravery, and luck,' his uncle was muttering hoarsely.

'What's that?'

Tyrfing tutted, and sauntered off. 'Sometimes I find it hard to tell the difference between them.'

Chapter 18

"Clap ye ears, lads, when the whales sing. Sing for ye soul they do, suck right of of ye body they will! Guard ye ears, boys, and keep that soul deep in ye chest, where it belongs."
Words spoken by Fishmaster Boon, recorded in the year 412

It was a fine night for singing, according to the whales.

It was a cold night, that was for sure.

The north had swallowed them whole. They were embedded in it like an iron arrow in pale flesh. To say it snowed would be a drastic understatement. This snow fell like the world had never seen winter. It fell lazily, in great blankets and sheets, so thick and fluffy that when it finally alighted on the water, it refused to melt, freezing into slush instead. It was hard to see where the sea ended and the edge of the ice began. Nuka was having trouble seeing the bow, never mind the ice.

Fortunately, the *Waveblade* had its whales. Their black fins and noses cut little paths through the slush as they clicked and whined and warmed up their voices. The big elder, whom Farden had imaginatively dubbed Scarnose after finding that his real name was something utterly unpronounceable, something with far too many clicks and squeals for the human tongue to cope with, called out for the ship to stop, and stop she did. Lines and hooks were dropped and the whales took them in their teeth. One by one they dragged them ashore and tethered the ship in place, nuzzling the ice with her sharp bow.

'We'll need some wind to break into the ice,' Nuka said, eyeing the fluffy sky.

'Or a push,' suggested Farden as he absently watched the cavorting whales.

Nuka made an uneasy face. Farden chuckled at his grumbling silence. The captain was still firmly clinging to that old whaler deep inside him, that old whaler that scowled and muttered every time one of the sleek beasts came near. He didn't trust the whales one bit.

Farden, on the other hand, had spent the day mesmerised by them. As the whales had led them a merry path through the fields of towering icebergs, he had ensconced himself in a lower porthole and watched them sputter and sail and surge around the ship, his pipe and a certain rat his only company.

The whales were the very definition of incredible. Graceful and dangerous all wrapped up in patchwork, monochrome skin. Teeth and thick blubber hiding tough muscle and old wisdom. Maybe Farfallen had been right... these truly were the dragons of the sea.

There had been other whales too that day, not just orca. A great grey whale had followed them for a time. A *humpback*, Nuka had called it. Longer than the ship itself, it had broken a small iceberg in half just for sport. Farden had tried to listen to the deep, sonorous words the two species traded. Though they were beyond foreign to him, their tone had sounded wary, and fearful too, and not because of the ship. Something else concerned the whales.

Farden suppressed a chattering of his teeth. He was wearing three jerkins and a shirt under his trusty cloak, but still the cold seeped in. His armour remained defiantly lukewarm, but underneath his left gauntlet, his missing finger ached, like it always did in the cold. He clenched a half-made fist and sparks of pain shot up his arm. *Curse that bloody Vice*, Farden hissed in his head.

Nuka wore a long, thick seal-fur coat that stretched down to his ankles. He looked warmer than a blacksmith's crotch, and smug to boot. He knew the north and her cold better than most, and had obviously packed for the occasion. Farden even spied a glistening of sweat on his brow. *Swine*, he inwardly muttered.

It wasn't long before the whales finished their slow dancing, and gathered around the ship in pairs. The sailors, Sirens, and soldiers clustered at the bulwarks to watch them. The whales were about to sing.

'I'm guessing you've never heard a whale sing before?' the captain asked. Farden replied with a distracted, 'No.' He was already leaning over the railing, thoroughly captivated. *What was it about these creatures*, he wondered? Nuka lashed the wheel in place and joined him.

'I suppose we're in for a treat then. Both of us, and the crew for that matter. I've only ever heard distant echoes. Sounds like wolves, normally, howling at the moon. Hence their name.'

Farden turned around. A glint of humour in his eye and lip. 'I wonder if we'll know the song?'

Nuka rolled his eyes.

The song of the whales was unlike any song any ear on that ship had ever heard, or could ever dream to hear. It was a song, but not a song. It had rhythm, and melody, true, but it had the depth of the seabed, the intricacy of a honeycomb, and the deafening pound of an livid storm, all at the same time.

It began slowly at first, slow as the snowfall. Each whale made its own tune. Some low, some piercingly high. All of them different. Some sang through the water, making the ship shake, while others spat tunes in bursts from their blowholes. Slowly, the song began to build and coalesce into a mighty tune. Fins slapped the slushy water. Huge tails lifted glittering streams of water, momentary waterfalls, only to dash them to the sea again as percussion. The elders rumbled and boomed with their heads buried in the water. Farden could feel the ship shake with every note. The young ones' whistling skittered over the bass notes as a topline. Every eye on the ship was painfully wide. Every ear strained. Every foot and finger tapping to the odd, displaced rhythm.

Any skald aboard would have hung himself in shame.

Roiks was the first to start singing. Unsurprisingly, he launched into a song about drinking. On hindsight it probably wasn't the most fitting tune to match the majestic orchestra of the whales, but it was Roiks, and his enthusiasm more than made up for it.

With a foot on the bulwark and a hand on his chest, he bellowed out the words for all to hear. It took mere moments for the sailors to join him. Then the soldiers joined in. Then the mages. Then the Written. Those who didn't know the tune, a smattering of mages and Sirens, just laughed and clapped along, throwing snowballs in the air and at the sails. On the aftcastle, even Nuka the once-whaler, banged his fist on the railing alongside Farden, singing as loud as they could. The only silent ones aboard were Tyrfing, whose throat was raw as a battlefield, and the two gods. But even Heimdall managed to shut his eyes and smile at the strange serenade swirling around him.

Unbelievably, the two songs fit. Like a sword in a scabbard they slipped into each other and were forged into one. The whales boomed and slapped while the ship yelled and capered. For the brief moments the song lasted, it was pure joy, stirred up from deep within, in that place not a soul can find, not until it comes alive with music and laughter. Perhaps those aboard knew what was to come. That was the last song they might sing. It made them sing all the louder.

As gradually as the song had built, it died away. The whales slapped their fins in a chorus of applause as the *Waveblade* finally caught its breath. The ship was still rocking from side to side in the echoes. In the silence that followed, all that could be heard was heavy breathing, the gentle crackle of the ice-laced waves, and the faint, feathery hiss of snow falling.

'What now?' Farden asked, to the silence and to the captain.

Nuka shrugged. His coat rustled. 'We just sang a duet with a pack of whales. Forgive me if I'm not completely sure what the next step is,' he replied sarcastically. Farden smiled wryly as he wandered down the slippery steps to the main deck, where a few Written made a space for him. They nodded respectfully as he murmured his excuses.

Farden leant over the ship's side and looked for Scarnose. Half of the orca had sunk into the icy depths, as if to cool themselves off. They were lost to the murky darkness of the sea and snow. Only a few elders remained, and Scarnose wasn't nearby.

Farden was about to call out when a black and white face appeared directly underneath him, rearing up with a muted splash. The whale lifted itself out of the water so much that its scarred nose of a namesake came almost level with the deck. Farden leant back involuntarily. There was a little rustle of awe through the crowd around him.

'Many tides pass since orca last sang with human. Many, many tides,' rumbled Scarnose.

Farden bowed respectfully. 'Too many, in my opinion. Perhaps when we return…?' Farden trailed off, hearing his own words in his ears. There was an uncomfortable silence from those nearby.

The whale seemed to sense it. 'Dark whispers in water, humans. Dark shadows beneath ice. On it, too. We hear drumming of feet across ice. Of claws. Of heavy, hurrying things. The magick draws them north. As it draws us.'

Farden couldn't wait to go meet it. 'Will you come north with us?'

Scarnose flashed a row of teeth and a pink tongue. He licked a few snowflakes from his rubbery lips. 'As far as ice allows. We may not be seen, but we are there.'

Farden nodded. 'And will you help us into the ice?' he asked.

'There is no wind.'

The whale began to slip back into the sea. 'We shall,' he said, and then added, strangely, 'magick man,' just before his head slipped under the surface.

Farden watched the creature disappear into the slush. Behind him, the soldiers slowly slipped away, back to their posts or back to their beds. The Sirens quietly disappeared below. Only a few remained on deck, milling about, unsure. Whether the crew felt it or not, a sudden air of danger began to corrode the joyous afterglow of the singing, and trample it into the dirty snow of the deck.

'Looks like we're getting a push,' Farden announced to Nuka, as he returned to the aftcastle. This time Lerel, Tyrfing, and several of the Written followed. The captain was unlashing the wheel. He didn't look that comfortable with the idea.

'It certainly does. These sea-wolves better be careful with my ship.'

Tyrfing stamped his foot. 'She'll hold, Captain. Don't you worry.'

Nuka bowed. 'Aye, your Mage,' he said. No sooner had the words tumbled from his mouth did the ship shudder. A couple of cries rang out from the deck. 'Steady as she goes!' he shouted. Roiks echoed the order as he strode about the masts in long-legged figure of eights, clapping his snowy gloves together.

'You 'eard the Captain, lads and ladies! Stop fannying around and get to work. Eyes sharp, legs steady, and keep your wits about you! We've got ice to break!'

More orders rang out from the mates. 'Reel in those lines, boys!'

'I want that ice chipped from the rigging. Don't make me come up there!'

'Mages, front and centre! Be ready with fire and light for the ice now!'

Farden leant close to his uncle as he felt the ship begin to move. 'I'm told you made this ship to break ice. What in Emaneska gave you the idea to make a ship that can break ice? Besides this mission, what's the point?'

Tyrfing had a scarf wrapped around his face. It puffed in and out as he talked. 'It was an accident, to tell the truth, nephew. I just wanted to make a ship that could cut another ship in half. This was a fortunate, but otherwise unplanned, application. It was actually Nuka that suggested it,' Tyrfing replied. His red-rimmed eyes were eagerly fixed on the thin shelf of ice that was getting closer by the minute. It only looked to be a foot or so thick, but that was plenty for any ship, even *Waveblade*. If he was nervous, he barely showed it. He just looked sweaty and feverish.

Farden was watching the ice too, he could feel that old fear of icy-cold water flooding back to him. 'So, you've tested it then?'

'Tested? Oh no. This'll be the first time.'

Farden slowly turned from the ice to his uncle, and found them both as worrying. 'The *first* time?'

'That's right, Farden!' Nuka called. 'Time to put the iron of this *'Blade* to the test.'

'She'll hold,' Tyrfing repeated hoarsely, not sounding all that convincing for Farden's liking. His gauntlets gripped the railing a little tighter as the whales began to push harder.

The edge of the ice disappeared beneath the bowsprit. There was a dreadful silence, full of clenching and waiting, and then a dull boom as the iron bow bit into the ice of the north. Any other ship would have had its keel staved in, split at the very least. Not the *Waveblade*. She lifted itself up and over the lip of the ice, and then hammered down on it with all of her massive, iron weight. The ice split like bad glass, and the *Waveblade* powered on.

It took more than a few minutes for Farden's unease to subside. In fact, it took a good half an hour, and a wincing journey to the bow to convince him that he was safe. The *'Blade* was too sharp and too powerful for the thin ice. She left a mottled, shattered path behind her, full of broken, sinking ice and curious whales. They kept pushing and the ship kept breaking.

Ilios seemed impressed. Farden absently stroked his feathers as he watched the ice splinter below. The noise was sharp, deep.

Two mages were straddling the bowsprit. They were lashed and roped into place lest they were to fall in the ship's shuddering. One dangled at a nauseating angle, staring down at the mermaid figurehead, while the other was busy staring out into the hazy, snowy night ahead of them. Bright light emanated from his hands, but it barely illuminated anything past the tip of the bowsprit.

Farden watched them for a while, curious. The snow dripped off their warm clothes and bodies, kept warm as they were by the light and their magick. Absently, Farden raised his hand, mildly curious, and went to clench it in that old, familiar way, but then he stopped. *No,* he warned himself. *Slowly.*

'Old habits?' asked a voice.

More than a little startled, Farden swivelled around to find the white-haired Written, Inwick, standing behind him with her arms folded behind her back. Farden didn't make any effort to hide his surprise. He began to pat his hips. 'Sorry,' he said. 'Should I have worn a sword?'

Surprisingly, Inwick smiled. It was a curt smile, rationed for politeness, but a smile nonetheless. 'I am simply here to talk.'

'Good. I'd hate to embarrass you a third time.'

'Gossfring told me I should expect some sarcasm. I see he's right, as always,' she said. She hesitated then. 'May I?' she asked, gesturing to the empty space between Farden and the railing. Farden waved her forward and she came to stand by his side, not too close, but close enough to keep her voice low and still be heard over the constant cracking of the ice below them.

'They tell stories of you, you know. Gossfring, Efrin, the others. Stories of a forgotten Farden, one that they met in the Efjar Skirmishes.'

Farden crossed his arms. 'Do they now?'

Inwick nodded. 'Indeed they do. They like to tell us newer mages the old stories of the Siren war, of Efjar and the minotaurs, of times golden and lost.'

'Any stories in particular?' he asked. Farden was gazing sideways at her, trying to figure her out. She had all the beauty of an icicle; her face paler than pale, and her nose and cheekbones were sharp and angular. When a snowflake landed on her cheek, he found it hard to tell the difference between it and her skin. She could have been made of porcelain, for all he knew. Only a light smattering of freckles across her nose betrayed her. Her hair was also white as a snow, and her eyes their curious pink. Farden had only seen a handful of albinos in his time. Usually a court jester or two, or a travelling minstrel or skald. Never a Written. Never even a mage. She must have been from a high family indeed.

Inwick rubbed her chin. 'One in particular keeps cropping up, I suppose. They talk of a certain mage, a young man. Scarred. Eager. Incredibly skilled with blade and spell. Call him the hero of Efjar most of the time.'

Farden pursed his lips. 'And why do they call him that?' he asked.

Inwick tucked her chin under the collar of her coat while she stared at the mages working on the bowsprit. Farden could have sworn her skin glowed slightly. Maybe it was her white hair and complexion in the glow of the lanterns, or perhaps it was her own spells at work, joining with the mages. Farden tried to feel that faint tingling in the air, the one he barely remembered, but it escaped him.

She let the story unravel, reciting it as she had heard it told many times in the decks below, in the canteen, on patrol, in the Spire before it had burnt down. 'They say that the entire camp was caught unawares. It was a misty morning on the marshes, so it might have been forgivable. The minotaurs crept in at first light, taking the watchtowers and the palisades before the alarms could be raised. They had the camp surrounded before anyone could crack an eyelid. They killed the ones that struggled and clubbed the rest back to sleep, and while they tied up their prisoners, they sat down to skin and butcher the ones that had resisted, roasting them in pieces over their own campfires, skin, bones, Book and all.

'Only one mage escaped their attack. He had fallen asleep under a low wagon, though gods know why. Hidden by the wheels and the shredded tarpaulin, the minotaurs had missed him in their searches. As the horrid smells of his own men wafted to his nostrils, he awoke thinking of breakfast. It took him only moments to discover what had happened. Through the mists he could see the shapes, horned and hoofed and carrying their mallets and hammers.

'The mage shuffled out from under the wagon and escaped to the edges of the camp, where he faded into the marshes and their mists. There, he realised he couldn't fight them all. This coming from a man who had wrestled a minotaur to the dust a year before and strangled the life out of it with his bare hands.' Inwick looked up at Farden. 'Am I telling this right so far?'

Farden rocked his head from side to side. 'I've heard this story before. It was a juvenile. Barely a teenager. But yes, carry on.'

Inwick made a mental note, and then carried on. 'So this lonely mage happened across an idea. Skirting around to the edges of the camp, keeping to the mist and the walls, while the smell of his cooking comrades lingered in his nostrils, he gathered wood, tinder, torches, and two copper pans that had been left in a pile of smouldering coals. He made his way to the north of the camp and began to pace back and forth through the thick bogs of Efjar's deepest marshes, marshes that can swallow a grown man whole.'

'Two men, I heard.'

'Two then. One by one he laid little piles of wood and tinder down in any dry patch he could find. He knew he had to be quick, for the air was wet, and he could hear screaming coming from the camp.

'Only when he had formed a line of almost a hundred piles of wood and torches did he stop. He was almost a mile from the camp now, and exhausted from his work, but still the screams spurred him on. Taking a breath, this brave mage began to hop from pile to pile, lighting them with his fire as he went. Galloping from bog to bog he lit them all, and every time he lit them he threw a burst of light and sparks into the air, yelling and bellowing at the top of his voice and banging those two pans together for all he was worth. He didn't stop until a wall of one hundred fires stood on the north side of the camp, stretching from east to west and turning the mists a bright orange in the morning light.

'Now minotaurs are quite skittish beasts, and fearful when outnumbered, and when the minotaurs saw the hundred lights they fled. Those who awoke in those moments remember hearing an army of mages hot on their hooves. Fireballs flew across the camp like burning arrows. The sound of steel swords on shields filled the air, echoing back and forth across the marshes. A hundred fire spells glittered in the mists, advancing on the camp to liberate it from the hungry minotaurs.

'Only when every last minotaur had fled into the mists did the mage reveal himself, covered in mud and soot and holding two copper pans, now beaten to a mangled mess. With a bit of fire and two pans, he had saved the entire camp from certain death. Sound familiar?'

Farden took in a long breath. 'It's an old story, that's for sure.'

Inwick turned around to face him. 'You know who you were in that story?'

'If I remember rightly, and it's harder than you think, I was the one at the end, holding the copper pans.'

'Apparently so. What I mean is, do you know *what* you were?'

'Lucky?'

'The hero of Efjar.'

'Ah.'

'What happened to him, hmm? I grew up on such stories. The older mages live to tell them. Stories of mages and Written like you and your uncle and heroes that have never been matched. Stories like that were why I begged my parents to let me train with my brothers,' Inwick said. She had an eager look in her eye. Half-angry, half-upset.

Farden rubbed his stubbled chin. 'I see. This is why you wanted to fight me, wasn't it? Either you wanted to see if I really was the man in that story, or you wanted to punish me for letting him die.'

'A little of both, I suppose.'

'And what did you find?'

Inwick paused to think. 'Judging by the stories and rumours I keep hearing on this ship, that man is being resurrected. Slowly. Surely. I hope.'

Farden smiled. 'And here I was thinking you were going to berate me, and harass me into being a better man.'

'Oh, I am,' said Inwick, flashing him a sour look. 'There is one thing still missing.'

Farden raised an eyebrow. 'Oh, and what's that?' Inwick slapped him on his back in answer. Farden could see her irritation building. 'That old chestnut,' he murmured.

She put her hands on her hips. There was a stern fire about her that he was starting to like. 'Do you know why I volunteered for this mission, Farden?' she asked.

'Because you're one of the best we've got, according to Gossfring,' Farden answered.

Inwick shook her head. 'No, because I didn't have a choice. There was no volunteering whatsoever. We Written are a dying breed,

Farden. We are the last of our kind. Do you realise that? What you see on this ship is what's left of us. Doesn't that bother you?'

'Well…'

'It bothers *me*, mage!' she snapped, the fire building. 'And the rest!'

'Of course…'

'It bothers me even more that you are unwilling to be one of us. That you obdurately refuse to put your Book to good use, and fight for the survival of your kind.'

'I am…'

'Unwilling to even try. A mage like you. Unrivalled!'

'It's more comp…

Inwick threw her hands up in the air in exasperation. 'Do you know what this is like, Farden? To see you waste such power, when you could be using it to help us?'

Farden dreaded to think. 'No…' he ventured.

'It's like you're the last man alive in the whole world and you're just too lazy to fuck to save your own species!' Inwick hissed. There was an awkward silence as she realised what she had just said. 'There,' she said, brushing her hair behind one of her ears. 'I have said my piece. That is all I wanted to do.' Farden didn't reply. He didn't really know what to do apart from stand there.

'Well,' she sighed, as she slowly backed away. 'I just hope you come to your senses soon, Farden. We Written need you. Not just Emaneska. Us.'

Farden watched her turn and go. Suffice it to say, he was a little shocked. Ilios whistled something low and confused, and Farden turned back to watch the mages work. Farden puffed out his cheeks, watching the snowflakes spin away in his hot breath.

Maybe, just maybe, Inwick was right. And Gossfring too. And his uncle. And Durnus. And all the bloody rest. Farden sighed.

'The hero of Efjar,' he spoke aloud. Ilios squinted at him,

intrigued. 'I remember him.'

The gryphon warbled.

'Young. Impetuous. Stubborn. Brave. Damn good at what he did,' Farden rubbed his stubble. 'Maybe I could be him again. A hero, like they used to say. I know what I need to do. Does doing it make me a hero, Ilios?'

Ilios clacked his beak and nodded.

'Though, a couple of minotaurs is nothing compared to what we're about to face.'

Another little warble, betraying the gryphon's joy.

'This hero just needs his armour first.'

part three
of snow and fire

1561 years ago

'Where is Lop?!' *Came the cry, echoing through the smoking crags.*

'Here!' *came the gargled reply.*

'Balimuel! Help him!'

The giant leapt down the hewn steps, puckered rock worn smooth with age and pilgrimage. His armour clanked as he stumbled into a rock, glancing harmlessly off it. 'I have him!' he cried. Strong arms looped under Lop's blood-soaked shoulders and hauled him to his feet. The man roared with pain as he was dragged upwards, hand clamped to his ripped neck.

'Damn you Lopia!' Gaspid was shouting. 'What possessed you to take your helmet off?!'

Lop just gargled in reply, desperately trying to wriggle his armour back on with shaking hands. His pauldrons greedily clasped at his helmet, and he was whole again. His armour would keep him alive, but only barely. The wound was disturbingly deep.

'Up, you bastards! Up!' Balimuel bellowed.

Up and up they climbed, step by frantic step, leaping two at a time when the rock allowed. Strength poured from their armour into their legs and knees, into their arms and hands, powering them up the smoking, sulphur-bled path. Gods, how they were tired. Gods, how they were desperate. Months of fighting had led to this moment, months of bloody, vicious fighting on the steps of the forts and the city walls and of the Froastsoar. They had seen more blood than a thousand hearts. More guts than an army of butchers. Heard more screams and prayers than the ears of a god. And still the greedy, *frantic hordes of Emaneska ploughed on, baying for their blood and metal. Korrin was tired. So very tired.*

Korrin stood at the crest of the volcano, where the razor rocks levelled out into a narrow path that lead to the blackened, jagged rim where the fires burnt. As the eight Knights climbed to reach him, he stared out at the ice fields, burning with the light of the Spine and the fires of war. Frostsoar was a hot brand in the distance, framed against the grey sky. Korrin could hear the great stones cracking over the rumbling of the volcano at his back.

Scalussen had been razed to the ground.

And all because of them. Because of their armour.

The Knights had held them back for a time. A few months at most. They had stood at the edge of Scalussen and reduced army after army to dust, fighting alongside the soldiers of the city. But as each new lord arrived, rubbing hands and heart thumping with greed and vengeance, the Nine had fallen back, inch by aching inch. Word had spread like disease across the south. Every man with a sword and legs that could travel had made his way to the ice fields, eager to claim the fabled armour of the Nine for himself. Emaneska had turned on them, well and truly. Immortality, it seemed, was too great a lure.

How silent Scalussen had stayed. How stubborn. Not a soul called for the armour to be relinquished. Not a mouth dared to entertain that notion. They had suffered the worst, to save Emaneska from a similar fate.

'Curse it all!' Korrin shouted into the hot air. He snarled at the world, bubbling with anger. He'd had it all. He had escaped his destiny with a shout of a name, become somebody that mattered, somebody with purpose, and now even that was crumbling around him. 'It isn't fair,' he muttered, over and over again. 'It isn't fair.'

Gaspid was first, wheezing through the gap in his visor. 'Gods, this air is foul, lad! We better keep moving.'

'We can't be serious, Gaspid!'

The man gripped him hard, eyes wild. 'We talked about this Korrin! We already decided! You were in agreement with us all!'

Korrin wrenched himself free. 'I'm changing my mind, Gaspid!'

Gaspid thrust him forward with a shove, almost driving him to his knees. 'Well, you don't get to! Now move! This way, Knights!'

And so they moved, negotiating the narrow strip of rock that led to the crater. They could hear shouts below them, and the harsh crack of sling-stones and arrows chasing them.

'Onwards!'

The Knights scrabbled over the rocks as fast they could. Lop was dragging his feet now. Gäel and Rosiff had leant Balimuel their hands, and together the three of them hauled him up the mountain.

'Here it is,' Estina sighed, as they reached the lip of the jagged crater. Their path cut a notch in the rim of thick, black, charred rock, taking them to the very edge of the volcano's fiery pit, where the Smiths had first learnt to forge.

'Here it is indeed, Knights,' Gaspid replied, his voice as heavy as the armour that clung to him. Heavy with tough decision and dread. They all felt it, all except Korrin, who quietly bubbled away in the background, angry and resentful.

Gaspid put his hand out, flat and shaking, into the middle of them. He raised his visor, and one by one, the others did the same. It was a solemn moment, there, perched on the lip of that fiery chasm. Molten rock roared below them. 'It is the only way.'

'The only way,' Balimuel nodded.

'The only way, echoed the others. Only Korrin stayed silent.

Shouts began to echo along the path behind them. Shadows flitted amongst the rocks. 'It's the only way we can put a stop to this.'

'Why not just the armour?' Korrin hissed. Even though he had spent the last five years dealing it, death was staring him in the face for the first time, and its breath was foul. He couldn't help but tremble.

'We've been through this, lad!' Gaspid shouted, as the volcano roared around them. 'There is no escape for us. You want to spend the rest of your life running?'

Yes. *Korrin spat, inside his head.* At least that way there would be a rest of my life. 'No,' he lied.

Gaspid nodded, reaching for his visor. It closed with a rattle of metal, as the armour locked itself in place. 'It has been an exceptional honour,' he said, before turning around. Before anybody could flinch, he was gone, plummeting into the molten rock far below without so much as a cry. Korrin felt something claw at his heart.

One by one, the others stepped up to the edge. Calm and silent they were, each betraying their thumping hearts and trembling lips. One by one their visors were closed, fists were clenched, and feet shuffled forward. Quiet Gäel was next, gone without a sound. Then Estina, lip curled to the very last. Chast cried out as he fell, a long tapering wail that made the remaining Knights shake even more. Lop hobbled up to the edge, dizzy with the loss of blood. His armour undulated in the hot light of the fire. He was gone before Korrin could blink. Demsin went next. Korrin thought he heard her sobbing before she fell. Then tall Rosiff, falling head first. It was only when Balimuel stepped forward that Korrin spoke up.

'No,' he hissed.

'Yes, lad,' Balimuel replied. He rested a hand on Korrin's shoulder.

'This is wrong.'

'It is the only way,' the giant echoed. His grip was tightening around Korrin's shoulder. He took a backwards step and his heel left the rock. As he balanced on his toes, Korrin was tugged forward, trapped in the giant's grip.

'Let go, Balimuel!' Korrin snapped.

'Come, lad. We'll go together. Like the warriors we are.'

'If we were warriors, we would be fighting our way out!' Korrin tried to push him off, but Balimuel was too strong.

'Accepting death is a fight, Korrin. You should know that!' Balimuel shouted over the roar. One of his feet was dangling in mid-air now. Korrin pushed and pushed, but the giant kept inexorably dragging him forward. Korrin pawed at the rock.

'No!' he yelled. As he felt his own toes meet the edge, he flailed frantically, swinging a fist up at Balimuel's hand. Balimuel's great fist came loose, and in a slow, painful moment, the giant toppled backwards, hand raised in a wave to the very last.

Korrin sobbed as he watched his comrade disappear into the hot, burning glow of the volcano. He was shaking like a leaf.

'There!' came a cry, from somewhere behind him. Korrin spun around. Black figures were scrabbling over the rocks towards him, steel glinting in their hands, grins on their faces.

'Spend the rest of my life running?' he asked, shivering. *'So be it.*

And he ran. He ran as fast as his legs could manage. He ran as fast as the rocks would allow. He ran like the fire that chased him.

Say one thing for the desperate. They can run.

Chapter 19

"The nomads of the ice fields share a striking similarity to the nomads and tribesmen of the Paraian deserts. The resemblance between their stature and bearing is most confusing, for they are two nations literally worlds apart. Were I not a learned fellow, I might assume they were related in some way. But I am no fool. Instead, it is plain to see that their elongated limb configurations are not a result of some common ancestor, but rather the simple result of plenty of walking."
Excerpt from Gatterfell's 'The Body Foreigner' - a lengthy disquisition on the 'anatomical peculiarities of Emaneska's more humanish of species'

'Can you feel it?' asked Lilith, as she awkwardly dismounted the spit-flecked flanks of the humongous wolf. She hopped around as she tried to drag her other foot down from its back, but her footing betrayed her and she collapsed in a snowy heap. Lilith could have sworn she heard the fenrir snigger at her. 'Hmph,' she sighed, as she got to her half-dead feet and brushed the snow from her anaesthetised legs. The jolting ride had knocked all the feeling out of her bottom half. Now she tottered about like a torso on cumbersome stilts as she attempted to get the blood flowing.

As usual, Samara wasn't affected by such things. She looked as though she had barely ridden a mile, never mind throughout the night and the following day. Although her cheeks were wind and cold-bitten, she strode about on legs as fresh as only young legs could be.

Lilith rolled her eyes and kept kneading her thighs. Her huge wolf leant down and snuffled at her feet, licking the snow for moisture, enormous teeth worryingly close. Lilith hobbled away from it.

The had decided that the fenrir stank. Perhaps it was their sweaty, matted fur. Perhaps it was their diet, whatever that was. Lilith dreaded to think. Either way, the smell of the huge beasts left a sour taste on her tongue. 'Can you feel it?' she asked again.

Samara was staring at the sky. The sun and the moon seemed to be jostling for ownership of the sky. One sat in the east, the other in the west. It was one of those rare days when the two pause in their eternal chase, and dare to be seen together. The girl wrinkled her nose at both of them. 'I...' she began, concentrating. She stretched out her hands and chips of ice and fallen snow drifted up to touch them. She let them hang suspended in the air for a moment before letting them fall. 'It's incredible,' she said distractedly. 'It's like nothing I've ever felt. Stronger, *sharper*. You wouldn't understand.'

'Of course not,' Lilith tutted. 'So, are you ready?'

Samara closed her eyes and fell silent. Lilith waited for an answer, but none came. Instead she looked around at the white wasteland, the one they had traded for the sandy brown wasteland. It was unbearably cold on the ice fields. Even with the daemon blood still swilling around her veins and joints, the cold was digging deeper and deeper into her flesh, making her shiver.

Behind them lay a shimmering, jagged strip of grey water, dotted with huge chunks of floating ice. At its edges was where the sea met the snow. It was a stark contrast, like a steel axe-head hacking at wool. In the far distance, she could still spot the line where the arid wastes had met the northern snow. Oddly defined; snow rubbing shoulders with frozen dust and scraggly plants. Not a single tree had been spotted since the huge pine.

In the west a great cloud lay across the horizon, maybe a blizzard or a storm. In the east, the sun had turned the wastes and distant ice fields into ruby gold. It shimmered with the strange heat of its morning glow.

Ahead of them lay the north: a barren, cold landscape, blindingly white even in the weak morning sun. It looked flat at first glance, and then the shadows began to betray ridges and hillocks and hollows. Far ahead lay a band of black and darkest green, where pine forests dared to interrupt the ice and snow. Beyond them lay dark clouds, or perhaps colossal mountains. The Spine of the World.

Lilith shivered. She couldn't wait.

Samara's fenrir pawed at the freshly-fallen snow and pounded the frozen ice beneath. He snuffled and sniffed at the wind, and then looked back at the girl, growling. Samara's eyed snapped open. 'I think we need to go further,' she said. 'We're barely onto the ice fields yet. The magick is flowing that way, like a river. I can feel it.'

Lilith shook her head. She'd been entertaining the vague hope of being able to complete their mission there and then, no mountains, no black rocks, no destiny. Once again, she was cheated. 'Lead on then,' she said, reluctantly returning to her fenrir's side. With a growl from the beast and a grunt from her, she climbed onto its back, instantly feeling the aches and pains of the ride quickly returning, even before the fenrir had begun to move.

Samara darted northwards without a word. Lilith's fenrir followed eagerly, springing forward so quickly that the seer was almost left behind. She clung on for dear life once again as four pair of paws pounded the snow, as two mouths puffed and slathered their way towards the distant mountains. To her doom.

❦

Midday found those paws silent, and hidden. Samara lay in a snow drift, eyes sharp and beady. Lilith lay beside and slightly behind her, snoozing fitfully. Half her face was buried in the snow. She was dribbling too.

A pretty sight, thought Samara, as she sneaked a quick glance at the old woman. A snore began to rattle in her throat. Samara gave her a kick, making her mumble, and turned back to her prey.

It still hadn't moved.

He must have been dead. He was face down in the snow, grey as a winter's morning. He had stained the snow underneath him a grimy, reddish brown, possibly the first splash of colour this part of the world had seen in decades. Samara decided to watch him for a little while longer.

When Lilith began to snore again, Samara decided it was time to investigate. She slid down the snow drift and out onto the thick patch of ice where the man lay motionless. She had her hands down and at the ready, glittering with light. She needn't have bothered. It took all of three seconds and a nudge with the foot to find that the man was utterly, completely dead. It sounded as though she were kicking wood. The man was frozen solid.

Samara bent down and unceremoniously prised his face from the ice. There was a ripping sound as some of the withered skin stuck. She raised an eyebrow at the sight of his face, sagging as it was. He was a Skölgard man, and from the look of his complexion, an old one at that. Scarred too. Samara lifted his collar and found ornate steel kissing her finger, cold and solid. She tapped his shoulders with her knuckles, then his back, then his legs, hearing the telltale clank of metal with every tap.

'What is it, girl?' called a voice. Lilith had awoken. She was staggering stiffly down to the copse, brushing the snow from her coat and the dribble from her chin. She joined Samara, sitting cross-legged by the corpse's side. The fenrir kept their distance, lingering behind the drift.

'Who's this?' asked the seer, halfway through a yawn.

Samara was busy staring into the distance, distracted. 'Not a clue,' she mumbled.

'Looks like he's been dead for a while. How'd he get all the way out here?'

'How? You're the seer.'

Lilith fumbled in her pocket for her stones. 'It don't work like that, girl, as well you know. That's past, not future. Past's awkward to grab at for us seers.'

'The magick...' Samara suggested, still distracted.

Lilith nodded. 'I'll try,' she said, as she brought forth her stones and cupped her hands around them. She blew on them to warm them up and then closed her eyes. After some mumbling, she cast them to the ice and watched how they fell and tumbled. A moment passed, full of some muttered swearing from Lilith. She scooped the stones up and tried again. Then a third time. It was then that they finally divulged their secrets.

'A lord,' she began, blurting out the images as they flashed before her eyes, 'an old lord of the Crumbled Empire. Chased from his castle. Banished by pitchforks and fire. Wandered the ice... three weeks. Saw a ship in the distance. Was trying to... to reach her. Ship, all grey and iron. Arka ship.'

Samara's fist dug into the ice. 'Them. The ship must be close. *He* must be close.'

Lilith was pawing at one of the stones. 'I can't tell,' she said, morbidly wishing she could.

Samara's fist was glowing now. The ice around it bubbled and steamed as it sank deeper into the ground. Her eyes had turned a dark crimson. 'Snow and ice. Can't be far,' she hissed. The girl got to her feet and began to pace.

'Calm yourself, girl. Farden's nothing compared to you.'

'Just you wait. Destiny be damned. I'll take him down, and then you skin him, while he's still wriggling,' muttered Samara. 'For *posterity*.'

Lilith didn't reply. She wanted to, but she couldn't think of anything good enough to say. All she could do was clear her throat. Her silence got more and more obvious as each second slipped by. Samara stopped pacing. 'It's not him, is it?' she demanded.

'Who?'

Samara put her hands on her hips. 'The one you won't tell me about. Your killer. It's Farden, isn't it?'

Lilith drummed her fingers on the armoured back of the frozen copse. 'Stones never lie,' she mumbled.

Samara stamped her foot, bludgeoning snow. 'One more reason to see his head on a plate!'

Lilith didn't have the heart to tell her that she wouldn't get that chance. That was another's duty. She had glimpsed that future too. 'Damn right,' was all she said. Samara went back to her pacing, back and forth, burning a path in the snow.

'Now I see why you were so keen to kill off the Written. You knew one of them would kill you.'

'Just not which one…'

'…Until a few years ago.'

Lilith had always wondered at the strange coincidence of it all. Here she was, bringing up her murderer's daughter. Her only smidgeon of satisfaction came from the fact that Samara had no idea Farden was her father. Vice's wish, it had been. An old lie, well-rehearsed. It was Lilith's accidental little dagger in Farden's side, her lasting poison. She'd cackled when she'd discovered it. 'The future is a slippery bastard, sometimes, girl.'

Samara grabbed the old seer by the shoulders, and looked deep into her eyes. 'I'll kill him for you, Lilith. If I can drag down the stars, I can stop him from killing you. I don't care what your stones say.'

Lilith's heart came up short once again. She spared a moment to meet the girl's crimson stare. She found the ferocity of it somewhat pleasing. Touching, almost. She met it for as long as she could, and then pushed her away. 'North with you, girl. Or those daemons will beat that bastard to cutting my throat,' she chided.

Samara just growled.

As they turned around to go back to the fenrir, they found that they were already halfway over the snow drift. They were hunched low and dangerous, their yellow eyes fixed on something nearby, something that had managed to pace through the snow without making a sound. Samara turned, quick as a flash, and confronted their visitor.

The odd man waved at them cheerily. 'Hullo,' he said, before babbling something in a language quite incomprehensible.

Samara strode toward him, angry that he had gotten so close without making a sound. She glared at him, taking in his white paper skin with its thick brown hair, his yellow eyes, his long, almost deer-like legs, and the curious shoes he wore, like nets stretched over an oval shape, tied to his hairy feet. Cheap tricks.

What annoyed her the most was that he didn't show a scrap of fear. Not for her, not for the wolves, not even for the bloody corpse lying skinned in the snow. He regarded the scene with a mild disinterest. Like a passing oddity.

Lilith marched right up to the odd man. She was forced to crane her neck to meet his nonchalant gaze. He was tall, nudging seven foot to her five, but he was thin as a sliver of willow. 'Who are you?'

'*Systrungur ert. Miknjil skegol?*' came the reply, a whispering, tongue-waggling mess. Samara made a face and prodded the man hard in the stomach. It was only then that his polite little smile faded, and his yellow eyes grew stony. '*Bashna,*' he said, so clipped and harsh now compared to moments before.

'Where did you come from? Hmm? Did you come with him?' Samara pointed at the dead mage behind her.

The man did not move. He just looked down at the girl and

narrowed his eyes.

'Answer me,' she demanded. 'Did you come on a ship? Are you following us? Are you with Farden and the rest?' The questions came like pellets. 'He's a halfwit,' spat Samara.

'He's a wanderin' type,' said Lilith. 'Snowmad. Icetreader.'

'I don't give a shit what he is, Lilith. He must know something about the ship. Where else could he have come from?'

Lilith sighed impatiently. 'They live on the deep ice, girl. Probably never even seen a ship in their lives. Come, let's leave.'

Samara scowled at the man, hands itchy for fire and the knife at her belt. His yellow eyes were cool and stony now. They goaded her. Her fury had found an unwilling target. She pined to teach this snowmad a lesson in manners. *Take her blade and show it to his throat*, she thought to herself. See if those yellow eyes don't drain white. Samara sneered and turned away.

'*Veglold. Bik,*' came the garbled reply. It sounded like a jibe, but she kept walking. Lilith met her halfway and then fell in behind her fuming strides.

'He can count his lucky stars we're in a rush…' Lilith was saying, right before an enormous boom shook the frozen ground. The seer collapsed to her knees as a brittle shower of cold snow rained down.

Samara was frantically wiping the snow from her face. She blinked like a blinded owl, half-expecting to see a smoking crater where the snowmad had been standing. Instead, there was a big dragon standing in his place. Something pink oozed from under its front claws.

Samara raised her hands, ready to show the dragon what she was made of, but to her surprise, it bowed its head to the snow, its gnarled metallic scales clanking like armour. It even closed its eyes, showing complete deference.

Two more dragons dropped from the sky. They fell a little less dramatically, but still the ground rumbled and shook as their claws touched down. One was a dull, rusty red, the other a milky brown. Each had a bare-chested rider on their back, wrapped in ice-bear fur. Some bore scratches and missing scales. One had a missing eye and a burnt patch where it had once been. They too bowed, and waited for the final dragon to land.

It was slightly smaller than the others, ever-so-slightly. It was a charcoal black with red mottling. Its horns had been painted red. As it landed, its rider, a muscled man with a ridged and scaly scalp, jumped effortlessly from its back and ran across the snow towards them. He bowed, albeit very briefly, but his dragon did not. Samara kept her spells simmering in her hands, dying to be unleashed, and waited for the man to speak.

The man approached her confidently. Samara found herself frowning. He too was tall. She was beginning to get annoyed by tall people. 'Here she is,' he was saying. 'And even younger than I had even imagined.'

Samara was about to spit something in reply when the man bent to one knee. It looked a foreign and odd movement for him, but somehow he pulled it off. 'It is an honour to meet you, my lady. Your ancient friends have told me all about you.'

Samara was still wary. 'Valefor?'

'And Hokus, yes. I asked them to meet me, and we bargained,' he said, somehow making such a meeting between a rider and a pair of daemons sound so casual.

Lilith had found her way to her feet. 'Bargained? What for?'

The man shrugged. He answered her, but kept his eyes on Samara. 'Our new home. Allegiance. The chance to prove ourselves. Not everyone on this rock prays to the gods. Quite the opposite, I hear.' A toothy smile, full of far too many teeth for any one mouth, spread across this man's face. Samara somehow found herself liking him. She crossed her ams, quenched her spells, and smiled.

'Quite,' she replied. 'And you are?'

The man got up from his knee. 'Saker, my lady. Lord of the North, master of Hjaussfen and the Castle of the Winds.'

'Hjaussfen, the Siren capital?' Lilith piped up again.

Saker flashed her a smug look. 'Until recently.'

'Not a very peaceful transition, was it?' Samara said, nodding to the blood on his arm and the marks on his comrades, both rider and dragon.

Saker flashed a look to the skies. 'It was, until we had some guests. Turned the Old Dragon loose and sent us on a wild wyrm chase north. Fortuitous, now that I have found you, but not finished. I shall bleed them ten different colours when I find them.'

'Mages, right? These guests' she muttered darkly.

'Two.'

Samara glowered at the east. 'Then we can bleed them both together. I'm starting a war,' she said, not bothering to hide her pride.

Saker looked behind the girl, at the mighty fenrir and the strange-looking, middle-aged woman. 'And that is why we are to accompany you. To the Spine, and to the roots of *Irminsul*. Where your destiny awaits.'

Samara clenched her fists and felt the magick make her legs shiver. She turned to the north and squinted at the black cliffs on the horizon. Something far behind them belched dark clouds. A tremble ran through her, and this time it wasn't the magick. Anticipation. Worry. The ache to prove herself. It was all of those things. 'Then let's not waste any more time.'

'Let us not, my young lady,' Saker bowed again. The muscles in his bare arms flexed as he gestured to his dragons. 'Dragon, or wolf?'

Samara smiled. 'Dragon.'

Chapter 20

"And yet another thing irks me about the Scribe, and has irked me ever since I came to the twin thrones. How exactly does he survive so much exposure to the mages' books? The scholars haven't a clue. Neither do the mages and instructors of the School. I damn well don't. Neither does Åddren. It's a mystery, and one that I will get to the bottom of, if I ever have any time to do so. This city already demands my every moment. Now this business with the stolen book, and this reprobate Farden. It is irksome indeed."
Excerpt from Arkmage Helyard's diary, found after his death in 889

The snow was merciless. The ship had grown a second skin of it. On the masts, on the railings, on the deck, on the hatches, on the steps, on heads, on shoulders, on feet, on faces… the snow sought to drown it all under its deceptively pure blanket.

Farden was helping some of the other mages and crew clear the *'Blade'*'s deck. It was an unfulfilling job. The trails that the brooms and heat spells carved were turned white again within minutes. It was more to stave off the boredom than anything else. Something to distract from the constant shudder and crash of the splitting ice. Not many of them had slept through such clamour.

'What a bastard,' Roiks muttered to himself as he sauntered past Farden. He had been idly writing his name across the port side in the snow, challenging it to see how fast he could spell it out without the first letter disappearing. Farden smirked, wondering if he could be bothered to join in. He was desperately tired. He had spent most of the night staring at the Grimsayer, staring at this Korrin and his lost armour. It had been worth the lack of sleep.

The only mercy was the wind. Although it whipped the snow up into a vigourous frenzy, it gave the sails something to grasp at. It had also given the whales a welcome break from pushing. The *Waveblade* was now barging through the ice on her own terms.

'Two degrees to port!' came another yell from the bow. There was a communal clenching of fists and jaws across the deck as the ship lurched awkwardly to the left. A dull boom rang out, and Nuka could be heard cursing on the aftcastle. The ice was getting thicker by the hour. Nobody wanted to admit it, but they were slowing down. The *Waveblade* was struggling.

'Njord's balls,' Roiks muttered again, only getting as far as the *i* of his name before the snow covered it. 'Give me seapspray and mermaids any day, mates, not this frozen shit this sky is givin' us.'

'Thought we'd all be used to it now, after the Long Winter.'

Roiks winked. 'Weren't no Long Winter for me, mage. I spent most of it sailing up and down the Paraian cost. Spice ship. Bloody Long Vacation, I call it,' he chuckled, absently trying his name again. This time he almost got to the *k* before the snow foiled it. 'Here. You try,' Roiks challenged the mage.

Farden shrugged and dug his broom into the slush. Its bristles hissed against the smooth wood of the deck below, leaving brown streaks. He spelt the letters with deft little strokes, as if it were a sword carving through a blanket. He finished and nodded at his quickly disappearing efforts.

Roiks was scratching his head through his hood. 'Fine and well, *Farden*, but who's Korrin?'

Farden looked down at the letters he had scraped. The snow had already seen to the first three. The other half were quickly fading.

'Er...' he began. He never got a chance to conjure up an excuse.

'Hard to starboard!' came the shout from the bow.

'Grab something!' Roiks bellowed instinctively as he grabbed the nearest rope.

Those who had heard were fine. Those who hadn't sprawled in the snow as the ship lurched into the air at a rather disturbing angle, and then came down hard on the ice. Ears perked up, waiting for the telltale crack of the ice giving way under the heavy weight of the iron bow. And still they waited. Nothing. The ice refused to budge.

Swearing floated down from the aftcastle.

'Think we're in trouble,' mumbled Roiks, as he helped another sailor to his feet. The man rubbed a sore nose, and agreed.

'Sounds like we're stuck,' he said.

Farden left his broom on the deck. 'Sounds exactly like that,' he replied, walking to the bow. A few Written had gathered around the bowsprit. A few well-placed fireballs plunged into the ice, but still nothing budged. Farden excused his way to the front so he could take a look.

Waveblade was stuck fast. The ice had bunched up like paper slid too fast across a desk, concertinaed into slabs each as thick as a banquet table. They were all slanted and jumbled at a crazy angle, and not one of them looked like it was ready to move. The north had become obdurate.

It took almost half an hour for the orca to break and nudge the ship free, and then another half an hour to push it back to a reasonable distance. With the mages pelting the ice with spells from afar, Nuka ordered the whales to drive the ship forward once again, this time at a different angle. The whales pushed and the wind mages blew, and the '*Blade* lurched forward almost as quick as it had escaping the Bitches.

All they got for their troubles was about ten feet. Maybe less. The ice crumpled up again and brought the ship to a sickening halt. The wood of her hull groaned for a full minute after the impact. Nuka even sent men below to check for leaks.

It didn't take long for the rest of the crew and the passengers to come gawp at their situation. Farden was still at the bow, holding court with Nuka, Tyrfing, and Eyrum as they discussed their options.

'What options?' Eyrum shrugged. 'I see very few.'

Nuka shook his head. 'Few? I see one.'

Tyrfing's throat was too raw to speak. He let Farden do it for him. 'And what's that?' asked Farden.

'It will take too long to turn her,' Nuka said, firmly, 'and too long to find another path. This is where my ship stops.'

'I thought you'd never ask,' said Farden. He cleared his throat and spoke a little louder. 'We go north then.'

※

It took an hour to turn the ship inside out. The white ice clasping the ship began to catch a rash, a rash of dark blankets and boxes, of crates and bags, people and feet. The cracks in the ice hissed and moaned as its unspoilt surface was unceremoniously disturbed.

The rash spread outwards from the ship as the supplies kept coming. Ladders were propped up. Ropes trailed. Sledges constructed. Mages forced poles for lanterns into the ice, and lit braziers to keep the others warm. People took to walking around the ship, testing the splintered edges of the *'Blade'*'s path, staring into the ink-blue water below and at the whales that cavorted there. Some of the children even had the nerve to make a game of sliding pots and pans into each other. The ice, given a voice, would have surely shouted at them to desist, and for the rash to retreat aboard its vessel. As it was, it had to be content with its creakings and grumblings, and being largely ignored.

Speed was of the essence. Noon had slid into afternoon, and was quickly turning into evening. The temperature, already nudging the depths of unbearable, was slowly and surely plummeting.

'Bless Thron and the gods for fire mages, that's all I'll say,' mumbled a passing Siren soldier, shouldering a crate. He nodded to Inwick, who was standing next to the brazier and massaging its tentative flames into life. She had the thing roaring in moments. Everybody in the vicinity, Farden, Eyrum, and several sailors catching their breath, shuffled closer.

'We can share as many of our furs and clothes as possible, but it will barely be enough to cover a dozen more,' Eyrum was saying.

'A dozen more is better than a dozen less,' Farden replied.

Eyrum shrugged at the obvious logic. Great beads of sweat clung to his brow, and yet still he was glad for the fire. Farden was sweating too, trying to hide how much he was trembling. They had been put to work carting supplies down the gangplanks. It was hard work, and yet it did nothing to keep them warm. The breeze was savagely cold.

Eyrum leant close and lowered his voice. 'What about you?' he asked, quietly.

'What about me?' Farden raised an eyebrow quizzically, conscious that Inwick was staring.

Eyrum sighed. 'I've spoken to Tyrfing. I know what you're going to do. Are you coming with us?'

Farden shook his head. 'I need to check the Grimsayer,' he said. 'For directions.'

'Well, mage. You'd better get to it. The sleds are almost full.'

Eyrum was right: the makeshift sleds the sailors and ship's carpenters had fashioned were bending worryingly in the middle, heavy with supplies and blankets and food for the journey ahead. If one looked closer, the glint of swords and shields could be seen amongst the provisions. They had more to fear in the north than the cold.

'Right you are,' said Farden, with a sigh. His legs ached. He swore he could feel the sweat on his forehead freezing. So far, he wasn't enjoying this excursion ashore as much as he'd hoped. What made it worse was that he had the distinct impression that this was going to be the high-point of the next few days. The calm before the storm.

So be it, he thought, as he strode up the gangplank.

He found the Grimsayer right where he left it, on the table beside his bed. With a heave, he lifted it onto the mattress and split it open with a creak. It was quiet in his room, deep in the ship. The heavily muffled thumping of busy feet was the only clue of the commotion outside. Farden briefly pondered locking the door and shuffling under the bed, falling asleep even. Hiding away from it all. He shook his head at his old, stubborn ways, and prodded the Grimsayer with his finger.

The magick must have been strong indeed in these parts. The lights leapt eagerly from the page, drawing waves and ripples around his fingertip. 'Show me the way to Korrin,' Farden spoke to them. 'Show me the way from here.'

The little lights obeyed with a will. They sketched a swift likeness of the ship and its new friend the ice, and then suddenly flew north, scanning back and forth to weave the endless, featureless expanse of the ice fields themselves. Suddenly there were rocks, and broken slabs of ice scratching at the sky, and then mountains. The lights stopped abruptly above a cracked plateau, swirling around and around a crown of tall rocks, and the mouth of what looked like a well in the ice. Even as a drawing, the mouth of the well sucked at the little lights, trying to tug them down into its darkness. Farden slammed the book on it, and hoisted it under one arm. 'Let's be off with you then, shall we?' he told it jovially. It rattled its pages in reply, and was promptly carted to the door.

Just before Farden reached the door, he heard a plaintive squeak from behind him. There on the bed was Whiskers, sat upright on his haunches and sniffing at the air. Farden sighed sadly as he made his way back to the bed. 'Not this time, old lad,' he said. 'Too dangerous for old rats. I need you here to keep an eye on the ship.' The rat looked up at him with his deep black eyes, and Farden couldn't help but think he understood. He teased his whiskers and patted his head. 'Keep the pillow warm for me,' he said, and went back to the door. Behind him, Whiskers curled up into a tight ball. The old rat watched the door long after it had closed.

Tyrfing was pacing up and down the corridor outside. Farden's confident smile faltered at the sight of his uncle. He was wringing his hands. His face was haggard. 'I still can't get hold of Durnus,' he croaked.

'Have you tried a hawk?' asked Farden.

Tyrfing nodded. He had tried two. 'No reply.'

'Is there anything else you can try?'

Tyrfing shook his head.

'Is there anything else you can do about it now?'

Tyrfing thought, and then shook his head again. 'It's a feeling I have…'

'Well…' Farden said. 'We'll just have to trust he's alright. It is Durnus after all. The pale king Ruin himself. With any luck he's halfway here already. We could use his help.'

Tyrfing gently pressed one of his fists against a bulkhead. 'Since when did you become the wise one?'

Farden laughed wryly. 'Since you let me.'

The two mages stood on deck and watched the last of the supplies make their way onto the ice. All around them stood heavily-breathing sailors and soldiers, scratching their heads and holding themselves against the cold. It was easy to see which ones wanted to stay, which ones wanted to go, and those weren't not with a lot of choice.

Nuka was sitting on the steep steps of the aftcastle, arms folded over his knees. He looked to Tyrfing, and the Arkmage nodded for him to go ahead. As he got to his feet, his eyes roved over his ship and those on the ice below. 'It's a first, for a captain to split his crew in half. Then again, it's a first when a captain finds his iron-clad ship being pushed through the northern ice by a pod of whales,' Nuka sniffed, no humour in his face, 'but if there is ever time for firsts, it is now. Firsts and lasts. You go to do what the rest of the world cannot. You go to do a noble thing, a brave thing, a necessary thing. Stay strong, all of you. And Njord, and all the other gods, be with you.'

There was a muted cheering as the captain sat back down again, eyeing the mountains in the distance with a wrinkled lip.

'Fine words,' muttered Roiks, as he shouldered his snow-covered pack.

'You're coming?' Farden asked, a little surprised.

Roiks winked bravely, but a tiny hint of something that might have resembled worry twitched at the corner of his mouth. Farden almost missed it. 'I'm a sailor through and through, but I'm also an Arka, and that means I go north with the rest of you sorry lot. Landstriding be damned. Besides, I ain't needed on this tub any more. She'll be waiting for me when I get back. Won't you, miss?' he chuckled, giving the ship a lingering look.

Farden reached for his own pack as he stamped his cold, half-numb feet on the solid ice. He cleared his throat. He abruptly realised that everybody was looking at him. Every mage. Every soldier. Every sailor. Every Siren. Even his uncle stood idly by, watching him, waiting patiently on his word. Four hundred pairs of eyes, waiting.

Farden quietly strapped his pack to his back, checked his armour, and then nodded. He took a deep breath, and shouted over the ice, as loud as his cold throat allowed.

'Let's go!' he announced, and one by one the makeshift army shuffled off. What a fierce, motley crew they made: the borrowed, the eager sailors and grim-eyed soldiers, war-shy ship's mages and Written armoured to the brim, Siren refugees and a strange smattering of others, two shadows of gods, a sick Arkmage, and his nephew, a mage but not a mage, leading the way. They left the *Waveblade* in their quiet wake, boots creaking, heads bowed against the snow, a lone gryphon circling above them.

Nuka watched them leave with a cold feeling in his heart. He couldn't help but count each figure as they disappeared into the snowy haze. Recording them for posterity maybe, or perhaps to see how many of them returned. The truth of war was always in the numbers. It is by numbers that victory is measured. The cold, hard, calculating of the math.

Nuka caught himself before he reached the end of the long line. Maybe he didn't want to know the truth after all. Nuka drummed his long nails on the wood of his ship and shook his head. 'I want half-hourly patrols of the ship. Chip the ice from the rigging. Batten the hatches. Keep those lanterns burning!' he yelled, distracting himself. 'We'll be ready for them, when they return.'

Trudging was what one did on the ice. There was no other word for it. One did not saunter. One did not skip. One certainly did not jolly or prance. One *trudged*, simple as that.

It was half the terrain and half the cold. The former made the going awkward, and the latter made the going slow. All the socks in Emaneska couldn't keep the northern cold out of their boots.

Farden had never longed for his magick so desperately. His uncle trudged behind him, periodically slapping his legs to force some hot magick into them. Despite his sudden sickness, he walked as only an old mage like him could in the snow: secretly warm and simply tired. Farden cursed himself one more time.

Roiks and Eyrum walked on his left and on his right, dealing with the cold in their own ways. Ever the true Siren, Eyrum stoically held his chin high, as if daring the cold to get even colder, Roiks seemed to be trying to fold in on himself. Farden knew the feeling. Lerel was behind with his uncle. Farden just kept his hands in his cold pockets and watched his feet plod.

Somebody was trying to sing at the back of the column. Farden had to applaud them for trying, he supposed, even if it was the singularly most annoying thing he could have imagined at that particular point. Annoyed elbows soon silenced the singer, and the column moved on with a few scattered mumblings.

Farden soon found a hand on his shoulder. It was his uncle. Tyrfing had wrapped a scarf around the bottom half of his face. Plumes of steam emanated from its mottled threads, as if he were finding it hard to breathe. 'Are you okay?' Farden asked him.

'I'm fine,' he croaked. 'Heimdall wants to know why you're not going ahead with Ilios.'

'Tell him it's because I'm needed here.'

'How so?'

'Somebody needs to lead these people.'

His uncle narrowed his eyes. With the scarf it was hard to tell if he was smiling or grimacing. 'Not putting anything off are you?'

'No,' Farden replied, with perhaps a hint of a lie. He knew what was coming. He couldn't deny the little tingle of fear. *A ship made of fingernails. A vulture's head...* his mind kept repeating it.

'Sure?'

'Indefatigably.'

'You put on a brave face, nephew.'

'So do you.'

Tyrfing fell back. 'Elessi would be proud,' he mumbled, before he left.

Farden's chest swelled with that. He pushed aside his thoughts with two names, repeating them with every step he took, like he used to on the flint roads of Fleahurst. *Elessi. Korrin. Elessi. Korrin.*

Samara might have sneaked in here and there.

Within the hour, darkness had fallen. Soldiers began to flank the column with their swords drawn. A few mages and Written walked up and down, their hands and skin shining like beacons. They made an impressive sight in the thick snowfall.

Talk of camp scampered up and down the lines. Eyes began to look into the darkness and long for trees or rocks or anything besides endless flat ice. They were nothing but disappointed. There was nothing there on the ice fields. And so, soon enough, the snow and darkness grew too thick to allow them to go any further. Camp had to be made.

Tyrfing strode up and down the long column, shining twice as bright as any of the other mages. Farden walked beside him, quietly helping the people tip the sleds onto their sides and set up lean-tos and tents to keep out the cold. Braziers and lanterns were dug out and forced into life. The smell of dried meat and warm broth soon joined the bitter breeze and the smell of tired bodies and trodden leather. Ilios came down from the sky, frozen almost stiff by the snow and the wind. Tyrfing spent half an hour snapping the icicles from his wings while the gryphon whined and whinged about missing his deserts.

For the most part, the people of the ship seemed quietly resigned to the terrible weather. They had bigger things to worry about. Nobody spoke of what was to come. It wasn't necessary. What was there to say, after all? Only the sailors seemed twitchy. Farden could see them longing for the sway of something wooden under their feet. They huddled together in thin little groups and sang quiet songs of waves and Njord's storms.

All the while, the gods stood like two statues in the haze at the head of the column. Like Eyrum, they stood with their chins and faces held high to the snow and the wind, almost as if they were tasting the air. Farden watched them from a little distance away, wondering what they were up to. Loki had his hands deep in his pockets as usual, while

Heimdall scanned the darkness with slow sweeps of his head. Farden could only imagine what he could see, so he decided to ask.

'What's out there?' he asked as he approached. Loki sidled away, still sour from their last encounter. Heimdall, of course, had heard him coming.

'Magick,' he replied. 'Great clouds of magick, streaming towards the north, like wind to a building storm. Clouding my senses,' Heimdall sighed as he waved his hand towards the heavens. Farden followed his hand but saw nothing but snow and a pitch-black sky beyond. He tried to paint a few colours onto it with his imagination, but gave up trying to figure out what colour the magick would be.

'I suppose you humans would see it as a mixture of blue and green mostly,' Heimdall said, as though he had heard Farden's thoughts. 'The Sirens call it the Wake, which is the path of the First Dragon. They are right, in a certain manner of speaking.'

'Why north?'

'It is gathering to the Roots. Growing with every step we take north.'

'I'll just pretend to know what that means, shall I?'

'The Roots and the Spine of the World are at the most northern point of this earth, where creation itself stems from, where the magick flows to, as it once flowed from. It is also where *she* is headed.'

Farden nodded. 'Where the giant fell.'

Heimdall winced as though Farden had uttered some dark blasphemy. 'I would not stoop so low as to refer to him as a simple *giant*, but yes, you are correct. Where he fell, and curled, and where the great ash withered on his back, until it formed the Roots. *Irminsul*, in the Siren tongue.'

'And it's not just her that's headed there,' said Loki, looking out into the haze.

'Loki speaks the truth. The ice shivers with the sound of creatures and beasts making their way north.' Farden peered into the night but saw nothing save what his imagination could conjure. 'An army is growing, the sight of which you humans have not seen in two millennia.'

Farden rubbed his gauntlets together. 'Well, I'd best get my sleep then.'

Heimdall turned to face him, looking irritated. 'You use your humour as a soldier uses a shield, mage. I should know, for I have listened to it for long enough. You shrug off importance and danger like a jester jiggles his bells. It does not befit the man I saw take the wheel of the ship so recently. Be serious mage, for these are serious times.'

Farden calmly thought his answer through. 'We can't all be stone-hearted and cold-thinking, Heimdall. I think a man is allowed a little humour, when the darkness needs to be kept at bay. It keeps us human. Keeps us from going crazy.'

Heimdall didn't answer. His eyes glazed over. Loki stepped forward to interject with something dagger-sharp and witty, but he was silenced by a hiss from his elder. Heimdall pointed into the distance, where a single point of light was emerging out of the haze.

'Arms!' shouted Farden, to the ring of steel. Fireballs and lightning sprang to life all along the column of tents and shelters.

'Who goes there?' Eyrum challenged, striding forward. An axe rested gently in the hollow of his shoulder, just like old times. He stepped out into the haze and yelled out again. 'I said, who goes there?!' he boomed.

Foreign words came back from the snow. '*Ragna! Olfjaarn bethest!*'

Every Siren within earshot visibly relaxed, while the others were left to look around, more than a little perplexed. Eyrum turned around and waved his hands. 'snowmads. They're friends.'

Eyrum was right. The newcomers couldn't have been more harmless if they had come bearing flowers on velvet pillows. Farden left the gods where they were and went to greet them with Eyrum. As a group of them came into the light of the camp, Farden couldn't help but be reminded of the Paraian nomads he met so many years ago; long-limbed and wild of face, almost half-animal, half human. These people were very much the same. Most of them were taller than Eyrum and had faces with long snouts. They had yellow eyes set into their pale faces, and manes of very fine, chalky hair. Their skin was so hairy that it almost bordered on a pelt.

'Well met, and good wishes,' announced Eyrum, bowing in an odd way, his hands outstretched beside him.

'*Asgarot, i beshemth snarvi da uglot. Siot af narla. Kurami,*' rattled off the nearest snowmad, a tall man with a goatee of braided hair and pine needles.

'He says hello,' Eyrum translated.

'All that means hello?' Farden looked worried. He dreaded to think how long their songs were.

'Hullo,' echoed the snowmad, with a beaming smile.

It didn't take long for the rest of the column to gather around these strangers. They were curious sights, to be sure, even for the most travelled amongst them. The snowmads' clothes were made of ice-bear pelt and white fox fur, with shoes and gloves of seal-skin. Some walked on shoes that had wide soles shaped in an oval, strung with sinew and string nets. With these they almost floated on top of the snow, barely making it move at all as they strode back and forth, jabbering in their foreign tongues.

As it turned out, Eyrum knew painfully little of their language. Fortunately, a few of the older Sirens spoke it almost fluently. They introduced Farden, Tyrfing, and Eyrum one by one, and then explained why they were there. It took almost half an hour to spit it out, with much eye-rolling and sighing on the part of the mages. Still the snow fell around them.

The most curious thing about the snowmads was their transport. It largely consisted of pelt-wrapped domes sat on rickety sleds made of driftwood, with runners made from the long, curving tusks of some unknown animal, very much like the one Farden had seen on Kiltyrin's wall. But it was the actual animal that was pulling the sleds that was most curious indeed. It seemed that nomads, snow, Paraian, or otherwise, had an obsession with obscure animals.

There was no easy way to explain it to the eyes. They were moles. Big, grey, harnessed moles. Farden had to rub his eyes to make sure he was seeing the right animal. Moles indeed. They sat contentedly in their harnesses and stared about short-sightedly as their masters went about setting up camp for the night. Farden and the others couldn't help but go and examine them.

Each of them was about as large as a decent-sized boar. Their fluffy grey coats were thick and well-groomed. They looked like docile beasts, with about half a dozen tied to each sled in little packs. Their long digging claws, each the length of a man's hand, were folded calmly in front of them, with their plump bodies splayed out behind. Farden watched with mild amusement as a group were unhitched from a nearby sled and led into a makeshift pen for the night. The moles were prodded into action with little poles. *A mole-pole,* Farden couldn't help but chuckle. The funniest thing was that they never seemed to lift their weight fully off the ice. Instead they shimmied across it in a frantic manner, digging claws and splayed feet shuffling feverishly, noses and whiskers twitching all the while. They practically flew across it. Farden pondered if they ever grew big enough to ride. He stored that question for later.

'Snow moles,' said Eyrum, as he joined Farden in watching the hairy creatures scuttle around.

Farden rubbed the snow from his forehead. 'And you say that as if it's completely normal.'

'Hmmm. In the meantime, we've found a snowmad who speaks our language.'

'Great news. Where is he?'

'Here,' Eyrum gestured to a buxom female. Her yellow eyes were round and nervous.

'Hullo,' she said, in a quiet voice.

'M'lady,' Farden said as he bowed, remembering his manners. 'I hear you can speak our tongue.'

'A little,' she shrugged. 'Not much.'

'Maybe you can help us answer some questions?'

The female bowed back, not quite understanding the protocol. 'Whatever you need, sirs,' she said.

'First of all, what's your name?'

'*Sapinjurskjafelli*,' promptly replied the female, as if she were immensely proud of the amount of syllables she owned. Farden was grimacing after the first three.

'Right. Sapin it is. What are you doing here, Sapin?' Farden asked.

Sapin pointed to her moles, smiling like a proud mother. 'We follow the storms across the fields. Storms chase the fish. Fish chase the storms. Our moles dig holes in the ice. We fish out the fish.'

'Makes sense,' said Farden. It really didn't. He was willing to let that go. 'What about the magick, Sapin. Can you feel it?'

The snowmad looked confused. She looked to Eyrum. 'Magick?' she asked. 'I know not this word.'

'Er... *Elexkjir*?' Eyrum guessed. He was apparently right, as the woman looked to the sky.

'Strange goings on. The ice is moving. Creatures going north. To fight. Darkness coming.'

'So I've heard,' replied Farden.

Sapin blinked her pink eyes. 'Do you go north too?' she asked. 'Because you point west. This line. You are headed west, no?'

'Well, we were headed north. Or so we thought,' Farden sighed.

'Snow can make eyes wander, and feet turn,' she advised, in simple nomad wisdom. 'Why north? It is dangerous there. Fire and ice and rock. War coming.'

'War is our business, Sapin. We need to find a girl, and a woman too. A girl with black hair, and eyes like mine. About this tall. A very powerful mage like me,' Farden asked, waving his hand about. 'Have you seen anyone like that?'

'No,' Sapin shook her head. 'But my brother, *Volskurskinha*, went east two days ago in search of storms. He will be back any day now. Maybe he has seen her.'

'He went alone?'

'We always send one to look and guide the way.'

Farden smiled, hoping this brother was safe. East was where Samara would be.

'And what about these?' Farden tapped his gauntlets. 'Have you seen this sort of armour before?'

'Never,' Sapin replied. She looked a little worried by his armour, as if it were some sort of sin to wear metal like that. 'No.'

Eyrum leant forward. 'And have you seen any dragons come this way? Nelska dragons?'

Sapin thought for a moment, and then shook her head. 'No. Only the northern, how do you say… group, band, no… Clan! Yes, clans.'

While Eyrum growled something to himself, Farden interjected. 'Finally, Sapin, could you help us find… Sapin?' Farden stopped talking. The woman had promptly crumpled into a prostrate heap on the ground. He was in the middle of wondering whether she had fainted when he noticed that the other snowmads around them were doing the exact same thing. All of them fell to their faces and flattened themselves to the snow. 'What in the…?' Farden muttered, spinning around. He soon found his answer, in the form of Heimdall and Loki standing nearby, looking blank and irked.

Sapin was tugging at Farden's bootlaces. 'The Skylights. *Shanaeh-yivag! Heaven dos rjint*,' she babbled on in her native tongue.

'It's okay,' Farden announced to those around him. 'They are with us.'

They barely moved. Loki seemed to be lapping up the attention, hands on hips and chin high, looking from snowmad to snowmad, as if to examine which one was more prostrate than the next. Heimdall, on the other hand, was slowly walking away. 'Come, Loki,' he ordered, and Loki sullenly did as he was told. As soon as they had gone, the snowmads got to their feet.

'You travel with the stars?' asked Sapin, yellow eyes wild like saucers.

Farden watched the gods retreat. 'In a fashion.'

Sapin slowly got to her feet. 'Then we help you in any way we can, *agmundr*,' she said, before walking away, a little paler than before, if that were even possible.

'*Agmundr*?' queried Farden.

Eyrum thought hard. 'Sounds like the dragonscript word for "protector" if I'm not mistaken.'

Farden turned to leave. 'How convenient you should know that word, old friend, and not many others,' he said, with a smirk. Eyrum raised his hands to the sky and shrugged.

'What am I, if not helpful?' he asked the snow and the darkness. They didn't say much in reply.

※

Night deepened and the noise of the shivering camp died away. Soon enough, all that could be heard was the snuffling of the sleeping, and the almost inaudible patter of the snow falling in the breeze. All was still in their little corner of the ice fields.

All save for one single shadow, treading softly across the snow.

Loki padded like a thief between the lean-to's and makeshift shelters. The lanterns and braziers had been left to the mercy of the cold, snuffed out by the snow. Now the only lights were those of the snowmad sleds and the mole-pens. Barely anything to see by.

The god crept to the nearest pen and gently undid the wire holding the gate shut. The moles were fast asleep, shivering gently in their dreams and in the cold. Loki took one by the scruff of its neck and led the half-asleep animal out of the pen and out of the camp. It snuffled at him as it shuffled along. Not a single eye followed them.

A few mages stood alone on the outskirts, glowing softly like fireflies as they kept watch. They were none the wiser to the shadow passing between them, heading out into the darkness beyond.

Loki paused barely a mile outside the camp. He craned his neck to listen to the night. He wished he had Heimdall's ears sometimes. He could have made better use of them. There were whispers that needed listening to, secrets that needed gathering.

Loki raised a finger to the sky and let the snow caress it. He could feel a little shiver run through him. Not the cold, no, something else in the air besides that. Something surging and undulating. Magick.

The god turned east and squinted into the near-pitch darkness until his eyes closed. Slowly, gently, he bent down to the snow and held the mole tight under his arm. The thing wriggled, but only gently, still half-asleep.

From one of his deeper pockets, Loki drew a thin blade, no more than a spike, and held it to the mole's neck. The creature barely made a sound as Loki pressed upwards into its windpipe and opened its neck to the cold. 'I know you will feel this,' whispered the god to the silence. 'I know you can hear me. Tomorrow, we will meet. They will all be here, just for you.'

Loki bled the poor mole until every drop of its life lay in the snow. With a sniff of disdain, he wiped his hands on its milky fur, and then walked away, feeling the magick change slightly as the darkness sagged, and faded.

☙

Faraway on the ice, a daemon got to his feet, and withdrew his claw from its hole in the ice. Hokus lifted it to his chin and listened to the melt-water hiss as he touched it to his neck.

'How interesting,' he said. 'Valefor?'

'Yes, brother?' he replied, unfolding from the night itself. Behind his smoky wake, two figures lay on a nest of dragon saddles and bear fur. One lay asleep. The other lay awake and counting the stars, occasionally plucking at the sky as if fingering unseen harp strings. In her other hand lay a half-sharpened blade, whetstone idly held at the ready.

The two daemons touched heads. 'It is time. You know what to do,' said Hokus. 'Call them.'

Valefor nodded, for once not a trace of mirth on his slippery lips. He wiggled his jaw from side to side, slowly unhinging it piece by piece until it hung at a sick angle. He then took a breath so big it sounded like his ribs would crack. He seemed to swell and grow until his body was ballooned out in every direction, ready to rupture. He grit his fangs together, and then let a roar, a great, screaming roar, burst forth.

Half the dragons took to the sky at the sound of it. The rest wriggled their spines and snarled as the roar deafened them. Lilith sat bolt upright and clapped her hands to her ears. It sounded like rocks being ripped apart. Only Samara stood still, blade in hand, smiling at the roaring daemon.

All across the ice fields and beyond, in the crags of the black Tausenbar Mountains and those beyond, in the scattered copses and frozen deep of the sea beneath, all manner of creatures stirred. Some crawled, dripping from their shells. Some began to pull themselves from their own graves. Some peeled themselves from the rocks, tasting the grit on their tongues and granite lips. Others felt their hackles rise, and felt their fur tingle. The rest weren't animal enough to mention.

All who heard it rose, and began to head north. The sides could be decided on the way.

Chapter 21

"The wild vampyre is a skittish beast, one that doth require the company of a pack, or a coven, for any hint of boldness! Watch ye for pale skin and raking nails, and the pointed ears which betray its nature. Travel only by sunlight in coven territory! Beware the fangs, tipped with a horrid poison. To be bitten is to be cursed, and should you survive the feeding, you shalt find yourself a beast, no longer a man!"

From "Death and all her Beasts" by Master Wird, an old-fashioned and rather outlandish account of Emaneska's creatures, first published in 504. Master Wird was a secretive fellow, a farmer by trade. He fell into writing by accident after he sent a letter to the magick council detailing the apparent existence of the so-called 'Weregoat' of the Össfen Mountains.

Farden awoke with a start.

Something was smothering him, trying to drown him in something wet and icy cold. Farden reached out and felt only asphyxiating cloth, heavy and dark. He could breathe, so he wasn't drowning, no, not yet, but he still couldn't get up. The darkness was bearing down on him, pressing down. He groped for air and found something hard and rough instead.

That was until somebody ripped it away.

Farden blinked in the sudden sunlight, finding the dark shape of Roiks staring down at him. 'Gods, you're an ugly one in the mornings,' he said. 'That's why we have private cabins, mage. Now stop floundering in your own tent and rise an' shine.'

Farden lay on his back like an overturned tortoise, gawping at the mid-morning sunlight. Reality blinded him along with the sunlight. He lifted his head and found a dark green, waxy tarpaulin half-covering him, heavy with the snow that had fallen in the night. Heavy and dark. Farden ran a hand through his wet hair and sighed. Just a tent, fallen in under its own weight.

Breakfast was some salted meat from the *Waveblade's* larders and a barrel of fish the snowmads had caught. They liked their fish half-smoked and stored in seal blubber. The smell of it bubbling and spitting in the iron pans of the column was enough to bring a man back from the dead. It dragged Farden to his feet in seconds.

He was surprised to hear the sound of whetstones sliding across steel accompanying the rattle of pans and the murmur of morning conversation. Roiks explained for him. 'Seems that everyone had a bad dream or two last night. A strange wind howled in the night. Or, might've been the cold. Might be somethin' else. Either way it's got 'em all on an edge.'

Farden sat down beside the campfire and grabbed a slice of bread and some of the oily, smoky fish. It was music to his stomach. 'It's a good thing. We're in dangerous waters now, after all,' he said.

Roiks grinned. There was a fish bone stuck in his teeth. 'Hark at ye, mage, sounding like a right sailor. You'll be cursing on Njord's balls before the sun goes down.'

Farden ate in silence while Roiks licked his plate clean. It wasn't long before the bosun was stoking the little fire up, trying to coax some warmth out of it. It was tough going, in the frigid northern air. 'So,' he said, conversationally. 'What's all this I hear about you going to rescue a soul or two, then?'

Farden paused, his fish half in, half out of his mouth. Roiks tapped his nose. 'Sailors talk, mage. More than women, they say. Gods know what women sailors are like. Have to ask Lerel, when she's up an' awake.'

'So everybody knows?'

'Not everybody, mage. Just a handful. Hundred or so,' he smirked.

'For f...'

'Are you really goin' to do it?'

'Yes,' said Farden, without hesitation.

'Then you're a braver man than I, Farden,' Roiks said. 'I leave the other side to the other side. Don't do to go messin' with souls and gods and all that.'

Farden couldn't help but notice how ironic Roiks' words were, with Heimdall sitting no more than a stone's throw away. He was probably listening. 'I never used to be,' he said.

'What changed?'

Farden gazed into the spitting pan. 'The old me was lost for a long, long time. Very lost, in the darkest places he could find. Then the old me died. I came back in his stead. Then I made a promise. Now I'm here.'

'Sounds simple enough,' Roiks said, unfazed by the vagueness of it all. 'An' I hear other rumours too.'

'Oh yes?'

'About the girl you're huntin'. It's your daughter ain't it? That's what the talk is. But that can't be true, I told myself, but then I remembered you at the table, that night before Hjaussfen, when...'

Farden cut him off. 'It's true, Roiks.'

The bosun sighed, eyes wide. 'Well, Njord's ballsack, what a pickle you're in, mage.'

Farden had never heard it put quite like that, but he had to agree. 'I am that.'

Roiks shook his head. 'I didn't think it were actually possible. Not after what you already been through. From the stories I 'ear about you, you've had quite a run o' bad luck, Farden. Not fair, if you ask me. If I were you I'd be still sat in Krauslung harbour, with me arms crossed, yelling I'm not going. Takes a man to make a promise. Takes even more of a man to hunt down his own daughter for the good o' the world.'

Farden nodded. The simple honesty of the bosun's words was almost as refreshing as the air. He didn't know what to say apart from, 'It's not over yet.'

Roiks nodded, and was silent for a time. He kept tapping the handle of the pan, making a strange sort of music between that and the silence. Then he piped up, and said something that Farden hadn't heard in a long time. 'Thank you, Farden,' he said solemnly.

Farden was more than a little overwhelmed. He struggled to swallow his mouthful of smoked fish, and then mumbled a quick, 'You're welcome,' before the moment got too long.

'Well,' said Roiks, slapping his knees. 'We're leavin' with those snowmad types soon, accordin' to that big Siren of yours. Better get packing I s'pose.'

'Mmm,' said Farden. He was still a little bit bewildered. He just kept eating, and tried to ignore the feeling of Heimdall's eyes upon him.

ቐ

'Don't think I've ever travelled by mole before,' said Lerel.

'I think you would know if you had,' Loki snidely remarked.

Roiks was sitting in the front of another nearby sled. 'Ain't there one missin' on yours?' he said, counting the moles of his sled, then theirs. 'Yep, one short.'

Lerel waved a hand at him. She nodded to one of the snowmads, who was kicking at the ice, head bowed low. 'Shh. The man's distraught. One escaped in the night.'

Farden strode up, and quickly hoisted himself aboard the sled.

'Well,' he said. 'Time waits for no mage.' The inside of the sled was strewn with warm seal-fur blankets and a myriad of pots and pans and other cookware. It was surprisingly warm, under its fur canopy.

'Except a dead mage,' said Loki.

Farden glowered. 'And you're sure there isn't another sled free, Loki?'

Loki quickly climbed the steps before anybody could object. 'What an abject shame for me that there isn't.'

'The shame is all yours,' Farden hissed. Lerel made a confused face, and decided to ride up front.

With the crack of whips and the frantic rattling noise of mole-claws on the ice, the sleds jerked forward at a surprising rate, far faster than any trudging could accomplish. Unfortunately, they were limited in their speed; there was not enough room in the sleds for all of the column, so the majority still had to walk. The sled drivers kept it slow to allow them to keep up.

Their sled was second from the front. Farden sat next to Lerel for most of the morning, talking through the years of her life that he had missed, and idly dodging the subject of his own years. Every now and again, Loki would throw in a sly or sarcastic comment, and was rewarded with icy stares from Farden. Lerel was polite. She knew what he was, and didn't dare share the same disdain for him. She kept it deep inside instead.

It was about midday when Farden finally snapped.

The mage whirled around, infuriated by yet another snide comment. 'Why are you even here, Loki? What purpose exactly are you serving?'

Loki smirked and looked away, meeting the disapproving eyes of Heimdall in the sled behind. 'Our reasons are not the business of mortals,' he sighed, aloofly.

Farden began to clamber into the back of the sled, but Lerel held him back. 'How about I make it my business?' he threatened.

'Calm yourself, Farden. You should be conserving your strength.'

Farden spat at him, and Loki wiped the front of his coat.

Lerel was wide-eyed. The man was a god, after all, no matter how annoying. 'There's no love lost between you two, is there?' she whispered, as quietly as she could. The rattling of the sled and scuttling of the moles drowned out most of her voice. 'Come sit down.'

'None,' muttered Farden. 'As far as I am concerned, he was brought to this earth simply to piss me off.'

'Maybe you've just answered your own question,' she suggested.

Farden shook his head. 'No. There's more to him than just being infuriating.'

'Maybe he's goading you for a reason. Trying to bring the magick out of you.

Farden shook his head.

'Then maybe he's heard the stories of the old Farden.'

'He met him already. And I think the new Farden is still very likely to slit his throat. If he asked.'

Lerel raised an eyebrow. 'There's a story in there somewhere.'

Farden shook his head, managing to smile ever-so-slightly. 'And it's not for you,' he said, awkwardly patting her knee. He didn't know why he made that gesture, but for some reason he did. Lerel didn't seem to mind. She caught his hand and traced the metal lines of the gauntlet for a moment, testing the limpness of its missing finger before letting it go. She looked up and sighed at the white wastes spread out before them. In the distance, something resembling a snow-trapped forest had appeared, and was growing bigger by the hour.

'It feels like we're getting nowhere fast on these ice fields. It reminds me of the dune seas of Paraia.'

'The calm before the storm,' replied Farden, and it truly was.

It was the itching period between clouds. The insecurity. The trepidation. The preparation. The worry. Farden felt it all. He pushed it all deep inside his mind where he wouldn't have to think about it, at least for now. Fortunately, it was something he was very good at. His stubbornness had been put to good use.

Lerel ventured a new line of conversation, the one she had been building up to for at least an hour. 'You're really going to do it, aren't you? Going to drag Elessi back from the other side.'

Farden rubbed his eyes, chuckling dryly to himself. 'Roiks has been talking again, I take it? Or was it somebody else? Maybe it was you who talked to Roiks in the first place...'

'So, why are you putting it off?'

Farden pursed his frozen lips. 'I'm not, and I'm struggling to see why everybody thinks I am. We're heading north this very moment, are we not?'

'Strange, to go by sled, when there's a gryphon,' muttered Loki, eyes shut, head leaning against the canvas of the sled. 'I thought this was a race?'

'Shut it,' Farden warned him.

Loki rubbed his palms together, as if he were the god of sarcasm himself. 'I am as eager as you are, Farden. You just tell me when, and we'll go,' he said. 'It will be like old times, back in Albion.

Farden turned around to glare at him. 'What makes you think you're coming with me?' he demanded.

'Aside from one questionable dream, one dalliance with the other side, you have no knowledge of where you're actually going, do you?' Loki asked smugly, outlining his ploy, like a glittering hand in a game of cards.

Farden could see what the god was angling for. 'And you do, I take it.'

'More than you. I know of the ship. The bridge. You did know about the bridge, didn't you?'

Farden's frown couldn't have got any deeper if it tried. 'So that's it, is it? Your grand purpose? Guide of the underworld.'

'I could think of worse callings.'

'I'd rather take Heimdall. Shit, I'd rather go by myself.'

'By all means. Suit yourself. We'll see what he says,' Loki said, already on his feet. He nimbly hopped to the back of the sled and jumped to the snow. In the blink of an eye, he was sitting in the sled behind and talking earnestly to Heimdall.

Farden clenched a red-gold fist. 'That bastard. If only he weren't a shadow, I could drive something sharp and ugly through him.'

Lerel's tone was scolding. 'He's a *god*, Farden. You should still show some respect.'

'I don't show respect to liars,' replied the mage, shaking his head resolutely.

'He lied to get you back to Krauslung, or so I heard. Wasn't that a good thing?'

'Maybe,' Farden said, instantly wincing. 'I mean, yes. It was. Is. Loki just enjoyed it too much for my liking. That god is not like the others. He's too… human.' And he stared back at the sled behind, catching the subtlest of subtle glances from Loki as he talked and gestured wildly at Heimdall, while the other god listened, and, irritatingly, seem to be nodding soberly. *Why was Loki so excited, all of a sudden?* Farden thought to himself. Lerel was still waiting for him to finish. 'I trust him as far as I could throw him. And I can't throw shadows very far.'

'Haven't you got enough enemies? What with Saker, the daemons, and your daughter, I would have thought you'd had your fill.'

'And what better time than now to come crawling out of the woodwork. Even those we don't yet know about.'

'He's a god, Farden. A god.'

'And as they say, they're not perfect.'

Lerel didn't respond. She simply reached out a hand, rough from the ropes of the *'Blade*, and rested it in one of his gauntlets. Farden didn't quite know what to do, so he just stayed still and enjoyed it, listening to the rattling of the sleds, the crackling of the ice, and the snuffling of the odd moles.

※

Evening fell a rosy pink on the ice. They had almost reached the frozen copse, its tall skinny pines all clad in white and permanent armour of frozen snow, from tip to root. It made them look like a phalanx of faceless knights, silent and dangerous. Frozen rubble poked out from the snow, here and there, dead pennants hanging stiff from forgotten flagpoles. The bones of a long-gone kingdom.

As the tired moles began to slacken in their harnesses, the snowmads reined them in and pulled the sleds into a long line that faced the faraway tree-line, like the shields of a brave little barricade. Farden couldn't help but notice the imagery.

There was one thing he wasn't noticing, however, and that was the magick that all the mages were a-whisper about.

'Bah,' was all he could say, as he strolled up and down the line of sleds to work some heat back into his feet. Loki's badgering had already put him in a foul mood, and now this. 'Bah,' he said again, watching the steam billow out of his mouth. *Let them whisper.*

Apparently one of the Written had singed his tunic, his Book had been burning so bright. Tyrfing had been shaking all day, and not from his fever. Every mile they crept towards the north, towards the giant black mountains on the horizon, the more the magick bit them, the more it ran through their bodies. The more it made the air shiver and the ice glow.

To all of them but Farden.

Even some of the sailors were feeling it. Farden could hear their laughter behind him. He knew exactly what they were up to. Holding their fingers in the fire of a torch and watching the flames slide harmlessly across their hands. Like children and a box of mudworms. Amateurs. *Lucky. Bloody. Amateurs.*

Farden put a bit more anger into his step, and began to stamp his feet instead of placing them. A horrible doubt had appeared in his mind, one that spoke of a legacy of his years of nevermar. A lingering idea of poison, and the terrifying word "permanent" had crept into his mind. It had been different in Albion and Krauslung. His magick had bee the root of his problems. But now that he had decided that he needed it, now that it was needed in the fight to fix those problems, he had finally been granted his wish: to have it banished.

Farden stretched out his hands to the snow lying trodden and trampled around his boot-prints. He stretched his hands out like he used to, fingers slightly bent and clawed. Rigid and tense. He tried to suck the magick from the base of his skull, where he hoped it still lingered. He tried to remember the little room in Krauslung, and his anger. But all that came was a sharp pain and a numb hand.

Farden wiggled his fingers. 'Screw it,' he said. He needed a drink to drown his mood.

※

'Cheers!' yelled the entire tent as the mage ducked under its sealskin flap. Farden just smiled weakly at them all, and they drank anyway. One of the Written handed him a cup of something clear and steaming. Worryingly, it had a slight yellowish hue to it. Farden didn't even want to sniff it.

'Er...' he began.

'Glassmelt,' said the mage, clanking his cup off Farden's with a smile. 'Snowmad's own recipe.'

'They have been making it since the sun refused to come up. We should count ourselves lucky. It is not for outsiders,' rumbled Eyrum from the bar, if it could really be called that. It was a crate barely covered by a cloth, with a three-legged mole curled up around its corner, snoring softly.

Farden pointed at it. 'Tell me you haven't got that beast drunk.'

Eyrum shrugged. He wore his axe between his shoulders. Its scarred blade shone in the torchlight. 'I can neither confirm nor deny,' he said.

Farden sauntered over to him, wading through the deep and hearty conversations that only strong liquor, excitement, and spare time can nurture. The Written were sprinkled here and there, being surprisingly social for their class. They shared tables with the Sirens. Soldiers sat around in clumps, polishing swords or armour and chatting idly while they worked.

'We made good progress today,' Farden said, tapping Eyrum's cup with his own.

'Slow but steady.'

'Wins the race?'

Eyrum shook his head. 'Must be an Arka fairytale. Ours are different.'

'How do yours end?'

'Dragons always win.'

'Makes sense.'

And so their conversation went. Stabs of humour and dialogue flew back like two fencers parrying and trading blows, circling something more solid and serious at their centre, like a pit filled with sabre-cats, or something, Farden didn't know. He just knew there was something niggling at his confident clarity. Something beginning to mar it.

'I could use a smoke,' Farden said to Eyrum, once their

exchange had died a little.

Eyrum dug into his jacket and fished something cracked and battered out of it. Farden squinted at it. Supposedly, it could be called a pipe, if a pipe were something that had survived a hundred battles and a ride down a cliff-face in the back pocket of a heavy, seven-foot tall Siren warrior. Farden fished his own out, a slender little skald's pipe, and led Eyrum out of the tent.

The difference in volume between the tent and the cold wastes was astounding. It was near-silent outside the sealskin. Around them, the other sleds and their tents sparkled like little islands in the rose-tinted half-dark. A few figures shuffled across the ice, minding their own business. Above, the stars were punching through the tender bruised sky and beginning to twinkle. Farden reached for his tobacco and handed it to Eyrum. The Siren wrinkled his nose. 'Never liked Arka stuff. Tastes like salt.'

Farden chuckled. 'Suit yourself. I could say the same of Siren tobacco. What's it made out of, seaweed?' he asked.

Eyrum smiled. 'Not entirely,' he said. He did a strange thing next. Strange, considering how much time had passed between them, and how habitual the casual movement was. Eyrum finished packing his pipe and offered the bowl to Farden, for him to light. He caught himself halfway there and made it look like an impromptu stretch. 'Sorry,' he grunted, sensing how obvious he had been.

'No need,' mumbled Farden. 'Just not the best timing.' He ducked inside and brought out a whale-tallow candle. The two men held their pipes to it.

Eyrum grunted again. 'I assume you are speaking of the other mages, and the magick in the air?' he asked.

'I am,' Farden replied between puffs.

'And I assume you cannot feel it like they can.'

'Two right so far. Try for third?'

'And that worries you.'

'We have a winner.'

'And here was I believing we came outside to be serious,' said Eyrum, running his hand over his grizzled face. His grey scales rasped against his rough hands.

Farden sucked his pipe and blew a smoke ring at the stars. 'We did. My apologies. Heimdall is right. I use humour like armour,' he replied, with a hint of a sigh.

Eyrum pointed at the twinkling lights above. 'Do you remember when you and I first looked at the stars?'

Farden nodded. 'It came back to me the other day. My memories are like that these days. Dribs and drabs. I remembered I pointed out the First Dragon.'

'That you did.'

Farden clacked the end of his pipe against his teeth. 'Now I look at them and I wonder which ones I can trust. Which ones are enemies. Which ones are walking amongst us now,' he wondered, trying to trace a myriad of shapes at once. They all jumbled into one. The stars in the north seemed different somehow, brighter, closer. He abruptly blinked his way out his reverie. 'Speaking of stars, where's Loki?' he asked.

Chapter 22

"Even daemons like to barter."
Albion adage

Loki was deep in the frozen copse.

Nobody had seen him leave. Not a soul. All far too busy with their drinking, or their shivering. The cold had come with the night, settling in like the cruel smile of a returning king. Loki felt it, but snubbed it. What was cold to a shadow? What was cold to a god?

Piebald ravens croaked in the frozen branches above. Little showers of powdered ice drifted down from where they hopped and scraped.

Other things lingered in the forest too. Loki could feel their presence now they were so close, and he to them. They were well masked, but he caught glimpses of their horns, their eyes, their teeth, their tendrils and hulking fists. Dark things, hiding in the snowy shadows. Old things. Lost things. Unspeakable things.

Loki found a glade made of ice, with stark trees like pillars, strewn with dead pine cones. The ravens held court above, peering down at this bold newcomer, this unwelcome visitor to their dark places. *He should have stayed with the lights!* They crowed in their own rasping tongues. *He would have been safe there! No longer!*

Loki could feel them before they appeared. He held his hands out by his side, empty and as white as the snow. He closed his eyes, and soon enough he felt the hot stink of the creatures creeping into the glade, drifting like smoke on a stolen breeze.

He barely flinched when the hot claws encircled his neck. Breath like grave-dirt rattled through fangs, mere inches from his nose. Loki opened his eyes and flashed a smile.

'Little god,' said Hokus, baring all his teeth in reply, many eyes winking in sequence. 'You are brave indeed.'

'Foolish, if you ask me, brother,' sniggered the darkness behind his wings.

Loki fearlessly pushed the claws aside, his hands stinging at the contact. 'Both, by my reckoning. And great things have been made on the backs of either,' he said, in a low voice.

※

Eyrum took in a deep breath of cold air through his nostrils. His chest swelled like a fermenting barrel. 'Who knows? In one of the sleds, I believe,' he said.

Farden squinted into the darkness between the sleds and beyond. A faint fog seemed to have risen from the ice, somehow. Night was truly falling now. Nothing could save it. 'It serves to keep an eye on that one,' he muttered. 'I've got a bad feeling about him.'

'And what of Heimdall? Do you treat all gods with mistrust or is it just Loki?'

'Heimdall is fine. Although he has disappeared as well.'

'I heard he is with your uncle. It seems the magick is having an adverse effect on him.'

Farden raised an eyebrow. 'How can that be?'

※

'Explain yourself, godling. Shadow-creature. Why have you

called upon us?' challenged Valefor. 'You, of all creatures? The other two I expected, but not a godling. One of the stars.'

'Because of *her*,' Loki said, pointing into the gathering darkness behind the daemon. If he was afraid, he didn't show it. He stared back at his sworn enemy with a cold, calculating stare, sneeringly confident.

The daemons looked around, as if they had been interrupted during an innocent stroll through an abandoned glade. 'Who?' they asked in tandem.

Loki folded his hands behind his back. 'Let's not play dumb, shall we? You wouldn't dare get so close with all of... *this*,' he said, gesturing to the things in the shadows. The edges of the glade creaked. The frozen pines had nothing to do with it. 'Without her efforts, the mages would be setting fire to it this very moment. Heimdall may be clouded by the magick, but it's not yet that strong. These woods reek of ancient malice. She must be smothering it.'

Hokus was now circling him. Valefor simply prodded him in the chest. 'Let us assume you are right, for now. So, godling. You called us. We are here. Why?'

'If you dare feed us lies, we will feed you,' Hokus said to the darkness, and it growled with a score of voices, if they could truly be called voices. The ravens squawked hungrily.

'Something tells me this shadow doesn't want to go back to the sky. Not yet,' Valefor chuckled.

Loki took a breath.

Farden exhaled and watched his breath rise into the diamond-speckled sky. 'So we're blind? He sees and hears nothing, due to the magick? Sometimes I wonder why these gods fell from the sky at all.'

'Because their fates hang on the next few days as much as

ours does. You are here. So are they. It is the way of it.'

Farden shrugged at the big Siren's wisdom, irrefutable as always. Immovable as the man himself. He stared out at the moonless night, peering into the cobalt-slate of the ice fields. Only a few shadows dominated the night, picked out by the eager stars, the dull reflection of the rocky mountains in the distance, and the silent pine copse barely a mile away. Farden stared at the latter and blew a smoke ring to frame it. 'It's too quiet tonight.'

'What did you expect, on the ice fields?'

'Something, at least. In the deserts, there was always something hidden somewhere. Skulking under the sand. Ensconced in a gap in the rocks. Skittering through the shadows just beyond the campfire,' Farden mused. He nibbled the end of his pipe. 'Sometimes I wish I had a dragon's eyes.'

Eyrum grunted.

The pines swayed like sick spears above them, reaching for the stars. Valefor tried his hardest not to look up at them. He could feel their stares already. No need to meet them when he didn't need to. He looked instead to Hokus, and found his comrade staring right back at him, wearing something of the same expression. It took a lot to surprise a daemon, and this was the third time they had been surprised in as many weeks. The daemon counted them silently.

First, the godblood armour on the girl's father.

Second, the call of the godling.

Third, the godling's demand itself.

Steam and smoke bubbled from Valefor's mouth as he exhaled. Even the edges of the glade seemed a little nervous suddenly. *Curse their ears, those that had them.* 'Let us get this straight.'

'Be my guest.'

'You want us, or rather, our esteemed companion,' at this point, none other than the esteemed companion herself, Samara, strolled from the shadows to get a better look at the audacious demand-maker, 'to bring *your* body down from the stars...'

'Where it should stay with the other corpses,' Hokus spat an interruption.

'...along with ours.'

Loki clicked his fingers. 'That's exactly right.'

※

Farden grimaced. He felt the unease in his gut. Every moment that he stared at the pine copse, a two-headed monster of suspicion and curiosity grew a little bigger in his mind. He kept his eyes on it, as though it might sneak off if he turned around, as he apologised.

'Sorry,' he said, quickly. 'I didn't mean to dredge up that conversation.'

Eyrum looked at the sky. 'They're somewhere. I can feel it. Towerdawn is a good Old Dragon. He would not have wasted their lives for any small reason. That, and he has the fastest of all Nelska with him. I highly doubt any of Saker's could nip at their tails. That *fjtchol*,' Eyrum muttered something better left untranslated. Farden didn't ask.

'I believe you. A lot has to be said for feelings,' he replied. His pipe had gone out. He tucked it in his pocket instead of finishing it. Eyrum was still puffing on his stubborn Siren tobacco.

'Whilst we are on the path of awkward subjects...'

Farden sighed. 'Oh, not you as well. I've already had this from Roiks, Inwick, Lerel... I'm dealing with it. You lot don't understand what I've set myself up for. It's...'

Eyrum put a big heavy hand on his shoulder and squashed the fire out of him. 'I know you can do it,' he said.

'I...' Farden paused. He hadn't expected that, but it was welcome all the same. 'I hope so.'

Eyrum sniffed, following the mage's gaze to the distant copse. 'What exactly is your interest in those trees, mage?'

Farden didn't know, but for some reason he started walking towards them. 'I have no idea, but it's bothering me. Too quiet. Too close,' he said.

※

'Well, isn't that something,' said Hokus. The daemons narrowed their eyes, silent. Samara spoke for them. She strode out of the inky darkness, bold as ever, and looked the god up and down. He was a small man. Shabby, by his coat and wind-strewn blonde hair. Tallish too, but he was a grown-up, and they always were. Intimidating? Hardly. She marched up to him and brought her face to his chin.

'Why should I help you, traitor?' she challenged.

'Because I have delivered your father,' shrugged Loki. An old woman, face creased in wrinkles and limp hand clutched to her side, emerged from the shadows behind her. She looked fearful. Loki saw her biting her lip.

Samara spat in the snow. 'You need to get your facts right, god. My father is dead.'

Loki smiled up at the daemons. 'Oh, did you not tell her?'

'Tell me what?'

Hokus waved a claw. 'The god is babbling, Samara, confused. What is it that you have brought us?'

'Why, I've delivered the whole group to you. The Written, Arkmage Tyrfing, my brother Heimdall, and Farden, of course. Minus only Ruin. No doubt why you've brought such, *hungry*, companions,' Loki looked around at the fidgeting edges of the glade.

'And what do you get out of this bargain?' demanded Samara.

Loki's smile faded all too quickly, replaced with something hard, like flint. 'Is there anything else? I was born a shadow. This earth gave me a thirst I didn't think possible. It's time this shadow felt flesh.'

※

'Farden? Where are you going?' Tyrfing coughed as he poked his head out of the tent. He had heard voices. Eager voices.

'Stay inside, uncle, where it's warm. We're investigating this forest.'

Tyrfing made as if to follow but began to cough instead.

'Stay inside, uncle,' Farden repeated. He strode to the edges of the camp. Others had gathered there. A Written. One of the sailors. A handful of snowmads. They were whispering to themselves, craning ears to the fog, scratching heads.

'What's all this?' Farden asked, making several of them jump.

'Voices sir, on the breeze.'

'What breeze?' Eyrum asked.

Farden turned around very slowly.

※

Loki was still talking. 'I can give you a power you haven't felt in millennia.'

'And what is that?' Hokus sneered, as if the god couldn't even give them a limp handshake.

Samara wrinkled her nose. 'What could you possibly give us?'

'Souls,' said Loki, as simply

Valefor cackled, the ravens with him. 'We take them as we

please. Like we always have. Along with the prayer.'

Loki sighed. 'By sword and claw, one by one. Am I right?'

'It worked well before.'

'I have something more dependable in mind.'

Samara looked to the daemons and then back to the god. 'Like what? What's this bastard talking about?'

It was Loki's turn to jab someone in the chest. He put his finger in the shallow of Samara's shoulder and kept it there. 'Just you worry about bringing my body down, when I ask for it. Understand?' Loki was lucky Samara didn't gut him right there and then. She would have managed it, judging by the venom in her eyes, if she wasn't so stunned by his boldness. Loki even had the audacity to wink. He pointed back through the silent trees, spying the lights and glow of the camp. 'Have fun.'

*

Crunch, crunch, crunch, went the ice under Farden's quickening boots. Eyrum pounded along behind him, a growing entourage of mages and snowmads behind them. Something was in the trees. Farden was sure of it now. His borrowed sword glinted in the starlight. A sudden wind whipped across the ice, bringing the creaking of wood and the chattering of branches to his ears. The chattering of teeth and fangs. 'Stay close,' he ordered. 'And be ready!'

'For what?' Eyrum whispered.

'Nothing, I hope.'

*

'Calm yourself, girl!' Lilith whined from the gloom of the pines.

'Farden will die tonight!' Samara screeched. She was beyond

listening. The wind whipped up the ice and needles into a frenzy around her as she stood arms stretched to the shadows. They whined and scratched the ground for her as the magick surged. The daemons looked undecided, but still they grew, swelling up to nudge the branches with their glowing shoulders. The pine copse shivered and howled around them.

Loki stood calmly amongst it all, watching the flashes of eyes and teeth as they flew from the shadow. He heard the tips of the pines crack as dragon's wings clipped them. He watched them all as they followed Samara out onto the ice, one by one. Her skin was already crackling with lightning, like a beacon in the night. Sparks of fury hissed.

Only Valefor stayed long enough to say anything. He spoke through his veil of burning smoke. 'We have a deal, god,' he said, before leaving. 'But you had best deliver.'

'Oh,' Loki smirked. 'I will.'

Chapter 23

"Carry with ye a silver mirror at all times! For the lycan is a terrifying foe, much more so that its vampyre cousin. Only a pure silver surface may deflect its terrible visage, and break the transformation! Ignore the tales of silver blades; only a mirror may save ye, verily, and a fleet foot. Travel only on a moonless night, as the milky glow of our heavenly sister doth hold sway over our lycan foe, and causes him to turn so! Unlike a vampyre, it is a creature caught betwixt its curse, half man, half beast, and never quite either. Its poison is held both in its fangs and its claws, and its roar can be heard for twenty leagues! Death is most preferable to the lycan curse. Should ye meet one bereft of a silver mirror, pray ye to the gods for a swift end!"
Another panicky excerpt from 'Death and all her Beasts' by Master Wird

To say the arrival of the dragons was well timed was nothing short of an understatement.

At the precise moment that the face of the copse burst into several thousand burning fragments of wood and resinous needle, splinters of ice and slush, the southern sky was turned orange by the belching fires of the arriving dragons.

Towerdawn was the first, skidding to a halt on the ice just long enough for Modren and Durnus to jump, or rather fall, from his side. There was no pretence of grace. The two mages' legs had turned limp during the ride. They slid from the Old Dragon's scaly hide and crumpled into two matching heaps in the snow. One of his captains was next, delicately rolling so that the still form of Elessi could be carried off by some waiting snowmads.

'Farden!' roared Towerdawn, sighting the mage standing against the blaze of the copse, the shadows suddenly alive with creatures from memory and nightmare. 'A delivery for you!'

Farden's reply was a flash of his sword. He had no time for reunions.

Where the mage was standing, it was all rather confusing. The silent ghost of a pine copse had suddenly exploded into life. A sinister army was pouring from its blazing trees. Giant wolves, shadows he couldn't even begin to name, swarthy ice trolls, ravens, something slithering, something crystalline glittering in the orange light, Lost Clan dragons, two daemons towering over it all, and in the centre, a slim, glowing figure, hair flying in her own storm winds. *Samara*. It was an ambush the likes of which he couldn't have dreamt up if he had tried, and she had orchestrated it all.

'Icewights!' yelled a nearby snowmad, pointing a shaking finger. Farden followed it, and found two glittering creatures at the end. They looked vaguely human in the light of the fire, but made of glass, razor-sharp and translucent. They slid across the ice as if it were part of them, far outpacing the rest of the chaotic mass galloping behind them. They raised their glassy claws and hissed as they came near. Farden was so stupefied by their appearance that he almost forgot to swing his sword…

…Almost.

The steel carved through the face of the icewight like a boulder through a pane of glass. The creature shattered. Farden grit his teeth and shielded his face as shards flew. Cold, sharp shards. The creature crumpled to the ice. The mage looked up to find the other in a very similar position, frantically clawing at the axe-blade that was embedded in its groin. Eyrum twisted, and the creature shattered like the first. Farden poked at the shards with his boots. They were swiftly melting, but still the snowmads behind them were cowering on their knees. Eyrum just shrugged. 'Easy as that,' he said, and turned to face the rest.

Farden felt the blast of wind as the dragons flew overhead. He heard, no, *felt*, the crunch and roar as they collided in mid-air with their Lost Clan foes. Several plummeted to the ice, ripping and tearing and trumpeting as they fell.

'Farden!' yelled a voice far behind him. Farden was about to turn when something resembling a boulder with arms and legs burst out of the fiery shadows. He stumbled back, sword glancing uselessly off a stone rib, curved like a tusk. *Who on earth was trying to strike up a conversation at this moment in time?!* he bellowed inwardly. It turned out to be his uncle, racing across the ice towards him. He slid to a stop just long enough to send a fireball ploughing into the boulder troll's stomach, and then he ran on. Farden ducked as the orb of flame sent the creature flying. He could smell burning hair.

When he stood up, a raven was flapping in his face, trying to peck at his eyes. A quick slash with the sword sent it flying across the ice in two separate directions. 'Next!' he yelled to the roaring, screeching paint-splash of orange and black that the night had suddenly become. It was madness. Pure, unexpected madness. Fire, ice, creatures, and his daughter in the midst of it all. He couldn't help but think at that moment that it could all still be traced back to him.

'Farden!' Tyrfing was still trying to catch up with him. He would have to try harder. Farden spun and slashed as the strange creatures kept coming, sometimes one at a time, others in packs of two, or three. He put his sword through the face of a white snarling fox, and then dashed another icewight to the ground. Something grabbed him from behind, something slithering and tentacled choking him around the neck. There was a dull *thwack* as Eyrum's axe bit into its spongy skull, and the thing went limp. Farden looked down to find out what it was and still drew a blank.

'What are these things?' he yelled.

Eyrum spun the axe like a toy. 'The scum and dredges of the old creatures, drawn by your daughter and her daemons,' he growled. A constellation of brown blood drops decorated his face.

'Speaking of,' Farden hissed, looked to his daughter, a few hundred yards ahead, wreaking havoc, flanked by the two daemons from Krauslung. He clenched his red-gold fists together and marched towards her. 'Enough is enough.'

'Farden!' Two voices this time. Farden ignored them as well.

'Samara!' he yelled instead, catching the eyes of his glowing, crackling daughter. The ground around her was a glittering pool of molten ice. It sparked like her skin, the lightning flitting away into the ice and the night. 'Samara!'

She had heard him the first time. She raised her hands and threw a wall of energy against him. Even at that distance, the shockwave still tossed Farden onto his back.

'FARDEN!' Three voices now, deafeningly close. *Who is that?!* he wondered, as three fireballs flew over his face, so close he felt his nose tingling in the heat. Shortly afterward, three pairs of hands dragged him upright.

'We need to leave. Now!' it was Tyrfing. His face was sunken and tired but his eyes were wild. He covered his mouth as he coughed. Farden stared at the orange-glowing faces of the men beside him. He had to blink several times to realise who it was. Towerdawn's shout suddenly made sense.

'Durnus! Modren!' he yelled, grasping them both. Durnus clapped him heartily on the back, whilst Modren just stood there stiffly. They both said nothing. Both were staring ahead at the daemons flanking Samara. 'I'm glad you could join the party,' he added.

'Well, it's time to leave it,' Tyrfing hissed.

'What?' Farden was confused. 'She is right there!' His head ached. Something was pounding on it.

Tyrfing pinched his forehead between his fingers. 'The armour. Korrin. We're not ready for this. We need to go, now!' Tyrfing explained, shaking his nephew by the shoulder. Durnus and Modren busied themselves with keeping the various creatures at bay. The night was filled with crying and yelping. Inhuman and very human sounds together, clambering over each other to fill the air. Tyrfing shouted over it. 'She's here for you, Farden. Nobody else. You and I need to leave.'

'Don't forget me!' cried a voice. Loki appeared out of the shadows behind them with an urgent, fearful look on his face. His coat was splattered with blood. Orange blood. There was a short dagger in his hand. The perfect alibi.

Farden scowled at him. 'Where have you been?' he snapped.

'Keeping out of trouble.'

'It doesn't look like it.'

'Farden!' Tyrfing barely resisted the urge to slap his nephew. Only another blast of spell saved him from doing so. Everyone but Durnus was thrown to the ice. They could hear the faint laughing of Samara and the daemons in the distance.

'Come face me, Farden!' came the cry. Farden bared his teeth and raised his sword, but three pairs of hands held him back.

'You don't stand a chance,' whispered his uncle's voice in his ear. 'And you know it.' Farden did. The truth was painful, but it was the truth. It often was. It was its business to be so. 'If we go now, then we can find the rest of the armour,' Tyrfing added, 'and come back to face her.'

'I have no idea what you two are jabbering on about, but it better include saving my wife,' Modren muttered.

'It does,' Farden replied, elbowing Tyrfing.

Loki tucked his dagger into one of his never-ending pockets. 'Well, are we going or not?'

Farden took a breath, and nodded. 'We are,' he said, and that was that.

※

The burning question went something like this: *what exactly does one take for an excursion to the underworld?* Farden was clueless. He stared dumbfounded at his array of supplies, tossed over the floor as they were in the overturned sled. There was a deep gash through the centre of the vehicle, suspiciously the same shape and size as a dragon's tail.

Behind him the battle roared on, half muted by the fur and the cloth. He grit his teeth on every clang and crash. Every flash of light that lit the snow outside the sled. He should have been out there, with the other mages. Swinging his sword like he was meant to. Fighting his daughter.

'Shit,' Farden swore, staring at his supplies like a cow might stare at a page of algebra. The sword was already strapped to his belt. His armour was underneath his cloak. His boots were sound. Did he take food? Did he take coin? What about a blanket? Was it cold in the underworld? Was it hot? Should he take a flint? The spyglass he had borrowed from Lerel?

'Farden!' came yet another hoarse cry. He was getting bored of hearing his name.

'Shit,' Farden cursed again, stuffing whatever he could grab with one hand into one of his haversacks and tying it to his shoulder. He took an extra blade, just in case, the spyglass, and the Grimsayer, of course. As he dashed outside, he nearly tripped over a fallen snowmad. The man reached up to him and gurgled something before slumping into the snow. Farden winced. He had seen enough dying men to know another one. There was nothing he could do. With a grimace, he tugged the blanket from his haversack and draped it over him. 'I guess I'll see you shortly,' he mumbled, mostly to himself, and then sprinted as fast as he could to the back of the camp, where Tyrfing was waiting with Ilios.

The gryphon was clawing at the snow, eager to be off. He had blood on his beak, all different colours. There was the hunter's fire in his yellow-flecked eyes. He kept clacking his beak and twitching his wings every time a dragon swooped even remotely close. Farden knew the feeling.

'Ready?' asked his uncle.

'As I'll ever be.'

'Good, and you, Loki?' Tyrfing asked, as the god emerged from behind Ilios. He nodded, patting down his coat.

'Better than ever,' he said, making Farden glare. The battle clashed on behind them.

'I don't know why you're insisting on coming, liar, but mark my words. You stay behind me, and you stay out of our way. If you're needed, then you're needed. If you aren't, you're just thin air to me. I won't spare you any breath. Spectator, is what you are. Guide, if needs be. Clear?' Farden said, aiming his finger like a spear.

Loki glared back. 'Crystal,' he spat.

Farden jumped onto Ilios' back before Loki could embellish his answer with any sarcasm. He smoothed the gryphon's twitching feathers as he dug the mighty Grimsayer from his haversack and lay it flat upon his lap. He spoke into Ilios' tufted ear. 'Let's finish this,' he said, 'now or never again.' He heard the gryphon warble something as his uncle climbed on, and then Loki, weighing no more than a feather. Nobody needed to say a word; the gryphon exploded from the ice and into the sky, winging high above the dying chaos below.

Farden eagerly looked down. The mages were cutting a path through the ambushers, led by a stoic Durnus and a fearsome Modren.

Samara still stood her ground, surrounded by a wall of fire twenty foot tall Only the daemons, and perhaps one other figure, hidden behind a rock near to the burning copse, noticed the gryphon fleeing north. They pointed and roared, but it was too late. Samara was too busy raining fire on the rest of the column to notice. Farden had escaped her wrath for a second time.

The night was cold out of the heat of battle. Colder still on the high winds and wings of the gryphon. Silent, the three faced the icy wind with grimaces. Farden hunkered down. Face painted orange by the Grimsayer, he watched his destination being drawn in light over, and over, and over again.

Chapter 24

"Friends make the very worst of enemies."
Old Arka saying

Morning found a lot of colours on the ice fields.

Black, from the soot and char of the burnt and burning pines.

Red, from the fallen, from the human ones at least, splashed and seeping.

Blues, of the snowmads' cloaks, as they went about cleaning the dead and their mess.

Green, from a fallen dragon, lying twisted in a heap.

Brown, the body of its opponent, their jaws still locked together in death.

And a palette of grey, the colour of the sky, of the pelts of the fallen wolves, birds, and creatures, of the fallen weapons and armour lying like the forgotten cutlery and crockery in the aftermath of a banquet. Of the moods of the people shuffling about.

It is easy to spot a veteran in the wake of a battle. They are the ones striding back and forth easily amongst the dead, picking up discarded weapons and armour. Emotionless and silent. They move like crows, from one body to the next. But these weren't scavengers. These were mages. Valuables went untouched, gawping eyelids were closed, and respect paid to those they recognised.

'How many fallen?' Durnus asked the cold morning.

Heimdall's eyes roved over the battlefield. He could still see the magick burning in some of the corpses, leaking away like the morning's mist, rising to join the rivers of it pulsing through the grey sky above. He winced. 'Thirty-six.'

'Who are they?'

'Soldiers, mostly. Ten sailors. Two mages. One dragon and her rider. The rest are snowmads,' replied the god, like a merchant totting coins.

'Bitch,' spat Eyrum, regarding the nearby fallen dragon with his one good eye. Towerdawn and the others were gathered around its corpse.

Durnus scratched his head. 'Why did she attack? Why now?'

'It was completely out of the blue. She must have been waiting for us in the trees. Caught us off guard well enough. Only Farden seemed to sense it,' Eyrum replied. He absently thumbed his notched axe-blade as he spoke.

'But why risk it now, when she could have just carried on north?'

'It is either anger for her father, or they are worried about our presence, and how we could hamper their plans,' said Heimdall. 'This is a good sign.'

Eyrum tugged his eye away from the dead dragon. 'With all due respect, my lord,' he began, bowing his head respectfully, 'it hardly looks like a good sign from where I'm standing.' Heimdall didn't reply to that.

'Any news from the sentries?' Durnus asked, as Modren sauntered up to them, snow clinging to his boots.

'Not a whisper,' said the Undermage. 'Wherever they've gone, it's not here. That copse is sticks and charcoal. Nothing in there. Still no sign of the missing Written either. His body's gone.'

'That is rather disturbing,' Durnus surmised. 'Why take the body?'

'She's always had a penchant for our mages. Maybe she eats them,' Modren scowled. 'I'd believe anything at this stage, after what I saw last night. Ice-creatures. Giant wolves. We should have stayed in Krauslung. At least Malvus I can understand. Malvus I know bleeds red if I stick him,' he said, kicking a patch of blue snow beside his boot.

'Then I take it that it's probably not the best time to discuss where Farden and Tyrfing are headed?' Eyrum sighed.

꙳

Modren dropped his chin in his hand and blew a sigh through pursed lips. 'And I thought you Sirens didn't have a sense of humour,' he said. The sled was silent. The only sound was the fidgeting of the two snowmads sitting in the corner, busying themselves with repairing a pair of bloody boots. Anything to keep the battle from their minds. It had been quite a night for all. The others couldn't help but feel for them. They hadn't asked to be involved with any of this.

Heimdall tutted. 'He is quite serious, mage.'

'Well then, I would say he was mad, if it didn't involve saving Elessi. I suppose I should be grateful, as well as confused,' Modren replied. This was all rather strange news to him. One moment Farden was leaving to fetch Siren healers, the next moment he was leaving for Hel.

It was news to Durnus too. A concerned look had fallen over his face. His brow had creased up like old paper, his lips tighter than a merchant's purse. 'And Tyrfing has gone with him?'

'And Loki too,' replied Heimdall. Durnus nodded as slowly as a person can nod. He stared around with his sightless eyes, not letting them linger too long on one spot lest the tears took their chances.

'So be it,' he said. 'He knows what he's doing.'

'I hope so. Somebody needs to keep Farden in check,' Modren

muttered.

Eyrum thumped his axe-handle on the deck of the sled. 'Actually, mage,' he said, 'Farden's been the one keeping us in check.'

Modren didn't even bother to hide his surprise. 'Then the world truly has been turned upside down.'

And so the four of them sat in silence for a while, ruminating on the night, on Farden, and what they both held in store for the world.

It was Durnus who sprang to his feet first. 'Tell me, Eyrum, can anybody amongst this crowd speak the language of these snowmads?'

Eyrum took his chin from the butt of his axe. 'A few.'

'Good. Will you find them for me?'

The big Siren nodded and got to his feet.

'What's on your mind, Durnus?' Modren asked.

Durnus flashed a tight smile and turned to Heimdall. 'You were headed north, were you not? Before we arrived?'

'We were,' Heimdall replied.

'North it is then. We need to be ready when Farden and Tyrfing emerge from whatever hole they're intent on crawling down. We follow Samara's trail, and buy them some time.'

'And if they don't return?' Modren asked, biting his lip. Durnus' smile tightened even further.

'Then you better pray for our souls, as well as your wife's, Modren, because it will be down to us. Now, muster your Written, Undermage,' Durnus commanded.

Modren got to his feet; leaden, but willing. 'Yes, Arkmage.'

'Good man,' Durnus nodded, as he listened to Modren's boots thump on the ice and stride away. 'Eyrum,' he said, 'find me somebody who can speak snowmad. It appears we have got an army to march north, and from what I remember of the ice fields, we'll need their help.'

Samara held the sword over the cliff, grit her teeth, and gripped it until her blood turned into flame. It melted the blade clean in half. She watched the molten scraps dribble from her hand and tumble into oblivion. 'We had them,' she spat. The wind whipped her hair into her eyes, but she stubbornly ignored it. 'We had them,' she repeated. 'We had *him*!'

'Calm yourself, girl,' hissed Valefor.

Hokus clacked his fangs together. 'Or it shan't just be the sword dribbling over that cliff.'

Samara whirled on the daemons, sitting slumped and impatient on the boulder behind her. 'Just you try it!' she cried, her anger drowning all need for respect.

Hokus made to get up, but Samara flicked her hands open and light exploded in each. 'Don't pretend I'm expendable, cousin. We both know I'm not.'

Hokus smiled a sickly little smile, and sat back down. Valefor spoke for him. 'They,' he said, waving his arms over the cliff and at the black smear of people far below on the ice, 'are not important. They are vermin to be squashed at a later date. A few mages won't stand in your way, not now the magick grows as fierce as it does.'

'And Ruin?'

Valefor and Hokus traded glances. 'He will answer to his father soon enough.'

'And Farden?'

More glances. 'They say blood is thicker than water. He's yours,' Valefor said. 'Kill him for us.'

Samara kicked a pebble into mid-air and watched it plummet. 'Well, I was going to last night, but he escaped, didn't he? Right under our noses.' *Thump.* Another pebble felt the wrath of her boot.

'Where's he gone to, anyway?'

Hokus looked north, as if he might just catch a glimpse of a heavily-laden gryphon. No such luck. The ice and the distant mottled mountains were empty, motionless save for the spurs of ice and mist flying like pennants from their peaks. Just the little slug of people below for company, creeping along across the ice, the dragons circling them. 'I don't know,' he said. It took a lot to worry a daemon, but this one was. So too was Valefor.

'Probably trying to head us off. Fools.'

There was a click of heels from behind them. It was Saker. He hadn't bothered to clean his sword after the night before. It dangled from his belt, free of its scabbard, a rusting streak of crimson along its tip. 'A storm is coming,' he announced.

'Damn right it is,' Samara snapped.

'No, my lady. A storm drifts southwards from the Tausenbar peaks. It will be with us within the hour. If we leave now, we can rise above it.'

Samara looked at the sky, as if ready to challenge it to a duel. With an exasperated huff, she reached up to tie back her thick hair, and nodded. 'Then let's go,' she said. As she passed Hokus and Valefor, she leant close to them, so close their sulphur almost made her gag. 'Next time I see him, he's mine, right? All mine? No distractions?'

'All yours,' Hokus nodded.

Samara stalked off. 'I look forward to it,' she muttered. 'Look forward to showing him the colour of his insides.'

Valefor sniggered fitfully. 'Sounds delicious,' he said.

The daemons waited until the dragons were in the sky before they faded into the blustery air, two clouds of jet-black smoke on the wind. Their voices joined the wind in its whining. 'We will see him again, won't we?' asked Valefor.

'I fear we will,' replied Hokus.

'In that case, brother, I hope she makes good on her word.'
'If she doesn't, we may have a problem.'

1561 years ago

his lips were dead.

The cold had kidnapped them, just like the sky had kidnapped the sun. He hadn't seen it in a week. He was beginning to fear for its safety.

His feet felt like hooves. Stumps of dead flesh to be stumbled over and wobbled on. The snow had frozen into the gaps in his armour. He was slowly being frozen solid.

Weeks, he had tottered about on the ice. No food. His only water was what snow and ice he could cram into his mouth and melt between his chattering teeth. His armour could no longer keep him warm. He was kept alive only by its stubborn, persistent magick.

Korrin rolled onto his side and looked back the way he had come. He could see his trail of awkward footprints leading back east. No dark shapes this time. No torches. Maybe he'd lost them.

No. He squinted again. It couldn't be. There, hidden in the distant snowy haze, a score of black figures stood in a line. They were moving slowly, probing every snowdrift with their spears.

Korrin thumped the snow with his fist, immediately regretting it as the numbness made his bones shudder painfully. He'd had enough of running now.

Korrin struggled to his feet and began to walk again. Pain shot through his legs with every step. He set his jaw and moved through it.

'Is it time?' he asked himself. Anybody will start talking to themselves after being alone for so long, so abandoned and lost. It is the mind's way of staying sane. Korrin bit his lip. He had never imagined it would come to this, but options were something he'd left at the lip of the volcano, to burn with the rest of them.

Korrin held his breath as the emotion caught in his throat. He sobbed once and then swallowed it.

With resolute hands, he grabbed his gauntlets and tugged them free. They dangled by his side for the briefest of moments before he tossed them aside, one to the left and one to the right, as far as his tired arms could manage. He grit his teeth as he heard them land in the snow. Please let that distract them.

※

It took another week to find the stones. Rising high out of the ice, on a shelf of rock above the ice fields, he found them. At first he thought they might shelter him from the icy winds, but as he staggered up to them, wheezing like a blacksmith's bellows, he saw they were bare and cold, spaced in a ring like a crown. The wind howled between them, cold breath sighing through granite teeth.

They were tall, that was for sure. Taller than one of his father's huts. Korrin slumped to his knees and gazed up at them. He felt the cold on his legs and forearms. Without the greaves and vambraces, the cold had gone deeper into his body. Slowly but surely he was freezing.

He collapsed there for a time. It was all he could do to put his face into the snow and let it numb him. His mind was rambling, capering through fields of the absurd, of guilt, and of sorrow. He let it ramble as he allowed himself to sag into the snow.

'This one's alives, brothers,' hissed a sickening voice, like silk being dragged over a fistful of nails.

'Alives indeeds. We've not hads visitors in so longs.'

Korrin tried to get up, but something heavy was pressing him down. He could smell it: old leather and rotting meat. He could feel its *claw clicking against his helmet. Korrin pawed for his sword before remembering he'd lost it three days ago.*

More voices now, horrid, slithering voices. Korrin guessed at five of them. 'Whats shall be done with its?'

'Meats, brother. We's shall eats it.'

'Like hell you will,' hissed Korrin.

'Ah, its speaks of Hels, brothers!'

'But our Hels, we wonders. Or anothers?'

Tap tap tap went the claw on his helmet. From what he could glimpse, these creatures were as big as dogs, made of black wings and fur. He spied a beak full of teeth, but he couldn't be sure. 'Have you comes to dies here, humans?' it asked him.

Korrin shook his head. 'I wanted to live.'

'Comes to the wrongs place for thats, meats.'

'To escape.'

'Likes the others?'

Korrin flinched. 'What others?'

Something breathed very closely to his ear. Its breath stank. 'More meats follows you. In the snows. Lookings for somethings.'

'Me.'

'You came heres to hides then?' asked the first creature. Tap tap tap.

'I don't know why I came here,' Korrin sighed. 'Everything's over. The others are dead...'

There was a silence as the creatures looked at each other, swapping furtive glances and ideas. The claw stroked the back of his helmet, almost as soft as a lover would. 'We's can hides you, ifs you wishes?'

'Where?'

'Wheres nobodys will ever looks.'

Korrin tasted the snow in his mouth. It tasted bitter. He was willing to try anything now. Even if it meant trusting these creatures. 'Hide me, then.'

'We's needs a trades, firsts.'

Korrin held what was left of his armour close. 'What could I possibly offer you?'

'Meats.'

'Meats?'

'Meats!'

Korrin bit the inside of his lip. He hadn't come this far just to be eaten alive. Hadn't trained and fought so hard just to give in and slump into the snow. Had never wanted something so much. He realised then that he hadn't just wanted to be alive, but to have a life. A life with meaning, not a pig farmer's life. He had carved himself a life with his armour, an existence. A purpose. How dare he let that crumble now, in his darkest moment. He wondered what his father Ust would say, if he were there now. He would have barked something fierce and bitter about doing what is necessary, no doubt. Korrin took a breath. 'Take those that follow me then. They are looking for me,' he muttered, weakly. 'I brought them here for you.'

'Presents?'

'We's accepts!'

'Meats!'

There was an eager little shuffling around him. The creatures were moving towards the stones. The weight lifted from his back but Korrin stayed where he was, sprawled in their centre. There was a muttering and a scratching around him. He glanced up to see the ugly things, all black skin and patchy fur, clawing at the puckered granite and its strange runes. Korrin felt the ice sag beneath him. A shadow grew dark under the ice, a bruised, hollow blue colour. Korrin pressed his hands to it and felt it shrivel under his numb fingers. It was melting away underneath him. He tried to quell the panic.

Before the freezing water took him, Korrin looked up at the grey sky, perched on the lip of the cliff hanging above him. The cloud had fragmented in the east, and in between the broken patches, he could see it: the pale northern sun. Finally returned, safe and sound. Korrin watched it until the ice vanished beneath his knees and hands.

And he sank like a stone.

Into a place no living eye had ever seen before.

Chapter 25

"Wrapped in a threadbare blanket, the rider shivered in the cold. It was bitter, there, in the north, where the ice clawed at the south. A great flapping sound made him stare at the sky. His dragon had returned. A golden drake was he, majestic, as any Old Dragon should be. The rider stood and stepped back, bowing as the dragon landed, claws crunching on the wet snow.

'My lord,' the rider whispered.

'Rider,' growled the dragon. The rider took a furtive step forward. Their camp was sparse. He had left the blanket in the snow.

'It is cold,' said his dragon. The rider nodded, trying to hide the trembling of his limbs.

'Have you tinder?' asked the dragon.

The rider looked up, shocked. 'What are you suggesting?'

The Old Dragon sniffed the cold air, sombre. 'It is time, rider. It is time you humans tasted our sacred fire.'

The rider bowed again, and folded to his knees. Hands shaking, he reached into his haversack and brought forth tinder and dry sticks, vestiges of a warmer, drier land. He laid them with reverence in the snow, and quickly stood back. No dragon had ever leant his flame before.

'Spread your hands, and be warm, rider,' whispered the Old Dragon, taking a deep breath. His chest swelled as took in the cold air, turning it to fire in his belly. Pursing his lips, he exhaled, and flame dribbled from his teeth, spilling on to the damp tinder beneath. Fire blossomed,

and the rider felt the warmth on his hands. He smiled. The dragon had given the rider his fire."
'How the Dragon first gave Fire to his Rider' - an old Siren proverb

As it turned out, Farden could have probably used that blanket.

Four days passed them by, and not by any means quickly. Time itself seemed to be affected by the cold. Traipsing past sluggishly, like a half-frozen beggar.

Farden had never been so cold in his life. Every day north they travelled, the colder it got. He spent the days hugging Ilios' back and praying for a second skin, or even just a second cloak. The nights he spent sitting as close to his uncle as physically possible, while Tyrfing tried his hardest to keep a flame burning in his hands for as long as he could. There was nothing to burn in the icy crags of the mountains, nor down on the ice, amongst the glaciers and ever-rolling snow fields, or the crumbled skeletons of old, frozen empires. They would have had better luck trying to strike a flint under the sea. Only Farden's iron pride kept him from asking Loki to produce a cloak or a blanket from one of his endless pockets. He would have rather frozen than ask for help from a trickster like him.

The Tausenbar Mountains were an inhospitable scrap of the world. Every inch of them seemed to scream "grave for hire" at one volume or another. They were a jagged bristle of black rock and sheer glacier, splayed east to west across the north. Young peaks, still waiting to be eroded and filed smooth by the ice-winds. Still saw-toothed and dangerous, miserly with caves or flats, barren and cold like the wastes they reared up from.

In their valleys the ice-fields wove and wandered, split into a thousand different threads by the rocks and foothills. Most ended in a sheer, black cliff or a wall of smirking, sapphire ice. Only a few led through the mountains to the other side, where the foothills stretched out into yet another wasteland of ice and snow, speckled with patches of frozen forests, rocks, cliffs, more rocks, and the occasional shard of black stone. But it was all just a preamble to the main event. A prelude. A warm-up act.

The real mountains sat in the distance.

The Spine made the Tausenbar look like a troll's rock-garden. Those mountains were monstrous things, the smallest of them easily as tall as Emaneska's highest peak, Lokki. Farden wondered why it still held that title, and then quickly realised why: nobody would have believed any adventurer if he had returned home telling of the Spine. Not even trusty old Wallium the Wanderer.

Ilios had taken them high above a storm on that day, to a peak so high they'd found it hard to breathe. They had seen the Spine instantly above the roof of the storm. A faint red glow pasted across the distant, jagged horizon, illuminating the peaks like the rotten, black teeth of a shark gnawing on bright crimson flesh. Plumes of ash sprouted up here and there between the monstrous summits, the remnants of the Roots. These were real mountains, like the gods would have wrought in their prime. Mountains that would have given giants a challenge of a climb. They were breathtaking in more ways than one.

Since then the sky had glowed constantly red. Even in the day the Spine turned the sky a rosy, bloody hue, like a constant sunrise. Farden hated it. He kept expecting to feel a little bit of warmth from such a glow, but the cold kept on being cold, and the wind kept on biting. More so with every wing-flap north.

Farden was just thankful for the gryphon. Ilios was not only transport, but warmth in the night as they crouched and lay against his feathery back. He had even kept their stomachs full on two of the nights. The first, he had caught a snow-fox. The third, he found a leathery rabbit, long-dead but perfectly preserved in a patch of glassy ice. Tyrfing had melted it free and cooked it with his bare hands. It was leathery indeed, like nibbling a boot, but it was food at least. Ilios had crunched the bones and fur, and seemed happy enough with that.

The fourth night found them shivering on the northern side of the Tausenbar, in the lee of a rocky outcrop, tucked into its hollow. There was a faint dusting of snow on the rock, like icing on a market cake. Farden was distracting himself from how cold his extremities were by drawing pictures in it. A minotaur with a broken horn. A fish with sails. A wolf with eight legs. As he moved on to draw a book with a hat, he wondered absently if he were going insane. 'Can you go mad from the cold?' he asked aloud, behind chattering teeth.

'We'll soon find out,' Tyrfing replied. He was warmer, though barely. He was trying to conserve his strength to fight off whatever illness was still plaguing him. His cough had returned with a vengeance. Barely a few minutes went by without him retching and spitting something on the rock. Tyrfing didn't tell. Farden didn't ask. It was a heavy lead lump between them. A bastion in the room.

On the other side of the hollow, Loki fished a small notebook from his coat, flipped through a few pages, and then put it back again. 'No,' said. 'Apparently you cannot.'

Farden had given up wondering about the god's pockets. They were as endless as he was annoying. If that was his only skill as a god, it made him about as useful as a feather in a sword-fight. Farden snorted to himself, and began to draw a feather with a sword-handle in the snow.

Ilios warbled something sleepily. The gryphon was curled up around the mouth of the hollow. Even with his thick feathers, he was still a desert creature. He wasn't made for the cold. Farden could see his claws shivering. 'Ilios wants to know how far we have to go. May I?' Tyrfing asked hoarsely.

'Be my guest,' Farden said, and slid his haversack over. Tyrfing opened it up, half-expecting to find the thick tome wrestling for space with supplies. It wasn't. It was practically alone in the sack. Tyrfing jiggled it free and heaved it onto his lap.

'You didn't bring much, did you?'

'What was there to bring?'

'A candle would have been good,' sighed Loki.

Farden rolled his eyes. A candle would have been good; he would have had something to carve. He contemplated drawing Loki in a noose. That was a little too close to home. 'Don't you have one in those magick pockets of yours?' he asked.

Loki clicked his fingers. 'Actually, I do,' he said, almost cheerily. It took him a moment of rummaging before he produced a fat tallow candle. He tossed it to Tyrfing, who had it lit in seconds. The faint, flickering yellow glow it threw out wasn't much, but it was enough to bring a little lift in mood to the hollow. And a little heat, too. Farden shuffled closer and practically put his boots in the little flame. He was about to ask if Loki had another, when a deep orange glow suddenly bathed their hollow. It was the Grimsayer. It was glowing brighter than it ever had before. It must have been the northern magick. Tyrfing asked it the way, and the lights went to work, throwing shapes on the rock above and around them.

'One more day,' Tyrfing announced, as he watched the route replay itself. 'One more day and we'll be there.'

Farden watched the lights and had to agree. He had to. He didn't want to believe anything else. He rubbed his hands together, trying to dispel the ache in the gap of his missing finger. He found Loki staring at it. 'What?' he asked.

'How did you lose that?'

'In a tavern brawl. Somebody was asking too many questions, so I cut it off myself and rammed it down his throat.'

'Sounds clever.'

'He thought he was.'

'Honestly, how did it happen?'

Farden sighed. 'Vice,' he said, 'Vice took it clean off in our last battle. When Durnus, Tyrfing, and I killed him.'

Loki nodded thoughtfully. 'It is a bit of a shame, don't you think?'

'What is?'

'How none of you managed to get what you wanted? How in the end you all had to share a piece of the victory, rather than having complete revenge?' Loki shook his head, as if it were truly sad news. Farden bit his tongue.

'I got what I wanted,' grunted Tyrfing. 'We all had a personal reason to see him dead. We each got what we wanted. Vice dead. That was it. Doesn't matter how.'

'Of course,' Loki smiled. He drummed his fingers together for a moment. 'But now it's a completely different story altogether, isn't it?'

Farden glowered. 'How'd you figure that?'

'This time, you each have your own daemon to fight, if you will pardon the pun. You with Samara, Ruin, sorry, *Durnus*, with his father, should he come down from the sky. Towerdawn has Saker. And of course you, Tyrfing, have that cough of yours,' Loki said, ticking off the names on his fingers. 'We all have our own separate battles to pitch and win.'

Tyrfing leant forward. 'I don't see you fighting any battle,' he croaked, deep in his throat.

Loki didn't seem fazed by the sharp look in the Arkmage's eye. 'Oh, I am. I'm right there with you,' he said. 'Don't you worry.'

Farden slapped the rock with his gauntlet, making Ilios jump in his sleep. 'Enough of this shit-talk, Loki, or I'll strangle you with the very cords you're trying to tug at. Go to sleep. Or whatever it is you god-shadows do. Just be quiet,' he ordered. Loki shrugged and just stared at the candle flame.

Another fit of coughing took Tyrfing, and Farden winced as he heard his uncle retch. His throat sounded as raw as a butcher's larder, like he was swallowing hot razors. He drew a circle in the snow and stabbed it with his metal finger until his uncle managed to catch his breath. Farden looked up. 'You okay?' he asked.

Tyrfing, eyes glistening with tears of strain, nodded, and even managed a smile. 'Fine,' he lied. Farden couldn't help but notice the tiny fleck of blood smeared across his uncle's lip. Tyrfing felt the stare, and wiped his mouth. Neither said anything. Farden went back to his drawings, Tyrfing leant against his gryphon, and Loki just smiled smugly to himself.

The world travelled through the bowels of night and came up for air in the morning. The sun made a cursory effort, barely summoning enough height to paint the sky a brighter shade of black.

Morning found Farden in a state of urgency. There were two burning issues on his mind that morning, as he rocked back and forth and muttered to himself. One was the cold. His toes had lost all feeling. His fingers were tingling. His lips were two strips of dead rubber. The cold had even seized his stubble, giving him a white beard of ice. It was unbearable.

The second was the powerful urge to piss.

The problem was simple. In a land where the breath froze in front of his face, what would it do to a man relieving himself? He had avoided the problem so far. It had been a smidgeon warmer the last time. Now he was afraid of freezing himself to the ground, or worse, freezing something else.

Farden got to his feet and strolled back and forth in what little space he had to manoeuvre. His boots kept sticking to the frost on the stone of their little ledge. Farden peeked over its edge at the black void below. *What a ridiculous situation this is*, he snapped at himself, *for a place to be so cold that a man is afraid to piss!* He did a little dance, making it worse. The cold now had a rival for unbearableness. He felt like he was going to pop.

'Oh for gods' sake. Come on, Farden,' he muttered, shuffling to the edge. 'Fortune favours the brave and all that.' Farden gasped as he felt the cold of his gauntlets in a place where no man should ever feel such a thing. For a moment, he thought the metal had become stuck, but it was just the numbness of his hand, sluggish to move. He breathed a sigh of relief.

And that was it. Farden threw caution to the wind, so to speak. He stood there, swaying, face torn between a mix of pleasure at the release, and of pain at the icy morning wind blowing around his nethers. Thankfully, it only took a minute.

When he was finished, Farden sat down right there on the edge, sighing and watching his breath turn to cloud. Some stars were still out and about in the lightening sky. Once again he found himself trying to guess their shapes, trying to figure out if they were friend or foe, and whether he would meet any soon enough.

It was then that a flicker in the sky caught his attention. A colour splashed against the black and grey of the morning, high in the cloudless rafters of the sky. Blues, swirling with deep greens. Disappearing there, dancing here, flowing like a ghostly river. The Wake.

Farden watched it for a time. It looked like what he imagined magick to look like, were it tangible. It was heading north, by the looks of it. Perhaps it was magick after all, he thought. He was in the midst of pondering this deep thought of thoughts when the Wake began to do something he had never seen before. Parts of it seemed to crystallise in the unreachable sky, and drift slowly to earth. Little grains of sand, blue, green, and white, fell like snowflakes to the ice below. They took an age to fall, and when they did, they lingered on the wastes, refusing to fade. Farden squinted. None had fallen near to their mountain, only on the undulating band of ice between the Tausenbar and the Spine. Farden watched them as they slowly began to drift north and slightly east, towards an outcrop of black rock that was separate from the two mountain ranges, standing alone like a lost cousin.

Farden got to his feet as if it would somehow aid his eyesight. The grains drifted so slowly in fact that it hardly seemed like they were moving at all. Farden suddenly remembered the spyglass he had taken from the ship, and whirled around to fish it out of his pack. He tugged the thing free and held it gingerly to his eye, careful of its cold metal rim. He swung it to the ice fields and scanned back and forth. Nothing. He looked up to get his bearings and a frown creased his brow. The grains had faded away. Farden was about to hurl the spyglass into thin air when a tiny glint of colour caught his eye, far to the northeast, by the lonely rocks. Farden lifted the spyglass and tweaked every lever and cog his fingers could find until the contraption focused. Even then it struggled with the distance and Farden had to rest it on his knee to keep it still. But there it was, trapped in his eyepiece. A single grain of light.

The mage watched it as it travelled across the ice. It was bigger than he had first suspected, more a lump than a grain, and a strange shape too. It fluttered like a half-snuffed candle. He could have sworn the thing had legs. It seemed to step across the ice rather than drift across it, plodding slowly and deliberately, as if it were in no rush, but knew it had a place to be. Like a condemned convict trudging towards his morning noose.

Farden squinted again, cursing his eyes. The thing had arms too. He could see them now. Hanging limply by its side. Did it have a head? Maybe. He couldn't tell. He looked again. The light it gave seemed to trail behind it, like the rags of a scarecrow in the wind. Farden snorted. What would a speck of light need with rags, or clothes, or hair?

Farden leant forward, almost forgetting for a moment that he had perched on the edge of the mountain. He watched, fascinated, as the light reached the base of a short cliff, where, if the shadows didn't deceive him, he spied a hollow filled with five tall stones. Farden got to his feet, nearly falling to his doom in the process.

Five stones. Five monoliths.

'Up! Get up!' Farden started pounding his gauntlet on his greaves, making a clanging sound. Ilios was up in seconds, claws at the ready. Tyrfing, his leaning spot suddenly transformed into an alert gryphon, floundered on the ground. Loki opened his eyes as if he had been awake the whole time. Both of them got to their feet and came to stand by Farden. He pointed at the tiny light in the distance, barely noticeable. They glimpsed it just before it faded into the ice. 'Gentlemen and gryphon, I think we've found ourselves a ghostgate,' Farden announced.

'What, there?' Tyrfing gestured for the spyglass. He winced at the cold of its metal.

'There indeed. Right where the Grimsayer said it would be. Barely a morning's flight,' Farden almost sounded excited.

'What was that light?' Loki asked, interested.

Farden shrugged. 'Well, I assume it was a ghost for the gate.'

'A soul, then,' Loki said, biting his lip.

'Whatever it is, it's where we're headed,' Farden paused as a shiver ran through his body. 'It's time to go,' he said.

❦

Pitted like pox-scars, the grey faces of the stones were a strange contrast to the black of the yawning hollow of the cliff behind them. They sat in a circle, an awkward, granite crown poking from the snow. Five identical stones, each of them massive and towering, no fewer than fifteen feet tall at a sound guess. Their points were sharp.

Their sides were sheer, ashen and sparkling in the morning glow. The runes and shapes that had once tattooed their surfaces were now eroded smooth and faint, whipped illegible by the wind and ice.

'Is this it?' Farden prodded the ground between the stones with his boot, making the snow creak. 'There's nothing here.' Nobody answered. Loki was silent and distracted. He stood a short distance away, facing south, his hands hanging limply by his sides. Ilios was off hunting. Tyrfing was also silent. He was busy scraping the ice away from one of the stones, trying to get at the runes beneath. He shrugged.

'Great. What's a gate that isn't a gate? A waste of time, that's what,' Farden muttered.

'So the light faded here, did it?' Tyrfing asked, casting around for something, anything. He had a cloth clamped over his mouth.

'Right here,' Farden stamped on the snow again. He took out his sword and prodded at the roots of the stones. Nothing budged. 'Nowhere.'

Loki turned around, his face catching the morning light and making his skin glow. Had Farden been in the mood to notice things, he might have noticed how strange it made him look. How solid it made him. 'Perhaps you have to be dead, to pass through the gate,' he said over his shoulder.

'By all means, god,' Farden snapped, 'be my guest.'

'That would be impossible.'

'Well, isn't that a sha…'

'Farden,' Tyrfing coughed, waving his hand. Farden raised his sword. He had heard it too. A scraping. A puff of snow falling down the cliff above them, trickling from one crag to the next, like a miniature avalanche. The two mages crept forward until they were under the lip of the cliff, backs to the rock. Loki stayed where he was, oblivious, or distracted, or both.

The mages watched the shadow of the cliff, a jagged black

line in the snow just beyond the furthest ghostgate stone. Farden pointed as a little shape popped up, and then disappeared. More snow trickled down. Another shape appeared, then another, and another, too small to be human, but too big to be a bird, or a rabbit. They could hear the scraping and tinkling of needle-claws on the rock above. Tyrfing and Farden pressed themselves against the cliff as something black and leathery flopped onto the snow in front of them.

It was a beastly little thing, that was for sure. All spindly limbs and feathers. Not quite a bat, but not quite a crow, and stuck somewhere in between. It was about the size of a cat, and had the tail of one too. Its beady little eyes hadn't seen them yet. They were fixed on Loki.

Another three of the little creatures came down to join the first. They crept forward, sniffing at the air, chattering softly, hungrily. Farden stepped forward, and calmly dug the point of his sword into the ice with a metallic ping. The creatures flinched. 'Stay where you are,' he warned, hoping they would understand. Surprisingly, they did. The creatures slowly turned to face him, baring clusters of jagged teeth, rammed into beaks several sizes too small for their faces. One of them shrieked at him, a horrible noise like a strangled bugle, but otherwise stayed put.

'Strangers,' it said in a hissing, bubbling voice, not unlike a pot coming to the boil, 'comes to stares at the gates.'

'We do,' Farden said. 'And what, pray, are you?'

The first shrieked again. 'We's ares the watchers. Watches the ghosts comes and goes.' The thing pointed the clawed stub of its leathery wing at patches of thin air. 'There's oneses. There's anothers,' it said, sniggering. Farden and Tyrfing looked around, wary. There was nothing except the stones and the snow.

Something rattled behind Farden and he felt a sharp pain on his neck. Another of the little creatures had jumped onto his back, sinking its claws through his cloak. Farden clenched his teeth and grabbed the thing by the neck. The others flapped and whined. 'Be quiet!' Farden yelled, holding the flapping, thrashing thing at arm's length. 'Be quiet, or I'll rip this one's head off quicker than you can blink.' There was a hissing as the things calmed, sagging into the snow. 'That's better,' said the mage. 'Now, what do you want?'

The first raised a claw, blinking its little black eyes. 'Hims,' it said, pointing at Loki. The god was still oblivious to all. 'He's not like yous.'

The creature in his grip squawked. 'Never mets a gods before!'

Farden threw the thing to the snow. It smelled like old meat and damp. 'He's none of your business. What are you creatures?'

'We's are the watchers!' cried the first.

'You said that, but *what* are you? What do you do here besides watch things?' Farden asked.

The beasts cackled amongst themselves. 'We's make sures the deads do as they's tolds.'

'Which is?'

'Go downs into the darks!'

'We's tells them their lives, if they wants to listens. Reads thems their pasts.'

'Ands their futures!'

'Eats their meats!'

Tyrfing sniffed. 'Fortune-tellers?'

The eyes of the creatures glittered. 'We's cans reads you yourses, if you pleases? For a prices!'

'Shrieks,' Farden muttered to his uncle. 'Fairytales were true after all.' He turned around to find the four Shrieks had gotten a little closer all of a sudden. They had gathered around his boots. Farden nudged one away with the flat of sword, but it crawled right back.

'Futures is all yous live oneses have,' one said.

'Pasts is all the deads oneses have,' another added.

Farden aimed a kick at the nearest Shriek. They smelled even worse in a group. They looked hungry too. 'Enough chatter. What do you know about the gate?'

'Everythings!'

'How do we get in it?'

'Impossibles for the live oneses!' cried the Shrieks, as one.

'Lies,' Farden grunted. 'It happened before. Korrin was his name. He wore armour like this.' Farden tapped his vambraces. The Shrieks fell silent. The breeze moaned through the stones, blowing a little snow in their faces. Tyrfing walked forward. His sword was out too. He flicked it up to hover barely an inch from the eye of the biggest Shriek.

'Show us the way, or we'll see to it that you never watch anything ever again,' he threatened, grunting his words. Farden nodded and twirled his own blade menacingly. They had no time to waste with politeness.

The big Shriek relented. 'Ones cames before. Before anys of us. Before anys of our eggs, or the eggs before that.'

'But you know of him?'

The Shrieks cackled, unfolding the story one by one. 'Storieses passed downs. Shriek to Shriek. We knows him. Korrins. Yesss.'

'Asked us for helps, he dids.'

'Asked us the ways in, he dids.'

'Helped hims in the ends.'

'Showed him the ways.'

'Gave us meats!'

Farden looked hungrily at the stones. 'Show us, like you showed him.'

The Shrieks fidgeted, creaking and rustling like slimy leather. A few moments passed. 'A prices,' one hissed. 'There's a prices for such knowledges.'

'Yes! A prices!' the Shrieks hopped up and down excitedly. 'He paid!'

'Whats can you offers us, in tradeses?'

'Meats?'

Farden smiled a very wild smile indeed. 'Of course,' he said, gently. Laying his sword across his knees, he slowly crouched down and bent a finger to the Shrieks. They shuffled forward eagerly to hear their prize. Farden looked at each and every one, still smiling all the while, before he answered. 'How about,' he began, 'you show us the way through this gate here, or we tie you all up in neat bundles, make you watch as we build a little roasting fire, and cook you all on spits. Alive, of course. One by one, so the rest can watch. You can even try a bit too, if you like. We're more than happy to share.' The mage grinned maniacally. 'How does that sound?'

The Shrieks had begun to shake by that point. The big one licked its beak with a blue tongue and nodded. 'We's accepts your kind offers. This ways please.'

Farden stood up and winked at his uncle. Tyrfing just nodded. Farden assumed he was smiling under the handkerchief wrapped around his mouth. It was stained with blood.

The Shrieks shuffled quickly into the circle of stones and spread out, each Shriek to a stone. They began to scratch around in the snow, looking for something. Whatever it was, they soon found it. The snow in the circle began to fizzle and spit, melting away until a hole had been cut in the ice, just wide enough to swallow a man. Farden went over to it, keeping his sword at the ready lest it be a trick by the Shrieks. But they were silent, busy hugging their stones.

Farden looked down into the hole, and was not entirely surprised to find it filled with water, At its ice-white rim, the water was a deceptively pleasant azure, but as the hole burrowed deeper, it turned the colour of a cobalt ink, painfully dark and disturbingly deep. Farden leant over to try to see the bottom. It was nowhere to be seen;

just the thick darkness of the water. He couldn't even tell if it had a bottom.

'What's this?'

'The gateses,' hissed the nearest Shriek.

'No, this is a hole full of water.'

'Thats *is* the gates, strangers.'

'Yous must jumps in. Be swalloweds.'

Farden nodded. 'Of course. What else?' he asked, throwing his hands up in the air. 'What else but a watery grave.'

'Farden, if...' Tyrfing stepped forward.

His nephew held up a hand. 'Not a chance in...' Farden paused, realising the irony of his reply. Before he could continue, the Shrieks hissed collectively. Loki stood behind him.

'What's this?' he asked, gesturing to the hole. He didn't seem bothered by the Shrieks.

'Our way in.'

Loki pulled a face full of mock-sympathy. 'Oh, and just to think, you don't like water,' he said. It was no surprise that he soon found Farden's fingers around his throat. Farden tried to grip him, but his fingers must have been numb. They barely responded. 'Mages first,' Loki said, nonchalantly.

'Gah!' Farden grunted. He slid his sword into its scabbard and stepped up to the edge of the hole. Some of the ice crumbled away and drifted down into the darkness. He met the eyes of the Shrieks. 'If this is some kind of trick...' he warned.

They all shook their heads solemnly. 'Korrins dids the very sames. Alls those yearses ago,' said one.

'It's the only ways!' cried another.

Farden nodded glumly. He looked up at Tyrfing. 'You still want to come?'

'I'll be right behind you,' said his uncle, sheathing his own blade.

'Well,' Farden muttered. *This was it*. The moment he had been dreaded ever since Nelska. His chest was already painfully tight, his breathing deep and panicked. His thoughts flicked back to the feel of a rope around his neck, and the spindly, skeletal arms of a tree reaching to the heavens above him. He closed his eyes, and pushed that all away, all except how quick it had been, how painless in the end. It had been like going to sleep.

It had been like going to sleep.

A vulture-headed ship made of fingernails.

Just like going to sleep.

A horde of dead things and shadows pushing him into the cold water.

Like going to sleep.

The helplessness, dangling in the wind like a ghoulish fruit, feeling his heart throbbing sullenly, slowly.

Going to sleep.

The feeling of numbness, of the cold, of the finality of it all. Of dying in a watery hole, bloated, useless, and forgotten!

Korrin.

Of death. Of feared, dreaded death. Here it was again. Everything he had always tried to escape, everything he had already escaped, and here he was, jumping back into it once more! Going back to Hel. *Hel*, of all places. Farden couldn't believe what he was thinking. He tried to remember the words of Roiks, of Lerel, of Eyrum, of Modren's handshake in the Arkathedral. Farden clenched his jaw. It was madness, but sometimes, madness is exactly what is needed, when all rational thought has faded.

'Elessi!' Farden roared as he jumped. The water swallowed him whole, with a barely a splash. In half a second he was gone, down into the inky-blackness. Tyrfing looked up at Loki, who was staring wide-eyed at the hole.

'I didn't think he would do it,' said Loki, seemingly

impressed.

'That's my nephew,' Tyrfing said. He took the handkerchief from his mouth and tossed it aside, accidentally throwing it in the face of one of the Shrieks. It hissed as he stepped up to the hole. He cleared his raw throat and jumped, no words or thoughts or roars for him. He was gone like Farden, in seconds.

Alone, Loki stepped up to the hole, ponderous and slow. The Shrieks were muttering something around him, chanting it almost. 'Tell me,' he said to them, 'have you ever read the future of a god?' he asked. He had been listening all along.

The Shrieks fidgeted, creeping a little closer. 'Nevers!' one burbled excitedly.

'Then what are you waiting for?'

And so they told him. Down to the last letter and detail, they shrieked and hissed his fortune, loud to the sky, and to the cliff, and to the rocks. Everything he had already planned, everything he hadn't, and everything else in between. One by one and all at once they spoke it unto him, and he listened hard.

When they were finished, Loki fastened his coat and kicked the edge of the icy hole. 'And to think,' he chatted idly, with a smirk, 'I'm the child of a lesser god. Who would have thought it?'

The sapphire water took him too.

Chapter 26

"Report to Lord Vice, year 885. From Durnus, minder of the 9th Albion Arkabbey.

Lord Vice, I trust this letter finds you well. In regards to the skirmishes in Efjar, I humbly request that you consider Farden for decoration at the celebration feast. Against all odds, and you and I both know to which particular incident I refer, Farden has persevered. Not only that, and by all verbal accounts, he has performed excellently and consistently in the face of tribulation, fear, and overwhelming odds. And let us not forget his outstanding feat of saving an entire camp of soldiers and mages. It is for these reasons that I wholeheartedly believe he deserves this decoration. Let it not be wasted on some jaundiced, high-born son of a council member. Forgive me speaking frankly.

Sincerely,

Durnus."

From a letter found in Arkmage Vice's rooms, after the Battle of Krauslung

Clunk.

The phalanx of Written dug their wide shields into the snow and readied their spells. There were swords strapped to their backs, ready for blood. Knives, daggers, dirks, all splayed across their chests. Pikes and spears waiting in the snow by their knees. They made a truly fearsome sight.

Behind them, Modren strolled back and forth, eyeing the sky between the black rock and the frozen waterfall. He watched the distant eagle circling for a moment, before raising two fingers to it. A few of the Written and the other mages chuckled.

'Another bloody spy, keeping us on our toes,' he spat in the deep snow, as gloomy as a stormy morning. 'Five days,' he said, 'and all we see is spies and shadows. Not a sign of a real fight, eh lads and ladies?'

'No sir!' grunted the crowd, the Written louder than the rest combined. *Twenty-four,* Modren counted again, wishing there were more. Around sixty mages stood behind him, and a couple of hundred soldiers and sailors beyond that. It was nothing but a handful, compared to what he would have liked, but what a mean handful it was. Calloused, seasoned, and strong. His Written were its claws. Sharp, they were, sharper than ever.

Modren could feel it just as much as the next mage. Every day they travelled north, the more and more they felt the magick. It woke them up in sweats. It made their hands shiver. It made their heads spin and pound. But more importantly, it made them stronger than ever before. Modren felt like a daemon himself. He itched for battle.

Hence his sour mood. Samara had disappeared from the face of the earth. She was no doubt far, far north by now. *Probably already surrounded by swarms of daemons and fallen stars,* Modren cursed. All they had seen of her and her army was shadows in the frozen trees, ravens and eagles circling above, cackles in the darkness, maybe a wolf or two circling their camp at night. Distractions. Hindrances. Every time something was sighted, they stopped, expecting another ambush. It made the going slow and aching.

'Five days,' Modren spat again, as he saw Eyrum leading Durnus to the front of the line. 'Five days,' the mage was ranting.

'Calm yourself, Undermage,' Durnus cautioned. 'We're close.' He gestured to the north, where he could see in his darkness a faint, yet gigantic blotch. Mountains, he had been told. The Spine itself. When the wind blew the right way they could hear the distant roaring of the fires and molten rock deep in the unreachable chasms of the Roots.

Modren lowered his voice to a whisper. He was angry, but he was wise enough to bear morale in mind. 'Not close enough, not for my liking. Five days is a long time by foot. She had dragons, last time I saw. And those daemons can fade in and out of wherever they please, if I remember rightly,' he said. 'They're miles ahead. Leagues.'

Eyrum had been listening to this sort of rant for the past three days. His stoic silence was wearing thin. 'And what would you like to do about it, Undermage?' he asked, also in a low voice.

Modren looked up at him and sniffed. Eyrum raised his hands. 'Shall we ask what dragons we have to fly these sleds north, one by one? Shall we abandon the snowmad women and children and sprint on, just the mages and soldiers?'

Modren crossed his arms. 'I know there's nothing we can do, Siren, but that doesn't stop me being angry about it,' he muttered, darkly. 'It's a shitty situation for all involved.'

'Such is war,' Eyrum shrugged.

'Such is survival,' added Durnus.

Modren tutted and stamped his foot in the thick snow. 'Up and in line!' he ordered. 'We're moving on. Double-time. Let's see if these dragons and moles can keep up!' he said, throwing Eyrum a look. He went to go march at the head of the column with his Written.

Apparently a dragon was well-suited to pulling a sled, so long as they didn't swish their tails. Only the snow caused a problem. After negotiating the Tausenbar, the ice fields had become more undulating, more treacherous, a landscape of snowdrifts, buried forests, and frozen rivers. The dragons' feet were suited to rock, not to deep snow, and like the boots of those that walked beside them, they sank with every step. It was tiring, bothersome, going.

The column was in the middle of negotiating a narrow pass between two spurs of black rock poking up out of the earth. Broken trees hung over them like strange ornaments, dark against the bright white sky. The only colour in the pass was the faint blue of the frozen waterfalls splayed against the rocks, one every hundred yards or so.

Eyrum and Durnus watched half the column pass before they met Towerdawn. The dragon glittered in the cold, afternoon sun. He looked tired, but he didn't dare pause. Eyrum and Durnus clambered aboard his sled while it was still moving. 'One more day,' he called back to them, 'and we shall be at the Spine. It is an age since we travelled so far north. An age.'

'And I am sure that none of us particularly intend to again. Not after this journey,' Durnus said. Towerdawn chuckled, a deep rasping sound in his scaled belly. He trudged on, making the ice snap and crackle with every heavy step. His breathing was loud. Steam gushed from his nostrils and open mouth, like every other dragon in the column.

For every ordeal, there was a blessing, and for the brave souls going north, it was the reinforcements that had gathered to them in the past few days. Snowmads of all tribes had come wandering out of the snow and darkness to join them. Some had brought their own sleds, others had come on foot, or by ice-bear. They had brought sabre-cats, white eagles, and even stranger beasts of the ice fields. And others too. Durnus had recognised their scent from afar. Wild men of Dromfangar, drawn by the magick perhaps, or the thought of war. They travelled apart from the column, not too close, yet not too far. They had chosen their side, and the Arka and Sirens were glad for it. Every man and beast counted.

Durnus had picked up another scent too. Vampyres. The odour was unmistakable. They travelled with the wild men. Perhaps even lycans too, if the wind wasn't lying to him. Tame, yet fierce, like he had been; more man than beast but just as dangerous as both. He kept silent about it, but found himself somewhat comforted. Every man and beast counted. Everything in between counted too.

Barely an hour passed before they had to stop again. A shout for them to halt trickled down the line, and everybody came to a sighing halt. Steam rose in great clouds from the column. Durnus and Eyrum got down from the sled with sighs of their own, wondering what eagle, or wolf, or fox, or fallen branch had brought them to a halt now. They had barely trudged a dozen paces when a dark shadow skimmed the tops of the sleds. Something huge and feathery. It screeched when it saw the two of them, and turned so violently that it would have made even the best of dragons vomit.

Ilios came crashing to the snow, whistling and burbling in a stream of agitated nonsense. Durnus held up his hands and found the gryphon's beak. 'Calm, Ilios. What is it? Slowly, boy.'

Ilios took a gasping little breath and began again, this time a little slower. Durnus' lips moved as the gryphon spoke, his mouth getting a little wider with every sentence. Modren came jogging back down the column, and caught the latter half of the conversation. 'And so they're gone?' he asked.

Ilios clacked his beak.

Eyrum scratched his head. 'And what is *that*?' he asked, pointing at the dead, dark lump in Ilios' claws. Ilios lifted it up between two talons and let it flop onto the snow, a little of its sickly blue blood splattering on the snow. He whistled. He hadn't a clue.

'What is it, Eyrum?' asked Durnus.

The Siren nudged it with his foot. 'It looks like a raven, but with skin instead of feathers. And a tail. A feathery, fluffy tail. Like a cat, almost. I truly don't know.'

Modren knelt down to prod it. It wheezed as he did so, dead air escaping from its lungs. It already smelled rotten. 'It looks like a scruffy sort of bat to me.'

Ilios warbled something.

'These were there when you returned?' asked Durnus. A confirmatory whistle. 'Did they speak? Could they speak?' Another whistle. 'Well, what did they say?' Ilios looked between the Siren and the Arkmage, and licked the edge of his beak. He made a low, growling sound.

'They said they were dead,' mumbled Modren.

Much to everyone's surprise, Durnus clapped his hands together and smiled. 'At last!' he cried. Modren let his jaw dangle open. The Arkmage looked sightlessly around. 'Do you not see?' he asked. The others shook their heads numbly. Durnus smiled even wider. 'They have done it. They have found their way in, or down, or whichever. Were their bodies by these rocks, Ilios?' The gryphon whistled a *no*. 'Then if they had been slain by these things, there would be bodies. The other side is for souls, not for skin. You leave that behind. Do you see now? Wherever they've gone, they've gone alive.'

'I have to say, your logic is pretty shaky there, Durnus,' Modren sighed.

'And I have to agree with the Undermage,' Eyrum winced.

'Doubt me all you want, gentlemen. I have my faith. Or at least my hope. And so should you, Modren. Of all people here,' Durnus countered. Modren looked suitably chastised by that. He quickly excused himself, chin tucked to his chest, and headed towards the end column, towards a sled pulled by an emerald dragon. The others didn't have to guess where he was going. They knew what, or rather, whom, lay in that sled.

☙

Eyrum put the whetstone aside and tested the edge of his axe with his thumb. Sharp enough to cleave a skull, that was for sure. And shoulders. And ribs. And anything else that got in its way. He licked his dry, wind-chapped lips and looked around, sniffing the air.

It was the middle of the night, more morning than anything else, and yet he wasn't alone in being awake. Half the camp, now swollen to a scattered thousand or so, seemed to be awake. The night winds were joined by the whining, scraping song of stones against steel. The clank and batter of mail being repaired, armour being fastened. The low mutter of voices. The stink of oil and liquid courage. The sounds and odours of an army readying to fight. Music to the backdrop of the constant and never-ending rumbling of the volcanoes.

'I swear I had another morning, just like this,' Eyrum whispered.

'And if I remember rightly, we were the ones springing the trap,' Lerel nodded.

Eyrum flicked his axe-blade with a fingernail, making it sing. 'Waiting to strike.'

Durnus was standing outside the sled, facing down the cold. He was staring northwards. 'I think I missed that one.'

'I remember it well,' Towerdawn rumbled. 'Only then I had Aelya, and my armour too.' He looked wistfully south. They could see the pain in his face.

Eyrum checked his armour, battered and frozen as it was. Half of it was clogged with snow that was quickly turning to ice. The other half was quickly turning to rust. He pounded his chest with his mallet-like fist and checked the straps. He wrinkled his lip. 'Looks like we'll have to make do.'

'Any sign out there, you two?' Lerel called. She was nervously fidgeting with a shortsword.

Heimdall grunted something incomprehensible and grumpy. The god was useless around so much magick, and it had put him in a dark mood. The world was just noise and light to him now. Making sense of it was like trying to listen to a harp in a gale, or catch a puddle in the ocean. It made his head want to explode. It was no wonder that he had a face like a storm giant's backside.

'Nothing,' Durnus said. It should have been easier, there in the foothills, where everything around them was painted a deep, dark red by the giant volcanoes of the Spine, the Roots. A deep, blood red. Disconcertingly so.

'Here comes another one,' Eyrum said, catching a flicker from the corner of his eye. Everybody turned to see yet another bubbling, sizzling rock rocket high into the black sky. It puffed and it spat, making a great fuss before it reached its zenith and plummeting downwards. Just before it came to its explosive end amongst the distant crags, it cast its light across the foothills just beyond their camp. Every head in the camp turned, every eye squinted, straining to catch a glimpse of something in the rocks. Anything.

Nothing.

Towerdawn said as much. The Old Dragon placed his chin in the snow and listened to it hiss against his hot lips. 'Not a sign,' he sighed.

'Curse all this waiting,' Modren said, appearing out of the crimson shadows. There were streaks on his face. Maybe dust. Maybe oil smears. Maybe tears. Nevertheless he was armed to the teeth. Two swords were strapped to his shoulders, followed by an array of various sharp and pointy objects stuffed through the belts across his chest. There was a bow in his hand, a quiver at his hip, and a throwing axe stuck in his boot. He looked on the verge of comical. His eyes dared anyone to say it. 'Curse it all,' he repeated. He perched on the yoke of the sled.

'They'll attack just before sunrise, when the light is poor and the shadows are at their longest. When they think we're still asleep. That's when I would do it,' Eyrum spoke as he stroked his axe.

'Well, in the meantime, I am sure you can all take in the sights. Not many in our history have made it this far north. Not many at all,' Durnus waved his hand across the sky, wishing he could see it. 'Think of where we are. The very centre of creation. The bones of our earth. These fires have never been extinguished. They have burned for millennia.'

'And longer,' rumbled Heimdall.

The others looked up at the dizzyingly high peaks that dominated the bruised sky for as far as the eye could see, for as far as the mind could imagine. Jagged crowns of black rock and soot, biting at the sky. Their sheer faces were aglow with the countless fires that burned at their hearts. Orange, murky red, sulphurous yellow. Rivers of fire and molten rock no doubt, swirling around their bases. Some of the mountains, far, far in the distance, even spewed fire from their peaks, or belched smoke into the sky where lightning came to flit and flutter. They could hear the rumbling of those peaks on the breeze, dangerous and thankfully distant. The Spine and its Roots were hostility incarnate.

'Are you sure we haven't travelled to the other side by mistake?' asked Modren, scratching his head.

Durnus pulled a face. 'No, we are still very much in the world of the living.'

'I for one, would like to keep it that way,' Eyrum grunted. He pointed at the sky. 'And here comes another,' he pointed at the sky.

They all watched as another rock rose and fell. It was a tiny one, and it sputtered out halfway through its fall. 'Pathetic,' muttered Heimdall, rubbing his eyes. A silence came with a gust of wind. Nobody could think of anything to fill it with. The Spine did it for them.

All of a sudden, the cold breeze turned unnaturally warm. It was a strange sensation after having frozen cheeks for so many days. Everybody in the camp seemed to feel it. Lights flickered in every sled in the column as feet slid into boots and cloaks were quickly wriggled on. Dark shapes began to fill the ice around them. Still nobody said a word.

In the wake of the wind came an almighty bang, loud enough to pop the ears of everyone in the camp. There were words aplenty now, fearful, agitated words, growing in volume as the northern sky grew hotter and hotter. The bloody red turned carmine, then scarlet, then a fierce orange. The ice changed colour with it. Yellow came soon after: a hot, sulphurous yellow that stained and smoked the sky. Black pillars of ashen grey smoke rose from the nearest peaks. The ice began to tremble under their feet. The dragons roared involuntarily, and so did the wild men. Their bellows and screeches joined the rumbling of the earth as the Spine belched forth rock after burning rock. They filled the sky like fireworks. Some exploded in mid-air while others tumbled, spitting fire as they crashed to the rocks below, unnervingly close now.

'Pull the sleds back!' Towerdawn yelled, and his dragons went to work. It was not a moment too soon. Little pebbles began to rain down on them, sharp little bastards that slipped under collars and into pockets and burned as they went down. Yells filled the camp. Indignant, confused yells. This was worse than war. A war they could fight, but a burning mountain? No. Foolish.

The dragons threw their weight into the sleds and shoved them back, a hundred yards at a time. The pebbles and stones clattered on their scales like heavy rain on a tabletop, bouncing harmlessly off. The dragons hauled sled after sled until the snowmads mustered their jittery moles and tackled the rest. 'Take the sleds back into the ice and form a line, east to west. A battle line!' Towerdawn roared to them, hoping they would understand. His spines prickled as he watched them turn about and retreat. Something was making his skin crawl, and it wasn't the stones.

Light splashed the snow. Slowly, he turned to watch an enormous missile rise up into the sulphurous sky, like a falling star changing its mind at the very last minute. It climbed high into the air, almost rivalling the tallest of the peaks, until at last its weight caught up with it. It teetered in mid-air, burning like a battling mage, and then exploded into a hundred sizzling fragments in a burst of brilliant white light. What was left of the night's darkness was unceremoniously tossed aside.

And there she was.

And there they were.

They filled every nook and crag. They stood knee-deep in the snow-drifts. They crowded on every slope and hilltop. Men and beasts stood silent and waiting.

She stood above them all, halfway up a tall hill, standing in a hollow shaped like the seat of a throne. Flanked by two dragons, two daemons, and two giant wolves, she stood with her arms crossed. Towerdawn thought he saw a smile on her lips as the light faded away.

The others had seen them too. 'Lines! Draw those lines!' Modren could be heard shouting to his mages. Eyrum was barking orders too, Durnus clinging to his arm as they sprinted across the snow towards the sleds. Sunrise, it seemed, had come a little early.

※

'Are you ready, girl?'

Samara grit her teeth. It felt like a storm was welling up inside her, burning her insides, making her bones shake. It had started in the night. Like a venom creeping into her veins. A sickening, dizzying venom, it wracked her body from head to toe. A glorious venom. One she had been waiting for. Magick, in all its glory.

'I said, are you ready, girl?' Hokus asked again.

'As I'll ever be,' she squeaked, through the pain. It had become too painful to keep it in, but thankfully, it was now time to turn it loose. She was ready to try again.

'Good,' Hokus grinned. He looked up at the yellow sky and

rubbed his hands. By his side, Valefor began to laugh. 'Then, by all means, my dear cousin, tear down the sky.'

Despite the pain, Samara managed a little smile. The roar of the volcano was loud in her ears. It sounded like applause, a countless crowd all clapping frantically for her, eager to see her begin her act. 'Better not keep them waiting,' she said.

Chapter 27

"The dead are dead and dead they will stay."
Siren proverb

It was a day of déjà vu for more than just Eyrum. Farden was feeling its poison too.

Breathe! his brain screamed at his mouth. His mouth refused.

Swim! cried his legs, but the cold was too gripping, his body too heavy.

Grab hold of something! he bellowed at his hands, feeling precious air escape his lips in a stream of bubbles, sliding over his numb face.

He reached out, half expecting to find a crate, or a cat, in his hands. But this was no storm, no sinking *Sarunn*. His hands met solid, sharp ice, and nothing but. It would have cut his fingers had they not been clasped in steel. He felt it rushing by as he sank, like a ten-tonne brick in the sea. He could feel the pressure mounting on his skull, on his ribs, as though a dozen trolls had set about turning him to pulp.

Farden dared to open his eyes and found them stung by the bitter cold. Water shoved its way under his eyelids and near ripped them off as it rushed by him. He shut them again, but not before he realised he saw how pitch black his surroundings were.

There was ice water in his veins. *How?!* his brain screamed again. He could feel it stabbing every joint and every bone as it swirled around his body. He twitched in the inky darkness.

Something kicked him in the head and he lashed out. But it was gone all too quickly.

Breathe! his brain commanded again, and this time his mouth obeyed, against all his might. Ice-water, so cold it felt like it would crack his teeth, gushed in and filled his throat. He swallowed, trying to find some saviour in it, but it was thick and oily and colder than any night on any mountain. Icicles stabbed his lungs, pierced his heart, and ran him through.

Farden swallowed again, and that time he felt an old, familiar friend in the water with him. A friend as cold as the water itself. A friend called death. It seized his flailing hands. It calmed his legs. It opened his mouth and let the water flood in. It even kindly numbed the pain for him as his insides gave up on him. Farden felt the water tug, but he didn't care. Something struck him the face, but he shrugged it off. The water was his friend now. As faithful as a grave.

I'm sorry, he told it. *I tried.*

※

Farden awoke by a river, a blue ribbon of a river lined with smooth, patchwork pebbles. Blue, grey, black, orange, they all quivered as the clear, cold water flowed over them. Farden listened to it burble. It sounded like words. A thousand different words with voices all swirled and mashed together. Farden listened to the voices, and smiled. So many of them, all of them telling their tale.

Soon enough he became aware of another sound: the gentle crackle of soft feet sliding carefully across pebbles. Farden sat up, feeling dizzy, and found himself in a huge cave, lit by bright lights he could not see. He heard the sound again and turned to see a faint outline of a crooked old man trudging across the pebbles, parallel to the calm river. It was not deep, and yet he seemed reticent to cross it, even at the shallowest points where the pebbles of its bed broke the surface.

Farden got to his feet, stumbled, and then tried again. His legs were foreign to him, as though he had borrowed another's for a time. He looked down and found red and gold steel staring back at him. Clean, polished, flecked with droplets of ice-water. They were marvellous things. He wondered whose they were.

Farden opened his mouth to call to the old man but his throat was too cold to work. He felt like a lead weight, striding across the pebbles, but step by step he did it. The man was hobbling so slowly that he caught him in no time.

'Old man,' he rasped, when he was near. 'Old man.'

The man was staring straight ahead, eyes beady and eager over a lip of a bedraggled old scarf. He was barely visible in the bright light of the cave. A mere shadow at most, but Farden could still see the sores on his brow, his cheeks, and his bare arms. He wore thick gloves and walked carefully, as if he were going to fall at any minute, as though a lifetime had been spent doing exactly that. A leper, if Farden didn't know better.

He looked old and beaten and Farden couldn't help but stare. He had seen this man before. 'Where are you going, old man?' he asked, through a throat that wasn't his. More bright metal caught his eye, and he looked down to see that his hands were wrapped in it. He clenched his fists, and the very end finger on his left hand remained upright. Farden moved to touch it, but before he could he heard the old man speaking.

'One step away from the grave. One step away from the grave,' he was mumbling.

'Come again?' Farden asked, but the man didn't answer. He hobbled on, and Farden was left frowning, searching for a memory that had never been, in a mind like a dark void. Farden followed. It was the right thing to do, though he knew not why.

The river by their side was running deeper now. The cave grew narrower. The lights became brighter. More shadows joined them, crowding between the cave wall and the shingled riverbank. Soon enough they were shuffling along in a group. Farden, and a bunch of shadows. He was glad to be one of them.

※

Tyrfing sat up with a start. Loki was standing over him, holding out a hand. The mage pushed it aside, struggled to his feet on his own, and then promptly fell over.

'The cold, I imagine,' Loki said, going to look at the river. It was deep and cold, its bank made of smooth pebbles.

'Where is my nephew?' Tyrfing hissed, from his position, sprawled in the pebbles. His throat was on fire.

Loki looked around, as if only just noticing that it was just the two of them. 'He isn't here,' he said.

'That's rather obvious,' snapped Tyrfing, as he tried his feet once more. They seemed sound enough this time. He walked in a wide circle, craning his neck to stare at the lofty roof of a long, giant cave, at the multicoloured pebbles, and at Loki dipping his fingers in the river. 'Well, where is he? More to the point, where are we?'

'I don't know, I just woke up. Same as you,' Loki said. Tyrfing wasn't quite sure whether to believe him. Farden's suspicions were rubbing off on him. 'But I would hazard an educated guess at Hel. The tunnels that birthed the daemons, when the first sparks…'

'Yes, yes, I know the stories. So we made it.'

'Look,' Loki pointed. Tyrfing looked.

Two shadows were making their way across the stones, heading away from them and upriver. They seemed nervous and careful, picking their way across the smooth stones with precision, as only the elderly would. Another quickly joined them, seemingly from nowhere, only this one was smaller, a child, probably no more than ten by her size. Her only clothes seemed to be a sack, stained black with coal or oil or blood. She traipsed behind the older shadows, matching them step for step.

Loki was after them like a shot. Tyrfing tried his best to keep up, wobbling from side to side on his numb legs. 'Where have you got to now, Farden?' he muttered to himself.

※

'What is this place?' Farden asked a shadow beside the old man. He was tall, rugged. A farmer by the looks of his clothes. He too was staring straight ahead, as though his eyes were glued in place. His lips moved though, and he spoke in a faint voice, stolen by an invisible wind.

'To the *Naglfar*.'

'Naglwhat?' Farden cupped a hand around his ear, feeling the cold of his metal hand. Strange, to be so dead and yet still feel so cold. He hoped it wouldn't last long.

'The deadship.'

'The crossing.'

'The boatman.'

'The other side,' came the whispers from all around him. The shadows jostled him as they walked. Their pace had quickened. Even the crooked old leper by his side was hobbling along as fast as he could. Farden followed suit.

At a bend in the river, the cave opened out into a huge vault, its roof so high that mist hung to the distant ceiling. He could barely make out its edges. Creamy stalactites punctured its thick tendrils, looking for all the world like upside down mountains. The river here was thick and wide and running fast. The shadows, the dead, gathered at its banks in their hundreds and thousands. Mist hung at the edges of the crowds too. There could have been millions there, buried in the haze. Farden gawped. All of them jostled for space. Never before had whispers been so deafening.

'I've been here before,' he said aloud. The crowd of shadows behind him laughed without smiling, or barely even moving their lips at all. One, a pale man with a face half-crushed and broken, shook his head.

'You don't get to see this place and leave, friend.'

'What is it then?' Farden asked. Something was itching in the back of his mind. Vacantly, he reached up to scratch his head, and then paused halfway.

'Where the dead come,' growled another, a huge minotaur with a twisted horn. Its lips had barely moved.

'The ship!' a thousand voices whispered around him. And there it was.

❦

'Where are they all going?' Tyrfing asked.

'I thought you knew the stories?' Loki sneered. For some reason he was walking very closely to the shadows, arms outstretched as if he were readying himself to hug one of them. Whether it was a trick of these ghostly lights, Tyrfing couldn't tell, but the god seemed to be glowing. Tyrfing squinted at him, and then huffed. *Trick of the light for sure*, he told himself.

'Forgive me,' grunted the Arkmage, 'I'm not that familiar with Hel.'

'That you aren't. These are the dead. They are making their way to the other side.'

Tyrfing looked around at the ever-growing crowds. His eyes ached trying to fathom their numbers. He was trying his hardest not to touch them. 'There are thousands of them. More.'

'Tens of thousands. Such are the dead.'

'And they all pass through here?'

'All by one ship.'

'Ship?'

Loki nodded. 'That's right.'

Tyrfing put the toe of his boot in the river. Even through the thick leather he could feel its deadly cold. 'A ship, in this?'

'Just you wait,' Loki said, distracted again by another crowd of shadows moving closer to the river. Closer, but not too close. The god pressed himself close to them. Tyrfing rubbed his eyes. Loki was shivering now, wriggling even, like heat rising from a flame, or a hand passing behind mottled glass.

'Curse this strange place,' he coughed. It was playing tricks with his eyes.

As it turned out, he did not have to wait long. Soon enough they came to where the long cave opened out into a cavern that would have swallowed the Arkathedral in one mouthful. Mist, cloud maybe, lingered at the top of it, wrapping the sharp stalactites like wool around teeth. Grey lichen clung to the rough, grey walls, climbing up into oblivion. The river grew wide here. Wide and deep. It hissed against the pebbles, adding to the susurrus of whispering and gentle crunching of the countless, endless, dead feet.

Tyrfing stared at them all, wide-eyed and disbelieving. He had never seen so many living people in one place, never mind the dead. They jostled for space as they pressed forward to the river, reticent to touch its waters, and yet eager to cross it.

It was then that the ship came. It materialised out of the dark fog on the far, far side of the monochrome cavern. Even from there, Tyrfing could see that it was a ship like no other. It was tall and imposing, sharp-sided like a knife on its side. Its dimensions were uneven and irregular, and its masts were crooked, bereft of sails.

Closer and closer it crept, unaffected by the rushing of the river, seemingly travelling at its own unhurried pace. Obviously, the dead could wait. Tyrfing pressed forward to see more of it. The shadows around him were cold. He swore he could feel frigid breath on the back of his neck. He pulled his collar up and stifled some more coughing. Loki was ahead of him somewhere, a solid pillar of life amongst a sea of ghosts. Well, almost. He was the closest thing Tyrfing had. *Where in Hel is Farden?* he wondered.

The ship pulled lazily alongside the shore, several hundred yards up the riverbank. Something ungodly and horrible was shrieking and screeching amidst the crowd, but what it was, Tyrfing couldn't see. Before he could ask Loki, the crowd surged like ocean swell, carrying them towards the ship. Loki seemed to melt into the shadows. Tyrfing pushed and shoved and fought his way along. He didn't like this one bit.

'Farden!' he began to call, as loud as his raw throat would let him.

Every step they took towards the strange ship, the more of it Tyrfing could make out. He grimaced as he peered at its rough, uneven sides. Stone? *No*, he told himself. Not possible. Metal? *No, too flaky, too rugged, pockmarked*. No smith could have made this. The crowd of shadows swelled, and suddenly he was at the riverbank, standing with his feet in the water. Tyrfing squinted at the ship, now barely fifty yards ahead.

Nails.

Of the finger and toe sort. Millions of nails stuck together with tar and resin and glue and things Tyrfing didn't even want to consider. Dead nails. He felt bile rising in his throat. *By the gods, the entire thing...* he inwardly gasped. He didn't dare look at the figurehead too closely. Out of the corner of his vision he saw it moving. Heard it screaming.

'Farden!' he cried again. He delved back into the dead and pushed them left and right, jumping up and down to glimpse anything that resembled something solid, something *alive*. 'Farden! Can you hear me?!'

There. He saw him, rushing headlong where the crowd was at its thickest. The roar of whispers was deafening now. Tyrfing barged his way through the pressing crowd, so cold even though they were so close and pressing in on him. His breath came in great steaming gasps. 'Farden!' he cried.

᳀

'I have seen this before,' Farden muttered again. If his feet were moving he didn't feel it. The crowd bore him up and carried him along, icy and clammy, just like him. Farden felt his eyelids grow heavy, his head loll. He could have sworn he had something to do, but it all seemed so distant, so forgotten now. So bothersome.

The ship came close to the shore and Farden heard the scrape of the yellow keel on the shingle. The dead pressed forward again as gangplanks were lowered to the stones. Farden looked at them dazedly. They looked like they were made from crushed shell, sand maybe.

'You're lucky,' said a voice in his ear, like cold worms slithering around in his hair. Farden didn't mind.

'Lucky?' he asked. 'How so?'

'Most wait an age for the ship,' sighed another. Farden didn't see their faces.

'The *Naglfar* will take us all in the end.'

Farden flinched involuntarily as a shriek ripped through the rustling and whistling. 'All aboard!' came the cry, a foul cry from a foul beak, rasping and thick with centuries of mucus. Farden could see something moving at the head of the ship. He blinked. A vague memory tugged at him. He held himself back against the crowd for a moment.

'Wait...' he said.

'Stop!' came another cry. Farden turned his head. He could see colours flashing through the translucent grey-blue of the crowd. Their shapes bent and warped by the blank faces and shoulders of the dead, like images warped by bent glass. Pink, brown, gold, silver, these weren't the colours of things here. Farden flailed his hands.

A shot of fire sprang up into the air. Just high enough to get attention. It crackled and puffed into smoke above the ship. Another flew up, and murmurs rippled through the crowd. Farden blinked owlishly.

'Back!' screamed the beast at the bow.

'Back,' Farden mouthed. 'You do not belong.' Words plucked from a dream by a curved and bloody beak. He shrugged. 'I tried. I tried,' he sighed.

'Farden!' somebody was shouting a name he half recognised. He floundered amongst the crowd like a sprat in a net, hopelessly useless against the surge of the shadows. As his boots crunched against the burnt-shard husk of the gangplank, something grabbed his arm.

※

'Farden!' Tyrfing yelled in his nephew's face, spittle flying like hailstones. Farden was as limp as a fish. Tyrfing shook him again as Loki tried to push back the dead.

'I tried,' Farden moaned, eyes glazed.

Tyrfing cupped his head to keep it from lolling onto his chest. His skin was winter-cold and clammy too. 'Damn right you tried. Tried to drown me, you did! Grabbed hold of my leg and wouldn't let go.' The Arkmage punctuated each of his sentences with a violent shake. Farden's teeth chattered together with each one.

'I can't...' mumbled the mage.

It was then that Tyrfing slapped him. Hard and open handed. A solid, wet thwack that made a tourist out of his jaw. When it returned from the opposite side of his face, Farden was blinking, mouth agape. There was a little bit of blood on his lip. He put a hand to his rapidly crimsoning face and coughed.

Tyrfing slapped him again for good measure.

Farden's eyes were rolling. 'What the fu...'

'And there he is!' Tyrfing cried. 'He's back with us.'

'And not a moment too soon,' Loki pointed. There was a scraping sound as the ship pulled away from the shore, gangplanks still trailing from its uneven bulwarks. Slowly it brought its bow around, giving them a full gawp of what had been nailed to the bow.

And what a nightmarish thing it was. Half a vulture, half a grinning man, it made the *'Blade*'s mermaid look like a kitten wrapped in velvet. This was a bad dream with a beak, with limbs like that of a skeleton. Their eyes started at its feet, emaciated bony appendages that dangled in the river's water. Then to its knees, thin pebbles with skin stretched over them. From the hips up, its ribcage was open and filled with splinters and broken fingernails, moss, and scraps of long-dead meat. From the chest the man became a black-feathered vulture. Its wings were splayed across the bow, held in place with bent, rusty nails and bits of yellow rope. Its head was barely more than a vulture's skull: a hooked beak and black eyes. Mad, black eyes.

'Hello again,' Farden said, crossing his arms.

The figurehead screeched as the keel nudged the shore. The creature loomed over them. The three had to fight the urge not to step back. 'Straddlers! You do not belong!' it cried.

Farden nodded. 'I think we had a similar conversation a few weeks ago.'

'You pretend to be dead! You do not belong!'

'If I may...'

'Straddlers! Back I say.'

Farden had become bored of being interrupted. He stamped his foot. 'How much?!' he bellowed.

The vulture snapped its beak shut. It took a while for it to open again. 'You wish to... to bargain?' it asked, almost a whine, and at a considerably lower volume than before.

'We wish to cross. What will it cost to do so?'

'Careful, Farden,' Loki could be heard whispering. The dead still clamoured and pushed behind him, but they had quietened slightly, almost as if they were intrigued by this debacle. 'Be very careful,' he said. He sounded so sincere that Farden almost turned around to check Loki hadn't been swapped for another god.

'What will it cost to cross the river?' Farden asked.

The vulture spoke no more. The stones crunched as the great ship turned on its bow and pushed its belly up against the shore. The gangplanks slid out again, burying their noses in the stones. Farden shrugged. 'I guess we'll find out once we're on board,' he said, and he was absolutely right.

The three shoved their way to the nearest gangplank and stared at it with disgust. Farden had remembered what the ship was made of. It was not crushed shell after all, but layers and layers of finger and toenails, just as he had seen the first time. He had hoped that part had been more a dream than reality, but there was no such joy. He stepped aboard with a crunch and a shudder. He tried his best not to wonder where they had all come from, and not to look down either. His stomach did a little turn.

Crunch. Crunch. Their boots played a sickening little rhythm on the gangplank as they climbed it to the decks above. Farden bit his lip with every step. The dead around him seemed indifferent. *I suppose you do, when you're dead*, he thought.

At the top of the gangplank they found a flat, crowded deck, and just like the rest of the ship, it too was fashioned entirely from nails. 'Remind me to tell Nuka about this,' Farden muttered over his shoulder. His uncle grunted. 'If we ever get out of here.'

The dead were packed tightly into every available scrap of space. They stood on the steps. They straddled the bulwarks. Some even hugged the spindly, sail-less masts creeping out of the deck like depressed oaks.

They heard a cry from the bow. 'Speak to the boatman!' it said, and they did as they were told, slowly worming their way through the crowds to the aftcastle, where a lonely raised platform stood overlooking the deck. A dark figure stood upon it, masked by a wheel.

Farden didn't really know what to expect in the way of crew. There was only one, as it turned out, the boatman, hidden behind his wheel. Farden squinted, wondering what sort of creature this boatman would be. Half-skeleton maybe. Perhaps part rat. A man with a wolf's face. After the figurehead, Farden wouldn't have been surprised by anything. Or so he thought.

As they reached the meagre stairs to the aftcastle, they saw him. Farden stumbled to a halt at the sight of a shock of blonde hair. 'Turns out the boatman is a boatwoman,' said Tyrfing, behind him, nudging his nephew forward.

The boatman was a woman indeed. She was almost a skeleton, as it turned out, but not quite. She was a tall and skinny bag of bones, white skin stretched over a frame, showing every joint and beam and lump there was to show. From her angular skull a waterfall of thick, tangled blonde hair cascaded, an ancient stranger to scissors by the way it fell past her legs and tangled around her bare feet on the deck. It dredged up a few memories that made Farden quite uncomfortable.

It was her face that captivated the mages. Even Loki seemed enraptured. Clutched between cheekbones, a jaw, and a forehead so sharp they could have given the Tausenbar peaks a run for their coin, was a face so vacant that Farden wondered for a moment whether she were a statue. Eyes black as tar stared into the distance. A thin scrawl of lips were drawn tight and had a faint, sad slope to them. Her nose was like the tip of a sword. She was beautiful in a way, in a forlorn and striking way. Cold and yet still warm at the same time. Forgotten and lost. A corpse of a pretty princess not long dead.

'Visitors,' she sighed, lips barely moving as they came up the stairs with slow feet and wide eyes.

'Madam,' Tyrfing bowed. By his side, Farden did the same. Only Loki stayed still, a frown on his face.

It was then that she turned to face them, gazing at them with eyes so black it was hard to tell if she were truly looking at anything at all. Her thin lips crept into an intrigued smile. 'Loki,' she said, 'what a surprise, brother.'

The mages turned to the god by their side, looking more than a little suspicious, perhaps a little shocked. They hadn't expected this. Loki nodded, still refusing to bow. 'Hel,' he curtly replied.

'Am I missing something here?' Farden asked, trying not to stare too deeply into the black eyes of this Hel woman.

Hel laughed then, a thin scraping of a chuckle. 'I first knew Loki when he was naught but a twinkling in the void. Before I was sent here, to ferry the dead.'

Loki spoke up. 'Mages, meet Hel, the dead shepherd, guardian of the realm of the same name, goddess of the road to the other side, and sister of Evernia,' he introduced, like a bored announcer. Hel nodded, and bowed her head very slowly, as if it pained her to do so, as if her neck hadn't moved so much in centuries.

'Evernia's sister?' Farden asked.

Hel raised her chin. 'Indeed I am. Though at times even I forget it. I have spent far too many years in this place. Far too many.' Her tone turned from proud, to resentful, to wistful all in one sentence. 'I assume you have not ventured down here for the stimulating conversation. What is your business in my realm?' she asked, her voice now hard and cold. 'How do you stand here, before me, so disgustingly alive?'

'The Shrieks showed us the way.'

Hel grunted something. 'Useless creatures. A shadow of their ancestors. They would have ripped you to shreds just for daring to look at the stones.' Hel looked disappointed. 'Well, here you stand. What hopeless mission brings you to my realm?'

Farden and Tyrfing looked to Loki to speak, but the god shrugged and turned away. 'We are looking for somebody,' Farden said.

'Two to be exact,' added Tyrfing.

'Two's right. A man and a woman.'

'Then these two you look for must be dead, surely, for no mortals are foolish enough to visit Hel before their allotted time, or so I thought.'

'One came here a thousand years ago. The other might just have arrived.' Farden looked at the crowd of dead on board the ship, and then at the teeming masses on the shore, still pushing forward to board.

'Names. Souls have them as well as bodies.'

'Elessi and Korrin.'

'Do you know of them?'

Hel wrinkled her lip. 'I know all the dead who cross the river. I am the only way across. They must all come aboard my ship. I have seen them all.'

'So you know them?' Farden stepped forward.

'Korrin, son of Hark and Ynin, both dead. Born in the village of Jukund. Elessi, daughter of Gastinsson and Florsi, both also dead. Born in Leath, Albion.'

Farden was close to shaking. 'Do you know where they are?'

Hel drummed her black nails on the crusted wheel of the ship.

It too was made of nails. Dust and dirt clung to its ugly spokes. 'She crossed a day ago, maybe less. She walks to the other side as we speak.'

Farden took another step forward. He resisted the urge to grab the goddess. 'So there's still a chance?'

Hel looked at him strangely. 'A chance to do what, master mage? What is your business here, besides looking?'

'I mean to take her back.'

Laughter. Cold, clammy laughter. 'How romantic.'

'I am very serious.'

'I am sure you are, master mage, but the dead are dead and dead they will stay, for as long as I am here.'

Farden crossed his arms. 'But she isn't dead. She was daemontouched.'

'As good as it then.'

'But not quite.'

'Once she reaches the other side, she will be.'

'But until that time, she is fair game, surely.'

Hel pouted. 'How dare you dictate to me, mortal. You have no place here. This place is reserved for the punished, those who know about death, not some mage like you.'

A look came over Farden then. A look as cold as any Hel could have given him. 'Punished, you say?' he asked, almost laughing. Down by his side, his hands slowly curled to fists. 'Let me tell you a little something about punishment, goddess. I've been punished since I took my first breath of cold Emaneska air. A forbidden son borne into a doomed house, snatched up and lied to for decades by a halfbreed bastard with delusions of chaos, who fucked me in more ways than I care to count. He took the love of my life and twisted her inside out, made me father a child with her before he let her die, a child that stands above us now, the bitch of some ancient prophecy. Just my luck. My only child from my only love, stolen and lied to and bred to bring the sky crashing down, daemons and all. I know what you're thinking. How does a man cope? Like this. The man banishes himself to protect all those he cared about. He buries himself in dirty work. Killing for coin, burying himself in blood and shit and tears until he's numb. Smoking and drinking until he's forgotten all but the pain. Surely that's it? No. Greed finds the man. Greed for his armour. Greed that hangs him from his own tree and runs him through. Leaves him to die. Somehow, by the skin of his teeth, he lives. He drags himself back to those he cares about, only to have one snatched away, by the daemons his very daughter summoned. A daughter who thinks her father was the very bastard who began all this. Quite a story, and you say I have no place here? I should be manning this ship, for all the death and punishment I've seen,' Farden spat, breathing hard.

There was an awkward silence. Tyrfing was staring at his nephew, his eyes bleeding every emotion they could.

Farden calmed himself. 'If she's not dead, then she's not quite yours. Am I right or not?'

Hel picked a nail from the wheel. It was a gross, yellow toenail, bigger than any toenail should rightly be. She flicked it over the side and into the river. 'I knew I could feel it on her. Like a stench,' she said, and then scowled. 'Fine. If you can find her, she is yours. Bring her to me, if you can. Though you have little hope, and even less time.'

'And Korrin?' asked Farden. Hel's scowl burrowed even deeper. She lifted a hand to cup her ear, raising a contemptuous smile to the ceiling of the colossal cavern.

'If you listen hard enough, you can still hear his heart beating. For a thousand years or more it has beaten. Thump. Thump. Thump. Sluggish, yet resilient. Foul it is. Sends shivers down my spine. A thousand years I have listened to that heart. It has no place here, and yet it taunts me. He refuses to die. Refuses to cross.'

Farden opened his arms wide. 'Fair game as well then!'

Hel flashed him a black look, literally. 'I know why you seek him. I see what you wear on your arms and legs, mage. Greed is a most despicable thing, as you say. Most of these,' she waved to the silently swaying cargo on her ship, 'are here due to greed.'

It was Farden's turn to scowl. 'Greed has nothing to do with it,' he growled. 'Sacrifice, on the other hand, has everything to do with it.'

Hel cracked a wide grin, full of black teeth. 'Sacrifice, you say? In that case, let us discuss your payment.'

The two mages swapped looks. 'Payment for what?' they asked. Behind them, Loki couldn't help but grin.

'For the crossing of course,' replied Hel, cackling. 'Every ferry has its fee, does it not? Did you think I would simply let you cross, out of the kindness of my own heart? Let you steal away my precious souls, for nothing but gratitude in return? Hah! Fools indeed.'

Farden reached for his coinpurse. 'So just how much exactly is this fee?' he asked, fishing for some larger coins with his metal fingers.

Hel laughed again at the sight of the mage rummaging for coins. She laughed long and hard indeed. So long and so hard, in fact, that Farden almost began to reach for his sword. When she was finally done, Hel wiped away imaginary tears and rubbed her bony hands together with glee. 'Why, master mage, the fee has nothing to do with coins, even though you delight in putting them on your dead, before the pyre.'

'Then what?'

The humour on Hel's face remained, even though her eyes turned cold. 'Why, everybody owes a death. Even you, who has known so much already.'

There was a moment of silence before anybody spoke. Farden scratched his head. 'So you're saying...'

'The price to cross to the other side is your life, yes. You may save your friend, of course, you may claim your armour, but only the dead may cross, and only the dead may reside here. That was Korrin's price, and so it shall be yours.'

Farden put a hand on his sword. 'I'd like to see you try to stop us.'

Hel clicked her fingers. 'Kneel,' she commanded. Farden was about to scoff when something heavy, impossibly heavy, pushed down on his shoulders and the backs of his legs. The next thing he knew, he was sprawled on the disgusting deck, hands splayed in the nails, knees pressing so hard into the deck that they ached. 'You have no power here, Farden, and neither do you, Tyrfing.' Her black eyes seemed to flick up to his uncle, who was standing with his hands at the ready.

Tyrfing raised a finger. 'Surely an exception can be made, considering the circumstances?'

Hel tilted her head. 'And what, pray, are they?'

'We need the armour to fight my nephew's daughter. The one he spoke of.'

Hel just shrugged. 'That is not my fight.'

Tyrfing's mouth hung open. 'But you're a goddess. Of course it is your fight!' he said.

Farden was wheezing on the floor. 'Selfish b...'

Tyrfing cut him off. 'Hel, we're asking for your help, a spot of kindness. Not just for us, but for your brothers and sisters,' he reasoned, pointing at Loki, who was still skulking nearby. Hel looked at him with a blank expression.

'And why should I help the ones who sent me down here? Banished me, to frolic with the dead?'

Tyrfing bowed his head, clenched a fist or two, and sighed. Farden grunted as he tried, futilely, to push himself up. Hel waited for an answer. Tyrfing cleared his throat. 'Can we speak in private?' he asked.

'If you so wish,' Hel said. She clicked her fingers again. 'Up,' she said, and Farden flew upright, boots stumbling against the deck.

'Give us a moment,' Tyrfing said to Farden. His nephew mumbled something derogatory and marched away, followed by a silent Loki. They went to stand by the bow, surrounded and jostled by shadows. The ship was full to bursting.

Farden watched the two figures at the stern talking. Tyrfing was waving his hands about in an urgent fashion. Hel looked on, still as a dead statue. Every now and again her mouth would move, and Tyrfing would wave his hands a little more.

'I wonder what he's saying to her,' Farden mumbled to himself. Loki wasn't paying attention, he was busy trying to grasp the arm of a nearby shadow. If Farden had turned around, he might have seen Loki's skin ripple with each attempt.

'Loki!' a shout rang out from the wheel. 'Leave them be. It is forbidden, even for I!' It was Hel. Loki whipped his hands back into his pockets as Farden turned around. He looked the god up and down quizzically.

'We sent her down here because she was mad,' Loki said, quietly. 'A nuisance. Unreliable.'

Farden snorted. 'Maybe they should have sent you instead.'

Tyrfing soon finished his conversation with Hel. He pushed his way through the dead, trying to stifle a cough.

'Well?' Farden asked, as he drew near. As if in answer to his question, the ship twitched beneath their feet. There was a loud scraping as the keel dragged itself clear of the shore.

'Apparently, I did it.'

'How did you convince her?'

Tyrfing tapped his head conspiratorially. 'It turns out that heartbeat is more annoying to her than two mages crossing the river without paying the usual price. If we can silence it, then she's agreed to let us cross. You, Loki, don't count, but you and I, nephew, have a return ticket.'

'And no dying?'

'No dying.'

'If only we had some wine to celebrate,' Loki muttered snidely. Farden went to shove him, but to his surprise, the god didn't move very much at all. He barely flinched. It was most unsatisfying. Farden rolled his eyes. *I cannot wait to leave this strange place. Even the shadows are solid*, he thought to himself.

'Well,' he said, clapping his old uncle on the shoulder, 'good work. Maybe politics does suit you after all.'

Tyrfing smiled a lopsided smile. 'Maybe,' he said. He waited until Farden had turned around before he let the smile fade. He retched and spluttered then as another wave of coughing took him.

᭡

Dark and fast, the deep water of the river took the ship in its grip and bore them away, out of the cavern and into a long tunnel of rock and mist. The lanterns hanging from the ship's side barely lit the way as they swerved to and fro through the twisting tunnel. The dead rode silently along, caring not a button for the rock flashing by mere feet from the bulwarks, or the gloomy ceiling hurtling past, threatening to knock a few yards off the masts with every turn.

Farden, Tyrfing, and Loki stood at the bow, trying to count the miles as they sped by. More than once, Farden glanced occasionally back at Hel, her face now masked by her wheel. She and it barely moved. It was almost as if the wheel were there for decoration only. That set a knot in Farden's stomach. The ship was at the river's mercy.

Tunnel turned to cavern and more dead came aboard. Farden didn't think it possible, but they swarmed into the dark holds below, to mingle with the toe and fingernails and the occasional mouldy coin, poking out of the decking.

Soon they were off again, hurtling into the darkness once

more. Cavern turned to tunnel, and then cavern again. Farden wondered how far they were travelling under the world, whether they were being borne far, far away from the north and its ice, and whether they could find their way back in time. As far as Farden could see, there was only one river, and it was only flowing in one direction.

After another handful of miles, the ship slowed, wrestling itself out of the river's strong current. As they emerged from their tunnel into yet another huge cavern, the ship drifted to nuzzle against the shingle of the shore. Farden looked over the bulwark, expecting to see yet another endless crowd of shadows clamouring to climb aboard, but instead there was an empty beach of shingle and rock, with faint paths leading into holes in the rock, like the mouths of rabbit warrens, filled with mist.

'Off!' screamed the figurehead.

Farden took a breath. 'Looks like this is it.'

'The other side.'

Hel was somehow behind them. The mages barely suppressed the instinct to jump. 'Not yet,' she said. 'That is over the bridge.'

'Bridge?'

'Through the tunnels,' she pointed to the holes in the rock, and then to the dead filing off the ship. They drifted across the stones, whispering to themselves. As eager as they had been to get on the ship, they now looked tired and listless, more like the dead should. They wandered with their hands limply at their sides, no longer pushing and struggling, but calmly sliding past each other.

Farden took another breath. He exhaled, and words came with it. 'Well, time is running out, gentlemen,' he said, and with that he began to push his way through the disembarking dead.

Loki followed. Tyrfing trailed behind. Just as he set his foot on the gangplank, Hel called after him. 'Remember our agreement, Tyrfing,' she reminded him.

'How could I forget?' he muttered, over his shoulder. She

waved as he disappeared over the side of the ship.
    'How could you, indeed?' she asked the silence.

Chapter 28

"Written Mages! We value our sanity and our health. Towels, tunics, or shirts to be worn at all times please, even in private!"
Old rule of the Spire, found gouged into a beam

In battle, seconds stretch to minutes. Anything can happen in them. All it took to start this battle was three.

One.

Samara raised her hands to the jaundiced sky, fingers bent and twisted like the gnarled branches of a lightning-struck tree.

Two.

The ledge of rock under her feet cracked. Then came a deep boom, one that almost matched the volcanos and their fury. The daemons and wolves jumped clear as it sagged into a crater of splintered rock, Samara standing shaking in its epicentre.

Three.

A shockwave burst outwards from the girl. A rolling wave of dust and ice, throwing all but the strongest to the ground. It made the earth shake and the ice crack as it bubbled outwards, flying faster than the eye could blink.

'Oof!' Modren gasped as he was tossed to the ground like a sack of meat. He gasped, the breath driven out of him. There was a great whooshing sound as the air rushed back in to fill the vacuum the shockwave had left in its wake. Modren felt his ears pop, half deafening him. Dizziness swamped him, and he floundered in the snow, listening to the dull, muted sounds of panic around him. He watched as a group of snowmads tried to keep a sled from overturning. It was cracking under its own weight. There was a distant crash, and the sled crumpled. Nearby, a mage was hauling an unconscious Siren back to the battle lines. He was yelling at others with every step, the faint echoes lost on Modren's ears. He looked north. He saw one of the two daemons striding across the landscape, unhinging his jaw to roar at the sky. Nothing more than a moan reached his ears, like a tired wind.

Fingers grabbed him and hauled him upright. Inwick was there, frantically probing his body for wounds. Eyrum was shaking him, saying something, Modren couldn't tell. His voice was a dullish rumble. Durnus was abruptly amongst them. He grabbed Modren by the skull, with both hands, and the Undermage felt something sharp run down his spine.

The world came back to him in a roar.

'By the gods!' Modren gasped as his ears popped again, painfully. 'What was that?!'

'Now is not the time to be discussing spells, Modren!' Durnus was yelling. 'We need to get everybody back to the sleds, now! It has begun!'

'Yes, your Mage!' Modren shouted in reply. The sound of the wind and the volcano was deafening. Ice whipped their legs and faces. Modren beat his sword against his chest. 'Written! To me!'

༒

The sound of the earth cracking was the least of Samara's worries. Her bones were more her concern. She could hear them cracking too.

Samara's spell was winding up to its fierce crescendo. Far

quicker than before. Too quick, for her liking. She had barely enough strength to keep herself from crumpling like a burnt twig.

She didn't dare spare a glance as she heard another boom beneath her feet. The hill lurched as she took a tighter grip on the sky. Her eyes were fixed on a cluster of stars, right above her. She reached toward them with her nails and slowly pulled her arms back.

Fire began to lick at her boots. Their leather had already been ground to dust under the pressure. Now the stone around her was being flattened and knuckled like wet clay. Veins of red popped out of its black skin as it crunched and whined, hot red veins full of molten stone. The fire leapt higher.

Inch by terrible inch her arms slid back to her sides. Samara could feel her knees buckling. She spared a desperate moment to push a spell into her legs, hardening her bones to keep them from cracking. It was not a moment too soon. She hauled her arms back and the weight of the spell drove her to her knees. She cried out as the hot stone cut her flesh. The spell was in full swing now. The fire howled around. Splinters of stone spun about her. The wind roared.

In her mind, all Samara kept seeing was the sharp teeth of her daemon kin, smiling and congratulating her for what she had done. She could feel their arms lifting her up above the crowds of daemons and their worshippers. She could hear her name like the crashing of a waterfall. *Samara! Samara! Samara!* They would shout it until the sun went down.

As the first stars flashed in the tawny sky, despite all the pain, she began to smile.

☙

'They're coming!' It was a useless shout. A young soldier or sailor no doubt, too terrified to keep quiet. Too excited to realise everyone else was pointing and gawping.

There was a collective crunch of ice and steel as everyone tensed. The whole line of sleds and soldiers, curved like a sour smile, clenched. A thousand pairs of eyes turned to the sky.

At first, the stars just twinkled and flashed, as innocuous and circumspect as any other bright stars on any other morning. Then they began to spit and flare. As each one punched through the atmosphere of the world, they grew from twinkling little gems to roaring, plummeting furnaces, flame and smoke streaming from their sides as they fell. Dull thunder echoed across the wastes below, each a star hitting the cold air.

It took them a full minute to fall to the ice. A full minute of gawping. A full minute of stern faces and wide eyes. A full minute of sore fingers strangling sword handles. Then they struck.

One, two, three, four, five... they hit the ice in devastating sequence, puncturing five smoking holes in a wide arc between the hill and the line of brave fighters. Clouds of steam flew like geysers as their inhabitants came to a shuddering, bone-shaking rest. A terrible moment followed, silent save for the roars of the wind, Samara, and the Spine. Then, one by one, claws and foreheads appeared over their blackened rims. Eyes of all shapes and colours. Hides of black, grey, ashen white, yellow, and red glistened in the light of the fire. Some were small, others as large as Valefor and Hokus. Some had bodies like that of men, others like that of nightmares. They looked hungrily at the line of men and women spread before them, barely half a mile away.

'Hold your ground!' ordered Modren, from the centre of the line. He could hear a nervous muttering running through the crowds, rustling like autumn leaves. 'Hold your damn ground!'

'More,' spat Eyrum, eyeing the sky. He pointed with his axe, and Modren followed it up to another section of the sky, where another dozen stars had begun to glow brightly.

'We'll lose them if we're not careful,' Modren hissed, looking about at the anxious faces dotted around them. 'They're only now realising what we're up against.'

'Bah,' Eyrum snorted. 'They should have seen the hydra.'

'And you killed that, didn't you?'

'Indeed we did.'

'Then by that logic, we'll be fine,' Modren said. He stepped out of the line and turned to face their army. He had his shield in his hand, his sword in the other. Men dragged their eyes from the skies to look at him. More whispers ran through the crowd.

'A speech?'

'Are we retreating?'

'He's going to barter for our lives!'

Modren was doing none of that. He looked up and down the line, noting the heads craning to see him. He raised his sword high above his head, and brought the flat of it crashing down on his shield with a loud clang. He did it again and again, beating out a solid rhythm, and all the while he looked up and down, looking, praying even, for people to join in. It was Eyrum who stepped forward first. Trusty Eyrum. He had a grin on his battered face. Modren matched it as the big Siren began to hammer his own shield with the head of his axe.

Inwick was next, beating hers with the pommel of her sword. The three drummed their rhythm proudly. Then it began to spread. The Written took up the beat, and then the Arka soldiers. The sailors, mostly without shields, began to shout and stamp their feet. Man to man and woman to woman the rhythm spread, like summer fire through ranks of dry trees. Fists punched breastplates. Shields met swords. Clubs and boots battered the ice.

Modren began to increase the speed of the rhythm. What had begun as a slow, plodding drumming now became a fierce thundering. Faster and faster they went, and as they drummed, shouts ripped from throats. War cries filled the air. The snowmads screamed strange songs. Roars from the dragons deafened any who stood near. Beasts snarled and screeched. The wildmen bellowed and grunted from the rear.

They were a storm, daring anyone to come near, and they knew it. They felt it now, every single one. The fear had melted away, if only temporarily.

Even when the next dozen stars fell, disturbingly close this time, the army kept on singing and drumming. The stars shook the ice from under their feet, but still they kept at it. It was only when one solitary star fell, later than the rest, did the thunder and noise die away a little.

The star fell in the very centre of the battlefield. Like a suicidal mountain it threw itself into the ice. It was bigger than the rest, it was easy to see that from the size of the hole it left. There was a deep rumbling in the seconds that followed. They could feel the ice cracking deep below them. Modren stepped back into line as the drumming died away.

A grey finger inched over the edge of the hole. No, not a finger, a claw. It fell back into the hole, leaving an oily smear behind. Then came a whip-like tail, waving like a flag in the gloom. Then a glow to rival Samara and the volcanoes, a hot red glow from inside the hole. A great gush of steam came up, and then the daemon lifted itself from the hole, stepping out onto the ice.

'And what about that?' Modren muttered into Eyrum's notched ear. 'How does that compare to the hydra.'

Eyrum sniffed. 'Still not as big.'

It was monstrous even so. A giant welt of a creature, a grey lump of flesh with cracks of red running through its skin like magma under stone. Its mouth was a blacksmith's forge, only with teeth, broken shards of teeth that looked more used to gnawing on granite than bone. It had a crown of twisted horns, and two that framed its face, pointing down into his mouth, as if any prey needed directions.

If that wasn't fearsome enough, it had two pairs of arms, each knotted with muscle and sinew like ripcord, and claws that would have made a scythe weep with embarrassment.

'Count yourself lucky that you can't see this, Durnus,' whispered Modren.

Durnus shook his head. 'Oh, I can.' He could see the fiery outline of it in the dark. That was enough. 'It is time,' he said.

'That it is,' Modren replied. He raised his sword. 'Mages! Written! Spells at the ready!'

There was a desperate shuffling as the mages moved forward. Fire, smoke, sparks, ice, water, and light began to trail around their wrists and fingers. Modren felt his ears pop one more time as the magick swelled. It was their turn to make the ground shake. 'Archers!' Durnus yelled. The creaking of several hundred bows added to the crackle and hiss of the spells.

'Fire!'

Perhaps it was an accident that everybody aimed for the giant daemon. Perhaps it was the fact that he was closer, or bigger. Perhaps it terrified them to their very cores.

Maybe it was all of these.

The daemon was turned into a flaming pincushion within seconds. Once again, time slowed as the army made the first strike. Arrows flitted past ears and helmets, like a swarm of angry, bladed hornets eager for blood. They soon found it. The daemon snarled and held up his hands as the arrows flew in. He was marching forward when the spells struck him. Fireballs struck him in the face and midriff. Lightning burnt the flesh from his black bones. Ice pierced him. He belched and bled smoke, filling the battlefield.

In moments, he was down, claws raking at the ground in frustration and pain. There was a whine as the last few spells struck home, and then the creature sagged into the snow, dead. The first blood had been drawn.

The army was about to raise an almighty cheer to the sky when they saw the rest of the daemons sprinting towards them. Wolves galloped alongside them. Dragons filled the sky above them. Creatures of all kinds, swarthy wild men, clansmen, bears, sabre-cats, ravens, rock trolls, ice trolls, tree trolls, and even a white giant charged by their sides.

'Spears! Spells! Fire at will!' Modren bellowed, summoning a huge fireball.

Seconds can drag into minutes in battle, but they can also shrink to nothing. A hundred yards were charged as though they were an inch, and before anyone could tense or take a breath, the battle had been joined.

Chapter 29

"Imagine if all the spell books in the world were to be taken away, whisked into memory, with the snap of a finger. How long do you think our songs can survive for, without them? How long will the rhymes stay lodged in the mind? The father can only whisper into the ears of his son for so long before the song is lost, or changed."
From the wildly popular book 'Mutterings' - author anonymous

'You would think it would smell down here,' Farden mused as they trudged through the seemingly endless tunnels.

'Smell?'

'Of dead things,' Farden said. He stepped aside as a huge minotaur lumbered past, vacant-eyed and faded. Farden couldn't help but reach for his sword. Old habits, he guessed.

'These are souls, not rotting bodies, mage,' Loki tutted.

'Of dirt then. Of mildew. It smells of nothing. There is nothing here but rock. I don't even feel warm or cold. Just nothing. It's as if my body doesn't acknowledge this place is real,' replied Farden, running his hands along the dusty rock. It certainly felt real.

Loki sighed. 'An interesting observation. Perhaps you're dead as well. That's why you can't feel anything.'

'Not likely,' Farden scoffed, rubbing his vambraces. Even so, he surreptitiously pinched himself to make sure. He winced. Still alive then.

They paused so Tyrfing could catch up. He appeared momentarily, leaning heavily on the rock, hand clamped over his mouth. Farden itched to keep going. Elessi had to be caught before she reached the bridge, if she hadn't already. He prayed that she hadn't, willed it with every inch of his being. They had been walking for hours and still there was no sign of any bridge. Just the slow, ambling of the shadows and the endless tunnels, lit by light unseen.

Farden stood in the centre of the tunnel, half watching his uncle, half examining the faces of the dead. *Man, man, troll-thing, woman... no, I've seen her before. Child. Man.* He counted each and every single one. Still no Elessi. Farden stamped his foot in frustration. They had to keep going.

'Tyrfing?' he hollered. His uncle waved and nodded, and made an effort to follow. Perhaps it was something about the tunnels, maybe the dust, but he had gotten worse in the past hour, ever since stepping off that horrid ship. Farden bit the inside of his lip as Tyrfing jogged to meet them. He was wheezing hard when he arrived.

'Any sign?' he asked.

'Not yet.'

Tyrfing shook his head and shooed them forward. 'Then let's keep going.'

Farden set his jaw. 'Just tell me if you n...'

'Nonsense, nephew. Keep up,' Tyrfing chided. He burst forward, making a go of trying to stay ahead, but he soon fell back again after a dozen paces. Farden knew his uncle didn't want to be fussed over, so he left him to it, and busied himself with checking the dead, running from shadow to shadow until he was breathless. *Woman, woman, child... for gods' sakes, where are you Elessi?!*

❦

'Tell me about this bridge, Loki,' Farden asked, as he was

barged aside by a gangly shadow. The dead were finding their feet again, quickening their pace. A fresh muttering and whispering filled the tunnels as it had the endless cavern. Farden felt they were near, though to what he had no clue.

'A bridge? Usually a structure, carrying a road or path across an obstruction or obstacle, perhaps a river, or fjord, or…'

'This is no time for your games, Loki!' Farden snapped. 'Tell me about *this* bridge.'

'The Bifröst?'

'Is that what they call it?'

Loki shrugged. 'Some do. We gods do. We built many bridges in our time.'

'You built this bridge?'

'Partly. The rest built itself.'

'How is that possible?'

'Where there's a need for something, the world provides. The dead, when there began to be dead, needed a way to the other side, to the void that all souls must go to,' Loki paused to squeeze between two shadows. He shivered, made a show of checking their faces, and moved on. 'This bridge was created to guide them there. We gods just helped it along.'

'And the daemons?'

'The daemons? They built this place.'

Farden nodded, remembering his uncle's stories. 'And so the daemons dwelt alongside the dead?'

'Worse,' Loki sneered, 'they used them.'

'Used them how?'

'Ever wonder why we gods took so long to defeat the daemons? It's because prayer is so weak compared to that of a soul. Both lend us power of course,' Loki said, letting his fingers pass through a nearby shadow, an old man hobbling along with a cane. He shuddered, but his face suggested it wasn't all that unpleasant. Farden eyed him suspiciously. 'But one is considerably more... *satisfying.*'

'So that's why Hel told you to leave the dead alone.'

'The Allfather forbade it. He created you creatures, both body and soul. He saw it as perverse to create a race purely so we could consume it. Rather, he saw it noble to create a race that could worship and fight. That could choose. I fail to see the difference. As did the daemons. They had, and have, no such qualms about consuming souls.'

'You know what? The more you talk about the other gods, the more it sounds like you don't like them very much.'

'Have you heard them speak of me? I guess it would sound the same.'

'Somebody's bitter.'

Loki ignored him, muttering something dark and poisonous. Farden relished in the point he had scored. Served the god right. Still, something in Loki's tone troubled him. Something in the way he stood a little straighter, a little taller. Something in the way he strode back and forth, idly checking the dead, his usual saunter injected with a little bit of swagger. Farden didn't like it one bit and it made him wary. Still, he was a god. A bastard of one, but a god nonetheless, and therefore bound to their morals. 'So this bridge? Is it near?' he asked.

Loki paused to watch the shadow of a wood troll wander past, its giant oaken limbs creaking faintly, emerald eyes still glowing stubbornly even in death. Intrigued, the god followed it around a corner. He was about to disappear from view when something stopped him dead in his tracks. 'See for yourself, mage,' he said.

'Tyrfing!' Farden called out as he bounded forward. It took him a moment to reach Loki's side, and when he did, a cold wind and a formidable sight joined forces to take his breath away.

'Might I introduce the Bifröst,' Loki muttered beside him, as he gawked at the edge of the world.

The entire end of the cave was missing. In its place was

nothing. Not a dark hole leading out into another cavern. Not a hole that led out into the countryside, wherever that may be. Nothing. Not even misty gloom. Just pure, simple darkness. At first, Farden thought it might be a wall, painted with the blackest paint imaginable, but then he took a step forward, and he saw that the void, for that was what it was, had a depth to it that suddenly made him feel very small, and very alone. It was a pit of darkness that had no edges, no limits, no end. No dust swam in it. Not even stars shone in it.

It was the other side.

Farden looked down the slope at the bridge that speared the void, one brave spit of reality bridging the gap between this world and the next, a single half-arch precariously clinging to the rock of the cave. Its join was so seamless that it looked as though the rock had spewed it out into the void, instead of being mortared into place. That was where the relationship ended. It was the bridge's colour that fascinated Farden. Instead of mirroring the cold, grey rock of the cave and the tunnels, the Bifröst was a shimmering... colour. It was hard to say which. It cycled through the spectrum faster than the eye could follow, glittering here and there with little curls of light and golden flame, like a rainbow on fire. Farden couldn't help but want to touch it. Would it be warm, or ice cold? Would it burn him? Was it metal, or stone? The mage wandered forward, leaving Loki behind. Had Farden spared a glance for him, he would have seen a jittery smile beginning to creep across the god's face.

The dead pressed towards the Bifröst, slowly, yet inexorably. They didn't fight and clamour like they had at the *Naglfar*, but rather they serenely took it in turns to step onto the bridge, in twos, threes, sometimes four together. Farden watched as an old couple set their feet to its glittering surface. They walked, still hand in hand, to its apex, where the void whisked them away. They didn't scream or shout. There was no violence in it; they simply melted into dust and faded into the darkness. It was all very orderly for the afterlife.

Farden looked across the crowds, wincing at the sheer numbers. They were pressed a hundred deep at the thinnest point, all tightly-packed and shuffling toward the bridge, always to the bridge. None of them looked back.

'Elessi!' Farden bellowed across the heads of the crowd. It was useless. Not a single head turned. He needed to find a rock, or a boulder, anything to climb up on. He pushed his way forward and dove into the crowd.

It was the boulder that found him, not the other way around. He didn't see it until he was sprawled over it, hidden as it was amongst the forest of shuffling legs. Nursing his groin, he clambered on top of it. It wasn't much, but it put him at least a head over most of the crowd. He shouted again, cupping his dusty hands around his mouth. 'Elessi!'

Nothing again. All Farden could hear was the incessant muttering and whispering of the dead. 'ELESSI!' he boomed, so loud his lungs hurt. His eyes frantically scanned the crowd. Still nothing, and every second that passed, another two or three shadows disappeared into the void. Any one of them could have been Elessi. It was like watching the sand run down an hourglass, except that at the bottom, the sand fell into an abyss, never to return. Farden could not have that. He had made a promise.

He jumped from his boulder and began to wade through the crowd again, pushing aside anything his hands came into contact with. It was like wading through deep water. The dead refused to move for him, and Farden soon found himself stranded, stuck in the middle of crowd.

'Tyrfing! Loki!' Farden shouted, jumping up as high as he could. He saw them in similar positions. Tyrfing was by the tunnel, swimming in his own patch of crowd. Loki was nearby, and somehow making a beeline for the Bifröst, effortlessly weaving in between the shadows as if they were nothing. 'Loki!' Farden yelled, but the god paid him no attention. 'Loki! Where are you going? Can you see her?!' he cried. Loki had already disappeared. 'Damn it, you bastard!'

Farden gnashed his teeth together. He felt drowned in the crowd. He shoved and pushed but the dead didn't budge. He held out his hands to brace himself and shut his eyes. If he had ever needed his magick, it was now. *Come on!* he inwardly roared. He muttered something to himself as a sharp pain ripped through his skull. 'Agh!' Farden yelped. He pushed again, grimacing as the pain grew and grew. He snarled as he felt the bile rising. He felt his fingers twitch. He cracked open an eye just in time to see one of the shadows stumble and fall. It wasn't much, but it was something. Reeling with pain, Farden rushed into the gap he had made and pushed on. Tyrfing was soon behind him.

'This is no time to be experimenting, Farden. I don't want to have to carry your unconscious weight back through those tunnels, you hear me?'

'I hear you. Now stop complaining and find Elessi!' Farden snapped.

With two to do the barging, they moved a lot faster. Tyrfing used his magick to cleave a path through the ranks. Farden followed closely, trying not to faint from the blinding pain in his skull.

'There's Loki!' Tyrfing shouted, pointing towards the bridge. Farden glimpsed a dark figure standing on it. 'What in Emaneska is he up to?'

That knot that had been forming in Farden's stomach tightened. A cold shiver washed over him as he spied the god standing alone amongst the shadows on the Bifröst, smirking and proud, watching them calmly as the mages struggled to the foot of the bridge. 'I think we're about to find out,' Farden hissed.

'Loki, what are you doing?' Tyrfing challenged him. There was a metallic whine as Farden drew his sword.

'Tyrfing, look,' breathed Farden, pointing with the blade.

Loki had Elessi by the arm. Farden's heart thumped. She was a faint shadow in his grip. She struggled only slightly, but he seemed to be having a hard time keeping hold of her. The apex of the bridge looked painfully close. Tyrfing turned around to hold back the dead while Farden moved forward. 'Let her go, Loki,' he ordered, moving slowly.

But Loki just tutted. 'Poor choice of words, mage. Why would I go and do a thing like that?'

Farden stepped onto the Bifröst. He could feel the thing vibrating beneath his feet, feel its heat rising up to warm his chin and face. Up close it looked like molten gold, swimming with gems and diamonds. His boots hissed quietly as its fire tested them. 'Give her to me, then,' he said, holding out a hand.

Loki nonchalantly thrust his spare hand into one of his coat pockets. He stared up at the roof of the cave and shrugged, rocking back on his heels. 'All in good time, Farden. All in good time.'

Farden waggled his sword at the god. 'Is this your way of punishing me? Something I've done to you? If it is, then leave her out of it. You and I can settle this another way.'

Loki flashed his teeth. 'All about you, isn't it? This entire voyage has been about you. You're so wrapped up in yourself, Farden, that you haven't even noticed who's sitting beside the bridge, have you? Waltzed straight past him, in a self-obsessed daze. Hardly respectful,' he said, standing on his tiptoes to peer over the Bifröst's wall.

Farden's blade fell. He edged backwards onto the rock and to the side of the bridge, where the wall of the Bifröst curled around in an arc. There, cradled in it, between the scintillating bridge and the dizzying edge of the rock, sat Korrin, in all his red-gold glory.

Farden barely resisted the urge to dash to his side. His armour sparkled with the Bifröst's fire. Farden's eyes grew large at the sight of the way it undulated and curved, at the way its scales slipped together in a metallic symphony, the way it… words failed him. It was simply beautiful. Farden could feel it calling to him. He felt his tongue running along the back of his teeth. He ached to go and touch it, but he didn't. *All in good time indeed*, he told himself.

'What do you want?' he asked, turning back to the god.

Loki almost looked impressed by the self-restraint. He was still wearing his smile. 'Many things, Farden. You mentioned punishment. We will start with that.'

'Punish whom?'

'Why,' Loki said, 'everyone, of course. Humans, gods, daemons. All of them will know what I've done. It's what an opportunist does, isn't it? Punish others by taking advantage out of a situation, changing the game, and then playing the best hand?'

Tyrfing was growling with the strain of holding up his spell. The dead were pushing harder and harder with every minute that went by. 'You sound more like a megalomaniac than an opportunist, Loki.'

Farden lifted up his blade again. 'You sound like Vice.'

Loki laughed then. 'That halfbreed? No, I'm the real thing. Or at least I will be,' he looked up at the roof of the cave again, 'in a moment.'

Farden lunged forward, hoping to catch him off guard, but the god was quick. He let Elessi slip further along the bridge. Farden caught himself and stopped short. He quickly lowered the sword. 'Don't!' he cried. At the sound of his voice, Elessi turned, as if she had heard the wind sighing her name. Farden caught a glimpse of her face and felt his heart thud even more. She looked so sad, so lost. She turned away again, and tried once more to break free and shuffle to the void. Fortunately, Loki held her firmly.

'What's gotten into you? What is this?'

'It is the beginning.'

'Of what? Explain yourself!'

Loki took a moment to think, smiling all the while. 'Of many things.' He looked up again.

Farden followed his gaze this time. The cave sighed as a hot wind rustled through it. A deep rumbling sound grew loud in their ears. 'What have you done?' he asked. The Bifröst began to rattle. 'What have you done, Loki?'

Loki raised his spare hand to the rock. 'Give my regards to your daughter, mage.'

'Farden, you better do something! I can't hold them!' Tyrfing strained. His spell was cracking. The rumbling grew louder. The Bifröst began to shake, and violently too. Farden found his feet slipping from under him as the earth trembled. His sword fell and skittered away. The rumbling sound grew to a deafening thunder. Sharp cracks, the sound of stone being split and hammered in to pieces echoed throughout the cave. Tyrfing fell to one knee as his spell waned. He was thrown aside by the dead. 'Farden!' he cried out.

Farden did the only thing he could think of doing. With a snarl, he dug his boots hard into the trembling Bifröst, grabbed his sword, and dived at Loki, blade held high and swinging down to strike.

He almost made it connect too.

The second before Farden's sword introduced itself to Loki's neck, a searing ball of light and fire came crashing through the cave's roof. Stone, molten and obliterated, rained with it. The fireball fell straight down, descending on Loki with a huge flash and a whip-crack of thunder. Farden met the fireball head on and was thrown to the bridge like a hammer to an anvil. There was a resounding crack as the Bifröst snapped, and fell away. He flailed wildly as he felt his boots kick at nothing, his stomach taking up residence in his mouth. He felt his hand bounce off something solid and he seized it. A sharp pain ripped through his shoulder. Something else slid past his arm and he grabbed that too, something cold and soft. Half-stunned and half-blinded by fire and smoke, he watched the flaming gold of the bridge tumble into the abyss. Lost.

Chapter 30

"The Spines have Roots, and in those Roots burn the molten fires of the old giant. Burned forever, they have, and will burn for forever more."
From a chapter of an old Scalussen book, found in the wreckage of the Hjaussfen library

Samara was shaking. Every fibre, muscle, sinew, and tendon in her body quivered. Every single one of them burned like torches. Her arms were lead weights. Her head was a boulder on shoulders made of glass. Her legs were twisted sticks, bent and broken.

And yet still she heaved on the sky.

Two more stars plunged into the ice, right in the middle of the enemy's line of sleds. Samara would have spared a moment to sneer if she could have. She watched out of the corner of her eye as one sled was reduced to kindling and burnt rags, sending men and corpses reeling. Moments later, a skinny daemon emerged from its smoking ribs, and with a roar, dove straight into the fray.

Another star fell, striking a dragon in mid-air as it plummeted. Lost Clan or Siren, Samara didn't know or care. The creature spun out of control and painted the snow with its bright orange blood.

'Samara!' came a shout from behind her. It was Lilith, cowering in the hollow of the cliff face behind her. She had come as close as she dared, and already the frayed strands of her cloak were smouldering in the heat.

Samara couldn't reply if she wanted to. Her teeth were clamped so tightly she suspected that they had fused together.

'Samara!' Lilith cried again. *What did the old bird want, now of all times?!*

'The daemons are calling you! That god has called to them! Loki! It's time!'

It took a huge effort to turn her head but she managed. There, below on the ice, stood Hokus, decorated with crimson. He was waving his arms at her, drawing a letter in the air. *L.* For Loki. Lilith was right.

Samara turned her head back to the sky. Dawn had now risen over the Spine, and the sulphurous belchings of the volcano had mingled with the lightening azure of the sky and turned it a faint green colour. The light wasn't much of an improvement. The mountains were still spitting fire and great plumes of ash, and with every falling star that rained down, more smoke and steam rose from the snow. A thick smog now hung over the battlefield. Swords, spells, and smog. A deadly combination. If the cries and roars were anything to go by, thought Samara, it was chaos down there. Delicious chaos.

Part of her wanted to be a part of it, but she had a job to do. Plenty of stars remained. One in particular was next.

Samara turned to face a patch of sky she hadn't yet touched. She squinted, finding her next prize. Slowly but surely she bent the spell to her will, clawing at the sky. She could feel the tug of the star as she latched onto it. Pushing magick into her legs and knees she pulled at it, scrabbling for purchase. It was becoming easier with practice, but no less painful. Samara let a strangled cry escape from her throat as she pulled the star from its resting place. As it began to fall, Samara tried to imagine the faces of the gods as one of their own was plucked from the sky, from right under their noses. Would they think it was a trick? A mistake? What would they do? Nothing, more than likely. Useless creatures. This Loki was a traitorous one, that was for sure. A cold betrayer. She liked that.

Only one thing remained, one reason her eyes sneaked furtive looks of the battlefield. *Where was he?* she asked herself, deep inside her roaring skull. She needed Farden. She needed his blood like her own.

※

'And another!' cried Lerel, as another star flashed in the sky. It was a useless shout. She was alone, after all, save for this snarling beast in front of her. She lashed out at the sabre-cat she was circling, catching it across the face. It hissed at her, slinking away. It didn't get very far at all. A ball of ice rocketed across the battlefield and punched it into the smoke with a howl.

Lerel raised her sword to the pale Written standing nearby. She nodded, and moved on to attack a nearby troll with another mage.

Samara was right. It was chaos on the snow. The lines had fallen apart under the daemons' onslaught, forcing the army to fight on all fronts, scattered and battling in little groups and wherever they could. With the smoke and steam, any concept of co-ordinated fighting had crumbled. It was every man, woman, beast, and daemon for themselves. The kind of vicious battle every soldier fears.

She found herself alone again in the smoke. All around her she saw shapes and heard the roars of battle. She spun around, waving her sword, feeling the fear drum in her chest. She looked up through the haze for the star she had spotted. She was about to shout out another warning when she noticed this one was different. It was not falling straight down, but at an angle, skimming across the mountains like a falling spear. Lerel followed it as it flew from east to west, completely missing the battlefield and the hill. She soon lost it in the smoke, but she felt its thunder in her feet as it collided with something several miles to the west. Perhaps the girl was slipping.

'Did you see that?' barked a loud voice, making her spin around with her sword. Eyrum caught it deftly on his shield.

Lerel blew a sigh of relief and wiped a hand across her brow, noting with pain the deep gash across her forehead. Bear claws were sharp indeed. 'I did,' she replied. 'Do you think she's losing it?'

'I hope so, because we're dying out here. We can't fight any more daemons,' Eyrum growled, and as if it had come to prove his point, a hulking figure stumbled out of the smoke behind them. It spotted them instantly. It snarled, and as it did so its skin rippled, leaking flame from every pore.

'Get behind me,' Eyrum snapped, lifting his axe, twirling it like a twig in lazy fingers. Eyrum was anything but lazy in battle.

He slipped forward, boots sliding through the snow, betraying his speed. The daemon sensed a lethargic opponent and almost squealed in delight. Claws unsheathed themselves like rusty iron blades from rock scabbards. Teeth dripped with black poison. The daemon poised, and struck, expecting the next thing he saw to be a lumbering Siren, skewered in his claws, ready to be crunched in his jaws.

Fortunately, Eyrum had slightly different ideas. Moving a dozen paces in the space of a second, he slid under the daemon's wide stance, a blur with an axe held high and swinging hard, aiming right for the creature's groin. There was a terrible whine as the daemon felt the sharp blade pass through several prized possessions. Eyrum slid free and jumped up, already swinging the axe like a whip, flaying the charcoal-black hide from the daemon's back. The creature took three hits, and then spun, knocking Eyrum to the snow. The Siren took the blow like the seasoned fighter he was, bowing into it, taking half the blow by leaning back. Even so, it sent him reeling. Eyrum blinked as he stared at the smoky sky above, breathing hard. The ground shook as the daemon strode forward. Eyrum raised his axe, raised a roar in his throat, and rolled to his feet.

Instead of a daemon ready to smite him, he found a wriggling, flailing heap. Three mages, all Written, advanced in an arrowhead from the right, Lerel at their centre. Fire and lightning streamed from their gauntleted hands, crooked fingers and sparks flying. They chanted their spells in deadly, rhythmic precision. It wasn't needed, but it was a formidable sight.

Soon the daemon was a shivering wreck, half dead or dying already. Eyrum put his axe through its iron skull. He tugged it free with a grimace, examining the thick chunk missing from its edge. 'Bastard notched my blade.'

The Written were panting hard. One looked up, eyes dizzy, half focused. It was the older mage, Gossfring. Two sharp flashes of light lit the fog, followed by two deep bangs. 'They keep coming.'

'Too tough.'

'Can't see a shitting thing.'

'Rotten battle.'

'Too many,' and so went their complaints. Eyrum could see the air shimmering around their hands and shoulders. Their polished armour was blackened and scraped. One Written had lost a long ribbon of his scalp. His face was a mask of blood and smoke.

They ducked as a Lost Clan dragon skimmed low, narrowly clouting one of them with its tail. 'And those too! Where are our dragons, when you need 'em?' shouted Gossfring, arms shivering with fire.

Towerdawn answered him with a roar. There was an ear-splitting thud in the spinning smoke where the Lost Clan dragon had faded, and then all of a sudden it reappeared. This time it was joined by another dragon, flashing molten gold in the battle's fire. Jaws snapped like fireworks as the dragons crashed into the snow together. Towerdawn had the other by the neck, and was clawing and raking at his unprotected belly. The noise of the two beasts drowned out the entire battle for just a moment. And it was just a moment. For that was all Towerdawn needed.

He seized his opening and his opponent's neck in one swift, lightning move. There was a crunch as his fangs met tough scales and broke them. Towerdawn's chest swelled and fire bubbled from his mouth, blasting the dragon from point-blank range. With his scales broken, the dragon was done for. He emitted one woeful trumpet before his throat was cooked and seared.

Eyrum yelled to his king. 'Old Dragon! We must be making a dent in their numbers now? Surely? Can you see from the sky?'

Three more bangs shook the air and the snow at their feet. Towerdawn shook his bloodied head. 'The girl is relentless. There are more now than when they first charged.'

Eyrum's face sagged like an old balloon. 'How can that be?'

'Can we not attack her?'

Towerdawn looked over his shoulder, gazing into the smoke. 'Durnus tries. She is too strong.'

Lerel took a knee and dug her sword into the snow. Hopeless. Nobody said it, but they all knew it. Lerel sighed. 'Fuck this,' she snapped. 'We need Farden.'

Nobody said that either, but they all knew she was right.

Chapter 31

"Even the brightest of stars fade in the daylight."
Old Siren proverb

Say one thing for the dead. They're accepting creatures.

There was no clamouring. No angry whispers. No pushing. No retribution. Loki pushed himself from his rock-dusted knees and stood tall. Like a man standing for the first time, it felt. Straight-backed and sure, shoulders rolling for the crowd. Flexing, testing, grinning, all the while grinning.

Loki was alive.

Loki was powerful.

He felt it in every pore, pocket, and follicle. Felt it in every vein, vessel, and tingle. He could feel the air, the dust, the ground beneath his cold and tough boots. Sensation, after a millennium of nothing, was euphoric. Loki looked at the dead milling about in front of him. If they were disappointed about the bridge, they didn't show it. They gazed at him like tired sheep, eyes saying nothing. 'I don't envy you,' he told them with a warm smile. He reached for the first, an old woman standing like a weary arch. Loki clasped her by the neck, took a deep breath, and savoured the soul's power flowing into him. 'Ahh,' he sighed, exhaling. The shadow was a little fainter for it, a little more crooked.

'And now to other business,' he muttered, turning on his heel, hearing the stone crunch. With a swagger normally reserved for drunken kings, Loki ran his fingers along the crumbled wall of the Bifröst, following its curves around and around, until he was leaning over where the rock fell away. He folded his arms, rested his chin on his hands, and smiled down at the man lying slumped against the bridge's broken wall.

Ignoring the armour, he wasn't that much to look at. A few scraggly tattoos, faded and bled with age, spiralled around his fingers and wrists. A long beard was in the middle of escaping from the chin of his helmet, like a frothing river fleeing a tawny cave. Only his face, framed by the red and gold of his open visor, was remarkable. Remarkably young, for a fifteen-hundred year-old man. Barely in his twenties, by Loki's reckoning, though there was an age about him that was hard to see without peering closely. It was the eyes that gave it away. Korrin's eyes were like marbles stolen from an older man. They had a depth and a hardness to them that youth couldn't buy.

Loki was about to speak when all of a sudden, Korrin chuckled. It was a dry old sound from a throat that hadn't tasted the faintest hint of liquid in the best part of five centuries.

'I've seen them all,' he rasped, with a tongue as shrivelled and dry as a boot in the Paraian sun. 'I've seen them all. I've seen creatures stranger than you'd ever care to wonder. I've seen men and women plainer than parchment. I've seen warlords nudge shoulders with thralls and peasants. I've seen princesses and kings mingle with their own servants, not a hint of recognition in their eyes. I've seen old men with young wives. I've seen young men with old faces. Young widowers and old bastards, them too. I've seen children, littler than you'd care to imagine. I've seen grown men by the drove. I've seen soldiers in their crowds, still lined up in battle lines. I've seen the ones snapped up before their time. I've seen dragons more ancient than some of these walls. The ones who died fighting, still painted in righteous blood. The ones who died cowering, still wearing the stains of their own piss. I've seen thieves sent to the noose. I've seen murderers on the run. I've seen judges, scholars, maids, teachers, farmers, bakers, butchers, smiths, sailors, and all the bloody rest. I've seen a few traitors too, in my time. And believe me, god, I've been here a very long time indeed. I know a traitor when I see one. Easy to spot, once you've seen a few.'

Loki was intrigued, he had to admit. 'Tell me, how do you spot one?'

Korrin flicked up two fingers, making no effort to turn them over. 'Two ways, aside from their actions. Two types, you might say. One's a fidgety sort. They wring their hands. They might have a twitch. Plagued with guilt.'

'And the other?'

'Your kind. The ones who beam with pride. Like pillagers counting the notches on their blades. You're easier to spot.'

'And tell me, Korrin,' said Loki, leaning close. 'How do you spot a deserter?'

Korrin chuckled again. He flashed teeth yellow like desert sands. 'I'll tell you this for free. Make a man sit in one place long enough, and he'll meet himself ten, a hundred, a thousand times over. With nobody but the dead for example, and nothing but his thoughts and actions to keep him company, there's nothing left to do but look inwards. I've met Korrin the deserter. I've met Korrin the hero too. I know them both very well. You can't shake me with your forked tongue, god. You're a thousand years too late.'

Loki's smirking face slowly switched places with an expression altogether more stony and dark. 'It seems my time here is short.'

'That it is.'

'Before I go...' Loki reached out for Korrin's helmet, curious. He wondered for a moment what it would feel like, to a god. He already felt alive, intoxicatingly so. Would it make him even more powerful? What would it feel like? Cold steel? Warm glass? It certainly looked like glass, up close. He wondered what…

'Agh!'

…in Emaneska had just happened. Loki clenched his fist as the burning sensation spread down his arm. The armour had stung him, seared him even. His fingertips were blood-red. Loki reached out again with his other hand, seizing a pauldron this time, and the armour bit him again. Loki clasped his hands tightly and growled, the sort of growl when no curses will suffice. Korrin snorted. 'Failsafe. Ask Heimdall, if you ever see him again,' he advised, sweetly.

Loki hissed to himself. What a cruel twist! How sweet, how victorious to be alive and real, only to then suffer its bitter twist: *pain*, of all things. How human! How dare it! Loki trembled with anger as he felt his power surge through his veins.

'I remember something about curiosity and cats…' Korrin commented wistfully.

'It really is time I was leaving,' Loki snapped. And with that, he went to fetch his coat, cast aside at the foot of the bridge. He snatched it from the ground and threw it on. A sliver of something red and gold caught his eye, a glimpse of fingers clasped tightly to the edge of the bridge. Loki licked his lips, edging the toe of his boot closer to the steel fingertips, ready to kick. *One nudge*, he thought, *one little nudge*.

Loki sneered. 'Not yet,' he smiled. He remembered what the Shrieks had told him. 'Not yet.'

'Tyrfing?' came a hoarse whisper from below. Loki stepped away.

'Tyrfing…?'

※

'Tyrfing?' Farden rasped. His tongue was numb. His teeth

ached and rattled in their sockets. His face was numb. Then again, how often could he feel his face? What a stupid thing to ponder, hanging from the edge of the world. 'Uncle, are you there?' His voice was like a file.

Something wriggled in his other hand and a shot of pain coursed down his body, from left shoulder to right foot, like a blade had just been dragged across him. Farden winced, feeling every corner of himself suddenly ache. He preferred the numbness. Definitely the numbness.

'Elessi,' he wheezed, 'hold still, damn it.' Farden look down to where the shadow of the maid hung from his steel grip. She hung like a pellucid fish on a hook, limply dangling into the void. Every now and again she would kick, or wriggle, or reach out for the darkness of the void.

'Fat chance of that,' Farden muttered. He looked up at the broken stub of bridge his fingers clung tightly too. It was all that was left of the Bifröst. Just a shattered lip of rapidly cooling stone. Its colours were dying with its heat, slowly turning to the hue of old, drab iron.

His shoulder had popped free of its socket, that was for sure. He could feel the bone and gristle scraping as he swung slowly back and forth. It was a wonder his fingers were still holding on, but he wasn't about to question them about it. It was a wonder he was still clinging to anything, never mind a dead bridge and a ghost. 'Stubborn luck,' he smiled grimly, thinking of the dragonscale pendant wrapped about his neck.

'Tyrfing!' he called, his tongue less dusty than before. He still sounded like a file. 'Are you there?! Now would be a good time to lend a hand!'

Silence. Not even the muttering of the dead. He had heard voices before, in his semi-conscious state, but they were quiet now. Farden winced as Elessi wriggled again. He had to try something else.

'Korrin!' he called. 'Can you hear me? If you're there, I need your help.'

Silence again. Not a rustle. Not a sound. Farden wondered briefly if he had gone deaf in the explosion. He decided to keep trying. 'Korrin, my name is Farden. You wouldn't know me. I doubt you knew any of my ancestors. I doubt you even know what I am, or have heard of where I'm from. All a little bit after your time, I suppose. But I know a lot about you. A great deal indeed. I'm something of your inheritor, I suppose. Your heir.' Farden looked up as he heard a scraping. A little crumbling of dust fell in his eyes. He kept talking. 'I've been looking for you and that armour for a long time. Years and years.' Farden winced. 'That's probably not long to you, but... Anyway. I'm not a thief, or a grave-robber, if that's what you've assumed. I'm not here to steal the armour for my own nefarious means. I need it. Everybody needs it. We need it to stop...'

'And I thought the dead talked too much,' said a voice. Farden looked up, and saw a face he had only ever seen painted in light. Farden let his mouth flap open, no words coming out.

'Better,' said Korrin, thrusting out a hand flecked with old tattoos, nails bitten and crammed with dirt. 'Give me the woman. Careful now.'

Farden took a few sharp breaths and heaved. Mercifully, Elessi was lighter than he had first thought. She still had some weight to her, more weight that a ghost rightfully should have, but still, he managed it. Heaving up and up, he raised her past his waist and chest, pausing only briefly as her face brushed his, a flash of something cold and not altogether there, and then up into Korrin's waiting hand. He dragged her onto the rock and disappeared. Farden spat the dust from his mouth.

It took an age for him to return, and a painful age at that. Farden managed to get two hands on the Bifröst's remains, but it still didn't alleviate the searing of his left shoulder. His feet scrabbled uselessly at the faceless rock below him. 'Give me your hands,' said a voice, more familiar than the last. Tyrfing, bleary-eyed and bleeding from the nose, popped his head over the edge. 'One at a time, if you please.'

Farden did as he was told, first the left, then the right. Tyrfing winced at his strong grip, the grip of a man who had spent the last half hour clinging to the lip of a cliff. Tyrfing hauled him up until his boots touched the bridge. Tyrfing sagged to the rock but Farden rushed to Korrin's side, sprawled as he was against the wall. Elessi was standing nearby, still like a stone. Not going anywhere.

Farden knelt by Korrin's side and looked deep into his grey marble eyes, impossibly deep. They flicked down to the mage's glittering wrists, his hands, and his feet. 'So, Farden. It appears that you were right. We do have much in common.'

'That we do,' Farden said, softly. His own eyes had wandered to the folds of the dusty breastplate, bright gold over blood-red. Scalussen scales, sharp, hard, and impossibly intricate. He looked at the whorls of the inlaid design, splayed across Korrin's chest. A lone wolf, hackles raised, baring its teeth at the gold tendrils of a lofty moon. *A lone wolf, of all things. How perfect.* 'More than I thought,' Farden dared a smile.

'You may not be a grave-robber, but you've certainly got the eyes of one.'

'It's been a long time…'

'…searching. I imagine.'

'You chose a good hiding place.'

Korrin looked around at his cave. He knew every rock and crack. He had counted them beyond a thousand times. 'Spacious. Company's terrible. Always talking, whispering. Thank the gods for this,' he sighed, tapping a finger to the side of his helmet. Farden hungrily took in its curves, the way the visor mimicked a face, how the overlapping scales formed horns and spikes that ran down to join the neck of the cuirass, like a dragon's spine. 'So, what perils face the world?'

'Daemons.'

Korrin nodded. 'Never fought those. Humans were bad enough.'

'Would you fight with us?'

'No.' The reply was like a stone dropping. Final. 'I made a deal with Hel. I stay here until I die, and then I'm hers. I had planned on crossing this bridge one day, but it seems that plan has been scuppered.'

Farden lowered his head. Korrin saw his fists clench.

'As you can imagine,' Korrin shrugged his armoured shoulders. 'Hel's been waiting a long time.' Farden couldn't help but crack a smile.

'What now then? What would you have me do?'

'You go to fight these daemons?'

'I do.'

'The gods have chosen you to be their champion?'

Farden looked up at the ceiling of the cave. 'In a fashion.'

'Then it is time you set me free, warrior. Heir indeed,' Korrin began to pant then, as if he were having trouble catching his breath. 'It has been too long.'

Slowly, respectfully, trying hard to hold back his hunger, Farden took the armour piece by magnificent piece. First the sabatons, folded over his boots. They wrapped around him like old friends, long lost, reaching up to meld with his greaves at the knee. Farden shivered, feeling that old familiar ice-water sensation as they tightened around him.

Shrugging off his cloak and jacket, Farden reached for the cuirass. His fingers found the latches, set deep into the metal, and they unfolded by themselves with a metallic whisper. Korrin's eyes were half-closed as he lifted his arms, letting the armour unwrap itself from his skin. He wore nothing but a dirty old tunic underneath, barely an inch from tattered, dusty rags. Farden felt a pang of guilt. Korrin sensed it. 'Put it on, hero. Put it on.'

Farden did so with a will. Ignoring the pain in his shoulder, he slipped the cuirass over his head, noting with a grin at how the breastplate's ribs expanded to let him in. Moments later it was tightening around him. The scales contracted and shivered into a tight, but not uncomfortable fit. The metal sucked itself in, following every contour of his ribs, his spine, and his shoulders. The pauldrons and rerebraces shivered as they unfolded and slid down to meet his trusty old vambraces. Scale met scale and intertwined like lovers. They couldn't have been a more perfect match. Farden almost bent double as the metal joined, feeling the dizzying rush of its power in his veins. His shoulder popped painfully as the armour forced it back into place.

As he bent his chin to the metal, riding the pain, euphoria, and everything in between, he looked down to find the wolf's eyes looking back at him, two tiny rubies embedded into the metal. Farden let his fingers touch them, and then he forced himself to his feet, riding the surge.

The helmet was last. Korrin had turned a frighteningly pale colour. Lines had drawn themselves in his skin. He was ageing now that the armour was being taken from him. 'The helmet,' Korrin whispered, through thin lips and fast-receding gums. He bowed his head to let Farden take it. Farden bent down and slowly lifted it free. He raised it high above his head, like a king receiving his crown. All but closing his eyes, he brought it down over his head. The world went dark as the helmet's visor slammed shut. Farden heard the scraping of the scales as they coupled.

It was done.

Farden lifted the visor, sliding it back along his forehead. Not a scrape, not a whine of rusty hinges was heard. The armour was as perfect as the day it had landed on the smith's table. Farden could barely keep from quivering, whether from the sheer joy, from the ice-cold sensation of the metal, or from the pain that was flashing up and down his body, racing through his blood, he didn't know. He couldn't tell if it was healing him or hurting him. He hoped the former.

Farden looked down at Korrin, a final, 'Thank you,' ready to tumble from his lips. But when he looked, he found Korrin dead, eyes open and lips frozen in a final little half-smile. Farden knelt down and reverently closed his eyes for him. 'Hero,' he whispered. 'I hope that I can be as half as good.'

'It's time, Farden,' Tyrfing whispered. He had Elessi by the wrist. He was already pointing toward the exit.

'That it is,' Farden replied with a sigh. He turned to Elessi, leaning close to her faded face. Her eyes didn't see him, they simply looked through him as if he were a pane of glass. 'We're not done yet,' he said.

☙

And they ran. They ran as fast as their legs could carry them, hurtling through the tunnels, barging through the crowded dead like spears through shoals of bewildered fish.

Farden was in front, Elessi in his hand. His red-gold legs pounded the rock as though he were a daemon himself. His breathing came in gulping gasps as they swerved left, right, then left again, weaving their frantic way through the tunnels.

Tyrfing was bringing up the rear. To his credit, he kept pace with his nephew. His breathing was atrocious. He hawked and spat and panted and coughed all the way.

And still they ran.

It was only when the river and *Naglfar* came into view that they slowed. Farden jogged ahead while Tyrfing stumbled to a canter, then a fast walk, then a pained shuffle, hands pressed to his ribs.

'Hel!' Farden was yelling. The dead were crowded around the ship, which was listing to one side, as if it had run aground. The dead were travellers without maps now, aimless and confused. They milled about in their clumps, telling each other their stories and lives in their quiet little whispers. A precious few looked up at the newcomers, vacantly confused at the sound of a man in full armour clattering by, dragging a shadow with him, and moments later followed by an older man, croaking painfully.

'Farden!' Tyrfing cried, but his nephew was oblivious. He was already at the ship. Tyrfing walked a little faster.

'Traitor,' Hel was hissing to Farden, when Tyrfing reached the bow of the ship. He put out a hand to steady himself and thought better of it. *Toenails*, came the thought. That, and the slimy legs of the grotesque figurehead were only a few feet away. It looked down at him, licking its vulture beak.

'What cost, he asks, what cost!' it was mouthing. Tyrfing scowled darkly at it.

'Which way did he go?!' Farden demanded, by his uncle's side.

Hel was leaning over the bulwark. 'He has escaped, Farden! It matters not where he has gone. He has broken it. The Bifröst! The dead are lost!' she cried.

'Then which way do we go? How do we get out?'

Hel was rubbing her pale forehead with her black fingernails. She positively shook with rage. 'Traitor,' she was saying. 'You hear me, sisters? Brothers? You sent down a traitor!'

'Hel! How do we get out of this godsforsaken place? Honour your bargain!' It probably was not the best choice of words given the circumstances, or their host, but Hel was too furious to notice. Anything but the last sentence, that was.

'Oh, I intend to, mage,' she said, looking him and his armour up and down. He glittered like flame. She threw an idle look in

Tyrfing's direction, then flicked a finger at the river. 'Enter the river, and you shall return to whence you came.'

'If this is a trick...'

Hel's eyes flashed with anger. 'There was but one trickster in Hel, and he has left. I keep my bargains, Farden Protector, now get out of my sight. In the river with you. Get out of my sight.'

'Protector?' Farden asked, as he marched Elessi to the shore. The vulture twitched its pinned-together wings.

'Protector, she calls you! For the armour! What do you think Scalussen means, in the old tongue? Hmm?' it squawked, seemingly proud of itself. Farden gave it a wide berth.

Together they moved clear of the listing *Naglfar*, and made for the edge of the rushing river. It was flowing much faster than before, as if it too shared Hel's wrath. Farden manoeuvred Elessi to the edge of the hissing waters and turned her to face him. He stared deep into her glassy eyes. 'You're going home,' he said to her, shaking her lightly by the shoulders. *Gods, her skin was cold.* She didn't seem to hear him, or even acknowledge he was there. She looked about, completely deaf, dumb, and blind to the mage. 'Well, here goes,' he said, pushing her gently outwards. She toppled like a frozen tree, half-heartedly flailing as she hit the water. The river swallowed her up in moments, and she disappeared into the shimmering waters.

'You next, uncle. This place is killing you,' Farden reached for Tyrfing's arm. Behind them, the figurehead cackled rather disturbingly, making the skin on Farden's neck twitch.

'No, you first, nephew,' Tyrfing smiled weakly, a little blood on his lip, gently pushing Farden's armoured hand away with his own, wrinkles around his mouth quivering bravely, and it was in that moment that Farden knew.

'It's you, isn't it? The cost of crossing...' Farden slumped. His stomach knotted up again in an instant, adding to the pain of the armour that still coursed through his body. He grimaced as he reached for his knees.

'I'm dying, Farden. My lungs are rotting. A tumour, the healers call it. No spells can touch it,' he smiled wider, eyes blinking hard. 'In a way it's a mercy to go out like this instead of, well, the usual Written way. I already lost my mind once. Can't have that again, can we?' Tyrfing chuckled dryly.

'Two goodbyes in as many minutes,' Farden was muttering.

'I'm sorry, Farden. At least we had one this time. And what you said to Hel,' his uncle paused, 'this armour is the start of a new life for you, nephew, I know it.'

Farden bit his lip until he tasted salt and metal, felt the hot trickle fill his mouth. He took a strangled breath, throat tight. He grimaced, showing the blood on his teeth. 'But we need you,' he said, making a half gesture at the river, at the roof of the cavern. 'Your magick...'

'I can't leave,' Tyrfing said. They heard a rustle above them, and turned to see Hel standing at the prow of the ship. Her face gave away nothing. Tyrfing clapped his hands. 'Besides,' he said. 'You have enough magick for both of us.'

Farden snorted, but his uncle put his hand on his shoulder. 'Don't you feel it Farden? That pain? That burning? It's been so long you don't know what it is. I can feel it coming off you in waves. Don't fight it.'

Farden shook his head, closing his stinging eyes. He took a deep breath as the pain surged around his chest and up into his head. *Yes*. That old feeling. That sharp pain at the base of his skull, like a blade to his spine. No, it wasn't pain any more, it was just pressure, just a rushing of blood and magick, burning the dust from his nerves, flushing out cobwebs and clutter like a broom across a forgotten floor. No wonder his back felt hot and clammy. No wonder his hands were shaking.

Farden opened up a shaking fist and felt his arm spasm as the magick tumbled down it, a landslide through his veins. Fire flashed into life in his palm, swirling like a tornado.

'See?' Tyrfing grinned as wide as he could, still gripping Farden by the shoulder. His nephew clenched his fist and put out the spell, then dragged Tyrfing into a near-crushing hug. It lasted only a moment, but they both knew it meant the world; a thousand words, what-ifs, and tears, anger, grief, and acceptance, all crushed into the clank and shudder of one short embrace. Sometimes that was all that people needed. Actions spoke when words were too hard.

'Go,' Tyrfing pushed him away. 'The others need you.'

Farden staggered back and jabbed a finger at Hel. 'You keep him safe,' he said, before turning back to Tyrfing. He slammed his visor shut, lest he see the tears. 'At least I know you're not going anywhere.'

Tyrfing smiled, and watched Farden turn, stamp the cobbles to death, and then dive headlong into the rushing waters with a giant splash.

Hel sniffed. 'He's a good man, your nephew,' she mused.

Tyrfing staggered onto his knees. 'No,' he said, shaking his head. 'He's a great man.'

Chapter 32

"No, I do not know what he was thinking. There isn't a scribble this quill can make that could describe by frustration, how exasperated I am with the man. To take on a Huskar chief's son in a fist-fight. Not for honour, no, but for pure greed. For the son's vambraces no less. Pretty they may be, exceptionally so in fact, but not pretty enough to jeopardise our tenuous political links with the Huskar tribes for. Not for all the Scalussen in the world would I risk another border skirmish with those savage beasts. I thank Evernia that the son instigated the bout. Thank Evernia indeed. Though I suppose it is worth noting that Farden did win the fight.
Regards,
Kospregr."
Extract from a report to the Undermage, from Sergeant Kospregr, of the School of the Written

'I feel sorry for her, y'know,' said the woman. She had a soft, fair face, with a birth-mark spread like a splatter of jam across her temple and forehead. 'Poor lamb.'

'Hasn't got much of a chance. Not out here. Should have taken her back to the ship. Who is she, anyway?' asked the other. She was quite the opposite in appearance. She had an axe-head of a face. Blunt and severe. Her lips looked to be having a contest of how close they could get to her nose.

The first woman rolled her eyes. The two healers were huddled around a candle on the bedside and like the woman on the bed they had drowned themselves in blankets to keep the cold at bay. They shivered all the same. 'I told you, it's the Undermage's wife. Poor lamb. Struck down on her wedding day too.'

'Her? How'd you know?'

'Cook told me.'

'Cook tells more lies than, than...' the second woman's lips twitched, flinging themselves at her nose in a wild effort. '...Than is right for one man to tell. Ship's full of 'is rumours.' She leant close and watched their patient's chest for any signs of movements. She squinted. It was hard to tell if there were any. 'If I didn't know better, I'd say she was already dead.'

'Nonsense. *Daemontouched* they said. Coma.'

'Daemonrubbish.'

'His Mage's own words.'

'If we were back on the ship...'

'Oh, here we go...'

'...If we were back on the ship, with a proper bed and a proper light, I might actually be able to do some medicinal good to this woman. Not sittin' here watching her freeze to death. Here, in this rabbit-hutch of a sled? On this ice? We're useless, we are. She hasn't got a chance. And who's going to explain to the Undermage, when he gets back? Hmm? Not me. *If* he gets back, that is. Then we'll be in hot water. We might as well have stayed with the ship. And another thing... BLEEDIN' NJORD!'

Two panicked screams split the air as the half-dead woman on the bed sat bolt upright. The two healers fell to the floor and scrabbled under a table. The severe-looking one reached for a butter knife, the other for a pillow to cover her eyes.

'She's awake!'

'She's possessed!'

Elessi retched and rasped. She flailed about like a mad thing, sending blankets flying all over the place. 'Far...den!' she choked.

'Farden?' cried the healers in unison.

Elessi turned around, eyes bloodshot crimson and wild with bewilderment. 'He's coming!'

※

Something was licking him. That was for sure. There was no other sensation like it. A wet slab of warm meat sliding and rasping across his skin, mingled with the feel of escaped breath, then a trail of cold following in its wake as the wet cooled in the icy air. A tongue. It had to be.

Farden opened his bleary eyes to find he was absolutely right. He just hadn't expected what sort of tongue, and the creature that owned it. He couldn't help but jump. He nearly made it to his feet, he flew up so fast. Instead he sank back on his knees, and watched the huge whale slide further onto the ice, rearing up out of its narrow waterway. Farden wiped his wet, slimy cheek, and pulled a polite smile.

'Where?' he began to ask, then his smile fell. His body sagged with it. Ice. Whales. Water. He was in the north alright, but days from the battle. That cursed Hel and her bastard ship. Farden put his fist in the snow, listening to it sizzle.

Then he heard it. That far off roar that could have been taken for a storm. But it wasn't, not to his seasoned ear. It was too sharp, too metallic. It was the unmistakable roar of battle.

Farden's head snapped north. There, cradled in a broken notch of the gigantic, blackened mountains, was a cloud of smoke and ash, its insides roiling with kaleidoscopic hues. Red turned to yellow, turned to blue, turned to green. The noise of it deafened even the flaming fury of the mountains and volcanos at its back. Farden watched as two bright, shining stars fell from the sky and dove straight into the haze. They exploded somewhere in its depths. Even at that distance the snow shook.

It was then that Farden spied his daughter on the hill, just on the cusp of the chaos. He could feel her too. Finally he understood. Shaking, trembling, the air was alive with her magick. It rose and fell for miles around like winter waves crashing on a snowy shore. Farden felt his head pound as he squinted at her. She was a bright star on a black hill, wrapped in fire and magick. His daughter. The paragon of magick. Apotheosis of power. Samara.

Farden got to his feet, shaking. He snarled. She would die like the rest of them.

'Ice is cracking,' hummed the whale, licking its dagger teeth. Its obsidian skin glistened in the dawn light.

'What?'

'Ice.' The whale slapped his flipper. 'Cracking.'

'Er…'

'We ride with it.'

Farden really wasn't getting the picture. 'Ride with what? Where?'

The whale waggled its fin as it slid back into the water. Farden could see dark shapes sliding along underneath, deep in the sapphire water. He suppressed a shiver. 'Into battle. Cracks are running under the mountains. Sea bubbles up. We fight.'

'Now?'

'Now! You ride with us.'

Farden slammed down his visor. Gods, he loved the feel of that. 'One question. How?'

The whale leant to the side so that his tall fin nearly knocked Farden in the face. 'I swim. You ride.'

Farden lifted up his visor again. 'I what?'

Samara shuddered. Not with fear, not with revulsion. She simply shook. Her body was failing. She could feel it. The sky was nearly emptied. Only a few dozen now remained, but only one could be next. It was time. She could feel him darkening the sky already, feel him pressing his mind into hers, commanding her, crushing her. Samara winced as she reached for him. It was his turn now.

Orion.

Samara's knees had long since failed her. She was now collapsed on her side, foetus-like in her black bowl of charred, splintered rock. The fire still spun, and the wind still howled. *Only a few dozen left,* she told herself for the tenth time in the last minute. Her eyelids felt as though they were made from hot lead. The feeling of triumph and power she had felt barely an hour ago had now all but vanished, burnt away by the searing, bubbling pain that wracked her body. She could still feel Lilith's worried eyes on the back of her scorched neck. *Only a few dozen left, then I rest, and ride on their shoulders.*

And she pulled. She pulled with all the might she had left to spare. Her arms were near ripped clean of their sockets when her spell found him. He seized her with iron claws like anchor flukes. Samara cried out as her shoulders inched further. She bit down on the magick and the spell bit back. Something snapped in her back, as the daemon came loose, prized from the void above.

She slumped into her hole, almost letting the spell cave in on her as she watched Orion light up the sky above. Hokus' ugly head appeared over the stone, a mask of teeth and blood that wasn't his. 'He is coming,' he veritably cheered. Samara nodded weakly. 'You have served your purpose well, child,' he grinned, turning to yell and roar at any of his brethren that could hear him. 'HE IS COMING!'

'Who's coming, brother?' Valefor looked up from picking the purple entrails from his claws. The two were acting like foremen, directing their bloody workers with roars, shouts, and slashes from their claws and nails. Theirs was a most gratifying job. From their little fire-smeared and blood-splashed pedestal they could watch their brothers and sisters falling from the sky with grins and welcoming arms; they could crush anything that dared come near enough to take a swipe at them; they could taste the roars, the screams, the destruction. It was what they had dreamt of for centuries. Salivated at in the darkness. Music to their stubby ears.

They had even dabbled in some fighting too. Their spoils lay spread across the rocks below. Two dragons, a bear, and countless little four-limbed insects. But it hadn't been all fun and games. Valefor had a chunk missing from his side. His left foot had been smashed by a big dragon-rider with an axe. Hokus was missing several claws and had a lightning burn across his chest from Durnus. The mages had struck early and viciously, but with every daemon that fell, they had been forced back into the smoke. Valefor and Hokus were enjoying themselves immensely.

'Who do you think, brother Valefor?'

'Our glorious king?'

'The very same.'

Valefor clapped his claws and raised them to the sky. Sure enough, there he was, hovering in the dawn-lit firmament, teetering like the jewel of a broken pendant, already beginning to fall. He would be there very soon indeed. 'He will be most pleased that we have left some for him. The Old Dragon, perhaps, should be kept for him. Ruin too, as he ordered.'

'Insects,' Hokus growled. A fireball flew out of the smoke and clattered against the rocks behind them. They heard a distant squeal from Lilith. 'They never stood a chance.'

Valefor giggled as he watched another clump of mages shuffle out of the smog at the foot of the hill, accompanied by a lithe black dragon. 'If you'll excuse me, brother.'

Hokus flashed his fangs, but waggled a claw. 'Overconfidence is dangerous, brother.'

'I'll remind them of that, before I sever their heads,' Valefor snarled over his shoulder, flexing his smoking wings.

※

Shivertread let the carcass of the huge wolf slide from his jaws and drop to the snow. The fetid creature hissed as its last breath escaped from its lungs.

'We should fall back,' hissed the dragon, fearfully. All around them, hulking shadows battled with pockets of resistance and bravery. There were too many to count.

'We should keep going, dragon,' Modren snapped, pushing Durnus on. 'We're close! We kill her and we may just have a chance!'

Modren was right. No sooner had he spoken than they emerged from the blinding smoke at the foot of the hill, where the black rocks rose out of the dirty snow, rising up to join the mountains. 'There!' the Undermage cried.

Durnus could see her now. He squinted at the bright, fiery spot in his blind darkness. It was Samara, slumped in the broken stone. Was she dead? His heart rose and fell in a moment, hope dashed on the rocks. He could still feel her spell shaking the air. He could still hear its roar over the noise of battle and the volcano.

There was a snarl from somewhere nearby. They had been spotted. Two daemons loped towards them across the snow. One was a muscular beast, half boar by the looks of his face, while the other was a slim, slender willow of a creature, all wings and oversized teeth.

Modren and Inwick went to work like the professionals they were, laying down a storm of sparks and lightning to keep the daemons at bay. Spells were the only thing that seemed to truly work against them. Blades took forever to hack through their iron flesh, and even then it meant getting close. The bastards refused to die quickly, fighting to the bitter bone. Oh, how Modren prayed for more mages.

Thooooom!

The air behind them shook as Durnus' spell flew from his hands. The Arkmage dashed forward, listening for its impact, watching the bright spark on the hill and praying for it to be snuffed. There was a booming crash as his spell collided with hers, fire meeting wind in an explosion of power. Blue flame curled around its edges. Durnus watched, catching his breath as the spark glowed brighter for a moment. Then, as the light faded, there she still was, untouched and still reaching for the sky. 'Curse that bitch!' he yelled.

Another daemon was coming for them, sauntering down the slopes. This one was a different sort. Modren recognised his gait, his wings, his grinning face. It was one of the three that had attacked Krauslung. Shivertread stepped forward, spinning his tail in a figure-of-eight like a whip.

'No,' Modren said, tapping him on his scales. 'He's mine.'

'As you wish,' bowed the dragon, turning instead to the other two. They were getting too close for comfort. Inwick and Shivertread forced them back, the dragon bathing one in fire, the mage bringing the smaller to its knees with a well-placed ice-bolt.

'Keep them busy!' Durnus ordered, taking in a deep breath. He spread his hands wide and fire sprang into life between them. Orbs of hot flame spun and melded into bigger spheres, building, building, ever-building into a colossal fireball.

Modren felt the heat of it on his back. His Book burned with it. He held out his sword at the approaching daemon. The hulking beast was now standing on the snow, not twelve paces from them.

Even from there, he could smell its stink. 'I know you,' he said.

'Lord. Master. Executioner. Take your pick, mortal,' it chuckled.

'You attacked our city.'

'It will not be the last.'

'How about I make it your last?'

The daemon didn't answer. It was looking with interest at Durnus and his huge spell. Everyone ducked as it exploded from his arms and sailed to the summit of the hill, where it crashed once again against Samara's storm. 'Ah, Ruin,' said the daemon.

Durnus' head snapped around to face the sound of his name.

The daemon flicked its eyes to the sky above, and smiled some more. Modren kept his eyes firmly rooted on the daemon, picking out the spots he wanted to drive his sword into. Face. Ribs. Groin. He skipped the heart; he had realised early on that these creatures were devoid of such a thing.

'It's fortuitous that we should run into each other, Ruin,' chatted the daemon. He twirled a claw. 'Your father will be here momentarily. I imagine the two of you have lots to catch up on.'

Durnus tilted his head to the sky and squinted. A shiver, somewhere far above. That was all he needed. He spoke slowly and carefully. 'Modren, call the others back. I think the time has come to beat a retreat to the sleds, as fast as we can.'

'But…'

'No, Modren, now!'

'Right you are. Inwick! Shivertread! We're leaving!'

'So soon?' the daemon called after them as they sprinted away, the dragon spraying fire in their wake. Durnus, his hand firmly clamped to Modren's arm, had begun to sweat.

'What's going on, Durnus?'

'Orion. He will be arriving very soon indeed. We do not want to be anywhere near him when he d…'

A chilling shout cut him off, ripping through the battle noise. It was a shout that nobody wanted to hear, at a time when they had enough to worry about with daemons and dragons and death, when they were sure in their knowledge that whatever happened, they were standing on solid ground.

'The ice is cracking! The ice is cracking!'

Wide-eyed, Modren glanced over his shoulder. The ice was cracking indeed, and rapidly at that. A dark line had appeared in the snow directly behind them, and was getting bigger by the second. Even worse, the daemon from the hill was now running to vault it, fire streaming from his jaws, claws outstretched, wings flapping behind him, eyes firmly fixed on them.

'Watch out!' Modren yelled, throwing the Arkmage to the snow, fire already simmering in his hand. He needn't have worried. The strange twists of battle were about to save him the trouble.

Nobody could have predicted a whale. Least of all Valefor.

The daemon pounded the snow with all his might. He could feel the fire in his lungs. In his peripheral vision he could see it dribbling from the corners of his mouth. His hands swung up and down like chopping axes, propelling him forward. He grinned wide as he saw Durnus pushed to the ground by the impetuous mage. Fool. *I will start with him*, Valefor thought, as he went to leap the crack in the ice, not even sparing a thought for the dark water bubbling up from below. *I will start with him, pulling each one of his fingers and toes off while Ruin lays in the snow, ready fo…*

To those watching, the surprise was painfully obvious. Valefor's hungry grin evaporated in a split-second as the ice to his left gave way to an enormous, shimmering whale, half-black, half white, and pink jaws open very wide indeed. The strangest thing was that there seemed to be a red and gold man clinging to its towering fin, holding on for dear life as the creature launched itself from the water and through the air.

Valefor squealed as the whale's jaws clamped down on his neck, half severing his head in the first strike. The whale bore him down to the snow, through the ice, and into the water with a crash and a damp hiss. All that remained in their wake was the red-gold man rolling through the snow to safety.

Modren let his mouth hang wide open as he watched the man stand up, shake the water off, and then march straight towards him. Modren didn't know whether to hug him or skewer him. Only the armour stopped him, that old familiar armour...

'Farden!' Modren cried. Durnus leapt up from the snow at the sound of his name.

'Where?' Durnus yelled.

'Right here.'

Durnus followed the sound of the voice, reaching out with his steaming hands. He found the metal of Farden's chest, and smiled. 'You did it.'

Modren barged in, grabbing him by the shoulders, caring nothing for the armour. 'Did you? Did you do it?' he demanded.

Farden raised his visor, exposing a wet and bedraggled face, but a stone-cold honest face at that. 'I did,' he said, barely finishing his words before Modren clasped him tightly around the neck. He said nothing, but Farden knew.

All around them, they could hear the cracking of the ice and the booming of whales, the roaring of daemons and the screams of everything else. Farden slammed his visor shut. 'I need a sword,' he barked, holding out a hand. It was Inwick that pressed one into his palm. She was trying on a smile for size. It didn't suit her, but at least she was trying. Farden nodded to her.

'She's summoned Orion, Farden. He is coming,' Durnus

pointed to the sky. Farden looked up through the smoke to see a bright orb glinting in the morning sky, getting bigger every second. They did not have long at all.

'Stay behind me. Far behind me.'

※

Farden was a whirlwind. Fire sprang from the cracks in his armour as he waded into the smoke like a man who had never heard of death. Farden would have cackled at that. As he had said to Hel, he knew it better than most.

The first daemon he came across was a monstrous bastard. It was in the midst of flaying the skin from a band of helpless snowmads. Farden beat his sword against his breastplate to get its attention. He got it almost instantly, much to the daemon's horror. The creature stumbled backwards as he saw the shining knight striding towards him, sword in one gauntlet, a ball of fire in the other. He could smell the armour, and something in it terrified him. He scrabbled to get away, but he didn't get far. Farden hacked the muscles of his legs into ribbons, and then cut him open across the stomach. The daemon burbled and wailed as Farden marched on, leaving him for the others.

'Godblood!' went up the cry, as another two daemons spotted him. They backed away from him, roaring at the top of their voices to warn the others. Two giant wolves lunged forward in their stead, so big they took Farden's breath away for a dark moment. But the armour had made him feel invincible. Whether he truly was or not, he could test that later.

The first wolf swiped a paw the size of a seat cushion at his head, catching a glancing blow across his helmet. The force made Farden stumble and he fell to the snow. The wolves dove upon him, jaws snapping at his limbs, trying to crack and pierce his armour.

Farden fought back the urge to laugh after his initial panic faded. The sound of their fangs sliding uselessly off the metal was almost comical.

An old habit called to him, and he slammed his vambraces together with a joyous cry. A wall of magick punched outwards from his skin, and the wolves were sent flying. One landed in a nearby crack in the ice, and was quickly snatched into the water by something long and sleek. The other was seen to by Shivertread, who strangled it in his lithe coils.

So it went. Daemon to daemon, beast to beast, Farden went, slashing, hacking, chopping, burning, and unleashing every pent-up ounce of his long-dead magick. Fire pulsed from every crack and pore in his skin as if it were dying to escape. Farden could feel his Book burning white-hot on his back. It was like nothing he had ever felt, not in all the years he could remember being a mage. He loved every burning second of it.

North he strode. Towards the hill he knew his daughter stood on. He could still feel her magick washing over the battlefield like an angry sea. Behind and around him, sensing the momentary turn in the tide, the pitiful few survivors began to swarm and clump together. Pitiful few indeed, and they were battered and bloodied but grim-faced, every single one ready to see this business finished. They walked in the mage's wake, pointing, cheering. Farden simply marched on, oblivious to all.

Another daemon dared to challenge him, a two-headed creature with long-flowing locks of black hair. Farden barely broke his pace as the daemon towered over him, swiping with her claws. Farden punched the air and sent her staggering with a shaft of lightning to her midriff. A sword followed quickly after, burying itself in her neck with a shiver of blue fire. Farden rode the beast to the ground as she toppled, and wrenched his sword free before she hit the ground. Farden grimaced. The bitch's spine had split the blade down the middle.

'Farden! Eyes to the sky!'

'Shit!' Farden cursed. Orion was falling fast now, a behemoth of fire and brimstone, hurtling towards earth. He could hear the roar over the crowd. The battle noise fell to a lull as every eye turned to watch the king of daemons fall. Both sides took a breath, and waited.

Farden broke into a jog. An idea had formed in his mind. A stupid, rash idea, but an idea nonetheless. A little inkling, a little gem of a chance. Could it work? Was he mad? Probably. Was he invincible? He had wanted to test it. *Not so soon!*

Farden's jog turned into a run. The star was plummeting faster now. The air was growing hot. The ground shuddered and cracked even more. Farden looked up and down, measuring where the star was going to hit. *The foot of the hill. Right on the main stage.*

Farden's run broken into a sprint. Daemons snarled as he passed. Farden flailed his sword at every one that dared try to grope or snag him. Severed claws and howls chased him across the snow. 'Foot of the hill!' he gasped. *Was he really going to do this?*

A daemon on the hill was pointing at him and yelling something, its eyes wild pinpricks of urgent fire. A dragon roared as it swooped down to grab him. Farden threw a hand in the air and sparks flew. The dragon swerved away.

Orion flashed past the peaks. The world had turned a blinding white. Farden hurtled on. *Was he really going to do this?*

'Stop him!' came the daemons' cries. He could hear them now. It was too late. Nothing was close enough. Arrows clattered off his back.

'Am I really going to do this?!' Farden yelled to himself, tasting his own panic.

He could feel the searing heat of Orion, painfully close above him.

Farden grit his teeth.

Too late now.

Farden let a roar rip from his throat as he threw himself into a desperate slide, directly into the star's path. Farden raised his sword above his head and clenched with every scrap of muscle and magick his body knew. In the moments before Orion collided with him, he dared to crack open an eye. Just before the fire blinded him, he swore he saw the daemon's face, a sour look pasted on it, one very much like fear.

The impact was indescribable. Farden would later try, on late evenings and drunken nights slouched in armchairs, or quietly to himself, in the darkened hours of restless morning. All he felt was the most incredible battering of his life. There was fire, he knew that. Thunder too. All the battlefield saw was a blinding flash of light.

The aftermath, once the fire had died away, and once the mage had prized himself from the hole, was simple enough to describe. It was a bloody mess, and it made the heart of every daemon present, for they do indeed have hearts, rise into their mouths and stick there like a fish-bone.

No eye could tear itself away from the gloriously grotesque sight: a mage cradling a molten sword, his glittering armour now charred and blackened by soot and burnt rock, kneeling in the snow, two halves of a gigantic daemon carcass lying either side of him. Bones and black blood arranged in a tortured little spiral, the work of some morbid artist. A face frozen in death, fanged maw open almost as wide as the eyes, staring up at the sky, as if they were wishing they had never come down at all.

Chapter 33

"If sorrow were a season, it would be winter - the numb blue of the ice, and the keen edge of the wind in your gut."
Old Albion saying

Farden's boots crunched on the cooling stone. Half of it had turned to glass.

'Hello, Farden,' spat the curled-up little creature in the centre of the mess. Farden twisted off his helmet and set it down. He perched on a scorched lump of rock.

'Samara,' Farden looked at his daughter. She was a shivering wreck. Half her clothes had been burnt to rags. Her hair was tangled and scorched. He swore he could see a bone sticking from the skin of her left leg and her knees were twisted in a way that brought bile into the back of his throat.

'Come to gloat?'

Farden shook his head. He ran a gauntlet through his sweaty, lank hair, noting how his daughter's hair colour was the same as his own. 'No, I've come to see you.'

Samara lifted up a hand as if to try to summon something to burn him, or shock him, or pierce him, but she was too weak, too spent. She let her hand fall, useless. 'You've ruined everything!' she hissed, venomous as a snake. Had her mouth not been scorched and parched she would have spat at him. Everything she had worked for, lived for, and dreamt of had ended in that last blinding flash. No applause for her. No parading around on shoulders. No shower of praise. No worshipping. Nothing. She had been deserted. A broken tool, left to rot alone.

Farden looked out over the battlefield. The smoke had cleared a little. For the first time, it was possible to see what carnage had been left by the fighting. It too made the bile rise. Black specks and shapes, some big, some small, littered the dirty snow, stretching into the distance. He sighed. 'Look at what you've done, Samara.'

'You deserved it, you and all your kind!'

Farden shook his head at the blind fury, wondering how many lies had been told for it to sink this deep. 'What have we ever done?'

'You? You killed my father Vice, my mother Cheska. You and the others. That uncle of yours, and Ruin! You all conspired to kill them. Murderers and thieves, worshipping those fake gods!'

Farden got to his feet, a deep frown on his dirty brow and a strange feeling lodged in his chest. 'We what?' he whispered.

'You heard me, mage. Thieves and murderers!' she yelled, thrashing around. Tears squeezed themselves from the corners of her eyes. The pain was easy to see. Farden watched her carefully. Her eyes shivered between colours, turning green as he stared at them, then to an angry red. Her back was broken. He could tell by the way she was curled. He dreaded to think what the black bruises on her side said about her ribs and lungs. He wondered how much time she had. No spell could save her. He realised then that she had been bred for one purpose only. She had never been meant to survive this.

'Samara,' Farden said slowly. 'Vice wasn't your father. I am.'

The look on her face was positively acidic. 'Lies.'

'Vice was the murderer. Cheska was his niece. He was not your father.'

'Lies!'

Farden stamped his foot, making her flinch. He could see the pain bubbling beneath her skin. He crouched down by her side. 'You know as well as I do what the daemons wanted you for, don't you?'

'A weapon,' Samara hissed, bravely, it had to be said.

'A tool,' Farden shook his head. He could see her eyes, his eyes, glinting with crimson anger at first, and then a reluctant truth, regal purple, then a crystal icy blue, like her mother's. He swallowed. 'That spell was never meant for surviving.'

Samara bared her teeth.

Farden sat down again. 'Fifteen years, and we barely get fifteen minutes together,' he sighed, plucking a splinter of glass from the ground. 'I looked everywhere for you. We all did, but I looked and I looked. Years went by and not a sign. Vice hid you well.'

Samara looked as if she were about to yell another round of 'Lies!' at him, but instead she held her tongue. Farden could feel her gaze roving over his battered features, looking at his hair, his grey-green eyes, his jaw. 'I loved your mother with everything I had. Loved her even though she worked with Vice to betray me, to create you. Would have loved you too, if I had managed to stop him hiding you away.' Farden smiled. 'I would have had no idea how, but I would have managed it.'

Samara tried to scowl. Her eyelids were fluttering now, weakly. There was something in Farden's voice that made her listen. Something she had never experienced before. Kindness. 'You would have, have... *loved* me...' The word was a lump of ash on her tongue, but her question was true enough. '...even though I was this? This tool?'

Farden took the chance to hold her wrist. She struggled at first but then relented. She was too weak. So weak. Farden tried to shove the similarities between this and another death from his mind. Farden talked between counting her pulse. It was sluggish. 'Durnus, you probably know him as Ruin, once asked me a question. He asked me are we the people we're born, or the people we grow up to be? I choose to believe the latter.'

'What were you born as?'

'Brawler. Drug addict. Bloody good with magick.'

'And now?'

Farden looked over his shoulder. 'Now they call me a hero.'

'I know what I was born to be. I've done my job. Now it's over,' she snorted. 'Some reward this is.' She knew now. Her whole life had been the product of a lie, of ten thousand lies. She wondered if she should be bitter about it, angry even. What was done was done. She had never been given a chance. Something caught in her throat. 'It's not my fault,' she whispered.

'Samara,' Farden said, leaning close. Did he dare touch her face? He did and she closed her eyes. She looked so small all of a sudden, like the fifteen year-old she truly was. *She'd never had a chance*, Farden thought, as he clenched a fist. 'You did what you were told to do. You knew no better.'

'Mhm,' Samara mumbled.

'Do you believe me now?'

Samara winced. 'I do,' she said. 'Father.'

'Tell me,' Farden whispered. 'Who fed you these lies?'

A single finger unfurled from Samara's hand and pointed to the flat face of the cliff behind them, where the hill crept up to join the mountain, where a ragged, crooked figure was crouching, clutching a thick book to her chest. The woman's face turned pale as the mage met her eyes.

'She did,' Samara mumbled.

Farden was after her like a bolt from a bow.

'Stay away!' screamed Lilith as she sprinted down the hillside, all thoughts of aches and pain and age suddenly, instantly forgotten. She could hear the clanking of the dreaded mage behind her. She flailed her hands behind her head, expecting a sharp pain in her spine at any moment. Her heart was in her mouth, trying to make good its escape. It didn't want to be a part of this debacle.

'Stop running!' barked Farden.

'Stay away, murderer!'

Farden had had enough of running for one day. He skidded to a halt and flicked his hand in a blade-like motion. The air wavered in front of it, a little wave spreading outwards, catching the woman square in the back and sending her flailing into the snow at the foot of the hill. She fell with a crunch, and fell very still indeed.

Farden made it to her side. He dug the toe of his sabaton under her shoulder and lifted her. He frowned when he saw the blood, and the broken sword blade that had caused it. It had gone straight through her ribs. Her frail old fingers were clasping it. She coughed, hard, and blood filled her mouth. Her eyes, mad with fear and pain, swivelled to meet his. Surprisingly she laughed.

'Just as I saw it,' she cackled, through a mouthful of blood. Farden noticed three stones lying in the snow, underneath her elbow. One white, one red, one black. A seer, then. 'Just as I saw it. Everything ends. And so will you, Farden, in good time!'

Farden was about to ask her who she was when she coughed once more and then fell still, her mad eyes still glaring up at him. Farden shrugged. 'And good riddance to bad poison,' he said.

Farden wandered back to the top of the hill to find his daughter had drifted away also. Her eyes were closed and peaceful. He sighed a shuddering sigh. It was hard to know whether to feel pain, or guilt, or gladness. Maybe all three would do, in equal measure. She had known him in the end, and that was the most important thing. She had known him as a father, albeit for a brief moment.

Farden watched her for a while and then walked away. Three goodbyes were too much for one day.

He found Ilios sitting halfway down the hillside, all quiet and watchful. The gryphon looked dishevelled, to put it politely. Farden slumped down by his side and plucked a frayed feather from his shoulder. The gryphon looked down and clacked his beak. Farden met his golden eyes, and he saw a sadness in them he knew very well indeed. The mage nodded, and Ilios turned away. Gryphons never cry. They cannot, to speak the truth, but like every other animal they have a heart that bleeds, and in that moment it was bleeding double for Tyrfing.

In any case, Farden let the tears flow for both of them.

When at long last he was done, when he had no more tears to shed, Farden leant back against the cold rock. He felt his armour grate on the stone, and took a deep, deep breath. It was all too much to think about. 'Sing me to sleep, Ilios,' he whispered. 'Sing me to sleep.'

epilogues

A pair of deep brown eyes followed the constellations of weary footprints south and into the distance. Gone. Disappeared. Alone. All these words pleased Loki.

He wove his way between the unburied bodies. The daemons, fallen in their droves, the Lost Clan dragons, crumpled and broken like strange, collapsed tents, and the ones that didn't resemble much at all. He tiptoed around each of them, staring at their freezing remains, looking for nothing in particular.

Upon the hill, he found a crater on a ledge of black rock. His boots split the rock open with every step, crunched glass, trod ash. He bent down to taste the char. *Magick, blood, and sweat too.* Samara had been here. His finger prodded the dirt like a spear. They had buried her at least. He had expected that much.

In amongst the rocks he found it, dropped in a hurry and left forgotten. Lilith's book. The one the Shrieks had told him about. With a smile, Loki found a seat under a fire-scorched ledge and rested the heavy tome on his lap. Rubbing his hands, he opened it with a flourish and examined its contents.

Skin. Pages of skin was what it was. They were oiled and tanned, but roughly done. A few hairs remained here and there. A crusting of blood in some places. What a grotesque little trophy he had found for himself. Loki rubbed the pages between his fingers and felt his teeth chatter. There was magick in those pages, he could feel it. Loki ran his fingers along the lines of strange script, finely tattooed…

A smile curved around Loki's face. He knew exactly what these pages were. It had all become clear. What a grotesque little trophy indeed. A grotesquely powerful trophy.

Loki hoisted the book under his arm and strolled back down the hill. He cast around for some of the bigger, more frantic footprints, leading off like thorns into the wilderness. These were the ones he needed. Loki looked up, eyeing the dark horizon. A solitary cloud, so lonely in the frozen skies of the north, passed momentarily over the weak sun. A long shadow threw itself on the ice. When it had withdrawn itself, the god was gone.

✢

'Close that door you oaf! We'll freeze down to our bones!' Seria scolded from the table, her hands firmly on her stew-spattered apron.

'Calm yourself woman, there's a bird out 'ere, trying to get in. Flapping like a flag in a storm he is!' Traffyd hollered over his shoulder. Sketched in the bright light spilling through the open door, Seria could see her husband's shadow flailing about madly, trying to catch something deranged and fluttering with a blanket.

'Well don't let 'im in! He'll be up in the thatch for hours!'

There was a cry and a thud and moments later, Traffyd came hobbling through the doorway, wrestling a quivering bundle of blanket onto the tabletop.

'There,' he whispered to it soothingly, whilst Seria fussed and bothered around him. 'Easy now, you mad bird.' The hawk was soon calmed. Traffyd had a way with animals.

'He's got a bag on his leg,' Seria jabbed with a spoon. 'See if you can get it off.'

Traffyd was slowly stroking the hawk's feathers now, holding the blanket over its eyes. 'You get it. I'll keep 'im calm.'

Seria puffed out her pink cheeks. 'I'm ain't touchin' that rabid thing!'

'He's a fine bird, Seria, not some mangy crow.'

Seria huffed but curiosity soon got the better of her. Her nimble fingers quickly saw to the twine around the bag's neck, and while Traffyd gently placed the hawk in a warm part of the kitchen, Seria gently shook the bag out on the table.

The note came out first. A thin square of paper. Traffyd pinched it between his soil-darkened fingers and peered at its scribbled words. He read them aloud, slow and steady, in a quiet voice not used to letters.

TO TRAFFYD AND SERIA. MAY THIS BRING YOU THE SAME LUCK IT HAS BROUGHT ME. IT SAW ME THROUGH DEATH AND BACK. TWICE.
THANK YOU DEEPLY.

FARDEN

Another shake of the bag, and a pendant tumbled out onto the smooth wood. Seria held it up to the firelight, letting it glitter.

It was a thin sliver of a dragon scale, sandy-orange in colour and sparkling as though it had been dipped in gold dust, dangling from a thin metal chain. Its colours danced in the glow of the fire. Traffyd rubbed it. It felt like rough metal.

'Well I never,' was all he could say. Then he began to laugh, slowly and quietly at first, but then louder and heartier, until he was braying to the rafters. Seria looked on, a severe frown on her blushing face.

'What are you laughing at, you old fool?' she chided.

'He's alive, Seria, alive and well! Don't you see? Jötun be damned. That mage has more lives than a cat!'

Seria tried. She tried very hard indeed, but in the end, it was futile to resist. As she clutched the dragonscale pendant to her chest, she began to laugh, slowly and quietly at first.

※

Dawn was a bitter sight, bringing a light drizzle and bad news. It came by hawk, exhausted, bedraggled, and half-dead by any rights.

The bird flopped onto the Nest and crumpled to a heap next to Malvus' right boot. It's glazed eyes, speckled with rain, stared up at the bony fingers of the marble trees above. Malvus nudged the poor hawk onto its side, and then bent down to rip the scrap of grimy parchment from its spindly ochre leg. Malvus wrinkled his lip as he unravelled the wet mess with the tips of his manicured fingernails. It was barely even a scrap, to tell the truth. Torn from a book, no doubt, charred on one side, ripped on the other, with its words scratched and spattered. Urgent. Angry.

Malvus' lips twitched as he read silently to himself. There wasn't much to read. An infuriating handful of lines, only three, but they told him all he needed to know in aching brevity. *Saker had failed. Orion was dead.*

'Problems?' asked a voice. A confident voice, considering the weight of Toskig's armoured hand resting on the stranger's shoulder, considering the guards hovering in the dripping shadows of the marble trees with their knives drawn and ready, waiting for a word.

Malvus pinched the parchment between two fingers and ripped it down the middle. He contemptuously tossed its halves over the edge of the Nest and watched them drift like dead feathers into the dark of the city below. 'None that concern you,' he replied.

'You don't seem too happy, milord,' came the reply. Still confident. The stranger's assuredness grated against Malvus.

'All has gone to plan,' Malvus lied. *Why hadn't that blasted seer told him about the failure of the daemons? Had she lied? Or had she not known?* Malvus clenched his fist. The daemons were but one chapter in his story. *All will be settled*, he told himself. Pasting a smile onto his face, he turned around to confront his visitor.

The stranger was a tall, thin gentleman, almost treelike with his spindly arms and skinny legs, like a winter-bitten willow escaped from a riverbank. His face was gaunt, his eyes a dark shade of brown, and his nose wide and crooked, a sign that it had been broken some time in the past. It hadn't been set well. His hair was shaved within a fraction of its life. Already the years were beginning to pull its dwindling borders back. Albion-stock, clearly. Malvus sneered. *Peasants*.

'So then,' Malvus began, superciliously folding his arms across his armoured chest. 'Jeasin says she knows you.'

The stranger smiled. 'We've crossed paths before.'

'Why?'

'She was some assistance to us, actually, in the endeavour I mentioned.'

'And who is *us*, exactly?'

'Duke Kiltyrin, of course, before he lost his mind.'

'I see.' *That mad fool.*

The two men stared for a moment, through the drizzle and the shadow, each trying to gauge the other. Malvus looked to the north while he rubbed his chin. 'You lie to me, and I'll have you drowned in the harbour, after I have the guards remove your tongue that is. Do you understand?' he asked, eyes like flint.

The stranger's head bobbed up and down. 'Clear as day, milord.'

'Now,' Malvus leant against the marble, 'you will tell me all about the Nine you spoke of.'

Loffrey smiled once more.

'Are you lost, sister?' Hel grumbled, watching the tall, faded figure emerge from the gloomy tunnel and make for the gangplank. Her dress and bare feet rustled softly against the pebbles.

Evernia waited until she was aboard before she answered. She shimmered, barely visible in the bright lights of *Naglfar*'s lanterns. A faint, fitful snoring came from the bow of the ship. Hel was sprawled against a bulwark, sullen and dejected.

'Not in the slightest, my sister,' Evernia replied. Her voice sounded faraway and lost. Hel shrugged. She pointed a black fingernail at the silk sack hanging from the goddess' left hand.

'What's in the bag?' she asked.

Evernia wasted no time with preamble or conversational foreplay. She knew her sister well, and she could see the mood she was in. Black as her eyes. With a flourish, she undid the cords of the sack and let it fall to the deck.

Hel sat up. 'Your scales.'

Evernia held up her golden scales, perfectly balanced as always. 'Indeed. Our new weapon.'

'I thought Farden was your new weapon.'

Evernia tilted her head. 'A weapon for a different sort of enemy.'

'Loki.'

'And his plans, whatever they may be. Heimdall watches him. He is furtive.'

'And you never saw this coming.'

Evernia bowed her head, truly upset. 'Never.'

'The scales then, sister. Divulge your intentions.'

'Hel has now been rendered a home for souls. No longer a path, but a warehouse if you will. This could be very dangerous in the wrong hands.'

'Or claws. I have fended some off already.'

'Indeed.'

'Your plan?'

Evernia crossed her arms. 'We provide another home. One out of the daemon's reach. We cannot take them all, but we take the ones we can. Haven and Hel. One above, and one underneath.'

'And we decide, how?'

'By weighing the souls,' Evernia said, laying her scales gently on the floor. 'Fear not sister, the balance is heavily tipped in our favour. These are my scales, after all.'

'So, the boatman has become the merchant.'

Evernia nodded. 'If you will.'

Hel took a deep breath, and got to her feet. She took a moment to dust herself off. 'The battle for the soul has begun then.'

'Whether we like it or not, sister. Whether we like it or not.'

Six days, it took them. Six days to find the *Waveblade* again.

Roiks nearly hugged the mast when he came aboard. He would have done, probably, had it not been for the broken arm he now wielded. Nuka hugged him instead. Him and every other of his sailors that had returned to him. There were a sorry few, that was the truth. At times like this, joy and grief are the best of friends.

'Home,' Farden said, when the whales had finally broken them free of the ice. The whoosh of dragon wings ruffled his hair. He blew it out of his face with a snort. 'What a strange word that is.'

'More so than ever, now that we can't go back to Krauslung,' Elessi sighed. She hadn't left Modren's side since he had found her sprinting across the snow towards their weary column, bare feet almost shredded from the ice. The Undermage had practically carried her all the way back to the ship.

'Where to then?' Lerel asked, leaning heavily on her own mage, Farden. Like Roiks, she hadn't survived the battle unscathed. She had broken a leg, and was insistent that Farden was the best crutch around. He certainly was the shiniest. He had yet to remove any of his armour besides his helmet. He glittered in the sunset, almost dragon-like himself.

They all took a moment to think.

'South? To Paraia?' suggested Durnus, leaning wearily against the railing of the ship. Nearby, Ilios looked up with an eager trill.

'Perhaps, at first,' Farden shrugged.

'Albion?' Elessi ventured. Everybody, even Modren, pulled a face, Farden especially.

'The sea is my home, and we have the whole of it to ourselves, ladies and gentlemen,' boomed Nuka, as he sauntered towards them along the deck. 'Let me show you the world one port at a time. Once you've seen them all, then you can decide...'

'North,' Farden announced, staring eastwards, where the Tausenbar faded into the creeping purple velvet of night. Heavy clouds lingered overhead, hinting of snow. 'That's where we'll go, when we're finished. To old Scalussen.'

Nuka clapped his hands. 'In the meantime, dinner is served. After you, Arkmage,' he said, gesturing to Durnus. But he held up a pale hand and shook his head.

'Farden and I will follow in a moment.'

'We will?' Farden asked. Durnus nodded in a way that made him not want to argue, even though his stomach rumbled chronically at the mention of dinner. Durnus waited for the others to file below before he turned to the mage, sightless eyes roving over his face. 'I could say a hundred words to you, Farden. I could say a thousand...' Farden wondered if this was a good moment to tell him how hungry he was, but he refrained. 'But all I need to say is how proud I am. You have really proven yourself. Not just with this,' he smacked him lightly on the shoulder, making his glistening armour clank, 'but for what you did for Modren and Elessi, even to the words you spoke a moment ago about Scalussen, and the way you spoke them. I think it is time.'

'For what?'

'To pass on my legacy, like Korrin did to you,' Durnus smiled. He gestured towards dinner. 'After you, *Arkmage*.'

Farden nearly fell overboard. 'You're joking, right?'

'Why ever would I? I am too old for this game, Farden.'

'What do you mean, too old? Aren't you immortal?'

'Aren't you? And still younger than I?'

'A fair point.'

'Well then, I rest my case. Of course, I will humbly accept the old position of advisor, or mentor, if it is still available. But otherwise, I am done. I pass the title to you, Farden. My decision is final. The Arka need a strong Arkmage now, more than ever. Even if it is to be an Arkmage-in-exile.'

Farden exhaled slowly while he shook his head, watching his hot breath escape as steam. There was a chill in the air. Clouds were gathering. 'What about Modren?' he asked.

'He has asked to be your Undermage.'

Farden exhaled a little more. 'Okay,' he said, after a moment of dizzying consideration. 'I accept.'

Durnus put his hand on his shoulder. 'I knew you would,' he whispered, 'I knew you would.' Farden might have been wrong, but it looked as though a huge weight had been lifted from his old friend's shoulders. He smiled, even though he couldn't see it. 'After you, Arkmage. Dinner awaits.'

'You are very persuasive, you know,' Farden muttered as they went below.

As they reached the door of the captain's cabin, Farden paused. 'I will be a moment,' he said, leaving Durnus' hand on the doorhandle. He turned the corner and found his cabin. He went in and locked the door, and then tugged something very thick and heavy from his haversack.

The Grimsayer landed on the bed with a grumbling thud, making the bed itself creak. A certain black rat looked up from its little hollow in the pillow, squeaked, and promptly went back to sleep.

Farden knelt down in front of the Grimsayer and gently lifted its pages. 'Tyrfing,' he said to it, and watched the lights go to work. It took them but a moment to draw him. Farden smiled at his uncle, kneeling there in the pebbles by a rushing river, smiling to the last.

Farden nodded, closed the book and went to the door. Just before he left, a flash of white caught his eye, in the little porthole next to the door. Farden pressed his face to the uneven glass, and smirked to himself. He had been right after all. It was snowing outside.

the end

acknowledgements

It's done. I couldn't be happier.

Emaneska has been a long and exciting road. Though rough and potholed in places, it has led me here, to the finale, to the culmination. Four years and four books later, I can't help but be proud.

And do you know what has helped me along this road? You. I'd like to acknowledge every single person thumbing this page or screen right this very minute. Give yourselves a hearty clap on the back. I want to thank you for enjoying the Emaneska Series. For picking it up and parting with your hard-earned cash. For sharing and retweeting. For the emails. For the stars and comments. For even just mentioning it in passing. You crazy lot keep me writing.

I'd like to thank and also apologise profusely to those incredible people that I have the pleasure of calling my friends and family. I thank you for putting up with my wild and excited rambling about Emaneska, about Dead Stars, and what fictional pools I'll be dipping my toes into next. And I apologise, mainly to your ears, for talking them to a raw pulp. I promise I'll stop. One day. Maybe.

I also owe my gratitude to those authors and other self-publishing indies out there that have inspired and educated me over the past four years. This industry is ever-changing, and indies are ever-working, and damn hard too. The alliances I have made and the communities I've been part of have helped me make some good decisions and helped me keep up the work I've been doing in the background behind the writing. Gods know there is a lot of it.

I won't be stopping writing any time soon. Not a chance. This may be the end of Emaneska, but it's only the start for this young author. Even now, as I sit poring over my laptop, congratulatory whisky in hand, the clock-face showing something ungodly, I'm itching to get working on the next book. It will be strange not writing about Emaneska, not manhandling our favourite mage through trial and tribulation, but it will also be good to try something new and different.

Who knows. Maybe I'll return to Emaneska another day, once I've got some of the other ideas out of my system. Maybe I'll write another series. Maybe I'll call it the Scalussen Chronicles. But who knows…

Thank you. To all.

Ben

Did you like Dead Stars Part Two?
Then help Ben out by showing your support.

For today's indie authors, every bit of exposure helps. If you liked **Dead Stars** and **The Emaneska Series** then why not tell a friend? By sharing and recommending, you support the author and help them to keep doing what they do best - writing books.

You can now follow and support Ben Galley on Facebook and Twitter:

Go to: Facebook.com/BenGalleyAuthor

Or say hello @BenGalley

Thank you for your support!

Dead Stars - Part 2